THE MAN OF HER DREAMS

"You are very beautiful," she told him, her voice dreamy and husky-soft. "I didn't know a man could be so beautiful."

Women did not say such things! Again his body stirred, again he ruthlessly forced his thoughts elsewhere. He refused to comment on her own beauty; it had been his experience that women who looked like this one were well aware of their charms and the power it gave them.

"I must be dreaming." She ventured another smile, the innocent sensuality of it making his heart begin to pound.

"I've never seen a man as big as you." She sighed. "And your hair, it's so long and thick. You know, you actually look more like a dark Viking than an angel."

"I am no angel." He laughed, a bitter sound, even to his own ears. "Far from it, in fact."

Then, to his disbelief, she crawled toward him, still shivering, but with fierce resolve plain in her small face.

"I want to touch you," she said, kneeling before him knee to knee. "This is my dream and I want to enjoy it before I have to go back to the real world. Except for in the movies, I've never seen a man as gorgeous as you."

Tilting her head, she laid her hand on his arm, stroking the hard muscles there, knitting her brow in concentration.

Kenric found himself holding his breath, trembling—yes, trembling!—as he allowed her touch.

When she moved her hand to his chest, parting the laces of his tunic and touching him with an untrained sensuality that drove him wild, he felt the last of his control slipping . . . .

Powerful Magic

Karen Whiddon

LOVE SPELL NEW YORK CITY

A LOVE SPELL BOOK®

February 2001

Published by

Dorchester Publishing Co., Inc.
276 Fifth Avenue
New York, NY 10001

If you purchased this book without a cover you should be aware that this book is stolen property. It was reported as "unsold and destroyed" to the publisher and neither the author nor the publisher has received any payment for this "stripped book."

Copyright © 2001 by Karen Whiddon

Cover art by John Ennis.
www.ennisart.com

All rights reserved. No part of this book may be reproduced or transmitted in any form or by any electronic or mechanical means, including photocopying, recording or by any information storage and retrieval system, without the written permission of the publisher, except where permitted by law.

ISBN 0-505-52432-5

The name "Love Spell" and its logo are trademarks of Dorchester Publishing Co., Inc.

Printed in the United States of America.

Visit us on the web at www.dorchesterpub.com.

To Lonnie, whose pride in me bolsters me,
whose love sustains me.

To Stephanie, who makes me proud.

To all my family—Scott, Sharon, and Alex, Dad and Betty,
Mom and Gloria, and Shawn. And my extended family—
Lavenia and Dennis, Floyd and Sarah, Cleveland and
Phyllis.
I love you all.

Powerful Magic

Prologue

Trembling, Megan waited exactly where they'd agreed to meet. She watched as Roger hurried across the freshly cut field, wearing a harried expression of distaste. In one manicured hand he clutched his wireless phone—it wouldn't do to miss any important calls. He hadn't wanted to meet her here, begrudging the time from his busy schedule. But she, in an uncharacteristic bit of bravery, had insisted. She had to do this, had to put an end to it while she had the nerve, before it finished her.

Above, the old oak tree spread its leafy branches, sheltering her from the summer sun. Though she knew it couldn't protect her when Roger heard what she had to say.

Even the weather seemed to mock her, the cloudless sky at odds with the turmoil inside her. Once she had thought she loved Roger, when she was foolish and naive, and blind to the dark sort of cruelty that could exist hidden away deep inside men like him.

Love. She wasn't sure she even believed in it anymore.

And Roger . . . Well, she thought he might not know the meaning of the word *love*. To him she was a possession, nothing more, a young and rich heiress. He meant to mold her to his every whim, to his will. Once she married him she knew she would gradually waste away, a shell of her former, vibrant self.

It had already begun to happen.

The sharp edges of the enormous diamond ring he'd given her cut into her palm. She'd taken the ring off and intended to give it back to him. It terrified her, this action that she meant to take. She was afraid; afraid of the anger that she knew could rise so swiftly within him, afraid that he would hurt her as he had before. She took a big risk; this she knew—a risk that he would refuse to listen, to take her words seriously. Or an even greater risk that, once he knew that she meant it, he would kill her this time.

He smiled as she got closer, the chilling kind of smile that made her freeze inside. She forced herself to continue walking, to show no expression. Most of all to show no fear.

She'd rehearsed what she had to say over and over; she knew the words well, though getting them past a throat gone parched would be difficult. Her heart pounded and, though there was a cool breeze on this gorgeous June morning, she began to perspire.

It occurred to her that she could have done this much more safely by telephone or by mail. But she would not run; the one thing she had left, though it was in tatters, was her pride. She would face him down somehow, and walk away with her courage and dignity intact. She hoped.

Almost there. She could hear her heart thudding inside her chest. Forcing her breathing to slow, she lifted her chin and raised a hand to greet him, wondering if he could see how she shook. He'd like that, she knew, so

she redoubled her efforts to appear calm and composed.
Unafraid.

Just then a loud crack sounded. At first she thought
he'd hit her, that he'd somehow read her mind and re-
taliated even before she could speak.

But no, it wasn't him, not this time. From the cloudless,
perfect sky a bolt of electricity snaked down, striking like
a relentless cobra. She knew a moment of terror, in that
instant wondering if this was fate's merciless retribution,
before everything went utterly, totally black.

Chapter One

The air smelled different—it held a crisp, moist, tangy bite that promised snow. And it was freezing, Megan realized, shivering in her denim overalls and short-sleeved T-shirt as she slowly took stock of her surroundings. Maybe heaven—or hell—wasn't like everyone thought. She had to be in one or the other—after being struck by lightning, she doubted she had survived.

Yet she still clutched her engagement ring in one hand. With a shaky sigh, she slipped it on her finger for safekeeping.

Moving slowly, she blinked and swallowed. Everything looked ashen: gray rock, slate sky, even the leafless oak tree had sooty bark. So maybe she'd landed in purgatory. It was supposed to be colorless, like this. But cold?

Cautiously she climbed to her feet, biting her lip to keep from moaning in pain. She had to grab hold of the tree to keep from falling, though its rough surface scraped her hands. She realized she hurt—badly. Every bone, every muscle, even her skin felt like she'd been cooked too long in a high-powered tanning bed, then pummeled by some sadistic masseuse. Though this could be a good thing—if she was hurt, then maybe she wasn't dead. Why, then, hadn't Roger taken her to the hospital?

Had she even gotten a chance to break the engagement? She couldn't remember. No, Roger hadn't even reached her yet when the lightning had zapped her.

God, she was cold. Or, she amended hastily, make that *dear* God. Right now she couldn't afford to take any chances of offending Him.

Still holding on to the tree—a tree, she noticed, that looked suspiciously like the very same one she'd been meeting Roger under, minus the lush leaves—Megan took stock of her surroundings. It was a barren winter land, she decided, her breath leaving her mouth in frosty puffs. The kind of place best faced in a down-filled anorak and thermal jeans. Desolate. Deserted. Dead grass covered the rolling hills, and the entire thicket of trees in the distance looked stripped of leaves.

But it was June, the end of spring, beginning of summer. Unless she had somehow been transported to someplace on the other side of the equator, it shouldn't be this cold. Not unless it was the middle of winter, or an alternate hell.

As if to prove her thoughts right, fat white snowflakes began to drift lazily down from the slate sky.

The thought occurred to Megan that perhaps she was dreaming. Maybe in reality she lay in some sterile hospital bed, hooked up to various machines, fed full of morphine or some other strong painkiller. She'd heard that people on drugs had some pretty strange and fantastic dreams.

Shivering in earnest, she discarded that idea too. If this were a dream, she would wish herself toasty warm. Or, at the very least, she'd give herself some kind of coat.

So then, where was she?

Snow began to fall in a heavy white curtain, soon obscuring the horizon from view. Letting go of the tree, Megan took one faltering step, then another, ignoring the pain that racked her body as she moved. She would have to decide later where she was—right now she needed to find shelter before she froze to death.

Kenric gave the warhorse its head, knowing the animal merely exulted in the crispness of the December air. As did he. God's teeth, it was good to be out of the keep, away from those who wanted only to use him. Though he rode dangerously close to his lands—he still thought of them as his, though another ruled there now—he felt far richer in his freedom than could be accomplished by any gold.

To remind himself that he'd nearly reached his goal, he'd brought along the bag filled with the payment that he'd accepted a mere two hours ago. He knew he ought to hide the jingling coins, but for now he counted himself safe. None would suspect a ragged warrior such as he of any kind of wealth, he thought ruefully. Though he did have his sword, more valuable than any gold. The great blade had been forged, some said, in magic and blood some two hundred years ago. It had been handed down from generation to generation, until his own father had placed it in Kenric's bastard hand as he lay dying.

Thinking of his father's end brought a black scowl. The death of his human family at the hands of the Faeries still tortured him, though four years had gone by now. Four long, exceedingly grueling years of him earning money as a mercenary so that he might reach his goal of owning land—human land. He wanted nothing to do with the Faerie land that those of Rune claimed was his by birthright.

He disowned that birthright; had disowned it on the day he learned who had killed his human father. Even if

14

the murderers had been, as the Faerie folk claimed, renegade Faeries, some evil faction that had chosen darkness over light, mayhem over compassion, he still wanted nothing to do with them or their magic.

Nay, he had his own goal: to be a human man with human land; to be a simple farmer, warrior no more. A goal, he reminded himself, controlling his eager mount's head with a light touch, that he had nearly enough gold to reach. Everything he'd earned was safely hidden in his cave.

None knew of this secret place, hidden in the rocky mountains of Wales on his own family's former land. It was now his home, the only way he could keep in touch with the soil and the land that still, in his heart, belonged to him.

Someday—someday soon—he would have land of his own. Then he would be able to keep the vow he had made to his father's grave. Bastard son or no, it was up to him now to continue the line. He, Kenric of Blackstone, was all that remained. So he fought and he saved, ruthlessly hoarding the money and waiting for the day he would have to fight no longer. After all, he could stomach waging other men's battles for only so long.

Though, Kenric conceded with a rueful chuckle, they paid well. He nearly had enough to bribe the king in hopes of being awarded a small parcel of rich Welsh land.

For now he would go to his hidden hideout, dangerously near the Welsh mountains, hunt up some meat, and rest. He was bone weary, tired of bloodshed and killing.

Slowing the massive steed to a walk, Kenric casually surveyed the surrounding hills. A light snow had begun to fall, which was good. It would, should anyone come looking, cover his tracks. Though no one would dare follow him, he knew, grinning at the thought of his surly demeanor when among the noblemen who had hired him. It was the same, wherever he went, whoever's battles he fought. Kenric of Blackstone, friend to no man, warrior of renown. They feared him and perhaps hated him, but they needed him.

As they would again. Though soon he would not have to answer when they called. Soon he would be through with fighting battles for other men, through with war, unless it was one of his own making. His sword, the one thing of magic he allowed near him, would not be used for deliberate bloodshed again.

Satisfied that he was alone, he dismounted, his heavy boots sounding loud on the hard, frozen ground. Trusting him implicitly, the warhorse allowed himself to be led into the dense thicket of yews. Together they picked their way over the stony ground, their breath making plumes in the frigid air.

Finally they came to the low outcropping of rocks, some as large as a man, that signified the rise in land. Ancient burial mounds, many of them were, and as a consequence other men avoided them. He was well satisfied with this.

Once more glancing around him, Kenric listened for any sign that he was not alone. There were none; all he could hear was the warhorse's labored breathing. Patting the animal's thick neck, he turned and led the way up, into the rock itself. Into a place where no man, were he sane, would think to go.

Here, hidden inside an outcropping of boulders, was his cave. His safe place, his refuge. And, for now, his home.

Because he had been here before, the horse followed him unhesitantly inside the dark entrance.

Once inside, Kenric stopped. Something—he knew not what—was wrong. Every inner sense told him things were not as they should be. His sanctuary had been disturbed, and recently. He could feel it. Even now, the faintly rich scent of some exotic flower, so out of place in this winter land, drifted in the frigid air.

He sighed, more annoyed than worried. No doubt some impotent mage had tried a new magic spell or trick. From past experience he knew no spell would work on him. This immunity was a remnant of a heritage he rejected. Refused in fact. Magic was an unwelcome and hated part of his lineage, his blood.

Bitterness welled up in him as he thought of it. Magic hadn't helped his family when they needed it. They'd all lost their lives in one fell swoop. While he, Kenric, bastard son and unbeliever, had been kept alive simply because he wasn't there. Damned to an eternity knowing he'd failed them. He no longer believed in things like magic.

He no longer believed in much of anything.

Best to make a fire. With the heavy snow, the smoke would not be seen or smelled. No man, had they a warm, dry place to sleep, would venture out in such a winter storm.

The war horse snorted a warning. Kenric froze, his hand going to his sword. They'd spent years together, and he trusted the huge beast's instincts. He heard a sound, a piteous mewling that could be human or not. Most likely it came from the abandoned offspring of some large cat.

Cautiously he started to move to investigate, then thought better of it. He would get the fire going first. That way, if the mother cat returned, fierce with the desire to defend her offspring, he would have the flames to protect his warhorse.

He needed his mount more than he liked to admit. The well-trained animal was his only possession other than his sword, the only companion he allowed himself. Though he would not let himself grow too fond of the beast; he needed no such weakness, no chink in the hard armor that kept him sane.

Once the fire was crackling merrily and he'd brought hay to his horse, Kenric grabbed a crooked branch and lit the end of it, creating a primitive torch. The mewling had not come again—perhaps the animal had died.

His stomach growled, reminding him of the need for fresh meat, though he knew hunting would be impossible in the storm. Luckily he'd thought to bring some dried bacon and several loaves of hard bread with him. For now, he would seek the source of the sound. Perhaps he might be able to end its pain.

There, in the farthest corner of the small cave, huddled under a ragged blanket that he used sometimes to cover his horse, he found the intruder. No wild beast, but a human, a young female near death from cold. She'd wrapped her arms around herself for warmth, but he could see from the pale gleam of her skin that they were bare, her long, pale legs too.

For a heartbeat he simply stared. He, warrior supreme and fighter of armies, did not know what to do. The tattered blanket did not cover much, nor did what little clothing she wore. In his experience, a naked female served only one purpose, and he had done without that along with everything else since the hated Faeries had brutally ended his other life.

This female, with her milky skin ashen and her lips blue, looked near death. She moved, shivering, again making that piteous mewling sound. Now he recognized it as a feeble cry for help, like that of a small child torn from its mother's arms in the heat of battle.

He thought that perhaps he should cover her and attempt to return her to the keep. No doubt that was where she was from—yet another silly girl sneaking off to meet a lover.

The howling storm told him that would be a foolish idea. He'd never make it, not in this blizzard.

Too, she'd found his cave. That made her a threat.

Again Kenric regarded her, noting her blue-tinged lips and uncontrollable shivering. She was near death from the frigid cold. The easiest thing to do would be to turn his back and walk away. If he did not help her, she would not live.

Yet he, hardened warrior, bitter loner, found he could not simply let the girl die. His younger sister had been about the size of this one. He hadn't been there to protect her when the invaders had brutally used her, something for which he'd never forgive himself. He, with his own capacity for great magic, dangerous magic, the only thing that would work against Black Faeries, had been unable to help her. Her death, along with the death of all the others, would lie forever like a thousand stones upon his conscience. He needed no more such deaths to blot his soul.

He had no choice but to help her, like it or not.

His decision made, he bent down and scooped her slight form into his arms. She weighed next to nothing, and as the thin blanket fell away, he saw that she was clothed, though barely. She wore some form of lightweight shirt, of a finer material than he'd ever seen, with a coarser fabric over it hooked together with some sort of metal fastenings. The coarse material, unfortunately for her, ended at midthigh, exposing her long, creamy legs to the elements. On her feet she wore a sort of leather sandal, open in the toe.

No wonder she lay near death. Only a fool would dress thus in the winter. Though, he reflected with a rueful shake of his head, only a harlot would dress so in any season.

As he brought her near the fire she stirred, but made no sound other than the harsh rasp of her breathing. Again her unusual scent drifted to him. Odd that it brought to mind spring, when the first stubborn flowers would poke their heads through the melting snow.

Spring was a long way off.

Studying her face, he thought she might be beautiful were her lips not so bloodless and her skin not so pale and sallow. She sighed, parting her mouth slightly—

enough for him to see she still had all her teeth and that they were white and strong.

Her age he could not guess at, nor the circumstances that had brought her to his secret cave, dressed in such a strange and inappropriate manner.

He would have answers later. For now all that mattered was keeping her alive.

He gently placed her on a recent acquisition, a thick and heavy bearskin. Wrapping it around her, he rocked back on his heels, wondering what he would do with her when she woke. After that thought came another: he found himself strangely curious as to the color of her eyes.

Fool. Chiding himself, Kenric added more wood to his fire, pleased as it crackled and danced in the modest stone hearth he'd created years ago in the rocky wall. It was close enough to the front of the cave that most of the smoke would flow out, yet near enough to the back to warm the entire small enclosure.

Feeling the warmth, the woman stirred. Her eyes fluttered open as she stared at the fire, then at the dim interior of the cave, and finally at him.

They were brown, he noted numbly, though a brown unlike any he'd ever seen. Gold flecks danced in them, and the upward tilt of her eyes made her look mysterious and very, very beautiful.

"Hell," she muttered, a foreign inflection to the familiar English. "I'm in hell. It figures."

Though he knew not what she meant by the last, Kenric moved closer.

She gasped and tried to move backward, the rock wall preventing her. "Who . . . who are you?"

It appeared she spoke English, though she spoke strangely. Perhaps the fear, so evident in the wide-eyed look of terror she wore, made her lose her capacity for normal speech.

20

"I am Kenric of Blackstone." Resigned, he waited for her to recognize the name.

When she did not show any outward reaction, he was startled to realize he felt relief. This meant, then, that she was not one of those who, by the grace of King William, lived in his family's former castle and feasted on food that should have belonged to him, but never would simply because he was a bastard.

The silence grew while she stared at him, still trembling. When she finally spoke, her tone was flat and lifeless.

"Are you some sort of devil, or"—her voice faltered—"a demon?"

Shocked, Kenric narrowed his eyes, his hand going automatically to his sword. He would challenge a man over such an insult. Forcing himself to relax his fingers, he inclined his head. Since she was only a tiny female, and obviously fought off some sort of madness, he would allay her fears.

"Nay, lady." His gruff voice vibrated with the anger he suppressed. "I am no devil, only a man."

To his amazement, she smiled then, transforming her heart-shaped face. Kenric stared, spellbound by her sudden beauty. He had not realized she was so comely. The fire made her dark hair dance with golden lights, and her long-lashed eyes glowed like precious gemstones. Color had returned to her face, enough to show him that she had skin the color of new-poured cream. And those lips, those lush, ripe lips . . . they parted to speak again.

"I guess that means I'm not in hell."

Cocking his shaggy head, he ran a hand over his rough beard and sighed. Either she was mad or she had injured her head while stumbling around in the snow in her ridiculous costume. That would explain her whimsical words.

He found himself hoping for the latter.

"You are not in hell," he assured her, though sometimes he too had his doubts. His life had become a sort of hell, ever since those from whom half of his blood came had taken everything that had ever mattered to him.

And could it be possible that she was one of them, here on another of Rhiannon's misguided missions? How else to explain her strange use of English, the foreign inflection in her voice? If Rhiannon thought to lure him with this one's sensual beauty, she was more of a fool than Kenric had thought.

"How came you here?" he asked her, still standing in his fighting stance, though he kept his hand away from the hilt of his sword.

"Here?" Blinking rapidly, she waved a milky hand around the dim interior of his cave. "I . . . I'm not sure. I think I was hit by lightning and when I woke up it began to snow."

She frowned, biting her full bottom lip. The look she gave him was one of fearful entreaty, the look of a damsel in distress expecting rescue, hoping and praying that her rescuer did not turn out to be the very thing she needed rescue from.

When she continued, it was in a low voice, almost as if she were speaking to herself. "Have you seen Roger? He was coming toward me when the lightning struck."

Kenric shook his head, though obviously she did not require an answer. Such nonsensical speech was what he would expect from one who'd suffered some sort of blow to the head. Or a madwoman. Whichever it was, it was clear her mind was addled. That well explained the strange garb. As to the talk of lightning, since a blizzard howled outside the cave, the woman would soon realize the foolishness of her words.

But this man, this Roger . . . now, this interested him. If she'd been meeting a lover, it was highly likely this man would be roaming around here somewhere, storm or no storm, looking for her. He himself would, he noted ruefully, were she of sound mind. A comely woman such as this one would be welcomed by any man, especially on such a cold night.

His body stirred at the thought, surprising him. He had forsworn such things. It had been a long time since he had allowed himself to enjoy the attentions of a willing maid. Not since he'd lived in his father's keep had he done so. Nor would he again, until the goal he devoted his life to had been reached.

Crouching on one knee before her, he lifted her chin with one hand. She shrank away from his touch, eyes huge in her heart-shaped face.

"What are you called?" With narrowed eyes, he waited for her answer. Fear he was used to, though he found he intensely disliked seeing it in her.

"Megan." she told him, swallowing. Her guileless expression told him she spoke the truth. "Megan Potter."

Megan was a Welsh name; Potter was not.

She made a mew of sound, trying to move away from his touch. He found himself moving his rough fingers to her cheek, caressing the soft skin there. His tender action so shocked him that he yanked his hand away.

"From whence do you come?"

"I'm . . . Dallas, Texas."

He had not heard of the place, whether within the mysterious mountains of Wales or in Great Britain itself. Perhaps it was in another country, like Italy or Spain.

"How came you here?" If she mentioned lightning again, he would know she needed some time to recover from whatever ailed her, and he would leave her alone.

Instead of answering, she only shook her head. "I must find Roger." Still shivering and chewing the nail on her index finger, the woman regarded him hopefully. "There is something important I need to tell him."

"You will not tell him of this place." It was not a request, but a command. Kenric knew he did not want to kill this slip of a woman, but he had to protect his sanctuary.

Megan Potter straightened her shoulders, fear still evident in the trembling of her rosebud mouth. "I do not even know where this place is. It is some sort of cave; this I can tell. But the only caves I know about are near Austin."

She tilted her head, seeming to dredge up enough courage from somewhere to let her gaze travel boldly over him.

It felt like her small hand touched him in those places where her eyes went. Oddly uncomfortable with her intense scrutiny, he looked away.

"You are very beautiful," she told him, her voice dreamy and husky-soft. "I didn't know a man could be so beautiful."

Women did not say such things! Again his body stirred, and again he ruthlessly forced his thoughts elsewhere. He refused to comment on her own beauty; it had been his experience that women who looked like this one were well aware of their charms and the power it gave them.

"I must be dreaming." She ventured another smile, the innocent sensuality of it making his heart begin to pound.

"I've never seen a man as big as you, at least in real life." She sighed. "Maybe one of those pro wrestlers, though I wouldn't know from personal experience. And your hair . . . it's so long and thick."

She fingered her own short, sable hair. "It's longer than mine. You know, actually you look more like a dark Viking than an angel. Pretty good, even for a dream."

Now he knew she was mad. What kind of woman would say such things, alone with a man in a cave? He remembered the lack of clothing and his earlier thought, that she was a harlot. Perhaps he had been correct.

Still, she aroused him beyond all reason.

He did not like his choices. She was either mad, or had been sent to entrap him. His jaw tightened. He could easily believe she had been sent to lure him with honeyed words and soft skin. That would explain her lack of clothing, and the appalling way she spoke to him, tempting him.

He would not give in. He could not. Yet, despite his vow, his blood thickened.

"I am no Viking." He clung to the insult, however unintentional, she gave him. "My family was English, though I was born here in these Welsh hills."

Slowly she nodded, never looking away from his face.

Outside, the storm increased in intensity, the wind shrieking and moaning. The entrance to the cave, small though it was, began to fill with snow. His warhorse shifted, snorting with unease. With a few quiet words, Kenric soothed the beast.

"A horse." The woman sounded surprised, as if she had just noticed the animal. "He's huge. And so beautiful. I didn't know angels rode horses."

She frowned, her gaze traveling over him again, heating his blood despite his intentions to ignore the attraction he felt for this tiny woman.

"And fur. You're wearing fur. Aren't you guys supposed to be vegetarians and antifur or something? Man, what a messed-up dream."

Angels. From demon to Viking to this, a messenger of God. And she kept talking about dreams.

Though she made no sense, and her accent made the strange English she used difficult to understand, until he knew more Kenric decided to act as if he took her words seriously.

"I am no angel." He laughed, a bitter sound, even to his own ears. "Far from it, in fact."

Then, to his disbelief, she crawled toward him, still shivering, but with fierce resolve plain in her small face.

"I want to touch you," she said, kneeling before him knee-to-knee. "This is my dream and I want to enjoy it before I have to go back to the real world. Except for in the movies, I've never seen a man as beautiful as you."

Tilting her head, she laid her hand on his arm, stroking the hard muscles there, knitting her brow in concentration.

Kenric found himself holding his breath, trembling—yes, trembling!—as he allowed her touch.

When she moved her hand to his chest, parting the laces of his tunic and touching him with an untrained sensuality that drove him wild, he felt the last of his control slipping despite his earlier resolve.

"Roger is nothing like this . . ." she said softly.

Roger. With an oath he put her from him, cursing his own unruly body.

"Know this, woman," he said in a snarl as he stood. "The storm outside is a mighty one. If your man is out in it, unless he has found some sort of shelter, he will not survive."

She gasped at this, her full lip trembling. "But it was warm when I went to meet him, and I didn't get a chance to tell him—"

So she *had* been having a tryst with her lover. Still, Kenric found her alluring, with the fresh color that bloomed in her cheeks, and the way her exotic eyes glowed.

"You really think that Roger is out in this?"

Roger. To regain a measure of steadiness, he fixed on the name. It was a good English name.

"Who is this Roger to you?" Folding his arms across his chest, he waited to hear her answer.

"My, uh . . ." She fumbled with the words, telling him again that this odd sort of English she spoke was not her original tongue. "I was supposed to marry him," she muttered, turning her magnificent gaze away to stare at the fire.

"Your betrothed?" His voice sharp, Kenric cursed under his breath. With her graceful, long-fingered hands and pampered skin, she was no serf. A noblewoman? That meant her lord would be trying like hell to find her.

Kenric narrowed his eyes and studied her again, trying to determine whether she lied.

As if to mock him, a gust of snow blew into the cave, making the fire sputter. They were trapped here together. There would be no leaving until the storm abated.

One thought cheered him slightly. He doubted anyone could find them either. His secret was safe, at least for now.

Moving closer to the fire, she held out her hands toward the warmth. As she raised her gaze again, her golden brown eyes were wide with the uncertain fear of a cornered doe.

"I am dreaming, aren't I?"

He ignored the question. In the space of seconds, she had gone from sensual temptress to frightened girl. It made no sense. Few knew of his goal. It would take more than a beautiful woman to turn him from his path.

Then she stood, the threadbare blanket falling from her slender shoulders, and his mouth went dry. He couldn't move.

Firelight reflected off her satiny skin, making it golden and warm. With her chest heaving and her head tilted up at him, her full, parted lips were more than even he, no angel at all, could resist.

So he bent his head and kissed her.

Chapter Two

In her glittering castle, Rhiannon, queen of Rune and all the lands that encompassed Faerie, paced. Though she tried to hide it, she knew her agitation was plain to those who loved her well, for she could no longer keep her impatience and pain hidden inside.

The pain was old, though usually she kept it locked away. The impatience . . . This was a new thing, and it brought great hope to her inner circle of advisers and friends. It seemed an eternity since their beloved queen had allowed any hint of emotion to cross the frozen perfection of her face.

"She is here," Rhiannon said, bitterness warring with hope in her bell-like voice. "And he is with her."

The three others assembled in her private chamber murmured among themselves—words of joy, of anticipation. Words that had not been spoken in the long, gray years since their queen had lost her one true love, her own soul mate.

Arwydd, a wizened Faerie who was perhaps the oldest of them all, spoke. "So what has been foretold will come to pass."

Rhiannon smiled fondly at her former nursemaid. "Yes." She knew the simple answer would be enough. No one in the Faerie Kingdom of Rune was unschooled in the prophecy.

"And your half brother, the changeling who is human-raised, will be the instrument all of our hopes are pinned on?"

The bitter tone came from Vychan, who had been most against any kind of relations with mankind. He did not believe the words of prophecy that said that the land of Faerie would die unless it came to terms with the land of humankind. But he was alone in this, for Rhiannon and the others believed. It was for this reason that Rhiannon, like her mother before her, had gone many years ago into the land of man and mated with a human male, the soul mate she had loved and lost.

Now her half brother was heir to all she ruled, though he claimed not to want it.

Rhiannon had hoped it would be a woman of Faerie who would win her brother's heart. But in a vision she had seen that this was not to be so. For it was a very human woman she had brought to him, a beautiful human female from another time and place.

"What of Myrddin?" This from Drystan, whose very name echoed his sorrowful nature.

At the name of their dreaded nemesis, the Faeries fell silent. Unutterably weary, Rhiannon made circles in the air in front of her in much the same manner as a Christian might make the sign of the cross. "He watches also."

None of them liked hearing this; indeed, it damped the very spirit of festivity that had been present a mere moment ago.

"And his power?" Vychan asked glumly.

She could tell them nothing but the truth. "Daily it increases."

"As ours weakens."

"Yes, but perhaps my half brother will be able to change that." Rhiannon had to interject a bit of optimism into the group. After all, this long-awaited event was the hope of all Faerie.

"Can you hasten it?"

Rhiannon shook her head. "You know better. Kenric and his woman both have free will. The choice must be freely made or it will have no power."

"And the love?"

Her heart ached. "My brother does not believe in love. Not yet."

"Love must flow between them for the magic to begin. Can you hasten that?"

Sadly, Rhiannon shook her head. "It must come to both of them naturally. Or not at all."

Vychan and Drystan exchanged glances. Each of them wore expressions of uncharacteristic gloom. "All will be lost if they do not love."

A murmur of sorrow, laced with the faint hint of tears, swept through those assembled.

Choking up, Rhiannon could not speak. To do so would betray her unseemly emotions. She was queen. They looked to her for answers. So it was doubly important that she show no doubt, that she believe. There was no need for her to answer that bleak statement. Every Faerie in Rune knew that it was the truth.

It wasn't a gentle kiss, not by any means. Stunned at first, Megan froze as his lips covered hers. But as his mouth claimed hers—plundered, actually—she began to respond, not totally against her will.

Though a large man, this Kenric didn't hurt her or crush her small body to his massive chest. Rather he kissed her with a desperate sort of possession, the heat of which she could not fail to answer.

She had never felt such passion from a man. Certainly not from Roger, whose kisses were more the chaste, brotherly sort.

Her knees went weak and, of their own accord, her arms wound up around Kenric's neck, her hands tangling in his thick mane of chestnut hair.

He was beautiful, she had to admit, and so totally male. And she, after all, was female, dreaming or otherwise. It felt good to let her body melt into his rock-hard chest, good to feel the restraint in his huge, muscled arms as he held her.

Though they were alone, she was not afraid, even as he deepened the kiss and his breathing quickened. Even as she felt his arousal, swollen hard against her belly.

It was he who pulled away, wearing a stunned look on his handsome face. Running a hand through his disheveled hair, he glared at her. Equally stunned, Megan stared back.

With deliberate care, he reached down for the blanket and handed it back to her.

"Cover yourself, woman." His voice sounded gruff, strained. "I will not lie with you, despite your brazen display."

Startled, she flashed him a look. Did he really think *she* meant to seduce *him?*

"Take it," he ordered, thrusting the covering at her.

With clumsy haste she did as he bade her, her fingers colliding with his big hand as she snatched the blanket from his grip.

Outside, the wind hissed and moaned. Save for a few feet at the top, the entire entrance to the cave was blocked with snow. Their small fire still burned, though it sputtered and sparked.

But she was not cold, not at all, not now. From one

31

kiss—one earth-shattering, wonderful kiss—her entire body felt ablaze.

Who was this man? Why did he affect her this way?

"You are betrothed." His deep voice, harsh and emotionless, broke the silence.

Because technically this was true—she hadn't had time to break things off with Roger before the lightning had hit her—Megan did not contradict him. Instead she looked away, recognizing the condemnation in his statement and wishing she knew what the hell was going on. Was she dreaming or not?

"And you?"

"I?" His dark eyes narrowed, making her wonder if she'd stepped over some invisible line. Still, he'd been the one to kiss her, not the other way around, and she supposed she had a right to know.

"Yes, you. Are you betrothed"—she stumbled over the strange word—"or married?"

He laughed at that, a bitter sound so utterly devoid of humor that she shivered. "I am alone," he told her.

The wind, finding some hole by which to enter, shrieked through the cave as if in agreement. The fire sputtered, danced madly, and nearly went out.

"What a strange way to put it," she mused, shivering. "What about your family?"

The silence stretched on so long she wondered if he meant to ignore the question.

When he finally answered, his words were as bleak as the winter landscape outside. "My family is dead. All of them."

Stunned, Megan didn't know what to say. "I'm . . . sorry."

But he had turned back to the fire, and if he heard her he gave no sign.

Her stomach growled, reminding her that all she'd eaten had been a cereal bar that morning. She'd been so worried and afraid about breaking up with Roger that she hadn't been able to eat much for days.

Roger terrified her. It had come slowly at first, the small slights, the put-downs, the sneers. When he'd begun hurting her, she'd slid into a kind of meek acceptance.

But recently she'd begun to realize she might be in even more grave danger. He'd begun pestering her to change her will. Then she knew she had to end things. Whatever Roger felt for her, Megan knew it wasn't love.

Now here she stood, feeling as though she were starring in some old episode of *The Twilight Zone*, with a man who looked like Conan the Barbarian. Freezing her heinie off.

Despite the increasing weirdness of her situation, the thought made her smile. Maybe she really was dreaming. That would explain the change of season and the reason she'd responded so strongly to the kiss of a stranger.

A gorgeous stranger, she reminded herself, but a stranger nonetheless.

If it were a dream—and really, what other explanation could there be—she ought to enjoy it. Obviously her subconscious had conjured up this hunk because he was exactly what she needed at this point in her life. He was nothing, she thought as she let herself eye him up and down, nothing whatsoever like Roger.

Thank God.

And until she woke up—if she woke up—and had to face her fiancé's furious face, she might as well have a little fun. At the very least, this big warrior would keep her warm.

Bold thoughts for a coward. The plain truth of the matter was that Kenric of Blackstone's kiss had left her hungry for more.

Still, trying to plot out one's own fantasy might be easier thought of than done. This man, this warrior, was one intimidating specimen. He had made it perfectly obvious he thought her slightly unbalanced, if not down-right insane.

But she'd seen the hot look in his eyes as he'd perused her body, felt his arousal when he'd kissed her. Her own body tingled, and her heart beat faster when she thought of it. She'd never felt like that before. She wanted to feel that way again.

If this wasn't a dream—and really, she reassured herself again, what else could it be?—she was in trouble. Megan Potter, twenty-eight-year-old heiress and straitlaced socialite, desired a man who dressed in clothes more suited for some sort of playacting group, whose hair was longer than her own, and of whom she knew next to nothing.

But she had been engaged to Roger for nearly three years and he'd never, ever made her hunger for a kiss as this man had.

Working up her courage, she moved closer.

His shaggy head came up, his expression fierce and wary. "What do you want?"

Now or never.

"I want you to hold me," she managed to say in a strangled whisper, feeling her face heat.

Disbelief flashed across his rugged face. Then, slowly, his gaze darkened and she saw the fire of passion heat his glittering eyes.

"Woman, be careful how you tempt me," he said in a growl. "I have already told you—"

"No." Still blushing furiously, she struggled to find words to explain—or an excuse. "It's cold."

"Cold?"

As if he hadn't noticed. Megan sighed. "I thought maybe . . ." Heaven help her, she couldn't do it, even if this *was* a dream. "Never mind."

"You thought perhaps the heat from my body would warm you?"

Miserable now, she shot him a look from beneath her

lashes. As fantasies went, this wasn't going exactly as she would have scripted. By now he should have swept her up in his muscled arms and kissed away any lingering doubts. Instead he stood there glowering at her as if she'd somehow insulted him.

"I said never mind." Turning her back to him, she shivered and held her hands out to the fire. She didn't remember ever being this uncomfortable in a dream either.

At precisely that moment an icy wind gusted through the cave opening, dumping wet snow on the small fire and putting it out.

"Perfect," Megan muttered. "Okay, that's it. I've had enough. Dream's over. It's time to wake up."

From behind her, she heard a muffled curse.

"Stop this foolishness." His gravelly voice sounded weary. "We must make another fire here in the back of the cave."

"But the smoke—"

"Breathing smoke is better than freezing to death."

To confirm his words, another icy draft whistled through the cave.

If he could pretend that she hadn't made a fool out of herself, so could she. Bowing her head, shivering so hard she could barely control her hands, she went to his stack and immediately grabbed up as much dry kindling as she could carry.

"Where do you want it?"

"There."

She could have sworn amusement flickered across his harsh features before he turned away to get more wood.

"Now what?" She didn't have a lighter, or even a match. And she'd never been a Girl Scout, so she had no idea how he meant to start another fire.

Ignoring her, he reached into a pouch and pulled out some sort of stone and scratched it on another. From a spark he coaxed another; before too long a small fire sputtered to life.

Of course he would know how to start a fire. And she'd lay bets that he'd never been a Boy Scout either.

"Warm yourself. Then we will eat. I have bread and meat."

Great. Now all that was missing was a jug of wine. Some imagination I have, she thought with disgust. At least she could have conjured up a lobster or even a thick, juicy steak.

Though she was beginning to doubt that this was a dream. What else could have happened, she couldn't hazard a guess. One thing was for sure: she was nowhere near Dallas, Texas. Nowhere near the good ol' U.S. of A. either.

The fire felt good, warming her still-frozen hands, though the heavy smoke that soon filled the small cave made her eyes water. Near the cave opening Kenric chipped away at the pile of snow. Hollowing out a tunnel, tamping and bracing it with rocks and sticks, she saw he'd created a chimney of sorts—at least until it filled with snow. It did alleviate some of the smoke, letting her breathe more easily.

Megan watched as Kenric, muscles working, hefted blocks of stone into his makeshift chimney. With his leather clothing he looked like something out of a fantasy novel. She thought of Mel Gibson in the movie *Braveheart* and smiled. With his looks, this Kenric had to be an actor or a model. Maybe one of her friends had hired him as a joke—like Sarah Frazier, who nagged her every chance she got that Megan's life was too staid, too predictable.

This was not predictable. Her grin widened. Sarah's husband had plenty of money. Enough to create a blizzard in June. Maybe that was it.

But the chill in the air spoke more of a harsh northern winter than a snow machine in Texas. And Kenric could win an Academy Award for his performance, if that was what it was.

She continued to stare blindly at the man while he worked. She had to figure out what was going on. So far she'd eliminated a dream, eliminated a practical joke. Then what, exactly, had happened to her after she'd been hit by lightning? *Had* she even been hit by lightning?

First, she needed to ascertain the facts: where this cave was located, the month, the year, the day.

"What year is it?" she blurted.

Kenric paused in his work to look at her, his piercing dark eyes inscrutable. "Did you hit your head?"

"No. Yes." Clasping the blanket around her, she drew nearer to the fire. "I can't remember the year, or the month."

"I see." His smile, when it came, was gorgeous! a movie-star smile, turning her insides to mush. "It is December."

It had been June. "December? What year?"

"The year of our Lord 1072."

It took a moment for his words to register. When they did, Megan's knees went weak. "You're kidding, right?"

He stared blankly at her. "I do not understand your words."

"I . . . Never mind." Now she did allow herself to sink to the ground, knowing her legs wouldn't support her another moment. No dream, this. What could it be? Medieval role-playing? In the middle of a blizzard, in some godforsaken cave? Somehow she doubted it.

Licking lips suddenly gone dry, she peered up at him, shivers still racking her body. "And where is this place?"

His eyes narrowed, making him look dangerous. "The whereabouts of this cave need not concern you, milady. Suffice to say you are still on English land, once belonging to my family, granted by King William. Now it is occupied by another noble family. Before that"—he paused, his mouth twisted—"it was Welsh."

She pounced on the one word; that might help. "Welsh, as in Wales?"

Obviously thinking she'd lost her mind, he gave a slow nod.

"King William?" she asked in a squeak, still trying to digest his former statement.

His lip curled. "The English king. We won this land fairly from the Welsh. Despite the Welsh people's murderous attacks, the English still hold it, and will continue to do so. Where have you been that you do not know this?"

"I told you. I'm American, from—" She stopped, remembering that the country of America had not existed in 1072. Columbus hadn't even discovered the New World, and wouldn't for another four hundred and twenty years.

She wouldn't even be born for over another nine hundred years.

Oddly, Megan felt suddenly old, even for a twenty-eight-year-old north Dallas socialite. Elderly, even. Still, she had to take one last stab at a rational explanation.

"Are you with an escort service?"

He shook his head before she even finished. "Again, you use words that sound strange to me, even though I make allowances since it is plain from the way you speak that this is not your normal tongue."

He thought *she* spoke funny? She wished she could mimic his speech, but one thing she'd never taken the time to study was language—*any* language, never mind some obscure and ancient form of Old English as he seemed bent on using.

Though, if it really was 1072, Old English wasn't ancient. It wasn't even old.

"No," she whispered, rubbing her temples in hope of warding off the particularly violent headache she felt coming on. Right now she'd give anything for a couple of aspirin and a battery-powered space heater.

"I thought not." He rummaged in a leather pouch and

pulled out a small loaf of crusty bread and a shriveled meat of some sort, wrapped in cloth.

"Do you wish to eat?"

Miserable, Megan nodded.

Tearing off some bread and cutting the meat with a wicked-looking dagger, he passed her a portion.

To her surprise, the bread tasted like the French bread she made in her bread maker, and the meat, while chewy, had a smoky bite to it.

After she'd finished, she was relieved to feel the pressure in her head easing. Her shivering, too, seemed to have abated. With the fire to warm her, she felt almost comfortable.

So she sat silent, watching Kenric eat. He ate with dignity, though she would have imagined a man of his time to eat with less finesse.

Of his time. She nearly snorted out loud. She almost had herself believing that she'd somehow traveled back in time.

"Why are you here?" She blurted the question, still hoping he could somehow help her make sense of this crazy situation.

He raised one eyebrow. "Here?"

"In this cave. Surely you have someplace else you could be. Someplace warm?"

His expression turned to ice. Too late, she remembered what he'd said about his family, about being alone.

"I have no home."

Odd, she remembered from her studies that most men, even peasants, belonged to some village, some castle, some lord. Judging from the way this man acted, he was no peasant. She would have expected him to rule over some small kingdom or, at the very least, his own castle with his own army.

Though the harshness of his tone warned her against asking further questions, Megan persisted.

"This cave"—she waved a hand around—"is it your home full-time, year-round?"

He went still, looking for all the world like a ferocious lion about to pounce on unsuspecting prey—which would be her.

Outside, the storm quieted. Even with the crackle of the fire, she thought she could hear his harsh intake of breath.

"Who sent you?" He stood, towering menacingly over her. "I would have truth from you now."

She refused to let him know how intimidating he appeared. He wasn't Roger. He wouldn't hit her. This was a dream.

"Calm down. Please. No one sent me. I don't even know how I wound up here."

"Speak English!" he said in a growl, his eyes dark and angry. "What of this Roger? Where is his holding?"

Something told her she'd better play along. "He comes from a place far from here." *There, that was a safe answer.* And, she thought proudly, she hadn't lied.

"You call England far?" Disbelief warred with anger in his aristocratic features. "It but borders us here."

Since Megan didn't have a response for that, she said nothing. Suddenly she longed for her comfortable home in North Dallas, for central heat and air and electricity and telephones. For normal people.

There had to be some way out of this. There had to be.

"You've got to help me." She knew she sounded desperate, but didn't care. Even Roger, with his myriad cruelties, would almost be welcome. At least he was familiar.

"Help me find Roger. I'm sure he'll make certain you're rewarded."

She watched as the musclebound giant flashed a cynical look at her.

"What kind of trick is this?"

"No trick, I swear it." Even if Roger wasn't willing to pay this man once she got safely home, she had funds of her own. She could pay—and would pay—well.

His dark brows lowered. "This Roger, he is wealthy?"

She nearly laughed out loud with relief. Money. Even in the supposed year of 1072 it all came down to that. Things hadn't changed that much in nine hundred years.

"Roger owns his own—" She almost said *company*. Instead she tried to find a word that Kenric could understand.

"Keep?" Finishing for her, Kenric again looked furious.

Strange word, that. "Yes." Megan licked her lips. "He owns his own castle—er, keep." Roger was nearly as wealthy as she was. The huge skyscraper on Stemmons Freeway could be considered a castle of sorts.

"Land?" He said it as if it were the most important thing in the world.

Since all of Roger's buildings sat on some very valuable North Dallas land, she nodded.

"All my life I have wanted my own land." Kenric spoke quietly, almost under his breath. "I am bastard born, with no hope of inheriting. Even before my family was killed, I wanted my own land."

Then Megan knew what she would have to offer him, even if she couldn't quite deliver it. It was this land he wanted, acres and acres of rolling green pasture most likely, not some lot on Cedar Creek Lake, or an industrial park in downtown Dallas. That kind of land was something neither she nor Roger had any way of giving him. Still, she had no choice.

"Perhaps"—her voice broke as she gagged on the lie— "Roger may reward you with some."

"His surname?"

She nearly choked. Luckily for her Roger was of English descent, though she had no idea if his name meant anything in this time.

"Spencer," she told him. "His name is Roger Spencer."

"*Lord* Roger Spencer?"

Swallowing again, she nodded. Roger, at least, thought he was some sort of royalty, judging from the way he expected everyone to jump to do his bidding.

Folding his muscular arms across his massive chest, Kenric still seemed suspicious.

"What proof have you?"

Proof. Great. She cast her mind back to every medieval movie she'd ever seen or book she'd ever read. A token. He'd need some token from her as a pledge that she was indebted to him.

She stared at her hands—left hand, third finger, to be exact. Her engagement ring, the gaudily sparkling, pear-shaped diamond that she hated, winked up at her. In its elaborate setting of gold knots flanked by oval sapphires, it had always seemed a bit pretentious to her. Roger had chosen it, of course. He liked things flashy. Now, though, it looked positively medieval, perfect for what she had to do.

Without further hesitation she slid the ring from her finger and held it out. "I can give you this."

Slowly he took it from her, causing her to notice how long and elegant his fingers were. Odd in such a big man.

Turning it around in his hand, he examined it with the bored expression of a man used to fine things.

"Did he give this to you?"

She nodded, trying to remember the wording she should use. Not that she completely bought into this traveling back in time thing, but better safe than sorry.

"By this token he will know that I am indebted to you." Holding her breath, she prayed she'd said the right thing.

Evidently she had, for his thunderous expression lightened. He inclined his shaggy head regally and accepted her ring.

"When the storm clears, I will take you to this Roger. Until he is found, I will protect you."

Chapter Three

Her heart stuttered at his words. Ah, if he only knew what he promised. "Thank you."

"Now"—Kenric indicated the fire—"we must rest."

Megan swallowed. "Where?" Wrapping the thin blanket around her more securely, she shivered.

"You may sleep closest to the fire." He spoke in the tone of one granting a huge favor.

She scuffed her foot along the hard, rocky ground and thought of her fluffy, soft bed at home.

"I don't think I can," she told him, her voice small and miserable.

Instantly he seemed to understand the problem. With a wry smile, he brought her his saddle blanket.

"This will give you some comfort. 'Tis what I use to sleep upon."

"But—" She stared up at this giant of a man, unable to read his expression. "If I take it, what will you sleep on?"

"There is straw that I can spread. The horse can spare it. I am well used to the floor of my cave," he told her, his tone brooking no argument. "Now go to sleep."

Her innate sense of fairness wouldn't let her, though even the coarse saddle blanket looked more inviting than standing and shivering. "I can't let you do that," she told him quietly. "We will share this blanket."

His head came up at her words, his dark gaze pinning her. "Be careful what you say, woman. For all you know, I might take you up on your offer. What then would your Roger think?"

Color flooded her face as she realized what Kenric had thought. "No, I didn't mean like that." To her dismay, tears pricked at her eyes. "I thought we could share the blanket for warmth. *Only* for warmth."

He muttered something under his breath, something fierce and guttural. Whatever it was, it did not sound complimentary.

"Forget it," she told him, her throat aching. It had all been too much for her and she could be strong no longer. She dropped down on the saddle blanket and rolled into a ball. She would rather die before she let him see her cry. Covering herself with the flimsy blanket, she swallowed convulsively and let the tears come in silence.

Megan felt it when he moved toward her. Ignoring him, she surreptitiously wiped at her eyes and kept her face covered. Unfortunately her nose was clogged, and her attempt at a discreet sniffle sounded watery and loud.

"What is this?" Compassion mingled with annoyance in his deep voice. "Why do you weep? Are you hurt?"

He thought she was injured. Fiercely she rubbed her eyes, glad. She'd rather he thought that than believe she'd given in to a spell of irrational female weeping, as Roger would have said.

"Go away." Though muffled by the blanket, she thought she sounded rather brave. OK, quavery maybe, but brave nonetheless.

Instead of moving away, or making cruel comments as Roger would have, he crouched down next to her. "Is there anything I can do?"

She shook her head, still keeping the blanket over her face.

With a loud sigh he scooped her up in his muscular arms. Rocking on his heels, he settled on the saddle blanket and pulled her onto his lap.

Megan went instantly, frozenly still.

Kenric said nothing, just held her close. She peeked up at him from under her soggy eyelashes. Instead of looking down at her as she'd half expected, he stared into the fire. The dancing amber glow of the flames made him look both beautiful and dangerous.

But he was warm, and it felt so good to be held by him. Gradually Megan relaxed into sleep.

Kenric knew the exact instant the woman went to sleep. Her slim body became boneless and her head drooped against his chest.

She weighed nothing, this tiny woman. She was not large breasted nor curvy like most of the tavern wenches he had known. Yet something about her lit a fire in his blood. Perhaps it was her very defenselessness, or her exotically fascinating face. Though she was not conventionally beautiful, she was lovely nonetheless. And her eyes—those amber eyes of hers hinted at secrets, tempting him beyond belief.

Because he'd given his word, something he hadn't done in years, to help her find her Roger, he was now bound by honor to protect her. Even from himself.

Outside the blizzard continued to rage.

Inside Kenric fought his own battle. How easy it would be to plunder those sweet lips, already parted, while she slept. He knew just how to awaken a woman with slow, sensual finger strokes and deep, drugging kisses until she arched against him and begged for more.

His body thickened and hardened as he thought of it. Asleep in his arms, the woman lay slumbering, unaware.

Resolutely he forced himself to think of other things. Her Roger would not appreciate a bastard, a hired sword, deflowering his intended. Kenric could not blame him.

Megan shifted in his arms, murmuring softly. Leaning close, he breathed deeply of her strange scent, more powerful even than the heavy smoke: the scent of flowers, the scent of spring. And here in his lonely cave with the howl of the wind promising retribution for his sins, he wondered where she had come from.

Morning came with a brightness of light that hurt Kenric's eyes. Somehow he'd managed to sleep, though little. The brightness of sunlight reflecting off snow told him the storm had finally ceased—that and the utter absence of sound from outside.

Their fire had died down to glowing embers that gave little warmth. Shifting his numb arms, he eased the woman onto the ground, ignoring his morning arousal, ignoring too how she sleepily, greedily reached for his warmth.

Standing, he gathered more dried kindling and built up the fire. When he finally turned, it was to find her sitting up, wrapped in his ancient blanket, watching him with sleep-filled, puzzled eyes. Still, they were the most beautiful eyes he'd ever seen.

He would do well to find her Roger and be rid of her. God's blood, he could not remember when he'd last been so tempted.

This confused him, for he allowed nothing to sway him from his quest. What irony, then, that the one thing that made him burn might be the means by which he achieved his goal.

She promised land. *Land.* For four years he'd thought of nothing else. For much of his life, he had been lucky, a bastard son acknowledged and loved by his father and family. Yet there was no help for the fact that as a bastard he had no claim to their keep, to their herds, to their land. He'd always known he would have to get his own by whatever method necessary. He'd thought that perhaps if he served his father or his half brothers well, one of them might gift him with a small parcel.

He had not counted on death robbing him of even that slight hope.

And now he had a duty to his dead father, to the brothers who'd taught him to fight and to laugh and to drink. He was the last of the family, the only one whose seed could bring continuance to a proud and noble name. Bastard born, yes. But his children and his children's spawn would be the future.

So he must do his duty, a promise extracted by his father as he lay, some two weeks after the attack, bleeding and feverish. His father had known then that all his right-born sons were dead. He had charged Kenric with the task of fathering the future of the line, given him the sword to seal the bargain.

To raise a family, Kenric must have land. The king had seen fit, in his shortsighted wisdom, to gift the land once belonging to Kenric's father to another family of noble birth, rather than to the bastard son.

Land must be obtained by another means.

Now this Megan had promised that her Roger would gift him with some land. Kenric would not have to purchase it with his small hoard of hard-earned gold. He would be able to use the gold for other things—to build his keep, to buy foodstuffs and supplies, even mayhap to hire a small army of his own.

So now all that he must do was find this Roger. And, no matter how difficult it might seem, return Megan Potter unblemished, untouched.

He grinned savagely. Put like that, it would be easy. All of these years—the blurry, bitter years since he'd learned of his family's obliteration—all these years of fighting for causes he did not believe in, for money that he hoarded and saved, and it had come down to this. One simple deed, one last quest, and his most cherished dream would come true.

He hardly dared to allow himself to think of it, so great was his elation. For this he would take her across the mountains in the dead of winter if he had to. For this he would even enter the stronghold of the Welsh, who knew and revered the hated Faerie folk, in the hope that her apparent high birthright would afford him some protection.

If all she wanted was to be returned to this Roger, some English nobleman who no doubt searched for her this very moment, he would be happy to oblige her.

Because she still watched him, he contained his glee.

"Where is"—she waved a hand, looking uncomfortable—"the bathroom?"

Kenric gaped at her. "You wish to bathe now, when water turns to ice and there is snow all around us?"

She colored prettily, catching her lower lip between her teeth. "Not bathe. I need to, uh . . ."

"I don't have a chamber pot," he told her, wishing he did not have to be so blunt but seeing no way around it. "I am always alone in the cave, so I go outside."

"Outside." She darted a glance toward the snow-packed entrance. "How deep do you suppose it is?"

God save him from feminine modesty. "I will make a path for you," he told her, glad of a task with which to occupy his unruly body. Grabbing the crude shovel he had made from an old practice shield, he began pushing the snow aside.

When he had completed a tunnel-like path, he turned toward the small copse of oak trees with their concealing outcropping of rock. Here he cleaned an area twice as long as his horse, and four times as wide. Once the woman had finished, he would need to bring the warhorse here also.

"Thank you." Wrapped in her pathetically thin covering, the woman stepped out from the cave. The quaver in her husky voice unnerved him.

Inclining his head in a nod, he moved past her. Inside the cave it felt warm; the small fire crackled merrily. His warhorse turned his huge head and nickered. No doubt the beast was hungry. Hay was in short supply, though luckily he'd thought to pilfer some grain from the keep's stores. He fed the animal, melting some snow in his helmet for water.

With a flurry of movement, the woman returned. She rushed to the fire, holding out her pale hands and shivering so hard that he could hear her teeth chatter.

"You will have to wear my clothing," he told her in a tone that brooked no argument. "Unless you have a gown hidden somewhere." He regarded her hopefully.

"No." Still shivering, she shook her head and flashed a miserable smile. "I have nothing."

Resigned, he went to the back of the cave, where he kept a wooden chest. Rummaging inside of it, he found her a heavy tunic and a pair of wool breeches. Watching carefully for her reaction, since it was common knowledge that only men of noble birth had such fine garments, he handed them to her.

She did not appear to notice.

"Thanks." Flashing him a wan smile, she pulled the tunic on over her own clothing, then stepped into his breeches. Of course, they were too large, so he handed her a length of rope to use for a belt.

When she'd finished rolling up the cuffs, she squared her shoulders, lifted her chin, and faced him. "What now?"

For a moment Kenric could not find his voice. Though the tunic was several sizes too big, fitting her more like a gown than a shirt, the way she wore it made him think of sleeping chambers and rumpled covers. He forced his gaze away, looking instead at the fire as if he might find the answers to all of life's mysteries in the dancing flames.

"Now." Choosing his words carefully, Kenric kept his voice level and emotionless. "You must tell me of this Roger. If I am to take you to him I need to know where he lives."

"Far away," she answered quickly.

Much too quickly, he thought, searching her face. "What is the name of the place?"

This time he meant to catch her in the falsehood. Well he remembered the name she'd given him, speaking as if the place were some country rather than a town. *I'm American,* she'd said, though he knew of no such place.

Before she even opened her mouth, he knew she meant to lie. Like a small child caught stealing sweets, she couldn't even meet his gaze. Then she mumbled something so low under her breath that he couldn't hear it.

"Where?"

She raised her head. He felt a jolt when her huge amber eyes met his. He could swear he saw defiance in the set of her small chin, the flash of her gaze.

"Dallas, Texas."

She'd told him that before. The first word sounded vaguely Roman. The second . . . he knew not what to make of it. The woman lied; of this he felt certain. But why? She wanted to find this Roger, did she not?

He, Kenric of Blackstone, meant to find this Roger too. Quickly, so that he might claim his promised reward. He would have the truth, even if he had to force it from her.

Intending merely to threaten her, he moved toward her. At his sudden movement she flinched, as though she expected him to beat her.

"You think I'm lying." The fearful misery in her expression stopped him as effectively as a sharp sword. What kind of man did she think him? Did she truly believe that he, a warrior, would actually strike her?

He forced himself to remain still, so as not to frighten her further. "Aren't you?"

She made a restless movement with her hands, shifting herself away from him. "No, I am not. But I think the place I come from doesn't exist, at least not yet."

More nonsense. He must remember that she'd somehow injured her head. "I see."

"No." Her tone was sharp, echoing in the confines of the cave. "You don't see. I am farther than mere miles from my home. God!" She shook her head, the motion sending her hair flying wildly. "Now I'm even talking like you."

"Calm yourself." Taking her arm, he guided her to where his saddle blanket still lay, spread on the ground near the fire.

"Come, sit and have some bread. You will tell me all you know of this Roger."

Reluctantly, Megan allowed him to lead her over to the fire. She didn't know what to do. He wanted to know about Roger, but anything she could tell him would seem like the ravings of an insane lunatic. Roger drove a silver Porsche 911, lived in a tony North Dallas house, and preferred to have his suits custom-made. He loved football, especially the Dallas Cowboys, and enjoyed finding small ways to torment her. Lately he had graduated to bigger and bigger torments. Most recently he'd given her a black eye and a broken rib when she'd refused to change her will, making him her sole beneficiary.

The thought sobered her instantly. Maybe she was better off here, for now. Safer, at least. She'd been a fool to think Roger would let her break their engagement. No doubt he would kill her if she returned.

She shivered. She was safe for the moment. Right now Roger had no idea where she was. He'd been walking toward her, and the sky had been that particular Texas shade of brilliant blue; then, *bam!* She'd been transported somehow to the winter in some godforsaken place, attended to by a Conan the Barbarian look-alike who honestly believed he lived over nine hundred years in the past.

It was hard to decide which was worse.

This Kenric meant to help her find Roger. Though in truth she had no desire to ever see her former fiancé again, this task was all she had to keep Kenric with her. Perhaps somehow he could arrange for her to return home. Though how, she wondered, was he going to take her across time? Yet she knew that if she mentioned that little fact to him, he would truly believe her mad.

At this point, she questioned her own sanity.

"I am waiting." With the tone of a man used to being obeyed, Kenric spoke. Still, he made no move to hurt her, reminding her that not all men were like Roger.

"Roger," she said, thinking back to what little she knew of medieval culture. If she remembered right, it was not uncommon in those times for a bride to know little about her husband before the wedding. She could use this, make it work for her, because what she knew of Roger she couldn't tell this man. He'd never understand.

"Roger is wealthy," she told him firmly, deciding to tell as much of the truth as possible. "I have known him all of my life."

Kenric cocked his head, his gaze considering. "And what value does he place on you?"

It took her a moment to realize what he meant. "He loves me very much," she said, gagging on the lie. She felt a pang of sorrow for the fool she had been.

She raised her eyes to find Kenric watching her.

"What is it?" His voice, though soft, seemed edged with steel. "What brings such fear and sorrow to your face?"

Startled, both by the way he'd been able to read her

so correctly, and by the fact that he even cared, Megan swallowed.

"N-nothing."

For the space of a heartbeat she thought he'd insist she tell him; then he simply nodded and waved one large hand. "Go on then."

Roger. She'd been talking about Roger.

"He's tall." She tried to think. Yes, Roger was tall, though not nearly the size of this giant. "Slender. And he has blond hair."

At Kenric's blank look she elaborated. "Hair the color of wheat. He is an important man. Others listen when he speaks."

"I care not what he looks like. Tell me of his holdings."

Holdings? Oh, he means land. Of course. But how did she explain the concept of twentieth-century Dallas to this man?

"The land he holds is important."

"To whom? The king?"

She noted the sudden sharpness in his gaze. Uneasy, she shifted her weight on the blanket. "I don't know the English king."

Kenric's handsome mouth twisted. "But you know of him."

Wondering what he would say if she told him that in her time a queen, rather than a king, sat on the throne in England, she shook her head.

"Not really." Heck, she had no idea even what monarch had ruled England in 1072. King William, he'd said.

Roger. She needed to get back to familiar ground, back to talking about Roger. What else could she say?

"Roger employs many people." Thousands, at last count.

"Employs?"

She did a rapid translation in her head. "I mean rules."

This time he looked more than skeptical; he looked disbelieving.

"Then these people of his must all be out looking for you. Combing the countryside, especially if this Roger of yours commands it."

"He doesn't have an army," Megan shot back, pleased with her quick thinking. "These people are mostly workers."

"Serfs?"

Calling Roger's employees serfs might be pushing it a bit far. But, when in Rome . . .

"Yes, serfs."

"Surely he commands his own men."

Though she knew Kenric meant warriors, she couldn't help but think of Roger's board of directors. Instead of seeing them dressed in custom-made suits, she tried to picture them clad like this Kenric of Blackstone, in tunics and leggings. The thought seemed ludicrous.

"Do you find something amusing?" Kenric's deep voice broke into her thoughts, making her realize she'd been staring off into space, a small smile on her face.

"Er, no." She schooled her face into a more somber expression. "Roger has twelve men who are his personal, er, force."

"Twelve." Kenric nodded, apparently approving of the number. "How many of them would he dispatch to search for you?"

Great. Now she'd gotten herself in hot water again. "I think they'd all travel together?" she ventured.

It was her luck that woman were not supposed to understand the ways of men and warfare.

Kenric chuckled, making him look approachable-handsome instead of forbidding-handsome. He muttered something under his breath that sounded suspiciously like *women*, proving that no matter what the time period, men didn't really ever change.

"What?" Megan couldn't keep from asking.

"Your Roger would not take all of his men with him to search for you. He would split them up, have them travel in different directions."

So much for that. Standing, Megan breathed the frigid air deep into her lungs, wishing she could get rid of the ever-present sooty reek of the smoke from their fire.

"All we have to do"—Kenric stood also, stretching in a way that made his muscular torso seem to ripple—"is find one of your Roger's men, if not your betrothed himself."

Transfixed, Megan couldn't help but stare, her mouth dry. She'd never seen a more beautiful man, or one more ruggedly attractive. It took her a moment to realize that Kenric had spoken. What had he said? Something about finding Roger. Roger was the last person she wanted to find. But the way to Roger was the way home. Did she really want to go home?

"Good," she muttered through numb lips. Her breasts tingled. God, she hadn't known a man could affect her the way this man did. Sexual attraction wasn't everything, but it sure didn't hurt.

"We will ride in the morning."

This got her attention. "Ride? Like that huge animal over there?" She pointed to his horse, wondering what he'd say when he learned she'd never been on a horse before in her life.

He laughed again, obviously thinking she was kidding. "My warhorse will not hurt you. Unlike most others of his kind, he is gentle and a good friend. He can easily carry twice my weight."

Looking at the massive animal, she didn't doubt it. She decided not to tell him of her lack of equestrian skills. Maybe she'd luck out again and he'd simply assume it was a problem associated with her being a woman.

Still, she'd wished she had her car.

"One other thing." Kenric folded his massive arms

across his chest. "When we leave here, you will become a boy."

"A boy?"

"Yes. Dressed in my clothes"—his gaze traveled the length of her, making her burn—"it shouldn't be too difficult."

Great. So he thought she looked like a boy. Glancing down at herself, clad in the too-large leggings and huge, shapeless tunic, she supposed she couldn't really blame him. Especially since he was most likely used to women in the ornate, formal gowns of his time.

"Your vassal?" she asked.

After a startled look, he threw his shaggy dark head back and laughed.

"Perhaps I missed it," he said, the amusement making him look ten years younger—and ten times more handsome.

Megan tried to clear her brain. It seemed to get a bit foggy whenever she looked at him. "Missed what?"

"When you swore your oath of allegiance to me."

OK, so maybe *vassal* had been the wrong word. She searched her brain, trying to remember what the correct term could be.

"Sorry. I was only trying to help."

At his brusque nod, she gave a sigh of relief, watching as he went to where he'd heaped his belongings. After a moment, he pulled out a long leather scabbard, carrying it almost lovingly to the fire. Even she, as ignorant of medieval things as she was, recognized it as a sword.

Slowly he withdrew it, the metal blade sparkling in the cracking firelight. Megan couldn't help it—she stared.

When he noticed her, he held it up so that the point faced the roof of the cave. It looked wickedly sharp, yet oddly beautiful. She wondered if Kenric would take offense were she to touch it.

"Yes, it is mine." His deep voice seemed to echo in

the small cave, reverberating with fierce pride and what she thought might be sorrow.

"It's magnificent."

He seemed to accept her words as due homage. "It belonged to my father, and his father before him. It was to have been my older brother's, had he lived." Lowering the blade, he began to polish it with a soft cloth, his large hands moving lovingly over the sharp steel.

Megan felt a twinge, wondering what it would feel like if those capable, long-fingered hands touched her skin that way.

"Does it have a name?" She was hesitant to ask, but felt relatively certain that she remembered this much from books. Or maybe only kings and princes named their swords.

Kenric did not seem to find her question ridiculous, however. Sheathing the sword, he carried it back to its place against the wall before answering.

"It does." Turning, he considered her, his eyes molten with reflected firelight, yet dark with his own memories. He looked like some pagan warrior, capable of slaying dragons and carrying distressed maidens off to safety. Capable, too, of breaking that same maiden's heart.

She would do well to remember that, even if this was only a dream.

"I cannot tell you the name." He gave a huge sigh, coming back to the fire and taking a seat alongside her. "For you to know the name gives you power over it. I keep forgetting you have injured your head, or you would know this. I will not tell you the name, but it means thunder."

Thunder.

Now it was she who felt restless, she who felt compelled to move from the warmth of the fire and pace the confines of the cave. Kenric sat too close, and though he could not know it, the temptation to touch him ran hot in her blood.

"The name suits you."

He frowned, obviously not liking the comparison.

"And the sword, of course," she tacked on hastily, at his grimace.

There was a wry twist to his sensual mouth. "Though I am but a bastard, great care was taken in naming me."

A bastard. In times like these that title carried so much more painful baggage than it did in her time.

Times like these. Did she really believe that? Unless she was the recipient of some bizarre, mind-altering drug, she had no choice.

"One more thing," he said casually, flexing his long-fingered, callused hands before him. "I am done with fighting. I would not like to kill again, even for you."

Kill? Conscious that her mouth had fallen open, Megan closed it. *Great.* One thing she did remember from her admittedly scattered reading about medieval times was that the men, both bandits and knights alike, were bloodthirsty. And she was stuck with a man who wouldn't defend her. Or, she amended, wouldn't kill for her.

Hey, this is good. Really. This was a sign of maturity, of civilization. Summoning a smile, she nodded at the big man who watched her silently, waiting.

"That's okay with me." On impulse, she grabbed one of his outstretched hands and squeezed it, noticing how different the hard, callused fingers were from Roger's smooth, manicured hand. "I wouldn't kill for you either."

Startled, he yanked his hand away. Fire flared in his eyes, the heat quite different from that of the flames that warmed them.

"Do you mock me?"

So the male ego had not changed at all in nine hundred years.

"Of course not," she soothed, wishing she'd kept her mouth shut. "I made a joke . . . er, a jest."

He seemed to accept this, stalking once again to his saddlebag and withdrawing their dinner.

They broke bread, again partaking of the odd-tasting dried meat.

He had some wine, sour and sweet at the same time, the taste of it metallic on her tongue. Drinking it helped ease some of her nervousness at the approaching night.

Would he hold her again?

She shivered. Though he'd behaved like a gentleman, she knew her own wayward thoughts had been less than ladylike. The sooner she could get away from him, the better. But for now she needed him to help her search. Not for Roger, as he thought, but for the gateway to her time. She had to get home, back to the twentieth century, where she belonged.

Chapter Four

Watching her, Kenric wondered if he'd imagined the look of contempt in her beautiful eyes. If she despised him, he could not blame her. All women had a right to expect that a man would defend them.

Not that he wouldn't; he simply did not plan to kill again if he could help it. And as long as he was the only one who knew she was a woman, he should not have to. No one ever bothered lowly squires. As a boy she was safe. Now, if only he could make his body forget the truth of it.

Thoughts of the coming night had his blood pounding heavy and slow. He wondered if he should hold her again, wondered if she would want him to, wondered if he dared.

When she came back inside, shivering from the cold, all caution left him. Holding out his arms, he waited until she was nestled snugly against him before lying back on the saddle blanket. Now he had but to prove that his mind could control his body.

She sighed, shifting once, then relaxed. The fire burned low, the dim orange glow making nameless shadows dance on the cave walls.

Gradually her shivering stopped as their bodies generated heat. He closed his eyes, trying to ignore the floral, feminine scent of her. A strand of her hair tickled his nostril; he brought his hand up to push it away. Somehow he found himself caressing the silky smoothness of her boyishly short hair.

Her breathing caught. Kenric found himself straining to hear her take another breath. When she did, it was a harsh one, low and very nearly a moan. His body responded instantly, and he cursed his traitorous longings.

Still, he did not move his hand.

With another half sigh, she relaxed into his massage. Eyes closed, she arched against him, a sleepy kitten under his fingers. The thin blanket shifted; his gaze went to her breasts and his breath caught in his throat. Her nipples were large, hard like pebbles, inviting the touch of his hand or his mouth.

If she moved again, she would know how she affected him.

He wanted her beyond all reason.

Yet she was the intended bride of this Roger, the man who would, for her safe return, gift him with his heart's desire. Land. He must remember that Roger would not take kindly to Kenric deflowering his woman.

He forced himself to think of the land, always the land. There would be other women. There would not be another chance like this.

Reluctant, his body straining against the front of his braes, Kenric deposited her gently on the blanket and pushed himself to his feet. He kept himself turned away from her, not wanting her to see his arousal.

"Where"—her voice sounded low, husky and sensual—"are you going?"

Though he knew he shouldn't, he could not keep from looking back over his shoulder at her. The firelight flickered over her tousled hair. She had the look of a woman in need of a man.

In disbelief, Kenric felt himself grow harder. Shaking his head, he headed out the small cave opening into the blowing snow and icy air.

Later, much later, cold and disgruntled, he returned to find her asleep. Disdaining the warmth of the shared blanket, he picked a spot on the opposite side of the fire.

Though he tried, sleep eluded him that night. The ground felt uneven and rocky, the smallest stone irritating his skin. Though he'd slept on this same ground a hundred times, though he'd bedded down in worse places, he could not get comfortable. Infuriating for a man, dangerous for a warrior. And he knew it was all because of this irrational, burning desire for a woman he could not have.

He had his gear packed and the warhorse loaded before she woke.

"Morning," she muttered, stumbling outside with her eyes half-closed and the ridiculously thin blanket wrapped around her instead of his warm cloak. He wanted to chide her, but thought it more prudent to hold his silence. If he kept things on a strictly impersonal level, it would be better for both of them.

When she returned he kept his back turned, checking the supplies one final time. With his chestnut coat gleaming despite the shaggy winter coat, the warhorse snorted, antsy, ready to go. He knew how the animal felt.

"What's his name?" Her soft voice came from right behind him, nearly making him jump. He cursed under his breath. Until lately, no one had been able to sneak up on him unaware. More proof that it was time to retire his sword.

"He has no name." Kenric sounded harsher than he intended; even his horse shifted sideways. He glanced at her—a mistake, he knew instantly. Though she'd finger-combed her dark hair, her cat's eyes still looked heavy with sleep. She blew a short gust of air from her lips, drawing his attention to her mouth—her lush, full, kissable mouth. Heat flashed through him, making him remember the raw, sensual taste of her.

"No name?" She laughed, reaching out one slender hand to touch the animal's thick neck. "Did you just get him?"

Setting his jaw, Kenric tore his gaze away. "I've had him for years." Since the day he'd found his family slaughtered, his father dying in the bloody, deserted keep, and the warhorse starving in his stall.

She fell silent, perhaps astounded by the fact that this animal that he so obviously valued had no name. When she spoke again, it was to ask a question that he should have anticipated.

"Why haven't you named him?"

Because he wasn't sure he could articulate the reason, and because the less she knew of him and his life the better, he chose not to answer.

"The sun rises," he told her instead, pointing to the gradually lightening cave entrance. "It is time we ride."

"Do I have duties?"

Kenric blinked, wondering what she meant, knowing she had not meant anything like the erotic thoughts that immediately came to mind. "Duties?"

"Yes," Megan said, her tone the exaggerated drawl all women used when they believed they spoke with limitless patience for the slowness of men. "What, exactly, does a squire do?"

Despite himself, he had to smile. "A squire serves a knight. Takes care of his armor and other things. Usually you would have your own horse, though a palfrey, not a beast of war."

She bit her lip, looking small and defenseless and less like a squire than anyone he'd ever seen. Protectiveness welled up in him, horrifying him. This desire to protect her was what he sought to escape. Especially since he knew he would ultimately fail, just as he'd failed to save his family.

Her tentative touch on his arm brought him out of his reverie.

"Are you all right?"

"Fine." With a brusque nod he clasped her around the waist, lifting her onto the broad back of his horse. To her credit, she made no sound, though her entire body might have become wood, so stiff did she hold herself. His hands seemed impossibly large, spanning her tiny waist. Suddenly he, a man fast on his feet, known as lightning with a sword, felt unbelievably clumsy, oafish even. To her he must seem a veritable giant.

And she was a female alone, weak and defenseless.

He wondered if she realized how lucky she had been, that he and not some marcher lord had found her. Or another hired sword, one with no honor. There were many men like that. In these parts, honor was in short supply.

With a start he realized he still held her and jerked his hands away. She watched him from beneath her lashes, her face pale and drawn. In the depths of her gaze he saw something, but he knew not what.

Then, recognizing it, he chastised himself for not realizing it sooner. Fear lurked there, barely masked. Of him? No, for in the next second she glanced at the horse's massive head, biting her lip. She would have to conquer her fear, for they had many miles to cover before they reached the nearest village.

Shaking his head, he mounted his steed, careful not to

touch Megan. The warhorse, eager to be off, tossed his head and nickered.

"Ready?" Scarcely waiting for her answer, Kenric tightened his calves, signaling the beast to move. The horse, surefooted and wise, picked his way among the rocks, increasing his stride when they reached flat land, still covered in deep, powdery snow.

"Where are we going?"

He pointed to the east, hoping she would not remember from what direction they'd come. "The nearest village is that way. It is to there we go, to see if your Roger has left any men to search for you."

They moved at a brisk walk, the horse's sturdy legs churning up the unbroken snowy whiteness. The cold air, though still, hung heavy with the promise of more snow. The leaden sky held no promise of sun.

And behind him, Megan sat so stiff, so frozen, that if it weren't for her carefully controlled shivering, he wouldn't have known she was alive.

He fell into his own thoughts, letting himself dream of the land that would soon be his.

More and more Megan felt guilty for lying to Kenric. Part of her wanted to tell him the truth, but she knew that if she did he'd think her insane. She wasn't even sure she wanted to go home, to wake up from this crazy Technicolor dream and find herself in modern-day Dallas.

But then she knew she didn't want to stay here, in this cold, barren land, for too long. She'd have to go home.

Without Kenric of Blackstone's help, she knew she'd never make it. Yet she, who prided herself on being up-front and honest, had to secure his help with a lie. Not just any lie either, but apparently his heart's desire. Land. Now how on earth would she pay him off? She didn't know. She knew only that if she found a way, any way, to get this man some land, she would do it. Once he'd helped her find her way home, of course. And maybe she could get him to make sure Roger left her alone as well.

They crested a slight hill and he reined the horse in. Wondering why they'd stopped, Megan craned her neck, trying to see around his broad back.

"There." He pointed, turning the horse sideways so she could see. "Perhaps someone there can help us."

In the valley below she could make out buildings, smoke rising from most of them. And people—she thought she could make out the tiny forms of people bustling around in the cold morning air below. But she saw no automobiles, no traffic lights, nothing to let her know they had returned to the world she knew.

It was as Kenric had said. Exactly as in a medieval movie, a bustling village waited below.

She tried not to let her spirits sink. If she had somehow been transported back in time, there had to be a way out. Maybe in this community, impossible as it seemed, there would be someone who knew how she could get home.

Eager to be off, the horse shied sideways. Megan tightened her grip around Kenric's waist.

"If you would not hold yourself so stiffly, you would be in less danger of losing your seat," he told her.

She could have sworn he sounded amused. No doubt he would find it highly entertaining were she to land on her behind in the snow. "I'll keep that in mind."

"When we reach the village, you must remember that you are a squire."

A boy. In other words, she needed to lose all trace of her femininity. Not, she thought, glancing ruefully down at her baggy pants and too-large tunic, that she had much left. At least her hair was short. Though with Kenric's long hair, maybe that was another oddity in this time and place.

"I will remember," she told him, lifting her chin, determined to make this work. It *had* to work, if she had any chance at all of going home.

"Good." With an invisible command, he urged the

horse forward and they plunged down the hill.

The villagers recognized Kenric. Several lifted their hands in greeting, their lined faces wreathed in smiles. Megan knew she shouldn't be surprised—obviously the man lived in the area—but part of her had expected people to act as if he were some lunatic bodybuilder with a fondness for medieval clothes. The same part of her steadfastly refused to believe she had somehow traveled back in time to the past. But everyone else was dressed similarly to Kenric. The women wore long, archaic dresses, their hair bound or flowing freely down their backs, and the men resembled long-haired barbarians— though none seemed as big or as brawny as Kenric.

No one seemed to mind the bone-numbing cold.

Kenric slowed the horse, pausing in front of a weathered stone building with a crudely lettered sign out front—a tavern.

OK. Megan rubbed her frozen hands together. Now they were getting somewhere. A hot rum toddy sounded wonderful.

"If your Roger has men searching for you, they will know it here." His chiseled features grim, Kenric dismounted, his cloak swirling around his broad shoulders.

When Megan made a move to follow him, he held up his hand.

"Wait for me."

With a resigned sigh, she nodded. For now she thought it would be best if she didn't speak, in case her voice gave away her identity. She knew she could deepen it if she had to, but wasn't sure it would pass muster.

Watching him stroll away, she marveled at his unconscious arrogance. If Hollywood were to get hold of him, he'd be a natural to play a king. Someone like King Arthur, perhaps.

No, Merlin, an inner voice whispered.

Stunned, Megan looked down at her hands. *Magic?* Now that she thought about it, there *was* something mystical about Kenric of Blackstone. Something magical. Something that gave him a look of authority far more powerful than brute strength alone could convey. Something that hinted of untold secrets that only the right key would unlock.

She wondered what it was, if it was only her imagination or a valid truth. She wondered if he knew it, recognized it, exploited it.

For the first time she wondered whether, if she told Kenric the truth, he would know how to send her back home.

The sky darkened, the wind picked up, and the temperature seemed to drop ten degrees. Snow swirled about them, stinging her face. Megan shivered. Something was wrong. Was another storm on the way? Or was it something more, something that was as weird and off-kilter as a stranded woman from years in the future?

Stop. Her foolish imagination would lead to nothing but trouble. Still, she did not like the strange expectancy that seemed to hover in the chilled air. Even the warhorse felt it, stamping his huge feet and shaking his head restlessly.

The warhorse. She couldn't understand why Kenric hadn't named the beast. Leaning forward, she gathered a clump of the chestnut-colored mane between her numb fingers. The horse turned to look at her, his ears cocked forward.

She tried to think of a suitable name. Obviously male, like Kenric, the horse did not look like an ordinary horse, at least not like any Megan had ever seen. For one thing, he was huge—as large as one of the Budweiser horses, and then some. For another, he was beautiful. Even his heavy winter coat shone with good health. His large brown eyes seemed full of intelligence and, though she had to admit it sounded silly, good humor.

For such a magnificent creature, no ordinary name would do.

If Kenric reminded her of Merlin, then his stead could be Arthur, or Gawain, or maybe Lancelot. *Lancelot. Yes.* She liked that.

"We can call you Lance for short," she told the beast, watching for Kenric and wondering what he would say about her choice of name.

Kenric burst through the door to the tavern, his cloak flying around him. Watching him take the few strides it took to reach her, Megan's mouth went dry. She'd never known such heart-stopping male beauty existed outside of movies and romance novels.

When he reached her, Kenric stopped, one hand on the saddle. "No one there has heard of your Roger, nor of any search for a lost maiden." His dark gaze narrowed in speculation. "Are you certain this Roger truly searches for you?"

Megan shook her head, wondering if he could see how she trembled and praying he would attribute it to the cold if he could. "What . . . what do you mean?"

Under his breath he cursed, a low and melodic sound. With an easy motion he swung himself up in front of her. "We will ride on to the next village."

He urged the horse forward, again with no discernible movement. Later, Megan meant to ask him how he did that. But for now she thought it best to keep silent. God help her if this proud warrior were to find out she didn't speak the truth.

Roger was not looking for her. At least not in this time. No matter how hard Kenric of Blackstone searched, he would not find Roger. Heck, *she* didn't even want to find Roger, just a way home. Though she detested liars, she had no choice. If she was going to figure out a way home, she would need Kenric's help.

They rode for an hour without speaking. The sun came out, weak but still warming. It made the day almost bearable, and twice Megan caught herself dozing, until the stiffness of Kenric's chain mail against her chin woke her. To his credit he said nothing, just stared straight ahead.

She contented herself with studying the landscape. She'd never been to Wales, or to Europe at all for that matter, and she found the gently rolling hills and thick forests beautiful.

She wondered if more than nine hundred years had changed the wildness of it, civilized the purple hills as it had tamed the people. At least her people. She knew nothing about the Welsh. If she got back—*when* she got back—she would have to do some research. She would like to find out if history contained any record of this man, this Kenric of Blackstone. At least then she could prove, if only to herself, that she hadn't lost her mind.

The weak sun did nothing to dissipate the white-gray air near the mountains. It grew thicker the closer they got. Megan wondered how this could be. She had never seen fog with snow.

"Look." Kenric pointed to a far-off hill nearly lost in the roiling mist.

Megan squinted. She could barely make out the outline of a forbidding building, stone from the looks of it, and nearly as immense as one of Roger's office buildings in North Dallas.

"It is Blackstone Keep, the place where I was raised."

She recognized the emotion in his voice, the fierce pride she saw on his handsome face. About to ask if his family still lived there, she remembered that he'd said they were all dead and closed her mouth.

Still, she had an inexplicable urge to comfort him. Megan leaned forward, placing a hand on his broad shoulder. "I think—"

"Quiet." The authoritative tone in his deep voice silenced her as effectively as a gunshot. Though he did not slow the horse's progress, it seemed to Megan that every muscle in Kenric's huge body was alert.

She listened too, glancing intently around them at the

70

shadows of trees and the insidious mist. Glancing up at the sky, she saw that the weak sun had vanished entirely.

Kenric's hand went to his sword. "When I tell you, you must slide from the horse and roll into the under-brush." The command came low, in a guttural whisper, and sounded urgent.

Megan goggled at him. "I—"

"Do you understand?"

Her heart pounding, she nodded.

With the sound of steel on leather, he unsheathed his sword. It seemed to her terrified eyes to glow in the dim light.

Then she heard it, the sound of hooves pounding the earth. More than one horse pursued them, from the sound of it.

His jaw set in a grim line, Kenric spun his horse around, turning to face the threat.

"Go," he told her, giving her a small shove. "Hide."

Somehow she did it—slid from the horse, landed on her feet like a cat, and ran into the frozen, shadowy un-derbrush. Dragging air into her lungs, she crawled under a dense bush, praying some hungry animal with sharp teeth did not hide there, waiting for her. It would have been par for the course.

But the threat that Kenric faced was worse, far worse.

Swords drawn, three evil-looking men on huge war-horses like Kenric's burst into the clearing.

"Welsh," Kenric cried, this time making the word both a battle cry and a curse.

Sparks flew as sword met sword. Hooves churned snow. They pivoted, spun, charged, the huge animals un-believably agile.

Though Kenric was outnumbered, she saw that he took care not to let them surround him. He fought fiercely, downing one man and scattering the other two. He was good, damn good. Exactly as she would imagine some-one who looked like him would be.

But how long could he continue to fight against such unfair odds?

One of the intruders noticed Kenric's sword and let out an unholy howl. Whether of pain or of fear, Megan could not tell. Kenric, who until now had been fighting grim-faced and determined, grinned. It was the grin of a man who knows the battle is over and he has won. Seeing it, Megan felt an odd sort of wonder and relief.

The two remaining warriors recognized it also and backed away.

"Thunder," said one in a loud voice that contained more awe than contempt.

Startled that he had spoken English, Megan crawled to the very edge of the underbrush, wanting to hear should anything else be said.

Still Kenric waited, his sword held ready.

The injured man on the ground moaned once, then went silent.

"We did not know." The tall man took another step back, keeping his sword lowered. "My lord, forgive us. We thought you were another English intruder."

"I am." Pride rang in Kenric's voice.

The other man shook his head, making a sign in the air. "You are also of this land. I beg your forgiveness." He began to back away.

Something in Kenric's stance told Megan he did not like the tall man's words.

No one spoke. It was still, except for the snorting of the horses and a quiet whimper from the fallen warrior.

Finally the tall man inclined his head. "There have been strange things happening here. Lightning during a blizzard, raw power in the air. Times are changing; the people have been restless, uneasy. Now they say powerful magic has occurred."

Glad they could not see her, Megan rolled her eyes. They were right about part of it—strange things had happened. Like her being transported nine hundred years into the past, for instance. But magic? Next they'd be calling her a witch and ordering her stoned, or drowned, or burned at the stake. What did they do to so-called witches in early medieval times?

She shuddered, remembering the witchcraft trials of Salem in her own country. And Joan of Arc—hadn't she lived around this time? No, maybe that had been in the fourteen hundreds or something. For the first time ever, she wished she'd paid more attention to history in college, instead of focusing on socializing. All the sororities in Texas couldn't help her now.

She had to perform a miracle and come up with a formula to help her pass through time.

Maybe witchcraft wasn't such a ridiculous idea after all.

Kenric spoke, drawing her attention back to the tableau in the clearing. "Take your wounded and go. I want no trouble."

"Nor do we, Kenric of Blackstone." Sheathing his sword, the tall man moved carefully to the body of his fallen comrade. The shorter, stocky man seemed frozen, undecided.

"Come on," the leader barked.

Still the other man hesitated.

"If you want to stay and fight, go ahead. But mark this: no man faces down Thunder and lives."

Puzzled, Megan frowned. Why did he speak as if Kenric's sword would do the fighting for him? Did he believe it to be magical, like the King Arthur's sword in the old legend?

Whatever it was, she couldn't help but be impressed. This Kenric was brave and apparently skilled. She couldn't have found a better man to help her, despite his earlier vow not to kill. How then, she wondered, would he defend himself in a fight to the death? Would he have let them kill him, rather than take another life? And her, what of her? Would he have watched while they ran her through with one of those shiny, sharp-looking swords? Somehow she doubted it.

The shorter man made up his mind, hurrying over to help the injured man stand. Somehow they got him on his mount and they all took off, the hurt rider hunched low over the horse's neck.

Crawling out of her damp hiding place, Megan brushed snow and dead leaves off her tunic.

"That worked out well," she said to Kenric's broad back.

Ignoring her, he stared off in the distance as if trying to make out the men riding away. When he turned, she was shocked to see the raw emotion on his face; whether fury or anguish she could not tell, though she suspected it was a combination of both.

"You fought them off, drove them away," she enthused, her heart racing, trying desperately to pretend she was unaware of the pain reflected in his expression. "And you didn't even have to kill to do it."

He gave a grunt, then strode to where Lancelot munched a bit of dead grass poking through the trampled snow.

"Come on." Without looking at her, he held out his hand. "We must reach the next village before nightfall. Mayhap we will find your Roger there."

Chapter Five

Once they were mounted and moving at a brisk pace through the packed snow, Kenric ignored her. She wrapped her arms around his waist and buried her face in the thick cloak he had loaned her, glad of the warmth. The landscape all seemed the same, more rolling hills, mist, trees, and, of course, snow.

Finally Megan decided to give in to her curiosity. "Why did they speak of your sword like it was magical?"

His only noticeable reaction was a slight stiffening in his carriage.

"Those men, they all seemed afraid of it." She pushed bravely on.

A muscle worked in Kenric's jaw. He shook his head, telling her without speaking that he didn't want to talk about it.

Typically masculine. Incredibly frustrating.

"I need to know this." Stubbornness was one of her worst faults, according to Roger. She reminded herself that Roger's opinion no longer mattered to her.

"If it is so dangerous that it frightens grown men into running, don't you think I should be warned?"

He laughed at this, a harsh bark of sound that seemed to absorb instantly into the heavy fog.

"Some call my sword magic," he told her. "And, as I told you, its name in Welsh is another word for thunder."

In Welsh? Though he'd mentioned the name earlier, he hadn't said the origins of it. Why would his sword have a Welsh name? He had made it plain that he despised the Welsh.

Struggling to understand, Megan nodded. "So it is both you and your sword that they were afraid of?"

With an arrogant smile, he inclined his head once in a curt nod.

Feeling brave, Megan pushed on. "Your sword . . . it seemed to glow." She felt foolish even saying it, but she knew what she had seen.

The muffled sound of Lancelot's hoofbeats and the fierce pounding of her heart filled the silence. She swallowed, waiting, but as they skirted the trees and rode down another slope, then straight up yet another, she realized Kenric had no intention of answering this particular question.

"I saw it." She lifted her chin, leaning around his right to try to peer up into the harsh planes of his face. "It glowed with a faintly silver light."

Now was the time for him to tell her she was crazy, that the head injury he suspected of happening had addled her brains.

"Some call it magic," he repeated instead, dragging the words out in a way that forbade any further questions. His expression might have been carved out of stone.

Megan knew enough to quit while she was ahead. Normally she wouldn't have believed him, or believed in his vague explanation of magic. Magic was tricks and mirrors, illusions and smoke. But something, some force, had sent her to this place, to this time, and if it wasn't magic then she didn't know what else it could be.

The wind picked up again, frozen gusts of it blowing snow flurries and the cold, wet fog in swirling eddies around them. Despite herself, Megan shivered. Would she never be warm again?

Kenric felt it. "Wrap the cloak tightly around you."

She did as he asked, wishing she had a knitted cap, some thermal underwear, and a good pair of waterproof, fully lined boots.

Soon they could not see. It seemed another full-fledged blizzard was in progress. Still, Kenric urged Lancelot on. Megan wondered how the horse found his way, because it was nearly impossible to see more than five feet in front of them. Unable to tell if it was day or night, she lost track of time. The cold snaked into her bones and consumed her, until even her teeth chattered and her jaw ached from trying to hold in her shivering.

But even if she begged Kenric to stop, Megan could see no place to take shelter. How she longed for the small cave and the warmth of the smoky, sputtering fire.

" 'Tis dangerous," Kenric muttered, his voice muffled by his heavy cloak. "I know not where we ride. I have to trust the horse to find a safe place to walk."

"Lancelot," she blurted without thinking, her voice trembling with her shivering.

Kenric turned to look at her while Lancelot kept plodding forward, head down. "What?"

"The horse." She wondered if the poor animal was as frozen as she. "His name is Lancelot."

Obviously thinking her deranged, Kenric shook his head. "My warhorse has no name."

Glad of at least one coherent thought to cling to, to push away the cold, Megan snorted. "He does now. I've named him Lancelot."

"Why?"

She wondered if the Arthurian legend was known in 1072. "Lancelot was a brave knight."

"Nay. He betrayed a king."

He did know the story. And while it was technically true that Lancelot had stolen the king's wife, all she could think of was Richard Gere's handsome and charming portrayal of Lancelot in the movie *First Knight.*

Kenric watched her, his eyes glittering shards of ice— the same way her hands and feet and the rest of her body were beginning to feel.

"He's a horse, for God's sake." Frustration and cold made her want to weep. "You don't have to take the name so literally."

He shook his head, the movement sending some of the snow that coated his dark locks flying.

"Are you all right?" he asked, the concern in his voice warring with the steely expression on his face.

She didn't know what to make of him. Right now she didn't much care. All she wanted was to find a place where she could get warm.

"No." She slid a frozen hand from under her cloak, daring to reach up and slip it under his, to the back of his neck.

He jumped. "God's blood, you are like ice."

Withdrawing her hand, she said nothing.

"There is no place to take shelter," he told her, while Lancelot continued to push bravely forward. "If we stop now, we will die. I do not know from whence this storm came—there was no sign of it when we left the cave."

Despite the truth she sensed in his words, stopping was beginning to sound lovely. An incredible lassitude seemed to have taken over, taking her past the bone-wrenching chills, the icy numbness, and the cold. She couldn't seem to hold her head up.

She, who had lived her entire life in the southern part of the United States, knew nothing of blowing snow, gale-force winds, or subzero temperatures. What she knew about freezing to death she had read or seen in the movies. It appeared, however, that was about to experience it firsthand. Megan knew enough to realize she should fight the sleepiness, that she should not let her eyes drift closed. But the desire to give into her fatigue was overpowering; it would be so simple to go to sleep for eternity, to finally escape the miserable stab of the frigid cold.

"Megan." The deep voice seemed to come from a long way off.

Bone weary, she forced herself to lift her head. "Cold," she mumbled. "So cold."

With fumbling fingers, Kenric reached beside him and withdrew his sword. Even the sound of leather releasing steel seemed muffled in this dizzying world of white.

Curiosity warred with the need to sleep. This time she fought the urge to close her eyes. The sword reminded her that she needed to live. Surely she had not survived a lightning strike and traversed so many years to die a frozen death. There had to be some reason for her arrival here, something to do perhaps with Kenric and his magical sword.

Thunder.

Opening her eyes wider, Megan peered around. She was so cold she no longer shivered, her teeth no longer chattered. She seemed to have almost transcended the world of mere mortals, feeling nothing now, not even the overwhelming need for sleep.

Again she heard it. . . . Had she imagined it, the deep rumble in the sky that preceded a thunderstorm? Surely she had, for though she didn't know much about blizzards, she didn't think snow clouds thundered. Or that lightning occurred, as the marauding Welsh riders had said.

Kenric continued to hold his sword up, his arm and the metal a straight line pointing to the sky. Again the weapon seemed to glow, a soft light that grew brighter as she watched, pointing a path through the swirling mist and snow.

Again she thought of King Arthur and Merlin and the powerful sword in the stone. For the first time she wondered if the legend had some basis in fact.

"That way lies safety." Though the words came from her throat, slurred, Megan knew she had not meant to say them. But Kenric, his dark shaggy head covered in white, nodded and turned the great horse toward the glowing beam of light.

They left the path and rode into the dense trees, Lancelot picking his way carefully. The snow did not seem to fall as heavily here; the close-knit branches formed a canopy of sorts. The light did not waver; as long as Kenric held the sword in front of them it lit the way.

The trees grew closer together, the going now more difficult for the large warhorse until finally he had to stop. They had reached a place where the trees grew so intertwined that they formed an unbroken wall.

"I like not the looks of this." Lowering the sword, Kenric once again sheathed it. The light glimmered and slowly faded; the snow and the otherworldly mist came up once more to swirl around them.

Megan shook her head. For some reason her lethargy seemed to have vanished. So had her chills. Blood rushed back into her limbs, making them tingle and ache so that she shifted uneasily behind Kenric. *Something about this place . . .*

"It's magical," Kenric said flatly, letting her know that she had spoken out loud. "I like it not."

"The mist?"

"This place. I sense magic here. Somehow the sword has brought us to a place of magic."

She couldn't see what the problem was. After all, he had said his sword was a magical sword. It only made sense.

"Do you think it will be warm?"

His face might have been carved from ice itself. "It does not matter. We will not go there."

The trees seemed closer, impossible to get through, either forward or back. Even if it was her imagination, she didn't see how he meant to turn Lancelot around.

"What are you going to do?"

"Go back." His voice sounded more frozen than the wind that howled outside the protection of their copse of trees.

"How?" She leaned in close to him, her breath making a plume of frosty smoke on his cheek. "Back the horse out?"

His expression left no doubt that that was exactly what he meant to do.

"I will think of a way," he told her.

Megan cast one final longing look at the wall of trees, from behind which she imagined she could see a soft glow of warm light. She had no doubt the barrier would somehow part for them, allowing them to enter the magical and safe—and warm!—place. Where this notion came from, she had no idea. But too much had happened to her recently for her to doubt her instincts now.

"I want to go there." Her hand held remarkably steady as she pointed. "I'm cold, I'm tired, and I want to get warm. I do not want to freeze to death in this blizzard."

After a moment of silence, Kenric laughed, a humorless bark of sound that seemed to echo in the still forest. "You speak with the tone of a queen."

She raised a brow the way she imagined real royalty might. "Maybe I am."

He did pause at that, cocking his head to study her.

"A queen?" he asked growling, looking annoyed and grim and maddeningly arrogant all at once. "Of what place, my lady? Perchance do you come from a place not of this world?"

Stunned at first that he believed her, it took a second for it to dawn on Megan that Kenric thought she came from the realm of magic, the realm of what—Faeries and Elves? To her this seemed even more improbable and fantastic than the truth, at least the truth as she knew it—that she'd traveled through time. But this man carried an enchanted sword. To him, she had no doubt that Faeries and Elves were real, even if he seemed to loathe them. More real than the year 2001 could ever be.

"It all fits," Kenric said under his breath, fury filling his face. "Your odd attire, the strange words you use. You are not Welsh. You are from the land behind the veil, the place where some say my sword was forged. And you say you are a queen? Or maybe only a princess who aspires to become a queen?"

"No." She refused to allow herself to panic. If this man, who seemed to abhor magic, truly believed she was some sort of elfin royalty, what would he do? Dump her to freeze to death alone in these woods?

She couldn't believe they were having this conversation, only minutes after nearly dying of frostbite. Then again, there was much about what had happened to her lately that she found difficult to believe.

His eyes narrowed in speculation. "A princess of Faerie."

"No," Megan said again, beseeching him with her gaze to believe her. "I am human, as human as you are. I don't know anything about magic or Faeries or any of that. And I was only teasing—er, jesting—about being a queen."

"As human as I am?" Kenric's voice dripped ice.

She swallowed as another thought occurred to her. "You are human, aren't you?"

Though he gave a slow nod, his frozen expression told her something was terribly wrong.

The chill of the air began to seep once more into her bones. Megan shivered and cast a look of longing toward the place that had, moments earlier, seemed so welcoming and safe.

Magical, he'd said. She really wanted to see this Faerie

world for herself, especially if it would get her warm. After all, maybe someone with a little bit of magic power could help her get home. Maybe even help her with the problem of Roger once she got there. But how could she convince Kenric to take her to this place behind the veil without his thinking she was some sort of Faerie herself?

Lancelot solved that problem neatly. The huge warhorse snorted once, then took the bit in his teeth and began lumbering toward the wall of trees.

Kenric cursed, pulling back on the reins. It made no difference—the horse ignored all of Kenric's efforts to make him stop.

"You." Turning to pin Megan with a furious gaze, Kenric put one hand on the hilt of his sword. "You had something to do with this, did you not?"

If looks could kill . . .

"No, I swear to you, I didn't. How could I?" She pleaded with him to understand. "I've never been on a horse in my life. I wouldn't even know how to make Lancelot move."

Again he shot her that icy glare. "My warhorse carries no name. Cease calling him Lancelot."

Lancelot came to the wall of trees. Instead of stopping, he plowed right into them. It came as no surprise to Megan that the trees seemed to part as if a powerful hand guided them, allowing them entrance.

Grim-faced, Kenric fell silent, and Lancelot, no longer plodding, seemed to prance as they entered the magical place. Megan saw immediately, with no small measure of relief, that here it was summer—bright, blazing sunshine, blue skies, and all.

Kenric, uttering a muffled oath, crossed himself. Behind them, the wall of trees seemed to straighten and reform.

"You'd best pray, my lady." His voice sounded bitter. Trying to restrain her delight, Megan loosened the heavy cloak and held her hands up to the brilliant sun. "For what?"

The look he gave her was filled with anger mingled with pity and disbelief. "Have you not heard the tales of mortals who wandered into the land of Faerie? 'Tis said years pass whilst they, unknowing, are bound by enchantment."

He lowered his voice, his eyes sharp, taking note of all around them. "Some never make it back."

Since what he said was too close to her present situation for comfort, Megan trembled. For the first time she wondered what she would do if it was not possible for her to go back home, back to Dallas in 2001, where she had electricity, a snazzy new red BMW convertible, and Roger.

The thought of her fiancé made her shudder. No doubt Roger was furious at her disappearance. Unable to believe that she'd simply vanished when the lightning hit, he probably had employed a team of private investigators to search for her. After all, she hadn't yet changed her will to make him beneficiary, as he'd ordered her to do.

Lancelot came to a halt, lifting his head to sniff the breeze. Stretching his thick neck forward, he whinnied, cocking his ears as if he expected an answer.

Dragging her gaze away from Kenric's hard face, Megan looked around her with wonderment. Stretching as far as the eye could see was a summer meadow of verdant green and gold. The long grass waved in the light breeze, and brightly colored birds flitted from the limbs of the leafy trees, their songs joyful and sweet. The scent of wildflowers and hay filled the air. For the first time since the lightning bolt had hit her, Megan felt warm.

"It's beautiful!" Unable to help herself, she laughed with delight. "Look"—she touched Kenric's shoulder, leaning close so that she might whisper in his ear—"there is a doe and her fawn."

"Beware, Megan of Dallas-Texas." Kenric turned to

look at her, his eyes as hard and cold as the land they'd just left. "This is a place of danger. Not all is as it appears."

She found it hard to believe. "All I know is that I'd much rather have awakened here than in that snowstorm." She sighed, wiggling slightly. "Can I get down?"

The big man in front of her stiffened. "No," he barked, his hand going once more to his sword. "You must stay on the horse. Trouble comes."

Peering around his shoulder, Megan gasped. A woman, her luxurious flaxen hair floating gently around her shoulders, strolled toward them. She wore a long white robe of some sort of gossamer material, edged with golden thread. Though she was still on the other side of the meadow, her very presence enhanced the idyllic landscape tenfold.

"She's gorgeous," Megan said softly as the woman grew closer. She was, without a doubt, the most beautiful woman Megan had ever seen.

"Aye, that she is," Kenric said glumly. He held himself as a warrior about to meet an enemy in battle. "It has been a long time since I've seen her."

He knew her? This vision of loveliness who approached them?

Suddenly, Megan felt positively dowdy in Kenric's faded, baggy clothes. "Who is she?"

His intent stare never wavered from the woman as she drew near. His mouth twisted bitterly. "Her name is Rhiannon. We shared the same mother. She is my half sister."

"Your . . ." Megan swallowed, hardly able to believe it. "Your half sister?" The idea that this rugged giant had a sister seemed shocking. She shook her head. Everyone had family, even arrogant warriors. But he'd said before that he had no family, that they were all dead. And if this Faerie woman was his sister, then what did that make him?

About to ask, she closed her mouth as the woman drew near.

"Greetings, my brother." With a soft smile, the woman hailed him. Her voice was lilting and musical.

Kenric slid from the horse, leaving Megan mounted on Lancelot's broad back. He made no movement to help her down. In fact, his eyes focused solely on Rhiannon's face. Tamping down surprise—that she was no longer afraid—and fury—that he should treat her as if she were not even there—Megan copied his movements exactly. She managed to land on her feet, looking almost dignified. That was, until her legs refused to support her and she had to clutch at Kenric's arm to stay upright.

He barely spared Megan a glance, his gaze never wavering from the woman who hailed them.

"Rhiannon, my sister." Kenric inclined his head, looking every inch the arrogant warrior. "How fares it with you?"

Astonished, Megan stared. This was it? This was the way he greeted his sister? Before she had time to think of it, she prodded him with her elbow.

"Give her a hug," she said in a hiss, close to his ear so that his sister would not hear it.

One corner of Kenric's mouth lifted. Imperceptibly, he gave a shake of his dark head.

Megan sighed, giving up. There was no way she could force him to be nice, not without making a scene. She supposed it was none of her business anyway. After all, she barely knew the man.

But she'd drawn his sister's attention. Long-lashed eyes the color of periwinkle glanced curiously at Megan.

"Who is your woman?"

The way Kenric's sister said the word *woman* endowed the simple word with another layer of meaning. As in girlfriend, wife, lover . . . Megan could feel her face coloring, especially under the other's curious gaze.

Kenric showed no surprise that his sister had seen

through Megan's disguise. "She is a displaced lady, searching for her betrothed. I am merely helping her." He clamped his mouth shut, his lips a hard line in a face that might have been chiseled from stone.

"And you?" his sister asked softly, her gentle smile never wavering. "What do you get in return?"

That seemed odd. Megan frowned, watching the interplay between siblings. Why did Kenric's sister automatically assume he would get something out of helping her?

As if he knew her thoughts, Kenric shot Megan a quelling look. Straightening his shoulders, he inclined his head. "In return she has promised me a grant of land. In the world of mankind."

"Ahhh." The woman's periwinkle eyes softened. "Human land. 'Tis what you have always wanted, is it not?"

He gave a curt nod, still ignoring Megan. It seemed he had no intention of introducing her by name. Very well, she could take care of that. She was a woman of modern times, after all.

"I am Megan Potter." Stepping forward, Megan held out her hand for Rhiannon to shake.

With slightly arched brows, Kenric's sister made no move to take it. Instead, she stared at the outstretched hand in apparent bafflement.

Megan felt herself blush—all over. She lowered her arm slowly. She should have known better. Women in medieval times did not shake hands.

Kenric grabbed her arm and pulled her into the crook of his. The gesture—meant, she felt certain, to be comforting—stunned her. But, she had to admit, it did make her feel immensely better. Perhaps this small token of compassion proved the hard warrior who'd found her did have feelings, after all.

"Megan hails from a faraway place," Kenric pronounced, as if to explain her strange actions. "Dallas-Texas. Perhaps you have heard of it."

Still silent, Kenric's sister watched them. Though she

shook her head, a smile curved her generous lips.

"Nay, I have not heard of this place." Her gaze drifted to Megan's face, her smile deepening. "I am Rhiannon. I am from"—she waved a graceful hand at the shining meadow, the sun glinting off her shimmering hair— "Rune."

"Rune?" The name was unfamiliar, and Megan could have sworn Kenric had told her they were in Wales. "Where is Rune?"

"Here," Kenric answered, his tone curt. "All around you. Rune is a kingdom in the land of Faerie."

Rhiannon tilted her head, studying Megan. This close to the stunning woman, Megan felt old, even though she knew she had to be the younger of the two. And plain. If this woman showed up in New York City, she'd become an instant supermodel.

"Kenric was born here in Rune," Rhiannon said softly, as though she had read Megan's mind. "He chooses to disavow this part of his heritage, but it all could be his. If he wanted it."

Not sure she understood, Megan looked at Kenric. From his set jaw and grim expression, she saw he would not explain. Still, she would give him a chance before she asked his sister.

"Kenric?" Tugging on his arm, Megan swallowed. "What does she mean? Are you some kind of—"

"Enough." Though he did not raise his voice, he might have shouted, so great was the command in the simple word.

"Sister, did you send this woman? Is she some minor princess from one of the other kingdoms of Faerie?" Drawing Megan closer, he put his big hand under her chin and lifted her face, his intent gaze fastened on her mouth.

Even to Megan, Rhiannon's laugh sounded a trifle forced. Still, it made Megan think of wind chimes tinkling in a light breeze. "She is not from Faerie."

"Did you send her to my cave?"

Color stained the other woman's porcelain cheeks, though she held her head high. "Why would I do that?"

Bending his head, Kenric touched Megan's lips lightly before replying. Though his mouth was warm, his eyes were cold. "To tempt me."

Though she knew Kenric mocked his sister, at the touch of his mouth on hers, Megan couldn't keep her breath from catching in her throat. Her heart tripped in her chest. Again, she felt color flood her face, making her curse her pale complexion.

"She is not from my kingdom." Her face alight with laughter, Rhiannon shook her head. Her long hair floated around her in a pale, golden cloud. "As you are of my blood, you know I would prefer you take a woman of Faerie to wife."

Megan couldn't help it; she gasped. With that simple statement, Rhiannon had answered two of her questions. If Rhiannon was a queen and, perhaps more important, a Faerie to boot, then that meant Kenric was . . . what—a Faerie also? Or a half Faerie? She didn't know much about Faeries, other than the fact that they weren't supposed to exist, but if they did she imagined they would have liberal use of magic.

Regarding the woman with new interest, Megan wanted to jump up and down with excitement. Magic might be exactly what she needed. Perhaps Rhiannon could help her get home.

As though she sensed her enthusiasm, Rhiannon patted Megan's arm. "Not now, Megan Potter of Dallas-Texas. You and I will talk later."

Kenric's lip curled. "So you two *do* know each other."

In the patient, loving manner of sisters everywhere, Rhiannon gave him an a indulgent smile. "Nay, brother, not yet. But I believe Megan Potter and I will know each other very well before the day is done."

Frowning at his sister's ambiguous statement, Kenric shook his head as if he needed to clear it. "Enough of this foolishness. I want to return to the real world, sister. Now."

Chapter Six

Rhiannon's violet eyes twinkled. "You cannot wish to be stuck in that dreadful blizzard again."

"No." Megan spoke up quickly, beating Kenric to the punch. There was no way she was going to pass up this opportunity to find out if this Faerie woman—*make that a Faerie queen*—could use her magic and help her return home.

Both of them stared at her with identical expressions of surprise.

"I don't want to freeze to death," she told Kenric, crossing her arms in front of her chest. "I want to stay here where it's warm."

"You don't know what you say." He growled. "This is not a place of reality."

"Just for a night." Emboldened by all that had happened, Megan moved closer and laid a hand on Kenric's massive arm. His skin felt warm, flushed.

"One night of warmth so that we can sleep. That way

we'll be refreshed if we start back out tomorrow."

"Time does not pass normally here." His gaze sharpened as he stared down into her upturned face. Something flickered in his expression. Anger? Desire? Then it was gone.

"One night can be a month when you step back out of the glade."

Megan found this hard to believe. But then, everything that had happened to her since she'd tried to meet Roger to break off her engagement was hard to believe. What was one more oddity?

Still, she had no choice. This might be her sole opportunity to get back home. "I'm willing to risk it."

He sighed, staring down at her with a shuttered expression.

She stared back. Even angry this man was beautiful, in a ruggedly fierce, thoroughly masculine way. Looking at him made her mouth water.

"Please." Leaning toward him, she unconsciously licked her lips, remembering his kiss. "One night."

He watched her the way a hawk watched an unsuspecting mouse. This time she knew it was desire that darkened his arrogant gaze. To test her theory, she moistened her lips again.

He caught his breath.

She held hers. In a second, he would kiss her.

Behind them, Rhiannon laughed, the light, tinkling sound making them both jump. Megan realized she'd managed to forget all about Kenric's sister.

"Come now," Rhiannon chided, her beautiful face alight with merriment. "There will be time for that later. For now, accompany me."

Without waiting for an answer, Rhiannon spun on her heel. Lightly stroking Lancelot's thick neck as she passed, she led the way, the huge warhorse following her, as docile as a newborn colt.

Megan slipped her hand into Kenric's large one, loving

the way his enveloped hers. He started, but did not pull away.

"Come on, let's go," she urged.

Rhiannon and Lancelot disappeared around a curve in the path.

"My own horse," Kenric muttered under his breath. With a muffled oath he allowed Megan to tow him after his sister.

Kenric tamped down his fury. How had he let it come to this? The one thing he sought to avoid all his waking hours—contact with the world of Faerie—had happened. And right in the middle of one of his simpler quests— finding the fair Megan's betrothed. A more perfect endeavor he couldn't have found, for it involved no bloodshed, no fighting, no greed or avarice or any of the other human passions that he, despite his wish to be only human, so abhorred. This detachment was part of his elfin heritage, he supposed. It was part of him, though he tried mightily to forget it, to pretend he was all human, all man.

The magic simmered always, just underneath his skin, tempting him with its power, letting him know that if he were to use it but once, he might have anything and everything his heart desired.

For this reason alone, Kenric had vowed he would never use the magic. It was too strong, too dangerous, too enticing a lure. He knew not what he might become were he to let his abilities loose in the world of men.

But he knew one thing: He would no longer be a mere man.

God's teeth. He ran a shaking hand through his hair— his left hand, since his right was currently wrapped around Megan's small, soft-skinned one. He had not returned to Rune since his tenth summer, by choice.

How had he let things get to this point?

Megan tugged on him, urging him to hurry. With a

sigh, he quickened his steps, allowing the tiny maid to drag him along after her like her personal pet. Now he knew how Lancelot—*no, not Lancelot*—his unnamed warhorse must feel.

He clenched his jaw. He'd rather face a blizzard—*nay, a thousand blizzards*—than face what he knew was to come. It had been a long time since he'd seen his sister's family, so long that he didn't even think of them as part of his family.

His family, his beloved human father and stepmother, human half brothers and sisters, lay dead and buried in the hard, frozen ground. Gone. And the ache inside of him would never go away until he secured his land and produced some heirs—human heirs—to continue the line and lay his father's ghost to rest.

No matter what Rhiannon wanted from him, he knew this duty came first, above all others. To fulfill his quest he had fought in wars whose causes he had forgotten. He had battled faceless enemies for pay, killed and bloodied until he knew he could bear no more. All for the land. Still, he had not amassed quite enough gold to purchase the kind of land he wanted.

But fate had sent him Megan Potter of Dallas-Texas, and with her, a much easier task—task with a reward that promised all he sought. He was so close, for once. So close he might reach out and touch it.

And into this, his time of certain peace, of near-achievement of his goal, came his mischievous, fey sister. Determined, he supposed, to stir up some sort of trouble.

He would not, he decided, let her. Squaring his shoulders, he matched his stride to Megan's smaller one, and followed the winding path into the heart of his sister's kingdom—into Rune, in the enchanted land of Faerie.

"Kenric!" Megan gasped, stopping so quickly he nearly knocked her over. Her small fingers dug into his.

"Look." Her voice trembled as she pointed to the crystalline castle that wavered and shimmered like an illusion in front of them.

Despite his misgivings, he smiled down at her. Her expressive face was alight, reminding him of a small child who had been handed some sweet. Except beautiful Megan, with her full mouth and wide, amber eyes, was no child.

Again he felt an overpowering urge to take her in his arms and claim her mouth with his.

Resisting, Kenric cast a suspicious glance at his sister. But she appeared to pay them no attention, focusing instead on greeting several of her retainers. They were elfin men, tall and slender and golden, all of whom stared with interest at his Megan.

His Megan? Kenric shook his head, bemused. Where had that thought come from? Probably more of Rhiannon's enchantment, meant to befuddle and confuse him for her own devious entertainment.

Even after all these years, he still did not trust her. He did not trust any of them, these people of Faerie, of magic. Someone from Rune had killed his human family. Someone from Rune had destroyed his world.

Megan, he couldn't help but notice, watched the elfin men with interest.

"Who are they?" she whispered, leaning close, her eyes wide.

Wondering if she knew how tightly she still clutched his hand, Kenric drew her nearer, until the curve of her hip was nestled against his side. Though the gesture spoke of possession, it was a message he felt it necessary to send, if only for the absentee Roger's sake.

"Faeries," he told her, nearly laughing out loud at the way her eyes widened.

"Are they . . . that is . . ." She swallowed, never taking her gaze from them. "Wow. I didn't really believe your sister was a Faerie, you know?"

God help him, he was beginning to understand her

strange dialect. He actually knew what she meant by that last, disjointed statement.

Rhiannon broke away from the group, her tinkling laugh grating on Kenric's nerves.

"Come, Megan Potter." Extending a hand, the queen of all Faeries beamed at them both. "Let me show you to your room."

About to protest, Kenric refused to release Megan's hand when she sought to pull it free. Unease prickled along his spine. For some reason he did not want to be separated from her. Long ago he had learned to trust his instincts.

"Kenric?"

Not sure if it was Rhiannon or Megan who had called his name, Kenric lifted his head and sniffed the balmy breeze. He smelled nothing but the pleasant odor of flowers and fresh-cut grass. Of course the danger he worried about must be imaginary, for no one would dare to hurt the half brother of their queen, changeling or no, nor his human charge.

Still, he did not wish to be parted from Megan.

"I will go too."

Rhiannon laughed again, making Kenric grit his teeth.

"Do not be foolish, my brother." Rhiannon reached out, touching the back of his hand lightly so that he felt it involuntarily open. Still, to his gratification, Megan did not immediately pull free. With an amused sigh, Rhiannon took Megan's hand in her own slender one.

"Kenric and I," Megan spoke up, her husky voice sounding strong, though it trembled, "stay together."

Feeling an inordinate amount of pleasure at her words, Kenric looked down at her heart-shaped face. It seemed this little Megan was wise as well as beautiful.

"That's right."

"My dear"—Rhiannon spoke with the patience of one who is sorely tried—"you must freshen up and put on some suitable clothes."

He saw Megan glance down at herself. Without the blanket, she still wore Kenric's too-large tunic and baggy pants. Her pale face colored at Rhiannon's comment, making Kenric instantly sorry that he had not thought of it himself.

"My sister is right." Though he did not like it, Megan had need of a gown, at least in this place. When they left, she could resume her masculine disguise, but as long as they were here there was no need of it.

Wariness in her gaze, Megan watched him. Something she saw in his expression must have reassured her, for she nodded.

"I will go with you," she told Rhiannon, once again speaking with the dignity of a born lady. "If Kenric says it is all right, then I will believe it is."

Hoping her blind trust wouldn't be misplaced, Kenric watched as his sister led Megan away. Who was this maiden, that she spoke so strangely yet comported herself with such quiet grace? Why, he wondered too, did she trust him so deeply on the basis of a few days' acquaintance?

Then again, he supposed she had no choice. He was all she had, until he restored her to her Roger.

Megan wondered if it was wise to let Rhiannon separate her from Kenric. She felt no danger in the other woman's presence, but with the strangeness of her life lately . . .

"Here we are." Rhiannon smiled, once again dazzling Megan with her loveliness. She pushed open a heavy door, made of some material that resembled leaded glass, and ushered Megan through the entranceway.

"Your bedchamber."

Stepping into the room was like stepping into a storybook. Everything was white, silver, or crystal. And though she would have thought those colors would make the room cold, instead it fairly vibrated with a glowing kind of warmth and serenity.

"Wow." Megan grinned, gingerly testing the over-stuffed bed with its downy white quilt. "I think I like it here."

Rhiannon's expression turned serious. "This is good. It is time for my half brother to embrace his destiny."

Uh-oh. Megan should have known there'd be a catch to all this.

"I'm sorry," she told the other woman, trying to pretend Rhiannon *was* just another woman, not a powerful Faerie queen. "Please don't try to involve me in your schemes for Kenric. I only want to go home."

"Do you?" With this enigmatic comment, Rhiannon tilted her head. "Perhaps we can be of help to each other."

Megan froze. She hardly dared breathe. "Can you—" Her voice breaking, she tried again. "Can you help me get back home?"

"Can you help me with my half brother?"

Now she felt as though she were in some convoluted game show or old movie; the hapless pawn who always made the wrong choice.

For a second, Megan closed her eyes, took a deep breath, and opened them.

"Kenric has saved my life. I would not do anything to hurt him."

"I am his sister." Rhiannon seemed to tower over her, shimmering and beautiful in the sparkling light from the crystal chandelier.

"I would not harm him either. But Kenric has great power, power that he must come to terms with to fulfill his destiny. He is a man torn—I only want him to find happiness."

Megan hoped Kenric would forgive her. She hated to pry into his private life, especially since he'd not invited any confidences. "And is he not happy now?"

The queen's eyes grew sad, her shimmer dimming.

"He is but a shell of a man, afraid to be Faerie, afraid

to be human. He doesn't believe in love, or hope, or magic.

"The Welsh revere him, though he hates them. They know of his mixed heritage. He carries a self-imposed burden so heavy that he is bowed beneath it, sentencing himself to exist on the fringes of life."

Thinking of the cave that Kenric had claimed for his home, Megan thought Rhiannon might be right. Kenric *had* said he had no family. He'd totally left out his sister, and any relatives he might have here in this strange and magical place.

"What is"—swallowing, Megan wondered why she was prying even as she realized she had to know—"this burden he carries?"

Rhiannon's luminous eyes grew wide. "He blames himself for the murder of his human family."

Murder? Megan swallowed, trying to remember exactly what Kenric had said.

"He said his own people killed them."

With a slow nod, Rhiannon confirmed this. "Aye. All here know of Kenric's great power—and of his refusal to use it. He is mentioned in prophecy, for his destiny is a path of greatness, if he will but take it.

"There are those of our kind"—she waved her hand, silver streamers of light following the graceful movement—"who hate him, both for that and the fact that he is half-human."

"And those were the ones who killed his family?"

Her expressive face full of pain, Rhiannon nodded. "We call them the Black Faeries, Faeries who are willing to fight and kill for their own dark reasons."

"But why?" Megan couldn't understand it. "What would they possibly gain by attacking innocent people?"

"One named Myrddin leads these Black Faeries. He believes the prophecy is about him, that it is he who should carry the power that Kenric refuses to claim. We believe it was he who went to Blackstone Keep to kill

Kenric and everything that made up who Kenric is. But Kenric was not there, so Myrddin and his followers destroyed everything else."

All that Kenric loved. Images of fire and savagery flashed in Megan's mind, though what she pictured was based on the movie *Braveheart*. No doubt the real thing was ten times worse.

"And Kenric?" she whispered, her throat aching. "Where was he?"

"Though bastard born, he was accepted into the family as a third son. Lord Madoc had sent him to train with another English lord. With part of the very power he despises, Kenric sensed what was going on and rode home. He was too late, returning in time for Lord Madoc to give him the sword Thunder, and die.

"For this, he blames himself."

Fighting back tears, Megan bowed her head. An ache started inside of her, as she thought of all the pain Kenric had endured, of the weight of the needless guilt he carried. This explained so much of the man's actions, though not all. "And Blackstone Keep?"

"The English king gave it to another English baron. As a bastard son, my brother had no claim to it, though he is the last of the Madoc line. This loss is why he hungers for land."

Megan racked her brain, trying to remember what she'd learned in college about medieval times and marcher lords. She had concentrated on her mathematic studies, the calculus and physics, taking the history and literature courses only because the degree program required them. She remembered very little. But she remembered enough to know that a landless man, especially a bastard son with no blood claim to his family's holdings, was reduced to hiring out as a mercenary.

"And that is why he fights—for money to buy the land." She didn't realize she had spoken out loud until Rhiannon answered.

"Yes. But this lifestyle has taken its toll on him. Fighting his own magic takes much strength. And he has killed, though killing is foreign to us, against all the very fiber that makes up our souls. Kenric is a man at the end of his endurance."

Megan had sensed that in him, an ironlike control that sometimes seemed ready to shatter.

She found herself wanting to find Kenric, to gather him in her arms and comfort him. Something about the man . . .

Wait a minute, she told herself, pinching her arm to bring herself back to reality. This entire thing was none of her business. After all, these events had happened in a long-distant past, where reality was very different. She hadn't even been born yet. She couldn't afford to care what happened here. She needed to focus on one thing, and one thing only—figuring out how to get home to her own time and place. And once there, she would have to deal with the all too real problem of how to get rid of Roger without his killing her. This stuff about Faeries and magic was too strange for her.

Still, the truth of where she wanted to return was even stranger. Yet she had no choice but to try to see if Rhiannon could help her.

"I am from the future," Megan said, watching the Faerie woman carefully for her reaction. "Over nine hundred years in the future, to be exact. From a place that doesn't exist yet, at least as I know it. Can you help me return there?"

Arching her perfectly shaped eyebrows, Rhiannon didn't seem surprised.

"Time is relative," she said, waving a hand dismissively. Again the silver slivers of light danced after her. "And magic transcends time. You were brought here for a purpose, my dear. Your purpose has not yet been realized."

"Brought here? By whom?"

"By the fates." Rhiannon looked away, a secretive smile curving her ruby lips. "It is your destiny."

More magical gobbledygook. Deciding to let that one go, Megan wondered if Rhiannon could really help her or not.

"Can you send me home?"

The other woman's mouth curled up in a swift smile. She countered not with an answer, but with another question.

"Are you certain that you really want to go?"

Ignoring the sudden pang of doubt—and fear—that the question brought, Megan nodded.

"Of course I do." Her words came out in a sharp tone. She took a deep breath and tried again. "I don't belong here. Can you or will you help me?"

"Will you aid me with my half brother?"

"But what can I do?" Puzzled, Megan wondered if Rhiannon might have the wrong idea about her and Kenric. "I barely know him. He has only agreed to help me find my way home."

"What can you do?" Rhiannon's laughter sounded incredulous. "How is it possible that you do not know?"

"Know what?"

Rhiannon stared at her for so long that Megan began to fidget. Finally, Rhiannon shook her head, her expression once again closed and remote. The Faerie queen.

"Know what?" Megan repeated stubbornly.

"Have you not felt it, in your woman's heart?"

"Felt what?"

"The pull he has on you, that tingling on the back of your neck that tells you that this man is different, that slow dawning of awareness that here, in front of you, might be the one?"

First magic, now romantic nonsense. Megan didn't know how she felt about magic since entering this world, but she held no illusions about romance. Roger had cured

her of any fanciful romantic notions a long time ago, the
first time he had hit her.

"No." Megan shook her head. Then, feeling an odd
compulsion to be truthful, she smiled. "Though I will
admit he is extremely easy on the eyes."

Rhiannon smiled back. "In this you are like him. Both
of you run from the truth. You and he were made for
each other. You, Megan Potter of Dallas-Texas, are my
half brother's rightful mate. He senses it, as you do. You
are soul-halves. Only together will you be complete."

Two hours later, bathed and dressed in a gorgeous gown
of some diaphanous blue material that seemed to float
around her legs, Megan tried to put the Faerie queen's
words from her head.

She didn't believe in destiny, in soul mates, and all
that sort of baloney. But then, she'd never believed time-
travel was possible either, or that such a thing as Faeries
existed, or magic.

Her world, in short, had been turned upside down. She
no longer knew what was real and what wasn't.

Rhiannon had never explained what it was, exactly,
that she wanted Megan to do. She'd waved her hand and
a fragrant, steaming bath had appeared in the white marble tub. In a similar manner the dress had appeared, the
vibrant cerulean startling against the stark whiteness of
the room.

Peering at herself in the crystallized mirror, Megan
knew she had never looked so beautiful. The long dress
hugged her body, swirling about her legs in a cloud of
sheer material. No matter that she felt as if she were
wearing a Halloween costume—the harem girl she'd always wanted to be but couldn't—she felt feminine and
pretty.

This, she reflected with a rueful smile, would be what
she'd dream if she had a choice. A beautiful Faerie kingdom, with the outside temperature an even seventy-two

degrees. No insects, plenty of tropical flowers, and warm sunshine. Gorgeous clothes that were comfortable as well as good to look at. And no doubt the food Rhiannon had mentioned would be a feast fit for a queen. Now this was the life. Forget that freezing snowy ride on Lancelot's broad back. Kenric could—

Kenric.

Her entire body flushed hot.

How would he react to seeing her dressed up like this? In a formfitting gown that seemed to be sexier in its enveloping curves than the tiniest minidress. This was the kind of outfit Kenric would be used to seeing on women. No doubt he'd approve; after all, he'd made it clear that he found her modern clothing odd and distasteful. But would she measure up? How could she possibly hope to compete with the perfect, shimmering beauty of Faeries?

Compete? Sinking down onto the bed, Megan groaned. This was Rhiannon's fault. Her ambiguous words made Megan long for things that couldn't be.

What could she be thinking? She had no need to attract Kenric's attention; all she needed from him was protection until she could get home.

That was all. No more. Despite the fact that he was the most gorgeous male she'd ever seen, despite the way her mouth went dry when she saw him, the way her bones felt as though they were melting when he put those massive arms around her, not to mention the deep, drugging wonder of his kiss. . . .

Whoa. Bringing her hands to her flushed cheeks, Megan realized she tingled all over. *OK, time out.* She needed to get a grip, to think rationally. So she was sexually attracted to Kenric of Blackstone—heck, who wouldn't be? He was every woman's fantasy man.

Again she thought of Rhiannon's insistence that she was Kenric's mate. *Not possible.* Obviously the Faerie queen didn't really believe Megan's tale of being from the future. If she did, she'd know that Megan had been born some nine hundred years too late.

No, somewhere out there in the world of 1072, some fair maiden lived who would be perfect for Kenric. All he had to do was find her, which shouldn't be difficult. Heck, if the women of this time were anything like the women of modern-day Dallas, they'd be standing in line for someone like him,.

Megan scowled. The idea seemed a bit . . . well, unsettling. But that didn't mean she had somehow become attached to the taciturn warrior. *Nah.* He was simply the only person she really knew in this time and place. Or, she amended with a grimace, in this utterly fantastical dream. Whichever.

Descending the stairs, which seemed to be made out of cut-glass blocks, Megan inhaled the tantalizing smells that wafted up the staircase. Food. Wonderful, delicious food, to judge from the scent of it.

She rounded a corner and ran smack-dab into the very man who'd plagued her thoughts all day. Kenric.

If she'd thought she cleaned up well—*man, oh man*—looking at him took her breath away. He wore a fresh tunic of rich golden material that looked like crushed velvet. His leggings were gray, which complemented his eyes, and outlined his muscular legs. Hurriedly she looked away, focusing her eyes on the center of his impossibly broad chest.

"Megan?" He sounded as stunned as she. One giant hand came under her chin, cupping it, caressing it, lifting her face to look up at him.

God help her, she felt as shy as a schoolgirl with a crush on a rock star.

His gaze traveled over her, disbelief warring with approval.

"You are"—he cleared his throat, his eyes darkening—"beautiful."

Because he said so, she believed him. For one perfect

instant, gazing into his dark eyes, she felt beautiful for the first time in her life.

"Thanks," she managed, her throat tight. She wished she could find the courage to say the same words back to him. "You look nice too," she said instead, unable to control the tremor in her voice.

Kenric held out his arm for her to take. "Now I might almost believe your claim to be a princess," he told her, low voiced, his breath tickling her ear.

She started, taking his arm with a nervousness that surprised her. "I'd forgotten about that. I was only joking—er, jesting with you." She'd also managed to forget the simple fact that Kenric, with his sister, the queen of Faeries, *was* a genuine prince. Straight from a dream.

Dangerous thinking. She had to concentrate on getting home.

"Remember, this is only temporary." Kenric's stern voice contained a warning.

Megan gasped. "Do you read minds?"

His short bark of laughter contained no humor. "Nay. Despite my sister, I claim no magical skills. 'Tis in your face, Megan of Dallas. The childlike wonderment at what you see here. Do not let the enchantment beguile you, for we ride away from this place at first light."

Chapter Seven

With a stiff, mocking bow, Kenric turned and led her down a long marble hallway. The tantalizing scent of roasting vegetables grew stronger. Her stomach growled, reminding her that she was starving.

She shot a glance up at Kenric from under her lashes. Once again, the cold, formidable warrior stood next to her.

They rounded a corner and found themselves surrounded by people—or Faeries—whichever was the case. Row after row of tables, made of some type of crystalline glass, filled the room, though the Faeries were not seated. Rather, they stood around in groups, laughing and chattering as though it were some North Dallas cocktail party. Except for the clothes. Megan had never seen such colors, such variety, except on television when watching the Grammy awards.

Kenric stopped, the expression on his handsome face

unreadable. As the room took notice of them, all conversation came to an immediate halt.

Kenric cursed under his breath. Megan could feel the sudden tension in the corded muscles of his arm. He glanced at her, a bold, appraising look, then nodded.

"Are you ready?"

In answer she squeezed his arm. Oddly, having him at her side made her feel protected, cosseted even, though she knew these people—Faeries—surely meant her no harm.

Right now, however, the silence seemed deafening.

As soon as Kenric began to move into the room, the assembled crowd resumed their conversations.

They headed straight for the banquet table, Kenric murmuring niceties but not stopping to make polite small talk as she would have. Megan tried not to gawk, but good Lord, it was difficult. All of the women were stunning, exquisite. She felt like a drab robin among peacocks.

And the men—oh, the men put even Mel Gibson to shame. Whether blond or dark-haired, blue-eyed or brown, there was not a balding, paunchy man in the crowd. They were all tall, all slender, some with wide shoulders, others leaner. She saw muscular men and wiry men, young men and men the age of Sean Connery. All in all, there were more gorgeous men in the room, than in any Chippendales calendar.

But none, she admitted reluctantly, could hold a candle to Kenric. It was an odd sort of irony that the best-looking man in the room was with the plainest woman. Ah, well, she was only human, while they were magical beings, who, no doubt, could choose exactly how they wished to appear.

The thought cheered her immensely. She was in the most divine fantasy land she could ever imagine, escorted by a gorgeous man, and wearing a dress that made her appear prettier than she ever had before. And the food—

the array of delicacies spread out on the buffet table made her mouth water.

To top it all off, Kenric had called her beautiful.

She felt as though she could eat a horse.

As if he read her mind again, Kenric handed her a plate.

Normally she would have taken time to examine the patterns etched in the sparkling crystal. Maybe she would later. But for now Megan moved down the table, heaping helping after helping of food on her plate. She didn't recognize some of the dishes, though they looked to be some sort of gourmet fruit or vegetable casseroles. She felt confident that they'd taste wonderful. Heck, anything would have tasted wonderful after the limited diet of dried beef and hard bread she and Kenric had shared. Though there was no meat—were Faeries vegetarians?— there were so many wonderful dishes that she knew she'd be stuffed. Especially if she went back for seconds.

"Is that for both of us?"

The amusement in Kenric's deep voice made her grin. She glanced down at her plate, then at his. While he had a large portion, fit for a man of his size, hers was easily twice that.

"Maybe," she answered, batting her eyelashes flirtatiously.

His husky laugh warmed her heart. And more.

"Come, wench." With his hand in the small of her back, he escorted her to a table. "I will enjoy watching you attempt to eat all of that."

Taking a seat in the chair he pulled out for her, Megan felt truly content for the first time in years. Ever since she'd finished high school, through college, and then after, she'd felt a gnawing sense of emptiness, an ache that nothing and no one seemed to appease.

For a time, she'd thought Roger would fill it. But after she'd agreed to marry him the abuse had started. It began in small ways—a disparaging remark, a direct order—then the first time she'd displeased him, he'd slapped her across the face. Hard.

It had progressed from there, such a smooth slide into hell that she'd never even realized she'd arrived. When she found herself driving to the emergency room, her arm wrenched from its socket, she'd realized she had to get away from Roger. It had just taken her time to work up the courage.

He'd been after her to change her will for the last few months, and she'd begun to wonder if he intended to kill her.

Glancing around her, at the unbelievably beautiful people with their gaily colored clothes, then at the rugged giant of a man who took a seat across from her, she found herself wishing that, if this was a dream, it might never end.

Kenric had never been at ease around the Faerie folk. Truth be told, he avoided them as if they carried the plague. They reminded him too much of the side of himself he tried the hardest to suppress. Ever since he'd been a young boy, taken in by his father at the tender age of five, he'd known he was different. So had all the other children of the castle, skirting him with wary looks and cruel taunts. As he grew older he'd told himself it was because he was the bastard son of the lord, but even then he'd known that was only the partial truth.

Though it was probably only some magical gift his sister had bestowed on him in secret, the fact remained that he was good at everything. Once he'd taken a fierce sort of pride in this. It was only as he grew older, more mature, and had come to realize what this meant, that he'd come to hate it.

Still, he could not help what he was. Hand him a sword, and he bested his opponent. Hand him an old manuscript, and he'd have it translated from Latin to English to Gaelic to Latin and back again in no time. His half brothers had at first despised him for it, though as they'd all grown older they'd come to regard him with a grudging sort of respect.

His brothers had ever been unsure what to make of him. He was taller then they, fairer of face and form, and the women flocked around him even though it was well known he was but a bastard, with no claim to any land rights. However uncertain they were of their feelings toward Kenric, he remembered with a small smile that they had appreciated it when he'd shared this abundance of feminine attention.

Kenric liked to think they'd formed a bond of affection in the end that, if not brotherly, was at least based on loyalty and their shared blood. This belief was all he could hope for, now that they lay dead and buried deep beneath the earth's fertile soil.

Like his father. When he thought of the man who'd sired him, Kenric had cause for regret. He'd always believed he'd have time, time to ask the endless questions that had plagued him since he'd become old enough to know the truth of his parentage.

His father had had a wife who, while a good woman, certainly could not compare to Rhiannon in beauty. His Faerie mother must have been beautiful. He'd never met her, since she'd chosen to vanish into the mists soon after his birth. He'd been told it was because his father would not marry her. Why, he did not know. He'd never asked his father, and his father had never spoken of the Faerie woman who had borne him a son out of wedlock.

Now that his father was dead, he would never know the answer to this question, or to any question he might have about their relationship.

If Rhiannon knew more than he did, he doubted she would ever tell. Nay, he would never ask. He did not want to know.

He wanted nothing whatsoever to do with Faeries.

And now, somehow, he'd gotten the Lady Megan of

Dallas-Texas involved in this. And she seemed to love it here. This was not acceptable, not at all. For she had charged him with a task: that of returning her to her betrothed. He would not let her become so beguiled of the land of Faerie that she forsook her journey. This he would have to impress upon her.

He pulled her jeweled ring from his pocket, turning it, examining it in the perfect light. Though it glittered and sparkled, he found the effect of the huge stone cold. The diamond reminded him of Rune, all flash and show and little warmth. For the first time he found himself wondering what kind of man this Roger was, though the size of the bauble left no doubt he was a wealthy man.

Wealthy meant he would have no problem granting Kenric the land that Megan had promised.

He would have to prevail upon Megan to leave this place, and soon. Even one night seemed too long to wait, especially knowing that one night here might be thirty in the mortal world.

So it was with great reluctance he found himself waiting for his charge to escort her to the banquet. Idly, he found himself wondering how Megan would look properly dressed.

In a moment he had his answer. She rounded the corner and ran straight into him, a vision in sapphire. His breath caught; his chest felt tight. Her beauty was ethereal, transcending even that of the Faeries who surrounded them.

She was beyond beautiful. Now he might almost believe her teasing claim of being a princess, and he told her so.

Raw desire mingled with need as a strange ache settled in his breastbone. He'd been around beautiful women all his life, but none had affected him the way this tiny woman betrothed to another did. It was not a good thing. Not a good thing at all.

The ring, all but forgotten, cut into his palm, reminding

him that she belonged to some man named Roger. A fellow Englishman, a wealthy lord. The sooner he helped her find this man, the sooner he could claim his land, and the better off he'd be.

With this in mind, he led her to the banquet table.

After they'd eaten—Kenric had watched in mild shock as dainty little Megan finished off a heaping plate of food—the music started.

Seeing his sister heading their way with a purposeful glint in her eye, Kenric shook his head. Next to him, Megan listened to the seductive thrum of the harps and mandolins, tapping one foot in time to the beat.

"Are you two enjoying yourselves?" Rhiannon beamed at them, her innocent expression telling Kenric she was up to no good. Some things, it seemed, never changed.

Megan flashed a sleepy smile, the guileless radiance of it going straight to Kenric's midsection. He shifted in his seat, suddenly uncomfortable.

For the first time he found himself wondering if he'd made a mistake in agreeing to help her. But then, there was the land. Always the land.

Raising his chin, Kenric met his sister's gaze dead-on, saluting her with his cup. "I am fine."

"Will you not ask Megan to dance with you?" Rhiannon asked softly.

He made the mistake of looking at Megan again. Her expression had gone dreamy, those wonderful eyes of hers soft, like warmed honey. With her chin resting on her hand, she listened to the music wholeheartedly, allowing herself to be drawn into the ancient rhythm, the timeless melody.

A dangerous woman indeed.

Kenric became conscious of his heartbeat, steady and slow. Of the blood that thrummed in his head, making him want much more than he had any business wanting.

"Well?" Amusement threaded Rhiannon's voice, telling him that his sister was well aware of his attraction.

113

"I think not." Lifting his cup of mead, Kenric drained it. He did not elaborate.

But Rhiannon was devious. "'Tis a shame, brother, that a woman as beautiful as Megan cannot truly enjoy the banquet. One dance will not hurt you."

As if the sound of her name pulled her away from her dreamy contemplation, Megan turned to look at him.

"A dance?" Her voice sounded husky and breathless, totally unlike the way she normally spoke to him.

Enchantment, no doubt. Still, knowing this did not keep his heart from leaping at the raw sensuality he heard there.

About to answer her, he found himself forestalled by Rhiannon.

"My brother does not like to dance."

The bright expectation in Megan's face faded. "Oh, I see." She swallowed, nodded, flashed a wan smile. "Well, I suppose that is good. I'm not sure I could do those steps anyway."

Without giving Kenric a chance to answer, she turned away to fix her attention on the musicians.

Oddly, he felt as if a cloud had obscured the sun.

"One turn around the floor," Rhiannon whispered, her expression carefully blank. "It would bring her such pleasure."

"Indeed," he drawled, wondering why he felt so apprehensive. He had, after all, danced numerous other times with women far more beautiful than Megan. One dance, if it pleased her, surely could not hurt.

"Megan." Rising, Kenric went to stand in front of her. When she lifted her lovely face to look at him, he was struck by the sudden, irrational urge to kiss her. Here. Now. No matter who might be watching. It was only by sheer willpower that he was able to push those thoughts away.

He held out his hand, praying she did not notice how it trembled. Without the slightest hesitation, she took it.

Her delicate fingers felt like they belonged in his protective grasp.

"Will you dance with me?"

Another woman might have simpered and flirted, or blushed and giggled. But not Megan of Dallas-Texas. Instead, she gave a regal nod and rose, leading the way to the other swaying couples.

Bemused, he let her, wondering at the way touching her quieted the sense of urgency, of danger, that he'd felt earlier.

Still, the instant he put his arms around her, he knew he was in trouble. Big trouble.

It could have been the way she wrapped her arms around him, as if she thought they were in the privacy of her bedchamber. Or the way she allowed her body to sway so close to him, touching in places she should not have allowed them to touch.

But—he thought, swallowing—if he were honest he would admit that it was more than the sum of these things. It was more than her admittedly lush body. Yes, he wanted her, desired her, but something inside of her called out to him. Something in her soul. He was a deeply mystical man—how could he not be, considering his heritage—and he knew in the place where certain truths resided unshakable that Megan could mean more to him than anyone ever had before. Or ever would again.

If he but allowed it.

She belonged to another. Such thoughts were beyond dangerous; they threatened the very foundation of his goal.

Deliberately, Kenric loosened his grip on Megan and tried to think of something else. He prided himself on his honor, and honor dictated that he return this woman to her betrothed, where even she herself wanted to be. He held no claim on her, nor she on him. And as long as he did not touch her . . .

Letting the thought trail off incomplete, he reminded

himself again of the boon she had promised: land of his own. Though he had saved a fair bit of gold, he knew he did not have enough for his purposes. If her Roger did as she had promised and granted him some land, Kenric could use the gold to build the estate of his dreams.

He would never again have to fight someone else's battles, nor kill without just cause. He'd best remember that.

Megan sighed loudly, her face resting on his chest.

His body stirred, warning him. Glancing down at her dark hair, he was struck again by the odd sense of yearning, of wanting something more from her, or maybe from himself.

It was another foolish feeling, and he shook it off, wishing himself anywhere else. Dancing with Megan of Dallas-Texas was too unsettling for his peace of mind.

As if in answer to some unspoken prayer, the music ended. He released her, reluctant to do so, yet glad he would be tortured no longer.

A male Faerie, one of his sister's high court, tall and comely, stepped up next to Megan and bowed.

"Might I have the honor of the next dance?"

Now Megan colored prettily, her gaze flying to Kenric as though she sought his permission. *God's blood.* Did she now think he was her lord?

With a curt nod, he gave her the approval she seemed to seek and strode away, cursing her Lord Roger for a fool. How could the man let a woman like her slip away? Were she his, Kenric knew he would never be so careless.

Were she his . . . He snorted, keeping himself focused on the crowd ahead of him, rather than looking back to where Megan danced. He found he had no desire to see her in another man's arms, especially one so golden and fair of face and form.

"You look thunderous, my brother." Rhiannon materialized at his side. "Is something wrong?"

Her pointed gaze made Kenric realize he carried himself stiffly, his hands clenched into fists, his jaw set and tight. Forcing himself to relax, he shook his head, still keeping his back turned from the dancers.

"Naught is wrong, sister. I am but eager to be on my way."

Rhiannon frowned. "You've only just arrived."

With difficulty, he bit back his impatience. "One night is all I promised. Megan must be returned to her future husband."

"Bah." Smiling prettily, Rhiannon laid a hand on his arm. "What is one day or two? The man must not value her highly or he'd have found her by now."

Since these words so closely echoed his own thoughts, Kenric said nothing.

"One more day?" His sister voiced the request in the most pleasant of tones, unlike the commanding way she usually spoke to him. This alone told Kenric she wanted it badly.

"How much time will pass in the real world?" he asked, keeping his own voice carefully neutral.

Her shrug was a calculated thing, warning him that she would not speak the entire truth. "I don't know. What does it matter?"

Though Kenric realized she knew exactly how much it mattered, he only shook his head. "I think not, sister. I have a task to complete and some land to see about collecting."

"Always this." She sighed. "Land, land, land. Such a base, human desire. Why must you act so much like them?"

"Because, my half sister," he explained with what he thought was great patience, "I *am* one of them. Do you forget that I am half-human?"

Her laugh sounded like crystalline bells. "Nay, Kenric. I do not forget. How can I, when you remind me of it at every turn?"

Since he had no ready answer, Kenric did not reply.

Instead he found his attention drawn to the dancers, even though he'd glanced over his shoulder only once.

"She is lovely, is she not?" Rhiannon asked softly.

He did not have to ask of whom his sister spoke.

"Perhaps." His answer came equally softly, though he edged his voice with steel. "Though she belongs to another man."

"Does she?"

"It is this man that I help her seek."

"I do not see it in her." Rhiannon watched him closely as she spoke.

Knowing his sister wanted him to ask, Kenric sighed with resignation. "See what, sister?"

"She does not pine for this man."

He shrugged. "There need not always be affection for there to be a betrothal. You know this."

She made a sad sound. "I forgot the foolishness of humans. You so seldom marry for love."

"We marry for wealth, for land."

"Land. One cannot own the land. It is all there for anyone to use or roam freely."

"In the realm of Faerie, perhaps." Kenric found himself watching for another glimpse of Megan. "But you know 'tis not the same in the land of man."

"So you tell me."

"So it is."

The music ended, the players bowing before they went to partake of refreshment. Kenric turned, watching Megan come to him, her hips swaying gently, and for a moment allowed himself to pretend that she was his. If she were, when she reached him he would capture her in his arms, lift her, and whirl her around until she was dizzy and laughing. Then he would kiss her until she grew senseless. Until they both grew senseless.

He became conscious of his sister's regard. Rhiannon eyed him with a faint smile. He had no time to reply, however, because Megan came to stand before him.

"That was fun." She slid her small hand into his and beamed up at him.

Kenric told himself to ignore the jolt he felt from merely touching her. "We leave on the morrow," he said in a growl.

Her smile faded, her clear-eyed gaze searching his, missing nothing. "What's wrong?"

"He fears but one thing," Rhiannon answered, forestalling him, her own expression disappointed, "and that is endangering that frozen lump inside him that he calls a heart." With that, she turned and stalked off, leaving them alone.

At Megan's puzzled frown, Kenric found himself smiling. He shrugged.

"She is my sister, and a Faerie queen besides. Who knows of what she speaks?"

"I see."

Despite Megan's hesitant smile, Kenric somehow doubted she was fooled.

They walked back to their table, Megan's downcast head telling him she wished to stay. It was usually this way with humans; once they visited the magical realm of Faerie, they wanted to remain always. He himself still fought the powerful tug of attraction this place held for him.

"Do you love this Roger?" Kenric heard himself ask, his brusque tone sounding as though it had been dragged from him.

Megan appeared shocked as well, her mouth dropping open as she gaped up at him. Color stained her pale cheeks. "Roger?"

Such a simple thing to make him furious, the sound of another man's name on her lips. He had to force himself to go on, knowing that the answer was somehow vitally important.

"Yes, Roger. Your intended."

"I . . ." She seemed incapable of speech, her lovely eyes wide and full of panic.

"Perhaps," he interjected smoothly, "you do not know him that well?"

At this she lifted her chin, meeting his gaze dead-on. "I have known Roger all my life."

"What will he gain from your union?"

It was a reasonable question, albeit an intrusive one. But Megan of Dallas-Texas did not appear to find it so, if the glitter of anger in her eyes was anything to go by.

"What will he gain?" She smiled coldly, though there was a tinge of pain there as well.

But her next words confounded him.

"What *will* Roger gain?" she asked, low-voiced, almost to herself. "He has it all—the huge, multimillion-dollar company, the properties, the land. But capital, that's another story."

Half of what she said made no sense to him, but he understood from the gist of her words that Roger was a wealthy man.

"Capital?"

"Money." Her mouth pursed tight, Megan did not seem to like her newfound conclusion. "Gold, if you will. There's the simple matter of my trust fund. I'm not sure exactly how much is in it, but last time I checked it was in the millions."

Though he knew she spoke of money, the numbers she used made no sense. Perhaps the currency was different in this land of Dallas-Texas from whence she came. But the concept . . . now, that was as old as time. Now he understood. It was as it should be.

"Ah, he needs your bride price." It had always been so: titled lords marrying wealthy heiresses to bring needed money to their aging estates.

"My bride price?" She spoke the words with distaste, as though they were foreign. "No." She shook her head, her eyes still flashing golden sparks. "He needs my money."

It seemed plain that the bump she had taken on the head still addled her wits.

Patiently, he explained. "A bride price is what every bride must bring to the marriage, especially when joining with a wealthy nobleman such as your Roger."

Before she could say any more, he took her elbow and guided her toward her room. With a heavy heart, he decided he could no longer allow doubt to interfere with the task he faced. He must return her to this Roger.

As for the powerful attraction he felt to her, he must ignore it. With Megan of Dallas-Texas, it was obvious he was far out of his league. A bastard son, he had no land, no title, nothing to give a noblewoman such as she. It should have come as no surprise to him that she would be wealthy in her own right.

Out of his league? No, he was out of his mind. The land, he told himself savagely; he must think of the land. It was his deepest desire, even though he found it necessary to continually remind himself of this fact when around Megan. The sooner he helped her find her Roger, the better off they would all be.

Chapter Eight

It had been, Megan thought as she flopped on the bed, sighing loudly, one of the most beautiful evenings of her life. Until the very end, when Kenric had unpredictably ruined it.

What had *that* been all about? Kenric seemed to believe she and Roger were some sort of lord and lady, for God's sake. She nearly giggled out loud, imagining some pompous footman announcing her as Her Grace, the Lady Duchess Megan of Dallas, Texas.

Whatever.

Though it would be better to correct his misconception, to tell him that she was American after all, and Americans didn't have such things as titles, she knew she couldn't. America didn't even exist at this point in time. If he knew she was from another place and time, he would know the land she promised him was worthless. At least to him.

And she needed Kenric to protect her, to somehow

help her get home, especially since his sister seemed disinclined to use her magical powers to assist in the effort unless Megan betrayed Kenric.

Which she would never do.

Rhiannon had said Kenric had magical powers of his own. But how could she get him to help her, especially once he learned she'd lied about gifting him with land?

What a mess. Closing her eyes, Megan allowed herself to remember the seductive chords of the music, the sensual lure of Kenric as he had swayed with her in his arms. Kenric made her feel things she'd never expected to feel, feelings she didn't know existed outside of the world of Hollywood movies and romance novels.

If Rhiannon was to be believed . . . *No.* She'd let herself believe in happily ever after with Roger, and look where that had gotten her.

Somehow things would work out. Kenric would get his land—oh, yes, she would figure out a way to do it, no matter what it took. Her ring ought to be worth something—maybe Kenric could sell it and use the money to buy some land.

Of course, that meant she would have to return home, and Roger would know that the lightning strike hadn't killed her after all. If she could ask for one thing, one thing besides the ability to return to her own time and place, it would be help in breaking things off with Roger—help staying alive.

Even thinking of Roger's reaction to her decision terrified her.

No, for now she would stay with Kenric, in his time, for just a bit longer. And if her heart beat faster when he was around, well, she would simply let herself enjoy it.

Megan drifted off to sleep, thoughts of a handsome warrior keeping her pleasantly warm.

The morning dawned with cheerful brightness.

Megan smiled, snuggling under her covers, and stretched.

The sun poured in, a river of golden warmth. All in all, it was a great way to start a day. She wanted to explore this beautiful place, meet some more people—Faeries—and . . . Then she remembered Kenric's dictate. Today they would return to the bitterly cold real world. She would not be able to remain here another day, unless she could convince Kenric otherwise.

Which, she decided with a grimace, she would have to figure out a way to do.

After she'd dressed—in another lovely, archaic gown that she'd found hanging over the back of a chair—Megan made her way downstairs. She had no idea what time it was. Her watch had not survived the lightning strike. Without it she felt curiously bereft, a fact she had not realized until just this moment.

She wandered the empty hall, searching for Rhiannon. Not finding her, she supposed she ought to go meet Kenric.

But her stomach told her it was breakfast time, no matter what the hour. She followed the same path as the night before to the dining room. There she found an array of vibrant, brightly colored fruits; puffy steaming rolls; and mouthwatering juices. Other than the food, which looked as if it had come straight from the glossy page of a restaurant advertisement, the room was deserted.

After heaping her plate—something about this place made her ravenous—Megan took a seat at one of the long banquet tables. She had barely sampled her food when a loud, clanking sound made her look up.

Kenric appeared, wearing his chain mail, newly polished, and a fierce, furious expression. Legs planted apart in a battle stance, he said nothing. Instead he merely glared at her. She hid her smile.

"Would you like a roll?" Megan held one up, wondering what had put him in such a foul mood. Surely it could not be something she had done; after all, she'd only just risen from her bed.

"No." Though perfectly modulated, the icy coldness of his voice told her he would have his say. "I would not like a roll. What I would like is your explanation, lady."

"Explanation?" Taking a delicate bite, Megan savored the taste of the bread before swallowing. "For what?"

"Did I not tell you we would leave this morn?"

She nodded.

"At first light?"

"Yes."

"So you did hear me say it?"

"Yes." Megan finished off her roll and started on a ripe apple. She had no idea where he was going with this, but she felt quite certain she would not like it.

"Then where were you?" These last four words he shouted, his voice rising until it seemed to echo off the crystal walls. "I have waited for you for nigh unto an hour."

"I was trying to find your sister."

"My sister will be found if she wishes to be found. Most likely she is furious that we dare to decline her hospitality one more day. Still"—his gaze, cold and hard, raked over her—"that does not explain why you did not meet me where I asked you to."

"I thought we should eat first." Actually, she'd wanted to forget all about leaving. She didn't want to go. "And anyway, how can I be late? It's barely sunrise."

"I broke my fast well over an hour ago." He narrowed his dark eyes. "Long before the sun rose."

So he was an early riser. How was she to know?

"I'm sorry," she began. "But—"

Kenric held up a hand. Apparently he was not finished. "Is it not customary to depart from the bailey?"

Since she had only the faintest idea what a bailey might be, Megan simply shrugged. "I don't know. Is it?"

Kenric moved closer, until he loomed quite threateningly over her. He was huge and fierce and devastatingly handsome. If she hadn't slept in his arms, she guessed she'd be frightened. But no, Megan *knew* somehow that he was different than Roger. Kenric would never hurt her or any woman. He needed a bit of placating, that was all.

"You didn't specify a time." Never taking her eyes off his, she laid a gentle hand on his arm and made her voice soothing. "And I have no watch. You should have sent for me or something. I don't even know where the bailey is," she confessed in what was nearly a whisper.

His eyes darkened. Before she could move, before she could react, he reached out and hauled her up against him. She gasped; then his mouth claimed hers.

The kiss was raw, hard, and furious, and spoke of his frustration. No doubt he meant it simply to punish her, but instead she thrilled to it. She found herself kissing him back with a kind of mindless, desperate need, her hands winding around his neck, keeping him close to her.

Kenric.

As her heartbeat thundered in her ears, her desire nearly out of control, he pulled back. His breathing as ragged as her own, he let her catch her breath before taking her mouth again. But this time the touch of his lips changed.

He gentled the kiss, slowed it, until she thought her legs would no longer support her. He possessed her and stroked her, all with his mouth. He made her want him with a mindless sort of passion; it consumed her so that she forgot where she was, even who she was.

When he pulled away again, she sagged against him, stunned.

Never in all of her life had a man kissed her like that. She'd felt cherished, cosseted, desired.

She wanted him to do it again.

He pushed her away, making a sound between a groan and a moan. He sounded like an animal in pain.

Megan opened her eyes. "Kenric—"

"Nay." Turning away, he shook his head. "I regret I have touched you in such a manner."

His shoulders stiff, he would not look at her. Instead he made a mocking bow.

"Finish your feast; then make ready to leave with all haste. After all"—he flashed a twisted smile that seemed more of a grimace—"your Roger awaits."

With those mocking words he was gone.

"Good Lord." Megan sank slowly into her chair. She picked up her half-eaten apple, but the fruit had lost its appeal.

Roger. Soon she would have to tell Kenric that she meant to break off her engagement. And that Roger existed somewhere in the far-off future. That, no matter how hard Kenric searched, he would never find Roger—not in this place nor this time. And, more important, that there was no land, at least not in any place that he might want land.

Yes, someday soon she would have to tell Kenric that the entire foundation of their relationship was based on a lie.

What a mess her fabrication was turning out to be.

She hadn't expected to want him so badly. Sure, he was gorgeous, tall, and muscular with thick hair the color of her new mink coat. But she wasn't like other women of her time; she wasn't the type who could indulge in random sexual affairs without risking her heart.

Even with someone as magnificent as Kenric.

Ah, but that kiss . . . Like the first time he'd kissed her, it had been, well, different. No, not merely that; it had been earth-shattering, enough to curl her toes and straighten her hair.

And, though she certainly wasn't experienced enough to be any authority on the subject, she was willing to bet that sparks like that didn't come around all too often. It had been more than a melding of mouths. It had been like coming home to a place she hadn't even known existed until now. Kissing Kenric of Blackstone was like joining souls.

Great. Next she would be buying into Rhiannon's strange pronouncement that they were soul mates. Even if such a bizarre thing were true, there was the simple matter of time that lay between them. In her world, Kenric had been dead for more than nine hundred years.

She kept trying to tell herself it was a fantasy, a dream. But this life, this time, this man had become all too real to her. If this kept up, she was in very real danger of being hurt.

And once she told him the truth, no doubt Kenric would hate her, for she'd promised him the very thing he wanted above all others.

Land.

Panic filled her, the kind of urgent, powerful panic that clouded the thoughts and made one think only of escape.

Leaping to her feet, Megan pushed back her chair and sprinted down the hall to her room. Kenric was right. The sooner they got out of this enchanted place and he helped her return home—or find Roger, as he thought she wanted him to do—the better.

Rhiannon appeared in her doorway just as she'd finished changing out of the borrowed dress and into Kenric's shabby old tunic.

"Kenric says we must go." Megan dared to take the Faerie queen's hand, clasping it and hoping Rhiannon would listen.

"But before I do, I need to know the truth. Can you help me get home?"

Infinite patience shone from the other woman's lovely eyes. "This is your home. You belong here, Megan Potter of Dallas. You, like your soul-half, have a task to complete."

Great. More riddles. Megan tried to hide her impatience. "What kind of task?"

Some of the serenity left Rhiannon's face. "Kenric faces great danger. Beware the one called Myrddin."

"Myrddin? The Black Faerie leader?"

Rhiannon nodded. " 'Tis not only Kenric he seeks to destroy. 'Tis me, and all of Rune with me. Warn my brother against him. He will hear your words better than he will hear mine."

"But I haven't even told him—"

Rhiannon pulled her hand free, the aristocratic expression back on her face. "There will be time enough for that later. But this is vital. Guard my brother, Lady Megan. Please. Guard him well."

Kenric said not a word as he helped her mount his warhorse, ignoring the sadness in her lovely eyes. He saw her glance around the deserted bailey and knew what she would ask before her lush mouth even framed the words.

"Where is everyone?"

"They do not believe in leave-takings."

Climbing on the horse in front of her was no easy task with the heavy chain mail he wore. He'd been surprised to find it lying on the floor in his sleeping chamber all polished and shiny.

At first he'd been afraid to touch it, believing it might be a thing of magic. But upon closer search, he'd discovered it to be his very own chain mail, brought to him by magic, but yet untainted by it.

His instincts dictated that he wear it. Danger lurked in the very air.

And Megan had no idea. Even now she regarded him with that steady gaze that would, if he let it, reduce him to a puddle at her feet.

Ignoring the roiling emotions inside of him, he settled himself on the warhorse's broad back. Luckily, the animal was sturdy and well used to carrying a lot of weight. He bore it all patiently, only the forward perk of his ears telling of his own eagerness to be off.

At last Kenric gathered the reins in one hand and urged the warhorse forward. *Lancelot.* He snorted. To think the woman thought she could tack such a name on his noble steed. He did not name his possessions, and that was all the horse was to him: a valued possession.

"Kenric." With her soft, distinctive accent, the Lady Megan commanded his attention. "Why didn't your sister come to see you off?"

"She despises good-byes," he told her tersely, not wanting to let her know that even now his sister glided along silently beside them, cloaked in her Faerie magic.

When they came to the edge of the meadow, he raised one gloved hand in silent farewell. He saw the answering twinkle of lights and turned to look over his shoulder at the woman sitting so silently behind him.

"Be prepared for the cold. We leave this place when I ride into those trees."

Megan said naught, simply nodding. He found himself admiring her courage; the snow and frigid air had been daunting even to him, and he was a man well used to harsh conditions.

The warhorse seemed to understand, needing no further urging to pick his way carefully into the mist-shrouded forest.

They rode through the last group of trees and Kenric braced himself, wishing he had more than an old, tattered cloak to protect the woman. He had decided, after that foolish, foolish kiss, to think of her not by name, but by the most general description, the same as his horse. She was only a woman, after all, an employer who had charged him with a task. It was the payment, the land that mattered, not the lustful thoughts that even now heated his blood.

He was Kenric of Blackstone, mercenary warrior. He had no human family, no land, nothing. Emotions and foolish dreams he could ill afford. Therefore, he would take control of his body and of his destiny.

He felt her stiffen behind him as they broke through the last bit of mist. The warhorse tossed his head, moving them into bright, warm sunlight much like the weather they'd just left.

Kenric cursed. The sun shone straight overhead in the azure sky.

"Springtime," Megan said softly, awe in her voice. "How can that be?"

"I told you, time passes differently in the realm of Faerie." He made no effort to hide the bitterness in his words. "What seemed but a day and a night to us was an entire season here."

She tensed, her arms tightening around him. "Months?"

"Aye." He thought of what this might mean to her, to them, and cursed again. "Think you that your Roger has taken another woman to wife?"

She was silent, finally relaxing her hold on him. "I . . . I don't know."

Kenric cursed a third time. He had the strangest urge to take her in his arms and comfort her. To kiss the tip of that downcast head, the sweet-smelling sable hair. He scowled. Maybe it was because she sounded so forlorn, like a lost, abandoned child.

Whatever the reason, he would not do it.

"We will find your Roger," he vowed, hoping his sister listened from whatever place she hid herself. "I promise you, we will find him. If the man cares for you at all, he will not have wed so soon."

The sound she made was a choking one, a cross between a laugh and a sob. Because there was naught else he could do, except that which he would not allow, Kenric urged the warhorse into a brisk trot. They had a lot of ground to cover before nightfall if they were to reach the next town.

Wrapping her arms tightly around his waist again, Megan did not speak. Her soft breasts bounced against his back in a way that, were it not for the protection of his chain mail, would have been a torment. All around them

131

were the scents of spring: the heady aroma of flowers, the scent of heather and of hay. The sun felt warm, and under his chain mail he grew hot. But he dared not remove it, not knowing when danger might approach. In these uncertain times, danger lurked at every turn.

The gait of his warhorse was smooth and would soon lull them into an unguarded state. For this reason, Kenric urged the horse into a canter. He had but one goal—to reach the next town safely and see if Megan's Lord Roger had ever inquired of her there.

The rocking motions of the canter were even more soothing and, from the way Megan sagged against him, Kenric thought she might have dozed off. He smiled, remembering the stark fear in her face when he'd first informed her she would have to ride his huge horse. She had struggled to hide it from him, never once complaining.

Now she and the beast had even become friends of a sort.

Ahead of him he could see rolling fields of green. Behind him were the thick forests. Aside from a few boulders, there was no place for an enemy to hide.

He allowed the warhorse to slow to a trot. Barely winded, the sturdy animal could go on for hours.

Imperceptibly, Kenric allowed himself to relax. At best, the next village was an hour's ride away. They would reach it long before dusk.

It was then, as he daydreamed in the warm sunlight, that the hair on the back of his neck rose. This was his only warning before the riders thundered around an outcropping of rock to circle him.

Cursing his unreadiness, Kenric yanked his sword free from the scabbard. This woke Megan, who came to with a startled, totally feminine-sounding cry. Kenric prayed the other men would see her only as a callow lad.

There were four of them, large, unwashed men dressed entirely in black. Not Welsh this time, they had the look of mercenaries; being one himself, Kenric thought he might have fought beside them or against them in one skirmish or another.

Behind him, Megan sat stiffly, wary and ready for whatever might happen.

Kenric remained motionless while he calculated the odds. He would go down fighting before he would willingly let them take his lady.

His lady. The thought gave him pause; then, because he had no time to dwell on it, he pushed it away. To all appearances Megan was a lad, nothing more. As long as she did not give herself away, she would be safe.

He hoped.

"What do you want?"

The leader cocked his head, considering him. "That depends."

There was something familiar about the man, devil take him. Kenric stared hard at him, trying to remember. He would not ask again. Right now the key was to appear unafraid. These men might respect that.

Then again, he knew not how much honor these men had. They might respect nothing but their right to take what they wanted.

He thanked God he did not carry much gold.

The leader urged his horse forward. "What do you have that we might want?"

He was a big man, dark of hair and eyes. His face wore the weary, jaded expression of a man who has fought one too many battles, uncaring of the outcome. It was a face that Kenric hoped and prayed he would not wake one morning and see staring back at him from a mirror.

Still, the hair at the back of his neck rose, warning him of great danger.

"I am a hired sword, like you." His hand still clenched around his weapon, Kenric gave a casual shrug. "I have nothing of value."

"That is a fine horse for a man with nothing."

Kenric set his jaw and swallowed. He would fight to the death before he would allow any man to take his horse.

"He is a horse, that is all." To any listening, it would appear he did not care. "But necessary for me to earn my living." With these words he told them he would not give up Lancelot—the warhorse—easily.

Several of the other men nodded, murmuring among themselves. To a man, they understood the need for solid horseflesh.

Still, Kenric saw the way the leader looked at his war-horse.

Behind Kenric, Megan squirmed uncomfortably. He prayed she would stay still and quiet, at least until the danger was past.

Kenric kept his hand on the hilt of his sword.

"I am Kern," the leader finally said, his avid gaze sliding past Kenric to Megan.

"Kenric of Blackstone."

One of the others, a tall, dark man with dead eyes, leaned forward, his stare intent and sharp.

Kern's expression narrowed, letting Kenric know that he had heard the name. "What of the boy?"

Kenric forced a smile, though he knew it to be little more than a baring of teeth. "He is my brother's son. I take him with me to teach him the trade." He felt a pang of sorrow as he spoke the lie. His brothers—and their sons—were all dead.

The leader threw back his shaggy head and laughed. "Then you go the wrong way, Kenric of Blackstone. We ride west, to join the English Baron Aldridge. He amasses an army and, rumor has it, pays well."

They were late. Kenric himself had collected his payment from the very same baron after successfully helping him wage war on a neighboring keep. But he could not tell the other mercenaries this; they would know he had gold and would try to relieve him of it. No matter that he had very little on him. They would merely torture him—and Megan—until they located the whereabouts of it.

"This I know. I merely ride into the village for supplies before joining him." He forced himself to chuckle, a harsh sound utterly without humor. "And it has been a long time since I have had a woman."

This brought guffaws from all four of them. Kenric took a guess that they had just left the same village after partaking in the same fleshly pleasures.

"We will meet up later then." Kern seemed to be taking his falsehoods for truth. Behind him, Kenric heard Megan expel a sigh of relief.

He would not let down his guard until the men had ridden off.

Kenric's warhorse stamped his hooves, shaking his head and making the bridle jingle. The others' mounts appeared restless too: one horse sidestepped nervously; another pawed the earth.

The mercenaries muttered among themselves, something that surely did not bode well for Kenric and Megan.

"I would have your horse," Kern announced in a loud voice.

Kenric lifted his sword. "I would rather keep him." He kept his tone polite. He still hoped, somehow, that a real confrontation could be avoided. Were it to come to a battle, with him against four, he would surely lose.

One of the other men, a huge, shaggy-haired fellow, laughed. "Methinks he spoils for a fight."

"Aye." One of the others, the man who had taken notice of Kenric's name, spurred his horse forward. With his narrow face and cold, empty eyes, he was the sort who fought only because he had nothing else to do, who cared not if he lived to see another sunset, who took little pleasure in life, or war, or anything for that matter. This utter lack of caring would make him deadly as a warrior.

Kenric was uncomfortably familiar with his kind; he himself had come too close to becoming one of the same. But there was something else about this man, something that hinted of great evil, of a dark rot festering in the soul. Kenric did not like this, not one bit. He had fought many men, some of them truly evil, but none wore the darkness about him like a cloak as this man did.

"Oh, leave us alone." Megan's cross voice, sounding childishly shrill, rang out.

Kenric winced. *God's blood*. Did she not realize how utterly feminine she sounded?

Kern narrowed his gaze. "Does your insolent whelp of a nephew issue a challenge?"

Behind him, Kenric felt Megan stiffen as she realized the full import of her words.

"Nay," he answered for her, cuffing her lightly on the arm in warning. "He is but a rash, impatient lad. He is unschooled in battle and useless in a fight."

This caused another roar of laughter, though Kenric noticed the man with the blank eyes simply stared, expressionless.

"Show yourself, lad," Kern called, false joviality in his voice. "I would see what manner of boy dares challenge such seasoned warriors."

Kenric could feel Megan tremble as she peeped out from behind him. Most likely she was terrified. He longed to comfort her, but he dared not. As long as she held silent, he might yet be able to figure a way out of this.

Instead, to his utter disbelief, Megan began talking. "You should be ashamed of yourselves."

Kern cocked his head. "What's that?" He grinned, a wolfish, evil smirk. "Does the little pup yap?"

"You're damn right I do," she shouted, her voice shaking with anger. "Why don't you bullies go pick on somebody your own size?"

Chapter Nine

Stunned, Kenric realized Megan trembled not from fright, but from rage. What was this? She'd always seemed such a sweet, docile little thing. What a time for her to choose to exhibit this side of her nature.

Luckily for them, the mercenaries found humor in her words.

"He seems about the same size as me." One of them pointed at Kenric, his eyes crinkling with laughter.

"Or me," said Kern, no humor in his voice or expression.

"Four to one are not fair odds." To her credit, this time Megan kept her voice low-pitched, so that she might pass for a green boy. But her next words were so totally feminine that Kenric didn't know whether to laugh or to cry.

"For shame," she scolded, even going so far as to shake her finger at them. "What would your mothers think?"

After a moment of stunned silence, the four mercenaries exchanged looks. Kenric prepared to swing his sword, certain now that he would need to use it.

"Our mothers?" This from Kern, his voice ringing with disbelief. "I have not seen my mother since I was about your size."

The others laughed—all except the man with the dead eyes. A coldness settled around his features, an utter chill that spoke of death and winter. When he spoke for the first time, Kenric knew his instincts had been right: the man was trouble.

"Something is not right here," the dark man intoned, his voice as flat as his expression. "Tell the boy to step down from the horse."

Kern did not hesitate one second before seconding the other's order. "Step down. Now."

Kenric had no choice; he could not defend her if she was on the ground while he stayed astride. When Megan would have obeyed, he put a hand on her arm to stay her.

"He will not." Kenric let his gaze linger on the man with the dead eyes, and his voice rang with challenge. He was through with the verbal sparring. If they wished to fight, he would have it over with.

"Let us pass."

Behind him, Megan clutched at his shoulder. With an effortless motion, he shifted his weight so that she was once again hidden behind him.

"Let us pass," he said again.

Kern laughed. "I think not."

Megan leaned around him, ignoring the warning glare he shot her. "The other men we met a few days—er, a few months—ago left us alone once they found out who Kenric is." Though she spoke bravely, her voice trembled.

Kern looked at them, then at the man who reeked of evil. "What say you?"

The dark man narrowed his eyes. "Kenric of Blackstone." His voice seemed layered, somehow profane, the threat thinly veiled. "I have waited a long time to find you. We have unfinished business, you and I."

"We want no trouble." Kenric elbowed Megan, sensing she was about to speak.

"What of the others, the men you met earlier?" Kern sounded puzzled. "We have been in this place for a fortnight and have encountered no others."

"They were Welsh." Dismissing them with a wave of his hand, Kenric kept his eyes on the other man, the man who, he now recognized, was the biggest threat. "They had no stomach for a fight."

Again Megan opened her mouth. Again he sent her a warning jab; this time his elbow connected with her ribs. Behind him, she gasped.

Kern glanced at his men, his gaze lingering overlong on the man in the back. "Mayhap we want to fight."

Kenric did not respond. Instead he dug his heels into the warhorse's side and rode around them.

Though he now doubted they were much of a threat, except for the evil one, still he kept his hand on the hilt of his sword. He would not entirely trust these men until they had ridden off and were but specks on the horizon.

They nearly made it past. Nearly. But as they rode by the last of the group, the man with the dead eyes, the man Kenric had deemed the most dangerous, reached out and, with one swift blow, knocked Megan from the back of the horse.

She cried out, forgetting in her terror that she was supposed to be a boy, and her shriek was undeniably female. Kenric spun the warhorse about, too late, and could only watch helplessly as she was nearly trampled under the other man's stout beast. The cap she'd crammed over her shorn locks went flying, as did the small pack she'd clung to ever since he'd found her nearly frozen in his cave.

Rage filling him, Kenric's first inclination was to attack them all. His second was to vault off his horse and assist her. Since this would give him a worse disadvantage than he already held, he simply kept his sword arm ready. With the other he directed Megan to a small rock outcropping nearby.

"Wait for me there."

Her expression grim, she did as he asked, looking, he thought, rather like a wounded sparrow. There was no possibility that the other men might mistake her for a young boy now, not when her vulnerable femininity was exposed for all to see.

The choice had been taken from him now. He would have to fight. Hell, he *wanted* to fight, to avenge the insult that had been given. As long as he could rein in his magic.

With a warning look at Megan, he raised his sword. The silver blade gleamed in the bright sunlight.

Kern grinned, drawing his own blade. After a moment's hesitation, two of the other men followed suit. Only one man, the man who had dared to knock Megan to the ground, did not.

"Draw your sword." Ignoring the others, Kenric challenged this man. If he had to die fighting, he would kill this one first.

"I have no sword," the other replied, a gleam in his cold gaze.

This gave Kenric pause. No man, if he wanted to live past the first flush of youth, went swordless in these times. What kind of fool was this man? Did he wish, then, to die?

"Borrow one." Kenric inclined his head toward the others, all with their blades drawn. "Defend yourself."

"He has no need of a weapon," Kern boasted. "Myrddin can kill with a wave of his hand and a word."

From the ground, Megan made a strangled sound of agitation. Kenric watched her as she stared at Myrddin as if she had seen the devil himself. Did she know this man? Perhaps he had fought for her Lord Roger. Though if he were a well-known mercenary, Kenric would have known him.

Myrddin. Though the man was not a mercenary, the name seemed so familiar. Kenric couldn't remember, but he could swear he had heard Rhiannon mention that name before. Perhaps this Myrddin had locked horns with her in some sort of magical contest.

A mage then. Having a Faerie queen for a sister, Kenric did not doubt that this warrior knew many powerful spells. But, from the look in his face, Kenric also knew that this shell of a man drew his strength from the dark, not the light.

Like the renegade Faeries who had murdered his family.

Eyes narrowed, he wondered if this Myrddin had been part of it.

One of Kern's men, overeager, spurred his horse forward.

"Halt." Sharp and deadly, Myrddin's voice carried a hundred times more authority than Kern's.

Instantly the rider halted as if frozen. All of them, Kern included, looked toward the mage and waited.

"He is mine," Myrddin said in a hiss, the words seeming to echo off the rocks. "He seeks to steel my birthright; thus he is mine alone to kill."

The breeze, formerly light and gentle, gusted. It carried a chill. From the west, dark clouds rolled in, turning the bright blue sky the color of slate. A storm was brewing Kenric could not help but wonder if the dark man had somehow conjured it up for his own nefarious purposes.

Magic. How he hated even the thought of it. Unlike that of his sister and her people, the magic this one used was dark and foul. Kenric could sense it in the roiling air, heavy with evil.

Magic. Good or bad, somehow he seemed unable to escape it.

If he would but acknowledge it, Kenric had protection;

evil spells could not harm him, not with his Faerie blood.

Faerie blood. He'd never before accepted it. Never wanted to, never needed to. He'd wanted only to be human, like his father and his half brothers. He could remember them taunting him as a child, calling him changeling and worse. How he had hated that.

No, he would be no changeling, no magical thing. Not ever. Especially not since his family had been killed because of what he was. He would fight as a man and, if necessary, die as a man too. This promise he had solemnly sworn after burying the bodies of his human family.

Megan made another soft sound, a cry of distress as if she somehow sensed his thoughts. Silently Kenric cursed. Somehow he had managed to forget her, if only for an instant *Damnation*. He had promised to help her, given her his protection.

The dark magic stifled the light, blotted it out, making breathing difficult.

Soon it would impossible to fight. Though fighting would be a waste of time against dark power such as this.

Only magic could prevail against one such as this. His sword contained magic, magic he could use without invoking his own powers, without using any of the Faerie magic that tainted his soul and threatened to overwhelm him.

He would use the sword only. The sword and its own magic would have to be enough.

The sky grew blacker, the chill more biting. Even from the back of his warhorse, he could see that Megan shivered. Though Kenric did not believe in such things, if this was a portent, it was an ominous one.

The dark man stared at him, one corner of his mouth twisting into a mocking smile. "Are you so ready to die, brother of Rhiannon, reluctant mage?"

"Rhiannon?" Ah, he hadn't been wrong then. His sister and this man were known to each other.

Myrddin laughed. "Aye, I know her well. And for you I have searched long and hard."

Many men boasted before battle; Kenric surmised that for some it was a way to hide their fear, while others thought to goad their opponent, hoping that anger would overtake caution and provoke recklessness.

This man, with his dead eyes and hate-filled expression, did not merely boast. Kenric sensed that he meant every word.

Four against one. It was not impossible. He had faced down such odds once before and won.

"Nay, one against one," Myrddin told him. Then Kenric knew that the other man had somehow read his thoughts.

"You and I. And our powers." His smile chilled Kenric's blood.

"I have no powers. Choose a weapon." If Myrddin would not fight with swords, perhaps he might be willing to do close combat with a dagger or a knife.

"I have chosen it." Myrddin laughed, his eyes glittering. He made a small gesture with his hands, somehow obscene, and lightning flashed over the plains. "Magic."

Magic. He had only to call upon his Faerie heritage for help.

With every ounce of his being, Kenric resisted. He had disavowed magic. He would not—could not—abandon every principle he had spent his life trying to hone.

He was human, a man. If the magic lay inside him, inherent, so be it. He would not call upon it, would not let it consume him, turn him into some kind of monster.

Fear and trust widened Megan's amber eyes. She trusted him. Kenric forced himself to look away from her.

He turned to face the wizard. With a smooth motion, he raised his heavy sword, feeling it hum with power.

"Fight, damn you." Gritting his teeth, Kenric issued the challenge.

The wind began to shriek and howl, buffeting him as

though he were a leaf clinging to a tree branch.

"The battle commences." Myrddin's twisted smile left no doubt that he meant it. "Now."

Kern and his other two men retreated, backing their mounts until they were a good distance away—near Megan.

Interpreting Kenric's warning look correctly, Kern grinned. "We will not touch her," he promised. "Yet."

Kenric hesitated, knowing that to hesitate could be death in a normal battle. But this . . . this was anything but normal. Myrddin's refusal to arm himself stumped him. He'd never struck down an unarmed man before. He wasn't about to start now.

"The prize"—with a dark smile, Myrddin tossed out the words casually, as if the outcome were of no importance—"is not the horse, though I am sure Kern will relieve you of the beast regardless. Nay, the prize is the woman."

As if he'd planned it for effect, lightning crashed, illuminating the gathering darkness. Thunder boomed, reminding Kenric of his sword's ancient name. Somehow Myrddin knew of Kenric's vow to protect Megan. That was why he had chosen to name as a prize the one thing that would make Kenric fight. No matter what else he was, Kenric was a man of honor.

Forsaking all else, he still had that. He'd clung to it, even as a mercenary warrior, choosing battles that he felt were justified—his honor.

And honor demanded he save Megan by whatever means at his disposal.

If Myrddin had been waiting for Kenric to agree to his terms, he waited no longer. The first blast of energy nearly jolted Kenric from the warhorse's back.

Lancelot trumpeted, staggered, then fell to his knees. Kenric had no choice but to dismount.

"Don't hurt the horse," Kern shouted.

Myrddin laughed, his face alight with an unholy glee. "Prepare to die, Kenric of Blackstone."

From her place on the rock Kenric saw that Megan watched, her eyes still huge, still hopeful. Trusting. Believing in him.

Kenric cursed. He had no choice. Just this once. He would use his inherent magic just this one time.

He readied himself, gathering his strength and his energy like a tattered cloak around him. For the first time he wished he had paid more attention to his sister's numerous attempts to teach him when he'd been small.

Focus. Ah, better. He felt it building inside of him. Lancelot—no, the warhorse—staggered to his feet.

The wind tore at him, as though trying to knock him from his mount. Around them the air became heavy with the promise of rain and . . . *smoke.*

Fire.

He felt it crackling around him, licking at his clothes. Consuming him, as he'd always known it would.

From a far-off distance he heard Megan scream.

There was no heat. No stench of burning leather and flesh.

Illusion.

The instant he thought it, knew it for a certainty, the flames vanished.

Desperately, he began again the process of gathering his energy, of honing his attention the way Rhiannon had tried to teach him as a young boy, so long ago. But he was rusty and long out of practice. The second he felt the stirrings of raw power begin to build in him, he knew he would not be able to control it.

Lightning crackled, the air sizzling with black energy. Demonstrating his own powers, Myrddin clearly had no intention of allowing his opponent time to do anything.

Again Kenric concentrated, focused. He could do this. He would do this. For Megan's sake, he had no choice.

All at once it filled him. His power, arriving so suddenly that Kenric felt out of control. His entire body vibrated as it coursed in him, through him, with him.

Focus, focus. He lifted his hands, gathering the energy like a shield around him. He could feel his sword, no longer separate, thrumming in tempo with the pulsating magic inside him.

Desperately he tried to harness his abilities, fighting the uneven pressure as the magic threatened to overwhelm that which was human, making him but an instrument, a vessel for its passage.

Nay—he would not give in to it. The violent tremors of his internal battle shifted his attention inward, so that he no longer saw the mercenaries backing away, their grizzled faces blanched with terror. Nor Myrddin, his eyes mere slits as he summoned up his own dark magic to counter the danger.

None of them knew—not even Kenric himself had realized—the breadth, the scope, the sheer might of the power within him. As he had feared, despite using all of his strength, his ironclad will, he could not dominate it.

With one last shuddering effort at resistance, he relinquished his control.

Violently, the energy consumed him, erupting outward as he screamed out one last warning before falling senseless to the ground.

When he awoke, all was quiet. No breeze chilled his overheated skin. The landscape once again looked pastoral: bright sunlight, azure sky, the sheer simplicity of a peaceful spring day.

As it had been before.

Off in the distance, he heard the rumble of faraway thunder.

Kern and his ragged band of followers were gone. As was Myrddin, the evil one, whose name Kenric felt he should know.

Behind him, the warhorse heaved a sigh. Kenric's

heartbeat steadied. He wiped the sweat from his brow and, with one final glance around him, sheathed his sword.

All was as it should be. And magic—if that blast of raw energy could be called such a thing—was no more.

Yet something . . . With a curse, Kenric recalled the woman he had put from him, meaning to keep her safe.

It appeared he had failed, for she no longer stood on the rock. In fact, he did not sense her presence anywhere nearby. Somehow, whatever his magic had done to the others had hurt her as well.

Megan had vanished.

This was ridiculous. Megan couldn't believe it. Traveling through time was one thing; meeting a Faerie queen and traveling to the land of Faeries was another. But an evil wizard? She was beginning to feel as though she were living in some skewed video game.

As heroes went, however, Kenric couldn't be beat.

Once the battle had begun, she couldn't tear her eyes away from him. Despite all his protestations against magic, the man positively resonated with it.

She'd been impressed, despite herself, when that Myrddin character had changed the weather. His dark visage was so blatantly evil that she supposed she ought to be glad that all he had done to her was knock her from Lancelot's back. And even then, he'd thought she was a boy.

Rhiannon had warned her against this man. Evidently Kenric was not aware that Myrddin had been the one who had led the Black Faeries against his human family.

Megan shivered, hugging her arms tightly around her middle. Myrddin had meant to kill Kenric.

And for a moment it had looked as though Kenric meant to let him. He had sat frozen, indecision clouding his eyes. Then he'd thrown his head back, his handsome

face contorted as though he were in agony, and she'd
seen the power course through him.

There'd been a blast of white heat and she'd seen nothing more.

Megan gradually gave up replaying the scene in her
mind and became aware of her surroundings. The light
had changed. She was no longer on the broad plain where
the battle had been waged. Instead, surrounding her were
gray stone walls, the rock weathered and rough. No fragrant grass lay under her feet; she stood on dirt, damp
and moldy. The stench was horrendous—bringing to
mind years of filth and neglect and, somehow, human
sorrow. She bit her bottom lip. It appeared she was deep
in the bowels of some castle. In the dungeon. The heavily
rusted bars that surrounded her gave that away rather
quickly.

Great. Could things get any worse? Hastily she erased
the thought, knowing they certainly could. To think she'd
once thought she had an ordinary, boring life.

Maybe no one knew she was here. Her heart leaped.
If she wasn't locked in, all she had to do was get out of
this castle and figure out a way to find Kenric.

Or could he find her with his magic?

Since she had no idea, she couldn't just stay in this
dank dungeon and wait for him.

Walking gingerly, she tried the metal door. With a hiss
and a moan, the door gave way.

Once he'd decided to use his magic to save their lives,
Kenric saw no reason why he couldn't use it again to
find Megan. She couldn't have gone far.

Closing his eyes, he focused inward, searching. He saw
only darkness—darkness and the unyielding, cold finality
of lichen-covered stone. He smelled a fetid odor like rotten earth and heard in his mind a horrible moan: Megan's
moan, Megan's voice.

His eyes snapped open as he scanned the empty plains.

Danger. His heart thudded once, hard, within his chest, then began to pound. Megan was in some sort of danger. And, since he'd somehow put her there, he had to find a way to save her.

The warhorse, sensing his urgency, surged forward.

Megan found herself in a long corridor. On the walls, torches flickered in the drafty air. Praying that no one would chance upon her, she hurried along the passageway. When she came to the narrow staircase, she climbed it without hesitation. Her luck held; no one appeared to challenge her.

When she reached the top of the stairs, she realized she was on the main floor of the castle. This would be where the greatest danger lay, for the castle inhabitants would roam this area freely.

Glad she wore the boyish disguise Kenric had given her, Megan hoped she would come across a large crowd and blend into it. In all the movies she'd seen, medieval castles appeared busy. But in this one, utter silence reigned. The silence seemed so pervasive that she wondered if everyone was asleep.

Or dead. She shivered, remembering those same movies and the savage butchery of the people of these times.

Surely not. Shaking off her trepidation, she forced herself to continue down the hall.

Where was Kenric? Why had he sent her here?

She reached the end of the hall. Now she could go either right or left. Listening, she heard nothing: no sounds of servants bustling, of children playing, of people. No sounds at all. Maybe, just maybe, she might make it out of here undetected.

Taking a deep breath, Megan closed her eyes, counted to ten, and plunged ahead to the right.

Smack-dab into the biggest man she'd ever seen.

She reeled back, her heart in her throat, gulping in air and spinning on her heel to run.

Hairy arms the size of tree trucks came up to grab her. "What have we here?" the giant boomed.

She quickly figured out that she couldn't get away. Escape was impossible. Even if she kicked this man in the shins, it would only anger him. Defeated, she let her shoulders slump.

He had wavy red hair that went past his shoulders, and a thick beard to match. His pale blue eyes were narrowed, though the corners of his mouth quirked up in the beginning of a smile.

Remembering her disguise, Megan took a deep breath. "I need to look for my"—frantically she tried to remember the proper term—"*liege* lord." It sounded phony even to her. And for all she knew there were no other lords in this monstrous castle besides the man who had his humongous hands clamped around her forearms. And wasn't *liege* a French word?

If she could have brought her hands together, she would have twisted them.

His eyes narrowed to mere slits. "Really," he boomed in a silky voice. "Which lord might that be?"

"You're hurting me." Instead of answering, she tried for a distraction. That, at least, was no lie. No doubt she would have bruises on her arms from this big lug's hands.

He made no move to release her. Instead he chuckled low in his throat. "A soft lad you are."

She knew a real boy would have bristled at that, but she was tired and hungry and really, truly frightened. She wanted Kenric. Odd how a man she'd known for only a few days made her feel so safe, so protected.

Megan hung her head. "I'm sorry," she murmured.

At that he released her, setting her on her feet with a thump. *Men. Who could ever figure them out?*

The giant continued to regard her with suspicion. "I have never seen you before."

"Do you notice every boy—er, steward—in the castle?"

His thick brows winged up. "Why shouldn't I, since it is my keep?"

Keep. Right. She should have remembered that. *Keep, not castle.*

Slowly she began sidling past him: one foot, then another.

"Hold."

Megan froze. Even though he'd spoken quietly, the command in his tone was unmistakable.

She raised her head, peering up at him with what she hoped was an entirely innocent expression.

"I will have the name."

For a moment she drew a blank. Then she remembered he'd asked the name of her liege lord. Well, there was no help for it. She knew the name of only one man in this strange place, if she didn't count Kern the bandit or Myrddin the evil wizard.

"Kenric of Blackstone," she said proudly, hoping he would not notice how her voice trembled.

His huge hand came down, clamping on her shoulder. "Come with me, boy."

Apparently using Kenric's name had been the wrong thing to do. Since she had no choice, she trotted along beside him, taking two steps to each one of his.

After what seemed an endless walk down the echoing stone halls, they came to a great hall filled with people of every size and shape. Megan immediately brightened. He wouldn't dare to hurt her now, not with so many witnesses.

"Good morning, Lord Brighton." Every person they passed hailed the giant.

So he was a lord. Megan tried to remember the hierarchy of the monarchy. If she remembered right, it went king, duke, earl, and then baron. Maybe. Anyway, this Lord Brighton wasn't a king, since no one called him Your Highness. That was good, she supposed, since kings seemed to be able to do whatever they pleased without any consequences. Including disposing of one insignificant boy.

And *insignificant* might be putting it mildly. As Lord Brighton dragged her through the crowded hall, no one even seemed to notice her.

But from the way people greeted him, Megan surmised he was well liked here in his castle—his keep, she amended silently. Another good thing, she told herself. Such a man would be less likely to do something rash or evil.

Not once did he release his firm grip on her shoulder.

After what seemed an endless march, they finally reached the other end of the hall. There Lord Brighton paused before an ornately decorated door. Fascinated despite herself, Megan studied the intricate woodwork. Made of hardwood, the highly polished design seemed mystical, almost holy.

Before she had time to wonder what it all meant, Lord Brighton pulled the door open and pushed her through.

Chapter Ten

Kenric vaguely remembered a keep situated to the east. He had never been there, though he'd heard tales about the place ever since he'd been a boy. What he hadn't remembered was how far away the place actually was.

He'd ridden hard all day and still saw no signs of the outlying village that surely would surround such a place. He saw an occasional crofter's hut, a shepherd and his dog guarding sheep, and still the winding road ahead showed him nothing but dust.

The sky remained a cloudless, vibrant blue, and the light breeze was warm. It would be a perfect spring day, if he were not in desperate pursuit of his vanished lady.

He would find her; he had to. Only once in his life had Kenric failed. He'd been absent when his father and his family were butchered, and for that he could never forgive himself.

For this reason, he would not fail again.

He would save Megan. He would return her to her

Roger, collect the reward, and live the rest of his days in peace.

For some reason, on the seemingly endless ride in the middle of nowhere, he found himself wondering what this Roger was like. What kind of man let his intended bride get lost and then made, for all Kenric could tell, no real effort to find her?

Perhaps this Roger did not want to marry Megan. Mayhap it suited his purposes better if she were to remain lost.

To his surprise, this thought angered him. Not because he would not be rewarded with land, as Megan had promised, but because he did not want Megan hurt. She had exhibited a strength of character and courage he had never seen in a woman, yet she was feminine and lovely.

If *he* were her betrothed—Kenric stopped the thought before it could take root. He had no room in his life for emotion, not now. Perhaps later, when he'd established his land and gotten his wife with child. All that mattered was the continuance of the line; he was merely the vessel by which it would continue.

Megan belonged to another. He would find her Lord Roger and claim his reward even if he had to wring the neck of the other man to do it. And, in the process, he would ensure that beautiful, sweet Megan was not hurt.

As he rode, the sun sank lower in the sky. Soon it would be difficult to see and he would have to find a place to stop. But the thought of Megan trapped in some dank and moldering dungeon haunted him.

He decided to press on, trusting his warhorse to find the way. After all, they but followed a road.

The moon hung high in the sky when Kenric, exhausted, brought the horse to a halt. He would have to sleep, and the animal needed a rest and something to eat.

By the light of the full moon he could make out a silvery sliver of water on the other side of a field. There he went, letting his faithful mount drink his fill. The lush grass served as ample feed, and, while the animal was munching contentedly, Kenric made himself a pallet and drifted off to sleep, his dreams haunted by the face of a woman who belonged to another.

It took a moment for Megan's eyes to adjust to the dim light in the small room. Candles flickered all around it, and some sort of incense burned as well. The exotic smell made her head swim.

In the back corner, reclining on a long couch, was an ancient man, judging from his deeply lined face and white hair and beard. He appeared to be asleep, though one gnarled hand rested on the head of an oversize gray cat.

Lord Brighton pushed her forward, clearing his throat loudly at the same time.

The ancient's eyes slowly opened.

Megan gasped. Totally unexpectedly in such a wizened face, his eyes were periwinkle, a purple of such brilliance and vibrancy that it humbled her. She had never seen eyes like his. After a second thought, she realized she had: Kenric's sister Rhiannon had eyes of the same color.

"Come closer, child," he whispered.

Because his expression was not unkind, and because Lord Brighton would surely push her again if she did not, Megan moved reluctantly forward.

"She has news of the one you seek," Lord Brighton muttered.

Megan wondered why this one would seek Kenric. Her knees trembled, though not from fear. Not exactly. Somehow the world that she had always taken for granted had changed. Not only had she traveled to the past, but the past didn't even match the history her own world recited as truth.

Magic existed here. Magic and Faeries and no doubt other things that were assumed to be only myths in her time. It challenged her concept of reality and absolutely terrified her. Yet at the same time she felt more alive than she'd ever felt in her life.

As if sensing her unease, the old man smiled. He lifted his hand from the cat's head and beckoned her closer. "I will not hurt you, child."

She believed him. And when a wooden footstool suddenly appeared next to his couch, she sat down upon it gratefully.

"I am Ed."

Gaping, surprised that one such as he should have such an ordinary name, Megan nodded.

"For Edmyg," he continued, grinning. "It means 'honor.' "

"I am . . ." Her attempt at keeping her voice low failed. She cleared her throat and tried again, this time in her normal voice: "Megan of Dallas."

Behind her Lord Brighton stiffened. "A female," he said in a growl. "That explains many things."

Megan cursed herself. She had been so awestruck by the power she sensed in this ancient one that she'd completely forgotten her disguise.

Edmyg waved Lord Brighton to silence. "Megan. Your name means 'strong and capable.' Are you?"

Though her Irish mother had always assured her that the name meant "pearl," Megan supposed it meant different things in different languages. In these times, perhaps it did mean what this man said.

"I suppose I must be," she answered reluctantly.

Edmyg smiled at that, his sharp eyes at odds with his jovial expression. "Where is he?"

Megan stared blankly at the man. "Who?"

"Your mate."

Immediately she thought of Roger, waiting beneath the old oak tree. He had wanted to be her mate, though she'd been zapped by lightning before she'd been able to tell him no. Then she remembered Rhiannon's words, telling her Kenric was her soul mate.

She sighed. "I have no mate."

Lord Brighton growled again, low in his throat. "She lies. When I asked her the name of her lord, she told me—"

"Enough." Sounding surprisingly authoritative for one so old, Ed pointed to the door. "You may leave now. I would speak with this one alone."

Despite herself, Megan shivered. Though she had no sense of immediate danger, she hadn't yet been able to ascertain if this man was friend or foe.

Lord Brighton bowed stiffly and left.

Was it her imagination, or did the shadows seem to grow deeper? The candles flickered, and the cloying scent of the incense seemed suddenly overpowering. Megan had an urge to run, to flee, to try to escape this weird place, this strange man, and most of all this time in which nothing was as it should be.

As though he knew her thoughts, the old man smiled. "Do not be afraid. I dreamed of Rhiannon late last night. In the dream she told me to expect you."

Rhiannon? This man knew Kenric's sister? And knew her well, if the naked longing that resonated through his powerful voice was any indication. Yet he was ancient, surely too old to care for the Faerie queen in the way his voice indicated.

"Yes." He chuckled, the shadows making his face look decades younger. "I know Rhiannon, queen of Rune. Someday I hope to look upon her lovely face again."

Wanting to squirm on her stool, Megan forced herself to hold still. She hadn't spoken, yet he'd answered the question she'd only thought. "Can you read my mind?"

"No, child. But there are things I know."

"How?" Interested despite herself, Megan leaned forward.

He tilted his head, appearing to consider her question. "Thoughts are patterns," he said finally. "As are deeds and wishes."

"And dreams?"

"Those too I can sometimes see."

Since she had nothing to lose, she decided to be blunt. "Can you help me get back home?"

He laughed, a dry chuckle. "You are home."

His cryptic answer made no sense. Rhiannon had said the same thing.

"Am I even on earth?" With all the magic and other weird things that had been happening, she wouldn't have been surprised to find out she'd space-traveled as well as time-traveled.

"Place is relative."

"Please." If this man knew the truth, she had to get it from him.

He sighed, giving her a look full of enigmatic sorrow. "Though it may seem to be at the whim of fate, everything happens for a reason. Your coming has been foretold for ages. You and Kenric of Blackstone are the stuff of legends."

That made no sense. But since she'd been able to make very little sense out of anything that had happened to her since she'd gone to meet Roger, Megan shrugged it off. Desperate times called for desperate measures.

"Please. I need to know if you can help me return."

His silence seemed almost a refusal. Behind him the candles flickered, the light wavering, the shadows dancing.

Why would no one help her? Not counting the evil Myrddin, she'd met two supposedly magical beings—Kenric's sister and this man—since she'd been here and neither one of them seemed the least inclined to help her. What she couldn't figure out was why not. It must have to do with this legend nonsense that both Rhiannon and Ed believed so implicitly. Odd how Kenric didn't know he was a legendary figure.

Gorgeous, magical Kenric. She started. For the first time it occurred to her to wonder if Kenric could use the magic she'd seen in him to catapult her back into the future, where she belonged. When she was ready to go, that was.

She'd have to ask him when he got here to rescue her. Somehow she knew he would. Whatever else he might be, Kenric of Blackstone was a man who was true to his word. He would be here. Now all she had to do was find out if this ancient man, this Edmyg whose name meant "honor," intended them any harm.

Raising her head, she found him watching her.

"What do you want with Kenric?"

"That is between him and me," the old man said, his clear eyes glinting with something close to amusement.

"Fine." Disgusted, Megan turned away and pretended to study the intricate tapestry on the wall. "I don't know why I even bother to ask, since no one around here will give me a straight answer."

Ed chuckled. "All will be revealed in time, child."

Time. The very word was enough to send shivers down her spine. Since she had nothing to lose at this point, she decided to try again.

"Do you know about me, where I'm from?"

He gave an immediate nod, his gaze sharp.

"Then you know how I got here?"

"Lightning," he told her promptly, smiling a pleased smile. "And the sacred tree. Two lightning strikes in the exact same place, though many years separated them."

For the first time it dawned on Megan how awfully old that oak tree must be. But it made no sense. If she was in Wales, she was a continent away.

Deciding to argue, she tilted her head. "It couldn't have been in the same place. I was in Texas; now it seems we're in Wales. How can this be?"

His eloquent shrug told her that he had said all he was going to say on the matter.

"Is it even possible to go back?" She held her breath, waiting for the answer to this one, though the odds were against him even bothering to answer at all.

"Anything is possible. Though your destiny is here."

Another riddle. Megan decided she was beginning to hate riddles. "Am I a prisoner here?"

Ed laughed at this, a dry and raspy sound that turned into a cough. "A prisoner? More likely an honored guest."

She wondered. "Lord Brighton doesn't think so."

He nodded wisely. "Ah, but he will. Once we have you outfitted as befits a woman of your stature, he will be surprised and pleased. Though a good man, he never was one for looking beyond the surface to the beauty below."

Inordinately pleased that this wise old man thought her beautiful, it wasn't until much later that Megan thought to wonder what he had meant by the phrase *a woman of your stature*.

As soon as the first golden fingers of sunlight began to lighten the sky, Kenric climbed on his warhorse and resumed his headlong rush of a ride. The night before he'd ridden until he could no longer ride upright. Finally he'd had to stop, knowing he would be of no use to anyone were he all but reeling with fatigue. Rest had been a forlorn hope though; his sleep had been fitful at best. All during the night he had been unable to shake a sense of pending disaster. Lady Megan was in trouble, trouble that somehow he had created. Though he had no doubt he would find her, he could only hope he would be quick enough to save her.

The few hours' break seemed to have refreshed the warhorse. He charged forward with renewed purpose. The closer they rode toward the keep, the more desolate the landscape seemed. Parched and barren ground gradually replaced the lush greenness of the empty countryside. What trees there were—and there were few—had gnarled and knotted bark and sparse, dry husks for leaves.

He saw no beasts here, no cattle or goats or even the occasional wild dog. Even the birds seemed to absent themselves from this place.

Kenric thought it odd that he came across no village nor people of any kind. It was his experience that the wealthier the lord, the more serfs he had dependent on him. Unless this lord was only recently installed, like the one who had taken over his own family's keep, a valued Englishman who had been granted Welsh land by the king in exchange for some sort of service or favor.

The possibility that the very kind of man he most despised might have Megan for a prisoner chilled Kenric to his bones. That, coupled with the fact that some kind of misguided magic of his own making had sent her here, worried him doubly.

The closer he got to his goal, the more intense the feeling of foreboding became.

When at last he sighted the keep, perched like some overweight stone gargoyle on the top of the desolate hill, he reined in the warhorse and stared long and hard at it.

The horse, until now stolid and steadfast, seemed to sense his growing unease and tried to turn back in the direction from which they'd come. With a heavy heart, Kenric restrained him.

"We go forward," he muttered, wondering at himself. Never before had he felt this uneasy, felt this gnawing sense of wrongness. The stark grimness of the landscape, combined with the slumbering evil he sensed in the air, made this a place to avoid.

No tenants, no farms. Not even a herd or two of sheep or cattle. Something was wrong here, something that most likely lay within the realm of magic rather than the real world he preferred to inhabit.

Magic. He grew weary of the very word. Ever since he had found Megan in his cave, he had been around more magic than ever before in his life. He would be glad when this quest was over and he could settle on his land, an ordinary man once more.

Then he thought of Megan's eyes, her beautiful amber eyes, and wondered if he would ever be ordinary again.

The slate stone of the castle seemed to glow in the setting sun. It was a somber, yet strangely beautiful place, though its very comeliness seemed to mock him. What kind of trickery lay within? And, more important, what did Lady Megan of Dallas-Texas have to do with it?

After her meeting with Edmyg, Megan was led to the upper floor of the castle and taken to her room. The young servant girl who showed her the way told her she should be honored, as this was the former sleeping chamber of Lord Brighton's daughter, married but two fortnights past.

Though it was nothing like her beautiful room in Rune, Megan sank down gratefully on the lumpy bed, letting her eyes drift closed and trying to dispel the worried feelings that still churned inside of her.

Where was Kenric? She knew as surely as the sun would set that he would look for her. And once he found her and came to this place, would he be safe?

Could Myrddin be watching them even now?

She let her eyes drift closed again and fell into a deep and dreamless sleep.

When she woke later, muddled and full of a nameless longing, two more serving women arrived, claiming they were there to help her get ready for the evening meal. Crossing the room, they opened an ornate chest and began pulling out dress after dress after dress.

"One of these will surely be to your liking, milady," the older of the two said, flashing a shy smile and bobbing her head.

Despite herself, Megan moved closer. The materials were well made, rich and heavy, and embroidered with a finer stitch than any machine could ever make.

Every one of them looked exactly her size.

And the colors—there was every shade of blue imaginable, a deep, forest green, and some lovely mahogany browns. But the gown that drew her, almost like a magical spell had been cast on it, was shimmering amber. It looked almost golden in the fading light.

It was a dress for a fairy-tale princess, a magical garment that promised to make the woman lucky enough to wear it more beautiful than any dream.

Though she knew it would fit perfectly, it suddenly seemed important that she try on this dress—just to see how it looked. Of course, any of the others would surely do just as well; it was only that this one seemed, well . . . made for her.

Megan shook her head. She certainly wasn't foolish enough to think an article of clothing would possess magical powers, not at all. Though in light of all that had happened to her so far, she wouldn't say anything was impossible. Not here.

Before she could change her mind, she reached for it. One of the maids gasped.

"What?" As she clutched the dress to her, Megan's heart sank. Both women wore identical looks of horrified fascination.

"Nothing, my lady," the older one stammered, her voice shaking as she looked down. " 'Tis just that . . ."

Megan waited. When it became apparent that the woman wasn't going to finish her statement, she sighed. "Please tell me."

"That kirtle, milady." The younger girl came closer, pointing to the gorgeous gown Megan still held in her arms. "It was to be for her wedding."

"A wedding dress?" Regarding the golden dress dubiously, Megan couldn't see it. "Did she not wear white?"

The two women goggled at her as if they thought she'd lost her mind.

"White, milady?" the older woman said hesitantly. "That would not have been a good portent."

Maybe things were different in this time. "So she did not wear this dress?"

"Her husband bought her a dress. A suitable one, of deep midnight blue."

Since they appeared to think she should understand this, Megan nodded. "Why did she not take this with her to wear another time, if it was her choice for a wedding gown?"

An expression of sadness came over the elder's worn face. "Take it with her?" She shook her head. "Like all of us, she could not leave. They have moved to new chambers. Aye, she is still here, and her husband grows unhappier each day."

Megan didn't comment, not understanding enough of the customs to say anything. And if Lord Brighton's daughter and her new husband were here, she did not want to gossip about them before even meeting them.

She fingered the beautiful material of the golden dress, not sure what to do. More than anything she wanted to wear it.

She lifted her chin, making a decision. "If it wasn't worn in the wedding, and she did not take it, I will wear it."

The two women exchanged a quick glance but didn't comment. Instead they came forward to help her, showing her the undergarments she must wear and offering to do her hair for her. Since she had no earthly idea what hairstyle might be fashionable, Megan agreed. When Kenric finally saw her he wouldn't know what to do with her. She remembered the warmth in his gaze when he'd seen her in the sapphire gown at his sister's castle— rather, her keep. Though he hadn't said so in words, he hadn't been able to keep the admiration from his expression. That night she'd known he found her beautiful—

not as some boyish-looking girl wearing his too-large clothes, but as a desirable woman.

For some reason, she wanted him to see her so again.

When she'd dressed and they'd put her hair up in some elaborate coil, the two serving women led her down the hall. Stopping in front of an ornately carved oak door, they informed her in breathless whispers that this was Lord Brighton's room. From the blushes and giggles, Megan gathered that both women found their lord to be uncommonly attractive. And, she mused, he might be, if one liked freckled, red-haired, blue-eyed giants.

Just as she thought that, the massive door swung open. Clad in a sky blue tunic that matched his eyes, Lord Brighton gazed at her, his mouth pursed in a soundless *oh*.

"My lady." Taking her hand, he pressed a light kiss to the back of it. Then, instead of releasing her as she expected, he kept her hand trapped within his huge paw and stared at her, a smile playing on his lips. "You are lovely."

Megan fought the urge to fidget. She shifted her weight from one foot to the other and tried to unobtrusively tug her hand away. She met with no success.

"Absolutely stunning," he said softly. "I had no idea."

As she darted a quick glance at his face, Megan's heart sank. In her desire to make herself beautiful for Kenric, she'd forgotten his instructions that she blend into the background. She'd wanted to see admiration on Kenric's face. Instead she recognized reverence on the florid face of the lord of this keep—admiration and more. Megan saw quite clearly, as she stared back at the man who gripped her appendage so tightly, an arrogant sort of lust. In that instant she realized Lord Brighton had decided to possess her, no matter what obstacles lay in his path.

Telling herself it was her overactive imagination, Megan finally succeeded in tugging her fingers free. As she did so, Lord Brighton immediately took her arm.

"We go to eat," he announced, the silky undertones of his voice letting her know that he had plans for her. Squeezing her arm and hauling her up against his side so tightly that she might have been plastered there, he left no doubt as to his intentions.

Megan swallowed and nodded, wishing with all her heart that she had chosen one of the other dresses, or perhaps remained in her drab and overlarge disguise. Lord Brighton's sudden interest in her could make things more difficult when Kenric arrived, which she prayed would be soon.

They descended into the great hall that Lord Brighton had dragged Megan across earlier. Long tables had been placed at intervals throughout the room, reminding her of a company banquet in some hotel ballroom. She'd attended several of those with Roger, outfitted in glittering designer gowns. Though none of those dresses, she thought with a sigh, were even a tenth as fine as the one she now wore—which, judging from the gleam of lust she saw in Lord Brighton's gaze, wasn't a good thing.

One table had been elevated above the others. As Lord Brighton pulled her along with him up the dais, she realized it was his table and he expected her to sit up there with him. Though she knew it would be considered a position of honor to these people, it also meant she would be on display. Everyone in the room would be able to study every move she made while she tried to eat.

Lord Brighton pulled out a chair and courteously helped her sit, all the while trying to look down the front of her dress. When he lowered his bulk into the chair next to her, he made a point out of moving his leg so that his massive thigh rested against hers.

Megan scooted her chair a little to the right.

Smirking, Lord Brighton did the same. Then, as she prepared to try to move her chair again, he put his arm around her shoulders, effectively trapping her.

"You are my honored guest," he said in a growl, his

166

expression stern. "All of my keep will see this as we sup tonight."

Megan began to pray that Kenric would hurry.

The hall began to fill. Fascinated despite her uncomfortable position next to Lord Brighton, Megan watched as people of every sort filed into the room. Closest to the dais were large groups of men—huge men, some in sweat-stained, bloodied tunics, others in some rough material that looked uncomfortable, even though it was clean. Something about the way they carried themselves reminded her of Kern and the mercenaries she'd met— and of Kenric, though none of them was nearly as good to look at as he was.

They looked like what they were: warriors. No doubt these men made up Lord Brighton's fighting force, knights or something. She hoped that Kenric would not have to fight them all at once.

Servants began bringing the food. The high table at which she sat was served first. The aroma of spices and roasted meat filled the air. She noticed that most of the people below shared odd-shaped, long bowls made of wood and referred to as trenchers.

Through it all, Megan barely ate. Instead she watched the door for Kenric. Surely he would show up soon.

Lord Brighton squeezed her shoulders in a viselike grip.

"Expecting someone?" he asked, still grinning. She saw from the expression in his eyes that he believed himself besotted by her. Realizing she would have to say something, do something to discourage him, she racked her brain for an idea. She had to turn him off, not make him hate her, because she certainly didn't want to end up in the dungeon.

Slowly, Megan nodded, still thinking. "I am."

"Kenric of Blackstone?"

"Yes." She gave a tight-lipped answer, because the

overpowering odor of the meat made her feel ill. "He will come for me."

"Ah." Lord Brighton exhaled, his expression intent, his breath hot on her skin. He ran the palm of his hand down her arm. "Are you his leman then?"

Megan had only the faintest idea what *leman* meant, but she knew it wasn't complimentary. She had to fight to keep from recoiling at his touch.

"No." She wished she had the nerve—and the strength—to push his huge body away from her.

"Really," he drawled. "Then why would he bother to come for you? You are pretty, 'tis true, but the world is full of pretty women. You are not his sister, nor his cousin, as I know for a fact all of his family is dead."

"He has sworn to help me," she blurted, then immediately regretted it as a look of glee flashed onto Lord Brighton's face. She continued doggedly: "He will come because of that, nothing more."

"I would speak to him about you," he said, dropping his tone so low that she had to strain to hear it. "If it is as you say, and you are nothing to him, then *I* may be able to help you."

"Help me?" Had the canny old wizard told Lord Brighton about her situation? How could he know, when she hadn't been able to discuss it?

"We are well guarded." Lord Brighton's voice rang with certainty. "He will not gain entrance unnoticed."

"Really?" Megan couldn't resist a small taunt of her own. "Maybe he will gain entrance the same way I did."

His smug smile faded. "Ah, yes. We will have to discuss that later, you and I. But for now, I think—" A commotion at the door to the hall interrupted him.

Her heart pounding, Megan could only watch as three of the burly guardsman dragged an unresisting Kenric into the hall.

Chapter Eleven

The instant he entered the crowded hall, Kenric spotted her. Dressed like royalty, she sat in a place of honor up on the dais next to the man who must be the lord of this place. Lord Brighton, according to the men who thought they held him.

Megan. When their eyes connected, he felt a shock of awareness, along with an overwhelming sense of relief. She was all right. Now that he knew that, knew that he had not failed in his duty to her, he could deal with this oaf of a lord and his foolish guards.

Relaxing his muscles, he felt their hands on him slacken. They thought he had given up, simply because they outnumbered him three to one. If, perhaps, one of them had heard tell of him and his legendary prowess in battle, they would think it merely an overrated battle tale, one of those that increased with each telling. They would not expect him to fight them—especially since they had taken his sword and one of them now wore Thunder strapped to his hip as though it were his right.

No one messed with Kenric's sword. Or, for that matter, with his warhorse, who even now remained hidden in the wood.

The room became utterly silent, all eyes upon them as he allowed himself to be dragged toward the high table. He kept his face impassive, hoping Megan would know that he entered this way because he had no choice, not if he wished to gain entrance.

He let them take him to the very base of the dais, practically at Megan's feet. She averted her gaze, causing his heart to sink. Surely she knew he would save her; surely she realized that he was stronger and more powerful than ten of these loutish idiots.

"Welcome to my keep, Kenric of Blackstone. I am Lord Brighton. Lady Megan and I have been waiting for you."

The first thing he would do after he got free, Kenric decided instantly, would be to wipe the smug smirk off this lord's florid face. He noticed the meaty hand stroking Megan's arm and saw red.

With a roar, Kenric shook off his guards. One he dispatched with a swift blow to the neck. To the next he gave a kick to take his feet out from him, then a blow under the chin. The third Kenric punched in the stomach; then, when the shocked man was doubled over with pain, Kenric relieved him of his sword.

As if the sword recognized his touch, Thunder seemed to vibrate in his hand.

Now he would show them what it meant to fight Kenric of Blackstone. But first he had to get to Megan.

It proved to be a simple thing. A step, a pivot, and then he had her arm and pulled her from the dais before Lord Brighton had time to react.

Two tables of men scrambled to their feet, going for their weapons.

"Hold," a voice rang out.

Kenric blinked. It was not the lord of the keep who gave the order. Yet every single man, including the lord, froze in his tracks.

Slowly he turned, seeking the source of the command. Although the voice had been young and full of power, an elderly man, hunched and bent nearly halfway, crossed the room in the ringing silence. He wore the heavy robes of a priest, though not the collar, and his eyes were sharp and wise.

A mage. Kenric nearly groaned out loud. It seemed he could not escape magic, no matter how hard he tried.

Keeping his eyes on the approaching man, Kenric motioned for Megan to stay close to his side. She obeyed instantly, her luminous eyes glowing with pride. He had the insane urge to gather her in his arms and kiss her senseless. Instead he shot the disgruntled lord a look that promised retribution, and waited for the mage to approach.

"Long have I waited for this day." The old man spoke in a surprisingly strong voice. "It has been many years since the name Kenric of Blackstone was spoken by these lips."

"You know my name." Kenric casually moved in front of Megan, ready to fight whatever threat this mage might tender. Magic or metal, it was all the same to him. The sooner the battle was fought and won, the sooner he and Megan could be on their way. He could return her to her Roger and collect his reward.

Though the thought of another man's hands on her creamy skin soured his stomach.

The mage came closer, peering up at Kenric with a direct look that made him instantly wary.

"Years ago Rhiannon and I talked much of you. The events you and your mate will put into place will greatly change this world."

More prophetic nonsense. It figured this mage would

know Rhiannon. Kenric couldn't seem to escape his half sister no matter where he went.

"Tell me what you want." Kenric deliberately made his voice carry to every corner of the silent hall. "So that I may take my lady and be on my way."

Lord Brighton took a step toward them then, a great, lumbering bear of a man. Rage mottled his face. "*Your* lady?" He shook his head, pointing. "She tells me she is nothing to you."

Behind him he felt Megan stiffen. "Keep him away from me," she whispered fiercely.

With an effort, Kenric kept control of his temper. "She belongs to another man. I but return her to him so that they might marry." His voice caught on the final word.

"Who is this faceless man?" Lord Brighton's gaze raked the hall, coming finally to rest on Kenric. "Tell me so that I might challenge him."

"Challenge him?"

The huge man nodded. "I want her."

Next to him, Megan clutched at his arm. "No."

Kenric tamped down the instinctive fury that rose in him at this man's words. "She belongs to another," he repeated.

"Who is he?" Lord Brighton roared. "I want his name."

Megan gasped. "Roger," she muttered, low enough that only Kenric could hear. "Roger Spencer. I don't believe this."

Kenric felt a blaze of hatred for her betrothed. In a way, he could understand Lord Brighton's words. Where was her Roger, that he let another man defend her honor and made no effort to reclaim her?

Still, telling this Lord Brighton his name could do no harm. Indeed, it might help in the search for the elusive lord.

"His name is Lord Roger Spencer."

Lord Brighton frowned, his anger fading. "I have heard the name," he conceded reluctantly. "Isn't he an earl?"

Megan opened her mouth to answer. Edmyg forestalled her.

"I would speak with you two." The elderly mage pointed across the crowded room to the ornate door that led to his chambers. "Alone."

Megan's grip on his arm tightened. Kenric imagined she must be terrified. Then again, so far she had exhibited more bravery than any other woman he knew.

With another look at the still-furious Lord Brighton, Kenric nodded.

"No magic," he demanded.

Graciously, Edmyg inclined his head. "Agreed. Come then."

Seeing no choice, Kenric took Megan's arm and followed, leaving Lord Brighton trailing silently after them.

Intent on every word and action, the crowd parted noiselessly.

He waited until the door closed behind them to sheathe his sword.

"Tell me what goes on here."

Lord Brighton made a sound of impatience. Edmyg waved at him to be quiet. "Lord Brighton is a good man, a just man. His tenants like him, though they have been forced to live in the keep for nearly a decade while the land goes untilled."

That explained the fallow fields. "Forced?"

" 'Tis the matter of a simple spell."

"Yours?"

Edmyg laughed, a raspy sound. "Nay. If I could remove it, I would." He peered intently at Kenric, one corner of his mouth lifting in a smile. "That is why I need you."

Kenric kept his face impassive. "Of what use can I, a simple warrior, be to you? You have dozens like me out there."

"It is not your brawn that we need, but your magic."

His heart sank. "I don't—"

Megan stepped forward, interrupting him. "He has a job," she said, her voice ringing with challenge. "Until he does it, he cannot help you."

Disbelief, that she dared to think she could speak for him, momentarily rendered Kenric speechless. Gradually, though, the wisdom of her words sank in.

"She is right," he conceded reluctantly. "I have given my word to help her return to this Roger."

At this both Lord Brighton and Edmyg exchanged a long look.

Finally Lord Brighton spoke, his tone resigned. "Be that as it may, in this neither of you has a choice. You cannot leave." He held up a hand when Kenric would have spoken.

"That is the nature of the spell. No one, once managing to arrive at Brighton Keep, can leave. Ever. The spell will not let them."

Later, when all had eaten and drank their fill and Lord Brighton had become occupied in a spirited discussion with Edmyg, Megan finally had a chance to talk to Kenric alone. She stood and quietly made her way to the end of the table, where he, having pushed his way through the sated crowd, stood waiting.

If she'd hoped he would pull her to him and kiss her, she was to be disappointed.

"Kenric," she said, soft-voiced. "I'm glad to see you."

"Are you well?" he asked, his gaze fierce and tender, loving and stern, all at once.

For such an expression alone, Megan would risk her life.

She told herself it was her imagination. "Fine," she told him, clenching her hands into fists to keep from giving in to the urge to reach out and touch him.

"Lord Brighton"—Kenric did not touch her either, his jaw set in grim lines, his eyes searching her face—"did he lay hands on you?"

"No," she hastened to assure him, not wanting any more trouble than they already had.

"He wants you."

She heard anger in the blunt tone, anger and something more. Because of this, she strove to sound lighthearted.

"Maybe he thinks he does, a little. But it's nothing."

"Nothing?" He swore under his breath, turning away from her.

"Nothing. You're here now." Glancing at him, she noticed Kenric held himself rigid, his hands, too, clenched in fists at his side. Did that mean he fought the need to touch her, the way she struggled against the desire to touch him?

She wouldn't think of it. That way of thought was too dangerous. It would be best to concentrate on the problem at hand.

"How are we going to get out of here?"

He expelled a breath, a gust of air that spoke volumes of his frustration. Megan nearly smiled, but when he looked down at her, the smile died on her lips.

Kenric looked . . . intense. And beautiful—too beautiful for a mere warrior. His dark eyes blazed; his chiseled features were fierce in anger. Was it anger? Or some other powerful emotion? Whatever it was, it set her heart pounding and made her throat dry.

His eyes darkened further, became molten. One hand on the hilt of his sword, he took a step toward her. Suddenly he seemed as dangerous as a lion on a hunt.

Unable to help herself, Megan took a step back. God help her, he looked magnificent. With that dark, shoulder-length hair, his broad shoulders, and his muscular body, he could have stepped from the pages of some fairy-tale romance.

Again she caught herself wishing that this were some sort of dream, for in dreams she would be free to cast away her doubts and fears and do what she truly wanted.

Oh, and how she wanted. She wanted to run to him,

let those corded arms wrap around her, let him crush her mouth with his. Her entire body heated as passionate images ran through her mind. Kenric naked, hard, and all man, his body covering hers. She wanted him; God, she wanted him more than she'd ever wanted anything, ever.

Something must have shown in her face.

Kenric narrowed his eyes. He took a step closer. Then, as if he'd read her mind, he took another, reaching out to her, crushing her to him as she'd hoped in her heart of hearts he would.

When his mouth took hers, she gave a glad cry and wrapped her arms around his neck. Her body sang; her soul rejoiced. She welcomed him, needed him, wanted him, and more.

With a searing kiss, he possessed her. She opened her mouth to him, her tongue meeting his with a sense of giddy joy. Desire, until now carefully banked, broke free. His hand came up, cupping her breast, caressing, stroking, until she thought she would die.

She moaned. He answered with a growl that spoke of possession and raw need. The dress slipped, baring one shoulder as she fumbled with the laces on his shirt.

Then, just as she spread her hands on his broad chest, exulting in the feel of the perfect, hard muscles she felt there, he pulled away.

"Megan." His voice was harsh—a plea, a command, she knew not which.

But it brought her to her senses.

Horrified, Megan realized that in another second she would willingly have let him take her on the stone floor of the great hall, in full view of the assembled crowd.

One glance reassured her that, as yet, no one paid them any attention. Most of the men lay, heads pillowed on rough wooden tables, drunkenly asleep.

Only Lord Brighton, his back luckily to them, and Edmyg, who winked at her when her gaze caught his, still stood.

Idiot! How could she have done this? Not knowing who watched, not caring that they had no protection, that once she found her way home, she would never see this man again.

The thought ripped at her soul.

"My God." With a shaking fist pressed to her mouth, she yanked up her dress, covering her shoulder, and turned away. She would not cry, could not cry; there was no reason to cry over something so beautiful, so wonderful . . . so *wrong*. Tears filled her eyes as she struggled to get herself under control.

She couldn't imagine never seeing Kenric again.

Overcome with emotion, Megan spun on her heel to go to her room.

Muttering an oath, Kenric grabbed her arm, stopping her.

She didn't dare look up at him. If she did, she would be lost.

He said her name, his rough voice making the two simple syllables into a caress as he pulled her closer, one hand clumsily smoothing down her hair.

She felt herself melting. Even more than passion, this gentleness from such a fierce man unnerved her. His kindness would be her undoing. She could feel herself weakening, knowing that if he led her away to a private room, she would go willingly. Eagerly, even.

Unless . . . Was it pity he felt for her? Wanting to know, needing to know, she sneaked a peek from under her lashes. She found him watching her, narrow-eyed, a look of perplexed wonder on his ruggedly gorgeous face.

Confused, was he? OK, she could identify with that. Her feelings for this man baffled her. And, even worse, she had no idea what to do about it.

As he watched her, his gaze hooded, all rational thought fled. How could she resist this man when every fiber of her being cried out for him? It was she who reached out for him, she who rose up on tiptoe to touch her lips to his.

But this time his kiss was gentle. This time he wrapped her in his arms as if she were infinitely precious to him. She knew he must have thought she'd been frightened and he meant only to soothe her, but the way he made her feel cosseted, cherished, was a powerful aphrodisiac.

Dangerous.

Despite that, despite the fact that Lord Brighton could turn at any moment and see them, she found herself wanting more. Pressing her body up against him, she moved suggestively against the rigid flesh she felt there. Never had she felt this sort of power, and it thrilled her.

Kenric's arms tightened around her, and he groaned deep in his throat.

The sound excited her. This time, though, she remembered where they were. Taking his hand, she pulled him toward her room. Edmyg watched them go, never pausing in his argument with Lord Brighton, who never noticed as Megan led Kenric out of the hall.

Silent, Kenric wore a shuttered expression as he allowed her to lead him. It was only when they reached the heavy oak door of her room that she paused, weighing the risk against her aching desire. She could get pregnant, since they had no protection. What did people do to prevent pregnancy in this time? Condoms hadn't been invented yet. In her other life, in the normal world, she'd been on the Pill, though naturally she hadn't been able to take any since the lightning strike had sent her here.

If this were only a dream, she wouldn't have to worry about such mundane facts as birth control.

Her entire body throbbed, protesting the direction her thoughts had taken. Kenric released her hand, waiting, watching, leaving it up to her to make the choice. Absurdly, this touched her. A medieval warrior such as he must be used to simply taking what he wanted.

178

Damn. She made a sound, a small cry of protest, a no that wasn't quite a no.

That apparently was enough for Kenric. With a slight nod of his head, he spun on his heel and vanished down the hall.

Stunned, Megan could only gape after him. He'd wanted her, she knew. She'd felt the force of his arousal, seen it in the darkening of his eyes, the harshness of his quickened breathing.

He'd wanted her, yet he'd walked away. Why? Was it possible he felt something for her, something more than just lust, something like she was beginning to feel for him?

He'd touched her with more than his body.

She'd never known a man like him. And she was very much afraid she never would again.

By the time he reached his room, Kenric's entire body hurt. With the scent of Megan still on him, he could barely walk. He felt as hard and randy as a lad of six and ten.

Megan's body fit his as though she were made for him.

Yet, despite the consuming desire he felt for her, he wanted more. More than he had a right to want, more than he could ever have, with her promised to another.

For the first time since he'd agreed to help her, Kenric almost wished that this Roger would never be found— almost, if it weren't for the promise of land, his reward.

All that he had ever wanted was within his grasp, yet now it no longer seemed enough. He felt hollow, confused. When he closed his eyes, instead of visions of verdant fields and rolling hills, he could see only Megan's amber eyes, dark with passionate promise.

By all that was holy, how had this happened?

Stalking to the window, he wanted to punch something, anything. If Lord Brighton had lists, Kenric would have been first in line to fight. As it was, he stared out into the moonlit night, over the oddly barren fields, and tried to make himself remember his dream, his plans. Doing so had always calmed him in the past; he would force it to be that way now.

Somehow he would have to banish these foolish desires and stick to the task at hand. Somehow he had to put thoughts of Megan, and the conflicting feelings she evoked in him, far from his mind.

That night he slept not a wink.

At first light Kenric paced the confines of his room. He had been dressed for hours, dressed and spoiling for a fight. Sleep had eluded him; instead of a respite from the day's demands, he had been tormented by erotic thoughts and a rebellious, needy body.

He needed to fight in the lists. He would see Lord Brighton and have something organized. Maybe once he'd trounced a few dozen men, he would be able to regain his normal calm demeanor.

As long as he avoided Megan, that was. Though how on earth he could manage to do that, he didn't know.

He headed down toward the great hall in search of something with which to break his fast. Lord Brighton was there before him. Kenric was thankful he saw no sign of Megan.

Standing before Lord Brighton, Kenric outlined his needs in a tone that brooked no argument.

Still, Lord Brighton had no desire to cooperate. "Lists?" he repeated, his scornful tone mirroring the disbelief on his florid features. "What need have we of lists? No one can leave. There will never be a reason to fight."

God's teeth. Was the man so blind to what went on in the world around him? Even now, Baron Aldridge to the west used armies to amass land. Who was to say when he might decide to turn his attention to Lord Brighton's unoccupied and unused estates?

Then Lord Brighton's words hit home. Though he had

mentioned this spell before, Kenric had thought it mere nonsense.

"You truly believe this, that no one can leave?"

The other man laughed, a guffaw so hearty his belly shook. "Edmyg told you. Anyone who enters this keep can never leave it."

Kenric didn't want to believe him, but something in Lord Brighton's voice bespoke the truth.

"Edmyg believes you can help us."

Narrowing his eyes, Kenric shook his head. "A spell such as this must be a powerful one. I have little practice with such things. I am a warrior, a fighter. Not a mage. I don't think that I—"

All traces of humor vanished from Lord Brighton's face. Uncaring that Kenric's hand still rested on the hilt of his sword, the older man gripped Kenric's arm.

"You have to." His stark expression reflected his desperation. "For if you don't, we shall never be free from this place."

The import of the other man's words sank in. Kenric refused to believe them.

"Go ahead and try." Releasing Kenric's arm, Lord Brighton waved a hand toward the window. "It is always thus, at first. My daughter's new husband thought to take her back to his own keep, until he found he could not leave. Mayhap you should go and talk to him."

"Talk?" Kenric spat the word. "I am tired of talk. I will have Lady Megan make ready and we will leave this morn."

Shrugging, the other man flashed him a wan smile. "Go ahead. Try. Seek me out when you have finished." Shaking his shaggy red head, Lord Brighton moved away.

Kenric stared after him. The certainty of the other man's convictions bothered him. Yet it made no sense. Why would anyone want to cast a spell to imprison people in a keep? Even a keep as large and prosperous as this one? With no crops from outlying fields, and no cattle or sheep, he wondered how they managed to eat and clothe themselves.

Grimacing, Kenric cursed. For a moment he'd almost fallen into the trap of believing in this spell nonsense. He snagged a hunk of cheese and a piece of bread and went in search of Megan.

After an exhausting night of tossing and turning, it was nearly dawn before Megan finally fell into a fitful sleep. Even then, she dreamed: dreams of Kenric, dreams that made her moan and writhe in the narrow, lumpy bed.

When she could stand it no more, she rose and splashed some water on her face. Running her hand through her tangled hair, she supposed she should be glad there was no mirror. If she looked as bad as she felt, then she must appear a hag. No wonder Kenric didn't want her.

She couldn't believe how badly it had hurt when he walked away after kissing her. Kissing her? *Hah!* It had been more of a possession than a kiss, as if he'd reached into her very soul with his touch and his lips. She'd been more aroused, more enchanted, than ever before in her life.

And then he'd stridden away without a backward glance. As if he hadn't wanted her at all.

His body, at least, wanted her. She knew she hadn't imagined his arousal. But she realized that would not be enough where he was concerned. She wanted more. She wanted . . . But then, she had no right to want anything when she fully intended returning home to her own time, her own people. To a life without Kenric.

Stunned, she froze. In desperation she tried to conjure up pictures of her trendy north Dallas condo, of the cute red BMW she drove. Of the clubs she frequented, the charity organizations where she volunteered, and the friends she hung out with, even the salon where she routinely had her hair highlighted and her nails done.

But it all seemed distant, like someone else's history. How meaningless, how trivial, it all seemed now. Her unpainted nails were ragged and uneven, and the highlights had no doubt faded from her hair. But she felt alive, carefree—and happier than she could ever remember being. This place, this time with its unlimited possibilities, gave her peace and joy.

This man, Kenric of Blackstone, gave her all she'd ever wanted in a man. Did she really want to give this all up to return to her former existence? To her bank statements and stock dividends, to the charities where she sat on the board, to the meaningless social functions and faithless friends among Dallas's social elite? To traffic and pollution and all the other hassles and problems that made up life in the modern world? To Roger, with his thousand cruelties and his burning desire to be made beneficiary in her will?

Suddenly having Kenric help her get home no longer seemed as urgent or as imperative as it had before.

A sharp rapping on her door startled her out of her reverie.

"Megan." Kenric's deep voice sounded angry.

She hurriedly smoothed down her hair and opened the door, glad she'd taken the time to step into one of the less ornate dresses.

He stood clad in what she'd come to think of as his mercenary warrior clothes. Formfitting, soft leather pants outlined his muscular legs. His white tunic with the billowing sleeves made him, with his rugged, dark features, look like a pirate of sorts. And then there were his smoky eyes—bedroom eyes, she'd heard eyes like his called once before.

Kenric of Blackstone was the sexiest man she'd ever seen.

While she drank in the sight of him, Kenric seemed to be doing the same. Of their own accord her nipples pebbled, as she remembered the kiss they'd shared and her own erotic dreams. Though she had never been bold, she found herself wondering what he would do if she were to pull him inside her room and throw herself at him.

"It is time to leave." Kenric sounded oddly strained.

Puzzled, Megan stared up at him. "Leave? What about the spell?"

His jaw tightened. "The spell is nonsense. Do you not wish to hasten back to your Roger?"

She opened her mouth to tell him the truth, but couldn't seem to force the words out. The best she could do was sort of stammer her former fiancé's name. "Roger?"

With narrowed eyes, Kenric let his gaze swept her room. "Gather your things. We ride out within the hour."

"Ride out? But where is Lancelot? I haven't seen him."

"The *warhorse* waits for me outside the castle. He is trained to come to me at my command." Pushing past her, he entered her room. "It shouldn't take long to—"

Megan was swept by a wave of desire so strong she swayed. All her life she had wondered what it would feel like to be a femme fatale, a seductive temptress who had the ability to make men desire her so much that they would risk anything, everything, for her favor.

Megan had never been bold enough, brave enough, beautiful enough to experience such a thing. But now, just once, she desperately longed to have such power— over one man only.

Kenric.

She took a deep breath. *Insecurities be damned!* She had traveled through time and space to be with this man. *Why not?* She had nothing to lose. Kicking the door closed behind her, she loosened the stays on her gown.

Kenric spun at the sound of the door slamming shut. "Megan . . ." he warned, then seemed to lose the capacity for speech as she slid the dress slowly off one shoulder, then the other.

Chapter Twelve

Her heart pounding, Megan pretended a nonchalance she didn't feel as she took a deep breath and dropped the dress, letting it fall into a pool of material at her feet. Then she slowly removed her shift, keeping her gaze on Kenric.

Totally bare and fighting the urge to cover herself with her hands, she tried to think of a Victoria's Secret catalog, unsure how to stand so that she looked sexier, unsure of what to do, how to make herself more appealing to him.

If the harsh intake of his breath and the dilation of his dark eyes were any indication, she wouldn't have to do much. So she simply stood before him, naked and exposed, while he stared at her in silence.

Finally he swallowed.

"Megan . . ."

At the raw need in his voice, she smiled a hesitant

smile, letting her eyes travel to the conspicuous bulge in the front of his braes.

"This may be our last chance." She moved closer, stopping a scant two feet away from him. Her nipples were hard and her breasts ached; indeed, her entire body seemed to ache for this man's touch. She could feel her blood thrumming in her veins, moist heat pooling inside of her.

Again Kenric swallowed. He looked like a man tortured. "I don't think—"

Then, just when she'd decided it was no use, he grabbed her, pulling her close so that her breasts crushed up against the rough material of his shirt. Trembling, she clung to him.

His hand slid across her bare back, caressing. With an expression both savage and tender, he gazed down at her.

"Megan . . ." he said in a growl.

The smoldering heat she saw in his dark eyes gave her courage. She began to slip her hands up his arms, reveling in the feel of the hard muscles, in the heat of his skin.

"Kenric." When she spoke his name, it was a wordless plea. "I want you to love me."

Startlement warred with desire, need with restraint as he expelled a harsh breath. Holding himself rigid, he shook his head.

"We cannot—"

Then, using an instinct that came from deep within her femininity, Megan moved against him. "Please," she whispered through parted lips. "One kiss."

With a harsh sound he took her lips, his mouth moving over hers hungrily. Joy exploded in her—joy and a desire so hot she felt as if her entire body were on fire.

One hand slid down the curve of her naked hip, searing a path. Megan nearly swooned. With trembling fingers, she loosened the ties of his shirt, tearing the material in her haste to have it off him. She wanted skin to skin, heat to heat, chest to chest, his hardness to her softness.

Squirming, she fitted herself against him, mindlessly needing, wanting.

He lifted his mouth from hers, his hands lingering on her shoulders. Now dark and intense, his gaze was full of heat.

"Megan . . ."

"No, no questions, no doubts," she whispered, standing on tiptoe and pulling his dark head back down to hers. "I want you."

Kenric made a sound then, guttural and full of need. Sweeping her up in his arms, he carried her to the bed. With a few easy motions he divested himself of his boots and braes until he stood proudly naked and erect before her.

Megan gasped, her breasts tingling. She held her arms up to him; she was wet and ready, aching and hot. He was magnificent, her warrior, and she wanted to feel him fully inside of her.

The bed shifted as he lay down beside her. Megan tentatively reached out and closed her hand around him, thrilling to the sheer massive strength of him.

"Hold." Kenric groaned, capturing her hand and stilling it. "Before I shame myself like a boy of ten and seven."

Then she knew that the desire he felt equaled her own. Her body clenched at this knowledge; she was more than ready for him to take her.

She moaned softly, an invitation, and arched her back.

"Ah, woman." It was a quiet curse, the sound of a man at the edge of control who knows he is lost.

"If we do this, it will change things between us."

It was both a statement and a question.

"Yes," she told him, nearly whimpering now. "Yes, of course . . ."

He reached for her then, his callused hands searing heat down the curve of her stomach, the length of her thigh. The sound he made was a sound of surrender, even as his mouth closed over one taut nipple and she nearly sobbed with relief.

With his hand he sought entrance first, and willingly she parted her legs for him, whimpering against his mouth as he claimed her lips again. He touched her, explored her; she was ready, long past ready, and still he stroked and probed and lingered, making her mindless in her need.

"Kenric!" She gasped, even as she shattered against his hand.

With one swift stroke he entered her then, possessing her completely as she clenched around him.

He was huge and hard and powerful. "You are mine," he told her fiercely, moving inside her. She rose to meet his thrusts, thrilling to the sensation of this man—with her, in her, of her.

They moved together; she matched his tempo until she could no longer tell where she ended and he began.

"God's blood." Curse or prayer, she could not tell; she could only watch as Kenric relinquished the last shred of his self-control, no longer able to slow his movements.

He became fury then, motion and heat and fire as he took her. This time the tremor built slowly, white flame flashing, then burst like exploding stars from deep inside her. She cried out her release, feeling the flood of it surround him, even as he shuddered and, with one last thrust, pulsed inside of her, filling her with his essence.

"Megan." He said her name like a benediction, gathering her close and stroking her hair. "My Megan."

And with those words Megan knew with an earth-shattering certainty that Kenric had claimed more than her body; he'd claimed her heart.

Standing awkwardly in the courtyard, Megan watched as Kenric shook hands with a smugly grinning Lord Brighton. Edmyg watched also, his expression guarded. No one else in the keep had turned out to bid them farewell. It reminded her, in a way, of their lonely departure from the Faerie castle.

She knew no one believed they would really be able to go.

The drawbridge had been lowered. Taking her arm, Kenric led her out the stone gate. Their footsteps thudded on the wooden bridge, and the morning air held a hint of mist. She smelled the freshness of the dew on the grass and the distant scent of the forest. Holding tight to Kenric's arm, Megan reflected that she'd never felt so in tune with life, so alive.

They finally reached the end. Ahead of them lay endless rolling fields of untilled ground. To the east the forest rose, shady and welcoming.

"I left the horse in the forest, so I could approach less obtrusively." Kenric explained.

Releasing her arm, he put his fingers to his mouth and whistled, a piercing, sharp sound. Lancelot, his chestnut coat gleaming in the bright sunlight, came charging from the trees. Running full out, the warhorse was both beautiful and terrifying. When he reached the rocky path where the drawbridge touched the ground, he reared, pawing the air.

Kenric strode forward—and staggered back as if he'd run into a brick wall.

Startled, Megan stopped too. "What is it?"

"They weren't lying." Running a hand through his dark hair, Kenric reached out a hand to take his horse's bridle, and couldn't. He pushed against the invisible barrier, muttering oaths under his breath. On the other side, Lancelot pranced toward them, then stopped at the end of the drawbridge, tossing his head and snorting.

"Edmyg was correct—we cannot leave this place. There is an evil spell at work here."

"Are you serious?" Megan couldn't believe it. She had no desire to remain in Lord Brighton's castle for the rest of her life, endlessly dodging the large man's determined pursuit.

"Try it and see."

"OK." Flashing him her most confident smile and hoping he didn't notice how it trembled around the edges, Megan stepped forward.

There was no problem. She felt nothing—no barrier, no invisible wall, nothing but the faint dampness of the mist and the coolness of the morning breeze.

Glancing at Kenric over her shoulder, she took another step, then another, until she reached Lancelot's side and stood close enough to lay a hand on his thick neck.

Triumphant, she turned to face Kenric and flashed him the thumbs-up sign before she realized he probably had no idea what that meant. Instead she inclined her head like a queen and grinned, beckoning to him.

"Come on."

Instead of smiling back, Kenric frowned. "How did you do that?"

She didn't understand. "Do what?"

"How did you get past the barrier?"

"There was no barrier." She shrugged. "Maybe it's all in your mind."

Setting his jaw resolutely, Kenric took a running step forward. He growled in frustration as he hit the same invisible wall and was thrown backward.

"I told you," Lord Brighton yelled from the castle gate, his booming voice filled with glee. "How did Megan get through it?"

"*Lady* Megan to you," Kenric said with a snarl, then glanced at Megan quickly. "I don't know."

Her heart pounding, Megan grabbed Lancelot's bridle and led him forward. Maybe Kenric could *ride* through whatever stopped him. Encountering no barrier this time either, she stepped easily across the drawbridge, but the warhorse stopped, nearly jerking her off her feet.

Try as she might, she couldn't make the horse go any

farther. Evidently, Lancelot felt the invisible boundary too.

Helpless, she let the horse go and crossed to Kenric's side. "I don't get it. Why can't you come with me?"

He watched her with narrowed eyes. "What magic do you possess, Megan of Dallas-Texas, that you have thought to keep hidden from me? Tell me the truth now. Are you Faerie?"

Stunned, she stared up at him. His craggy face wore a furious expression.

"Magic? I don't have any."

She could see from his set expression that he didn't believe her.

"Really," she insisted. "I didn't even believe in magic until I met you." And until she'd found out she'd somehow traveled to the long-distant past.

On the other side of the barrier, Lancelot tossed his head and pawed the ground. If horses could talk, Megan would have sworn this one urged them to hurry.

With a clenched fist, Kenric reached out toward his warhorse—only to have his hand come up against the same invisible force. No matter how hard he pushed, he couldn't get his hand through.

"Walk through it again," he ordered.

With a sigh, Megan did as he bade her. She felt no barrier, no tingle of magic, nothing.

Lancelot snorted. Megan reached up and patted his long, muscular neck. "Come on." She held out her hand to Kenric.

"I cannot." His low voice echoed his rage.

She didn't understand. "Use your magic."

"My magic."

"Yes. The same magic that somehow transported me to the dungeon of this castle . . . er, keep."

Kenric's expression darkened. "Mayhap you got yourself to this place."

She'd had enough experience in dealing with men to

191

realize that his male pride had been offended. Searching her brain for a way to make him understand, she realized what she would have to do.

"OK." Flashing him a bright smile, she remembered he might not understand her twentieth-century slang. "All right. I guess I'll just have to go on without you. I'm sure you won't mind if I borrow Lancelot, here, will you?"

"What?" he roared.

Trying not to laugh, Megan affected a serious, wide-eyed expression. "I still have to find Roger."

"I will deal with Roger. You are mine," Kenric stated arrogantly. "As is the warhorse. You will go nowhere without me."

Despite herself, Megan liked his warrior's confidence. Eyeing the magical sword, she wondered if it would somehow help him break the spell. Hands clasped in front of her, she waited, confident that her warrior would find a way to her.

Her warrior. Her heart skipped a beat. She liked the sound of that—liked, too, the way Kenric claimed her as his own.

Under his breath, Kenric muttered a few words.

The breeze picked up. Kenric drew his sword. The sword began to glow.

He rushed forward, the weapon ahead of him. His sword pierced the invisible barrier. He did not. He reeled back from the force of the blow, his sword clattering to the ground on Megan's side of the barrier.

With an apologetic look, Megan stepped forward and picked it up. The sword was heavier than it looked, so she could barely lift it. Instead she held it gingerly by the engraved handle, its point pressing into the ground. Though it might have been her imagination, it seemed to vibrate.

She chewed her bottom lip, trying to figure this out. Kenric's magic—indeed, all magic—seemed to her to be a hit-and-miss thing. She would have thought it would be more . . . well, controllable.

Raking his hand through his hair, Kenric shot her a frustrated glare. "Any other ideas?"

Silently, she shook her head. Beside her Lancelot whinnied. Evidently the horse didn't understand why his master wouldn't leave the drawbridge.

Why could she cross and he couldn't? Did the spell somehow recognize that she wasn't from this place, from this time? That was the only valid explanation.

Telling Lancelot to wait, Megan lifted the heavy sword with both hands and crossed the barrier to Kenric's side. Without a word she handed him the sword, watching as he grimly sheathed it.

Behind them she could see Lord Brighton doubled over, his large belly shaking with laughter. Only the mage continued to watch as if he still believed something could be done.

Something *had* to be done. They had to come up with a way out of here. She wasn't about to stay here; nor would she leave Kenric.

"Take my hand," she ordered softly.

Kenric stared at her, his stormy expression reflecting his disbelief. As she slipped her hand in his, his pupils dilated. Megan felt her own breathing quicken as she realized he was remembering the lovemaking they'd shared. She shivered, amazed that he could arouse her with merely a look, but accepting it. After all, that was the way of it when you were in love.

In love? Gasping, she tried to pull her hand free, but Kenric would not release her. Though she'd sort of known it after they'd made love, thinking the words like this shocked her.

Why had this happened and what could she do about it? She didn't belong here, though she'd thought to stay until she . . . Until she what? What exactly had she thought? That this was infatuation, or lust? That Kenric

193

would be a casual affair, the kind her North Dallas friends giggled and gossiped about so easily? But Megan had never been that kind of woman, had never been able to pretend or lie, which was why she'd been breaking it off with Roger in the first place.

She loved Kenric. She loved a man from over nine hundred years in the past. God help her. Rhiannon, with her Faerie magic, had been right. Megan now knew Rhiannon's words had been true: Kenric was her soul mate, the other half of her heart. How on earth did she think she could live without him?

Something must have shown in her face.

"What is it?" Low-voiced, Kenric cradled her chin in his other hand, his dark eyes searching her face. "Are you all right?"

Numb, she nodded, though she wasn't all right. Not by a long shot. Pushing away her rioting emotions, she focused on the problem at hand—getting Kenric off the drawbridge.

He pulled her close, letting her pillow her head on his broad chest. Closing her eyes, Megan let herself pretend for a moment that everything was normal, that everything would be all right.

"Megan." He muttered her name, one hand smoothing down the back of her hair. It was a gesture of love, of need, even as she felt his body thicken against her. "Do not forget that you are mine."

It came to her then, with this declaration, spoken so boldly without heed of the consequences: Megan knew how to get Kenric through the magical barrier. He might not know it yet, or admit it, but she believed he loved her as deeply as she loved him. And she'd always heard that love was the most powerful magic of all. Though she had no knowledge of magic, no idea even where this thought had come from, she knew it to be true. After all, it had brought her to this place, this man.

She raised her head to look at him. "Hold me close," she whispered.

Since he was already doing so, he merely smiled, the smile so full of masculine arrogance that it took her breath away.

"Walk with me, this way, to the end of the bridge."

Kenric merely lifted a brow and did as she requested.

They moved as if they were slow-dancing, stopping and embracing and gazing deep into each other's eyes. She felt a slow heat begin inside her, making her languid and feverish, desire for him strong and fierce. She forgot about spells or castles or old wizards. She forgot about everything but the ruggedly beautiful warrior who held her in his arms, the man whom she loved.

It was only when they bumped into Lancelot that she realized they had made it across the drawbridge.

Kenric released her when he realized it. "You did it," he told her, the heat in his dark eyes becoming wariness. "Yet you claim you have no magic."

It was both statement and question, and Megan knew he required an answer. "I did not do it alone," she told him, finding herself suddenly unable to look at him. What if he didn't feel the same as she; what if lust alone drove him, or some other masculine emotion for which she had no name?

"Explain."

She decided to take a chance. After all, he had told her that she belonged to him. For now, that would have to be enough.

"Love did it, Kenric. Love is more powerful than any magic."

He was silent for so long that she had to raise her head and look at him. Instead of outright shock, or horror, or any of the expressions she might have expected, he merely looked thoughtful.

"I—"

Whatever he'd been about to say was cut off. Shouting,

Lord Brighton galloped toward the drawbridge. Moving at a more sedate pace, Edmyg followed close behind.

"How did you do it?" Lord Brighton asked excitedly. From the speed of his pace, Megan saw that he expected to find the barrier dissipated. She was afraid that he was about to be sadly mistaken.

Behind him, Edmyg struggled to keep up. For an old man, Edmyg could move.

His lips drawn back from his prominent teeth in a triumphant grin that was nearly a grimace, Lord Brighton crashed into the barrier at full speed. The impact was enough to toss him back onto his ample rear end.

Edmyg screeched to a halt before running into him.

Megan couldn't help it; she started laughing. From the corner of her eye, she saw Kenric turn away to hide his own grin.

Plainly shocked, a red-faced Lord Brighton picked himself up. Glaring at Kenric, he advanced as far as the barrier would allow, Edmyg trailing along after him.

"How did you do it?" Lord Brighton demanded again, his hands clenched into fists, his face mottled with impotent rage.

"Love," Kenric replied. "She has told me that that is the manner in which she broke through the spell."

"There is no such thing!" Lord Brighton roared. "Only warbling bards and simpering women believe in that nonsense!"

Then Megan knew that Lord Brighton might not ever be able to leave his enchanted keep.

Edmyg moved forward, stretching out one hand toward them. "I knew such a love once," he said, his voice quavering. "But it has gone now, never to return except in my dreams."

"Only love is strong enough to conquer this kind of magic," Megan said quietly when Kenric held his silence.

All three men looked at her, bewilderment and shock

plain on Lord Brighton and Edmyg's faces, a stony stubbornness on Kenric's.

"We ride now," Kenric pronounced, tight-lipped. Then, helping Megan up onto Lancelot's broad back, he swung up after her.

Her heart sinking, Megan wondered if he was as stunned by what had happened as she. As to the depths of her feelings, love was an emotion she'd never before believed she would feel for any man. Until this man, now.

With Lord Brighton gaping after them, and Edmyg sadly shaking his gray head, Kenric urged Lancelot forward. The warhorse stepped out eagerly, tossing his head and looking for all the world like a proud papa carrying his two children on his shining chestnut back.

Before too long Lord Brighton's keep had faded in the distance. Once again the fertile land began to show signs of human activity, the occasional crofters' huts and plowed fields a welcome sight.

They rode in silence, each lost in their own thoughts.

Then, reining the horse to a stop, Kenric turned in the saddle, capturing Megan's mouth in a hard kiss. His lips moved over hers, slow, drugging, possessive, until she grew breathless, until her head swam and she could no longer think straight. When he finally lifted his mouth from hers, he grinned broadly.

"What was that for?" she whispered, wishing she were bold enough to pull him back and make him kiss her some more.

"For the gift you have given me," He told her cryptically, turning and urging Lancelot on once more.

Did he speak of love? More than anything she wanted him to say the words, to tell her that he felt the same as she. But fear held her back—fear and the knowledge that she had bound him to her with a lie. Until she was truthful with him, she had no right to want more. So Megan held her tongue, pushing away the guilt and the longing, so raw, so new.

For the first time in his life, Kenric knew uncertainty. Always before, he'd been able to fixate on a goal and stay with it. Up until he had made love to Megan's sweet body, he had actually believed he would be able to find her Roger, relinquish her to his care, claim his land, and continue on with his life.

Now he knew that to be a lie. He wanted Megan more than he'd ever wanted anything or anyone. He would have to find this Roger and see if the other man would relinquish his claim on Megan. He, Kenric, would of course relinquish his reward—the land.

The land. Briefly he closed his eyes. He hungered for Megan, yet still he yearned for the land. He could not help it.

Though greed had never been one of his faults, he wanted both—Megan and the land. God help him. One would be meaningless without the other. He needed land to build his keep, to raise his family. He needed Megan to keep him sane. And, he concluded, smiling to himself, to be his helpmate and bear their children.

But love? Despite Megan's claims of its power, he was not certain he believed in such a thing. Respect, admiration, even fondness he could well understand, having shared such a thing with his human father. But love? Nay, it had to be—

Only love can save the land of Faerie.

The thought came out of nowhere, blindsiding him. Gritting his teeth, he shook his head, willing the thought away. Rhiannon again, with her Faerie trickery and her misguided claims that Rune needed him. No, it was best he concentrate on what was real, in the here and now. Best he focus on how he could get Megan's intended to break his betrothal.

By now he calculated this Lord Roger should have

given up the search. Though, were Kenric of Blackstone the one who searched, he would never rest until she was found. But in all their time together, not once had he seen a single sign that this Roger even sought her. Perhaps Megan did not matter to him.

Amazed at the lightness of heart this thought brought, Kenric forced himself to think realistically. It was not easy, not with Megan's arms wrapped tightly around his waist, her full breasts pressing into his back. *God's teeth.* He wanted to stop the warhorse and take Megan now, in the fragrant grass under the warm spring sun.

Because he knew he would hold her in his arms again that evening, Kenric forced himself to think of other things. Like his very real problem—if he gave up the promise of land that would have been his reward for bringing her to Roger, how could he marry her? Where would he keep her, how could they begin a family? How could he have both his heart's desires?

"Magic," Megan murmured behind him. Her voice sounded low, husky. Perhaps the warm sun and the rocking motion of his horse's canter had made her drowsy. He waited for her to continue.

"How is it that magic is so real here?"

He couldn't help it; he had to laugh. "Is it so different in the place you come from?"

"Yes." She sighed, her breath stirring the hair at the nape of his neck. "Very few believe in magic in my ti—er, place."

"But just because one denies its existence, magic still exists." Though he spoke arrogantly, with the knowledge of experience, he was not prepared for her response.

"I think there must be belief"—she sounded sad—"for it to work."

"No." This time he did rein in the warhorse and turn to face her. "I have spent most of my life trying to deny its existence. Yet still, magic will not leave me. I think

199

it is there always, hidden just below the surface, waiting for me to tap into it."

She gave a slow nod, without any real enthusiasm. Her huge golden brown eyes looked so serious that he wanted to kiss her and make her forget her doubts and fears. Instead he found himself recalling to her his sister's words, spoken to him when he was a child and callously disregarded until this moment.

"Each of us has the potential for magic. After all, magic is nothing more than enhanced reality. When you free your higher self from doubts and fears, you free that which has been available to you all along."

Disbelief still clouded her face. "I don't—"

Seized by an urgency he did not understand, Kenric grasped her shoulders. Why was he, who had spent his entire life denying magic, trying to make her believe in it?

"You led us from Lord Brighton's keep, remember? What was that if not manifestation of your magical potential?"

Her expression cleared. She favored him with a slow smile so sensual that it set his blood boiling.

"That was love."

He swallowed, keeping his eyes fixed on hers. "Magic," he said firmly.

When she did not dispute this, he reluctantly removed his hands from her and turned away. If he gave in to the urge to kiss her, they might never go forward. Her next words, however, stopped him cold.

"I love you, Kenric of Blackstone."

He closed his eyes, knowing he must hurt her by his silence, but determined not to make any false declarations. He needed her, desired her, wanted her—that would have to be enough. But even so, he could not tell her. Until he had found her Roger and had the betrothal dissolved, he could not even tell her that he, Kenric of Blackstone, meant to make her his wife.

He was only a landless bastard, and had no right to such lofty expectations. Until he had the land, until he could keep her safe, he could make no promises. For now, he had no choice. He would do nothing to let her think he had turned from his original course.

Chapter Thirteen

At first his silence hurt her. Her heart heavy, feeling as though a stone had somehow lodged in her chest, Megan did not speak again. As they rode into the brilliant sunlight, she found herself remembering Rhiannon's words and thinking of the weight of the burdens Kenric carried.

He had lost his entire family.

Too afraid he might lose something if he came to care for it, he hadn't even named his horse. No wonder he still refused to call the animal the name she'd chosen. The desperate control that he held over his emotions was rigidly in place.

She could understand that; after all, losing one's entire family—*Myrddin*. Kenric didn't know that Rhiannon suspected Myrddin had been the one who had killed Kenric's human family. She had to tell him about Myrddin. But when? How?

One thing she knew for sure—she would have to tell

him soon. One secret between them was more than enough.

After riding hard all day and into the waning sunlight, Megan was relieved when Kenric finally reined in a lathered Lancelot and announced that they were to stop for the night. The air smelled of lilacs and grass, overlaid with the deep, mysterious scent of the forest. Of necessity, Kenric had told her, they stayed close to the trees in case they needed to vanish quickly.

She watched as he brushed Lancelot down, enjoying the play of Kenric's muscles as he worked, laughing out loud at the way the horse closed his eyes and tilted his massive head in pure sensual enjoyment. When this was done and Lancelot had begun to graze, they built a small fire.

"Kenric," Megan whispered, wanting only to be held as she figured out a way to tell him. But Kenric deftly sidestepped her clumsy attempt at a hug and, with a few muttered words, disappeared into the woods. He'd gone to hunt small game for their supper. This was reasonable, yet Megan could not shake the empty feeling that had sprung up at the way he avoided touching her.

Had she given her love too freely? She thought of his lack of response to her avowal of love, and the fear inside her became an ache. Would he hold her tonight? Make love to her? He had told her she belonged to him, but what did that mean to a medieval man? What did that mean to him?

The sky gradually darkened and still she sat, alone but for the warhorse munching nearby. Several times her eyes filled with tears, which she blinked away in determination. She wanted Kenric. She *needed* Kenric.

When he finally returned with a rabbit, she held her breath, still hoping he might come to her, if only for warmth, as the night air had grown brisk. But, avoiding her eyes, he busied himself with skinning and setting the animal to cook, and then with making a bed on the other side of the fire. In stunned silence she watched him, waiting for a look, a word, a smile—anything. She might have been invisible, for all the attention he paid her.

The rabbit he'd killed turned on the spit, filling the night air with the scent of roasting meat. Her mouth watering, Megan glumly watched him tend it. His expression grim, Kenric concentrated on their meal as though his life depended on it.

"That smells wonderful," she ventured.

He grunted.

OK. So he has some male version of PMS. No doubt her declaration of love terrified him. But why?

Roger. Kenric thought she was still engaged to Roger. Though technically she was, since she hadn't had a chance to break it off before the lightning struck her, if she wanted to split hairs, the engagement had never happened, at least not yet. Roger and modern Dallas were hundreds of years away, not to mention a continent.

Kenric removed the rabbit from the spit, slicing it with a wicked-looking short dagger into a hollow, wooden trencher. This he placed between them, rocking back on his heels and indicating with a sweep of his hand that she was to eat.

How could she tell him the truth when he acted as if he wished he were somewhere else, anywhere but with her?

Still, she had to try, while she still had this newfound courage. "Kenric—"

"Not now." His tone left no room for argument. "Eat."

Fuming, Megan grabbed a handful of rabbit meat and crammed it in her mouth. She nearly gagged, trying not to think of Peter Cottontail. By pretending it was chicken, she managed to choke it down.

Then it dawned on her—it actually tasted pretty good. Surprised, Megan took another handful, smaller this time.

She chewed it slowly, savoring the taste. *Not bad. Not bad at all.*

Reaching for more, she found Kenric watching her, a reluctant sort of smile curving his hard mouth.

Ah, the end of hostilities was in sight.

"What?" She looked at her greasy fingers, popping another piece of meat in her mouth. "I've never eaten rabbit before."

His dark eyes reflected his disbelief. "Never?"

"Nope." She went for another slice, unable to keep her hungry gaze from roaming over him. "It's not half bad."

He nodded, helping himself to more meat. Though he didn't speak again, his craggy features seemed much more relaxed. Now was as good a time as any.

"I'm not going to marry Roger." She blurted out the words, figuring she had to start somewhere.

His head snapped up.

She felt herself color. Since the fire provided a dim sort of light, with luck he wouldn't be able to tell that she looked like a ripe tomato.

"Of course not." The arrogant certainty of his tone pleased her. "I told you, you are mine now."

OK, that was her cue. Megan leaned closer, giving in to the temptation to touch him. She let her hand roam up the corded muscle of his arm, loving the steel she felt underneath the warm skin.

To her delight, he shuddered. "Megan—"

"There are some things I need to tell you," she said, nervousness making her voice quaver. "But first, what do you mean, exactly, when you say I belong to you?"

With a sound of impatience, he captured her hand.

"'Tis all that I can say, for now," he told her, his features once again remote and hard, as hard as his voice. "Until some things are settled, I cannot make promises."

This sounded suspiciously like the medieval form of "I don't want a commitment."

How could she tell him now, when she had no idea

what he meant to do with her? What would he do once he found out she was from another time, that there was no Roger in this time and place, no reward, no land?

Confused, aching, and anxious, Megan tried to eat more rabbit, the once succulent meat tasting as dry as ashes in her mouth. When she finally fell asleep, a hard knot of dread coiled inside her stomach.

Hours later, she awoke. Though it was still dark and the moon still hung full and ripe in the sky, she was wide awake. Faintly, she could hear Kenric's even breathing, telling her he still slept. She heard the far-off sound of an owl hooting, then nothing. Still, the skin on the back of her neck prickled, warning her that something had changed.

"You are right." The soft tones were those of Rhiannon, Kenric's sister and the queen of the Faerie land of Rune. "My brother's mind is in as much turmoil as your own."

Megan slowly lifted herself up on her elbows, then sat up. She smoothed her unruly hair with one hand and pulled the blanket around her more securely with the other. "Somehow I'm not surprised."

Rhiannon laughed, that lovely tinkling of bells that made Megan smile. She glanced at Kenric, fully expecting this sound to wake him, but he slumbered on.

"I have used a light spell." Rhiannon shrugged, one corner of her shapely mouth lifting in a grin. "He will not awaken until it is time."

Megan nodded.

"I have come to talk to you about us helping each other." The older woman's lovely eyes were sharp, her expression both serious and regal. "Have you given it any thought?"

On the slight breeze, Megan caught the scent of wild-flowers. "I . . . I don't know." How could she tell this woman—this Faerie—that she had begun to doubt her own destiny? How could she tell Rhiannon that she was no longer certain she wished to go back to modern-day Dallas? How could she state in simple terms the love she now bore for Rhiannon's half brother?

One look at the Faerie queen's sympathetic gaze and Megan knew she wouldn't have to.

"You are soul mates." Rhiannon nodded sagely. "It was inevitable."

"But I am from the future." Desperate to make her understand, Megan reached out and touched Rhiannon's hand. "I am not supposed to be here. What if something I do changes things in the future?"

"Everything happens for a reason."

So Ed had told her, back in Lord Brighton's castle. It seemed that neither he nor Rhiannon could understand. "This distance that separates us is too vast."

"No obstacles are too much for soul mates to overcome. You must be together, and that is that."

"But this is *time*." Pleading now, Megan leaned closer. "Time *and* space."

"Time is relative. So is space."

"Good Lord." Agitated, Megan sprang to her feet. "You sound like Edmyg. Why is it that no one will give me a straight answer?"

"Edmyg?"

Megan realized that Rhiannon had gone very, very still. And her skin, normally a soft, glowing peach, had become the color of chalk. "What's wrong?"

"Edmyg. Where did you hear this name?" Rhiannon's voice trembled. A haunted look, filled with sorrow, flashed across her beautiful face.

Stunned, Megan could only stare. Great, any minute now Rhiannon would tell her that Edmyg, whose name meant "honor," was some sort of evil wizard or something.

"I met him in an enchanted castle—er, keep—a day's ride from here. Kenric met him too."

Rhiannon's sigh contained a wealth of meanings. Unfortunately, Megan couldn't decide which ones they were.

Her head bowed, Rhiannon stood silent. Her eyes were closed and her lips were moving, as if in silent prayer.

Megan waited, wondering what tangled knots she had unraveled now. "Is this good or bad?" she finally asked, when Rhiannon went silent.

The other woman seemed not to hear her. "Edmyg. Blessed Goddess, I have searched for him for years."

She raised tortured eyes to meet Megan's gaze. "Somehow, for some reason, he has been hidden from me. That explains why I could not find you—the spell must have hidden you from me even as it kept you safe from Myrddin."

Myrddin! Good Lord. Megan still had to tell Kenric about him.

"We ran into Myrddin," Megan said slowly. "He fought Kenric."

Rhiannon appeared to shake off her sudden melancholy. "That explains the disturbing ripples we felt in Rune. Ripples of power, great power, untamed power. I though it might be either Kenric or Myrddin."

"It was both."

Sagely, the Faerie queen nodded. "So it will be once again, in the final battle."

Megan waited for Rhiannon to elaborate, but the Faerie queen fell silent, lost in her thoughts. Things were beginning to remind Megan more and more of some giant weaver's loom, like in the myths of ancient Greece. Edmyg and Rhiannon, Myrddin and Kenric, and she herself, all mysteriously entwined, rushing toward some inevitable conclusion. Eventually Megan supposed that this too would come to light.

"Do you still wish to return to your home?" Pitched low, Rhiannon's voice was serious. "To your own time?"

The question caught Megan off guard. She found herself unable to meet Rhiannon's eyes, choosing instead to stare at her hands, which, for some reason, she found herself twisting in her lap.

Did she want to go back? She thought she might already know the answer to that. More important, did she have the right to stay?

Megan realized she had to give some sort of an answer. "I don't know," she finally said.

"Ah." The beautiful Faerie queen nodded wisely. "Do you love my half brother?"

Whoa. Admitting it to herself, and even saying it out loud to Kenric, was one thing. Saying it out loud to Kenric's sister was another.

At Megan's silence, Rhiannon smiled. It was a gentle smile, full of sympathy. "I understand you are betrothed to another."

Roger. "I was about to break the engagement when the lightning sent me here. He is an evil man," Megan admitted, relieved to have the truth out at last. If only it were that easy to tell Kenric.

"Then why do you have my half brother seeking this Roger?" Nothing but mild curiosity colored Rhiannon's voice. Megan got the eerie feeling that Rhiannon already knew the answer to the question she asked.

"I didn't know what else to do. I woke up in the middle of winter, freezing, in some isolated cave with a giant man who dressed like a barbarian. He wanted land; I needed protection. It seemed like a good idea at the time."

"Kenric would not hurt you. For him, it would be like hurting himself."

Thin slashes of rose appeared in the sky to the east. Soon the sun would rise. Megan was seized by a sudden fear that Rhiannon would vanish with the morning. This time she needed some answers before the Faerie queen left.

"I need to understand what is going on. Do you know what happened to me?"

Her expression grave, Rhiannon gave a slow nod. "You were needed."

Megan waited for her to say more. When the silence stretched on, and Rhiannon didn't seem inclined to elaborate, Megan realized she would have to ask pointed questions if she had any hope of getting answers. "Needed by whom?"

"Kenric needs you."

Not a complete answer. "And?"

"We need you." Was that reluctance that colored Rhiannon's silky voice?

"We?"

"All of us." Every inch the regal queen now, Rhiannon waved an arm at the lightening sky. "Especially Rune and the land of Faerie."

Now they were getting somewhere. "Why?"

To Megan's surprise, Rhiannon closed her eyes and lowered her head. " 'Twas not of our choosing. Even Myrddin, who believes he acts only from his own desire for revenge, is caught in the web. It is ancient legend, prophecy come to life."

This was not what Megan had expected to hear. An awful suspicion made her stiffen. Looking down at her hands again, she forced herself to hold them rigidly still. She asked the question through lips suddenly gone dry. "Was it you that made this happen? Did you and your magic bring me here?"

Silence.

Raising her head, Megan realized she was speaking to empty air. The Faerie queen had vanished. Rhiannon was gone.

Though he had an iron control over himself during the bright light of day, Kenric could not keep himself from dreaming. And what dreams they were! In them, Megan

210

and he lay entwined, slaking their passion again and again. When he awoke he was hard and aching.

Megan still lay sleeping, curled on her side with one hand under her chin. In the faint light of dawn she was breathtakingly beautiful, her skin creamy and glowing, her hair a tousled cap of dark silk. Hell, he admitted, merely looking at her took his breath away. It had taken every ounce of will he possessed to keep from taking her up on the seductive invitation she'd issued the night before.

And now? Unaware of his hunger, she slumbered, the sensual curve of her shoulder an invitation of its own.

How had this woman come to mean so much to him? Grimacing, Kenric forced his stiff muscles to rise. Better he should ponder the mysteries of the universe. She belonged to him and, conversely, he to her. That was the way of it, and his time would be better spent figuring out a way to have her and his other heart's desire, the land.

After he'd washed, he went to wake her. Standing over her, his heart pounding in his ears, he knew he dared not touch her. So instead he stomped around, talking out loud to the warhorse, banging the knife against a stone, and, in general, making enough noise to wake the dead.

Megan stirred, making mewling sounds of protest. Unable to tear his gaze away from her as she yawned and stretched, Kenric found himself hard again. He cursed under his breath, telling himself to turn away. But he was only human, and, though he might deny himself the pleasure of her touch, he could not help but watch her. Even though watching her made him ache.

When she stood, running her fingers through her short sable hair, and offered him a sleepy smile full of innocent sensual promise, he turned away. It was one of the hardest things he'd ever done.

"We ride out shortly," he told her, his voice harsh, his breathing raspy, even to his own ears. "Take a few minutes to ready yourself." This was time he would need as well, to get his errant body under control.

When they were once again mounted on the warhorse's broad back, after breaking their fast with chunks of hard bread and leftover rabbit, he held to a surly silence. To his surprise, Megan did not speak either. He found he liked the quiet, feeling a camaraderie that he had experienced with very few people since his father. If only her closeness weren't so distracting. The light floral smell of her kept him on the edge of arousal. He wondered how she did it without scented soap or lotions.

"Have you talked to your sister lately?"

The question startled him. They'd been riding two or more hours without exchanging a word, then out of nowhere Megan asked this.

"My sister?"

"Rhiannon."

God's blood. With Megan pressed against his back and her soft breath stirring the hairs at the nape of his neck, he could scarcely think.

"No." Curious, he twisted in the saddle so he could see her eyes. "Why?"

Her shrug seemed too casual, and she would not look at him. Suspicion made him rein the warhorse in.

Before he could ask, she lifted troubled amber eyes. "She came to see me last night. I think"—she swallowed hard, biting her bottom lip in a gesture that sent the blood roaring through Kenric's body—"she has some sort of plan for me and you."

Pretending her nearness had no effect on him, Kenric nodded thoughtfully. Though Megan looked boyish in his overlarge tunic and faded cap, he knew what lush curves the ugly clothes hid. Knew and longed to touch them.

"My sister is full of intrigues and schemes. Do not let her distress you overmuch."

"She knew Edmyg."

"Who?"

"Edmyg. The wizard from Lord Brighton's castle."

"Ah, the old man who had not enough magic to break the spell." Kenric shook his head. "That is nothing to worry about."

She sniffed. "She knew that Myrddin person too. She told me it was he who set that band of Faeries against your family at Blackstone Keep."

Kenric saw red. He could not speak; he could not even think. To know that he'd had the man responsible for killing his family in his grasp . . .

"I will destroy him," he said with a snarl.

Megan's eyes were huge, the amber turning to pale gold in the bright sunlight. Her voice shook. "He means to kill you, Kenric. Last night Rhiannon said it was something to do with an old legend."

"Last night?"

Megan paled even more. "While you slept, she came to me and asked for my help. She even hinted that she could help me get back home, but only if I would help her."

"Get back home." The emotion stabbing through him at the thought was an unfamiliar one. Jealousy was not something Kenric of Blackstone had ever experienced, though he did now. "To Roger?"

Breaking the gaze, Megan looked down. "To my time."

Since this made no sense, he let it pass for now. With his finger he lifted her chin until she faced him once more, battling away the rage the thought of Myrddin brought and the terrible, aching fear that exploded in him at the thought of her leaving.

"Tell me, Megan, do you still want him?"

"Roger?" Her lips parted as she looked down. "No, Kenric. I intended to break it off with him, but before I could I was sent here."

Relief flooded through him, so intense it nearly made his head spin. But something . . . there was something in

213

her words, something in the way she avoided his gaze that alerted him that there was more.

"*Sent* here?"

Still keeping her face averted, she nodded. "I think Rhiannon had something to do with it."

Another kind of anger filled him at those words. "I suspected this from the beginning, did I not? Next will you be telling me that it is one of Rhiannon's spells that binds me to you?"

Megan blanched at that, misery and pain shadowing her mobile face. "I would hope not," she told him quietly.

"But you cannot swear it is not so."

"No." Tears filled her expressive eyes.

Kenric forced himself not to let the sight of them move him. His half sister had talked about legends and prophecy ever since he could remember. She wanted him to embrace that in him which was Faerie and renounce mankind forever.

He, of course, would have none of it. Especially since it had been Faeries and their magic who had destroyed his family.

"We will talk more later." Turning his back to her to indicate the conversation was done, he once again urged the warhorse into a trot.

Behind him, Megan heaved a great sigh. "What Rhiannon had to say seemed important, Kenric."

He didn't answer. Where Rhiannon was concerned, everything seemed important.

"She said it concerned the entire fate of Rune."

If Megan thought to gain his attention by such a dramatic statement, she was sorely mistaken. Years of hearing his sister's dramatic pronouncements had inured him to such things.

"She said"—Megan's voice was soft, so soft he had to strain to hear it—"that you needed me."

Startled, Kenric nearly turned to look at her. At the last moment, he stopped himself, knowing that if he looked at Megan now, she would be able to see the depth of his emotion in his eyes.

Instead he swallowed and took a deep breath. "Mayhap I do," he told her, his voice steady and calm as he thought of the land and the family he hoped to raise. "In that my sister is correct."

It was not a declaration of love; Kenric knew Megan realized that. In time she would come to value his truthfulness. He would not lie to her, would not speak honeyed words that would ring false upon her ears. This was all he could give her—the truth. And the truth was that he needed Megan in a way even he did not pretend to understand.

"We near the border of England and Wales," he told her, hoping to distract her.

Instead Megan fell silent, lost in her own thoughts.

Kenric watched the landscape, alert for any signs of danger, and planning what words he might use when they finally found Megan's Roger. The words would have to be persuasive, for, if Roger had half a brain, Kenric knew the other man would not willingly let a prize like Megan go. Even if Megan had planned to break off their betrothal.

He longed to put an end to this farce, this search for a man who didn't seem to want to be found. Therefore, though it would be a long ride, he would go to the one place a man of Roger's stature could not hide: London.

Though Kenric himself had never left Wales, he had many connections in the large town, from his father's and half brothers' days at court, and wouldn't hesitate to use them. Even if Roger did not wish to be found, in London Kenric would find him.

Once Kenric went into his taciturn mode, Megan knew from experience that asking any more questions would be futile. Instead she pondered his comment that he needed her. Needed her how? Needed her body? Needed

215

her for the reward she had promised him, the land? Did he really intend to return her to Roger, even though she'd told him she intended to break the engagement?

Her heart grew heavy at the thought. Kenric had taken her body, and her heart and soul as well. He had told her that she belonged to him, but in medieval times that could mean anything. He could have meant simply that she was his ward until he relinquished custody to the man who would become her husband.

Thinking about such things made her head spin. Feeling the beginnings of a monster headache, Megan concentrated instead on the scenery.

This land of so long ago seemed pristine. Rolling green hills dotted with sheep, the occasional crofter's hut, and the endless blue sky. She'd always heard it rained a lot, but so far the stretch of brilliant sunny days seemed unbroken. White, fluffy clouds dotted the blue sky, and the light breeze contained the fresh bite of early spring. No doubt it would be different in the cities and the villages. The lack of plumbing and ignorance of hygiene made the thought daunting. She was glad they'd never had to go to a city so far in their travels.

Then the thought hit her. *England.* Why would Kenric be taking her there? Because he thought her Lord Roger was English, and meant to find him by any means possible.

She had to ask. "Kenric, where are we going?"

He didn't even turn his head. "London."

Her heart sank. *Great, just great.* "Why?" she asked, her voice coming out as a squeak.

"I have connections there."

"Connections?" This kept getting worse and worse.

"Aye. Though I am a bastard, my father was a baron. His name is known in London. I will use that to locate your Roger."

She wished he'd quit saying *your Roger* in such a brusque tone. After all, she had told him she meant to break off the engagement. In this, at least, she hadn't lied. Closing her eyes, swaying to the rocking movement of Lancelot's gait, Megan tried to decide what to do.

Kenric would make a fool of himself asking among the noblemen of medieval London for a man who didn't exist.

She owed it to him to tell him the truth.

But would he believe her? And would he hate her afterward?

"How long is it to London?" Deliberately, she kept her tone light. She needed to know how long she had to prepare some sort of acceptable way to tell him. All she needed was for Kenric to think she'd lost her mind. Or worse, to leave her by the side of the primitive road.

" 'Tis a long ride. But there are many villages between here and there. Mayhap in one of those we will find news of this Roger."

Panic flooded through her. Somehow she would have to find a way to tell Kenric the truth—and make him believe it.

She had to tell him the truth. But how to say it? Did she just blurt it out, as in, *Hey, Kenric, guess what? I'm from the future?* As she ran the words through her mind, Megan knew one thing: if Kenric didn't immediately question her sanity, he would be furious. She knew how important the land was to him; knew too that it was only the promise of this land that had kept him traipsing all over the countryside with her.

She had promised him his heart's desire and now would yank it away. A low ache settled in her breastbone, near her heart. Though she hadn't known Kenric then, dangling such a carrot in front of a man like him now seemed inexcusable. But what else could she have done? She thought back to her abject terror, waking in the freezing cave with a huge barbarian warrior towering over her. She'd said anything she could think of, anything that would keep him from harming her. Then, once she'd realized he would not hurt her, she'd said anything to keep him by her side.

Now it was time to pay the piper.

Chapter Fourteen

"Kenric," she began, "there is something I—"

As if in answer to a prayer, or maybe only bidden by Megan's turmoiled thoughts, Rhiannon appeared on the road ahead, shimmering in the muted sunlight.

Megan's heart skipped a beat. Rhiannon knew the truth. Maybe she could help convince her brother.

With a muttered oath, Kenric reined Lancelot to a halt.

The Faerie queen inclined her head. "Greetings, my brother, Megan."

There was no warmth in Kenric's reply. "What is it now, Rhiannon?"

"I must speak with you." Her periwinkle eyes traveled to Megan, doubt and worry clouding them. "Both of you. It is a matter of great urgency."

Kenric snorted. "Everything is a matter of great urgency where you are concerned."

She held up one pale hand. "This is truly serious."

Megan frowned. Was it only her imagination, or did

Rhiannon's normal shimmering aura seem dimmed? She heard too the barely veiled panic in the Faerie woman's voice. She would have to convince Kenric to listen to his sister.

"Kenric—"

His voice hard, he cut her off. "We go to London. It has become imperative that I find this Lord Roger who is betrothed to Megan."

Despite her best efforts, Megan felt herself color. Especially when Rhiannon's piercing gaze found her.

"You have not told him?"

Megan slowly shook her head.

In front of her, Kenric went still. "Told me what?" Though he did not turn his shaggy head, his icy tone left no doubt what his reception to the truth would be.

A feeling of dread coiling inside of her, Megan opened her mouth to respond. "I—"

Rhiannon forestalled her. "You will not find this Roger in London."

"What?" Kenric roared. This time he did turn, impaling Megan with a furious glare. "Is this true?"

Shaken, she nodded.

"When did you think to inform me of this?"

She swallowed. "I was going to, once we stopped for the night." Best not to tell him she'd spent the day trying to work up the courage and find the right words. Remarkably her voice came out steady, totally belying the jittering mess of nerves that she felt inside.

"Kenric, Megan." Something in Rhiannon's soft tones silenced them both. "The hour grows late. It is long past time we had a talk, all three of us. What say you to making camp for the night here?"

"I think it's a great idea," Megan said. Without waiting to hear Kenric's answer, she pushed away from him, sliding down from Lancelot's broad back unaided.

Afraid to look at him, afraid something in her expression might give her away, she stumbled into the woods.

With luck they would think she needed to relieve herself and would give her a few moments of privacy. Which was good, since she didn't want to disgrace herself. Any minute now, the meager contents of her stomach were going to come up her throat.

Once she'd gained the shelter of the trees, Megan sat down on a log and tried to think. She didn't know if having Rhiannon there would be a hindrance or a help. Kenric seemed to regard his sister with, if not outright hostility, then at least blatant suspicion. Surely finding out that Rhiannon was privy to Megan's secret while he was not was bound to infuriate him.

When she made her way back to the clearing, she found Rhiannon seated on a folded blanket, by a small campfire, while Kenric took care of Lancelot.

"Come," Rhiannon greeted her with a broad smile, "sit with me."

Megan sat reluctantly. She cast a glance at Kenric, who continued to pretend they didn't exist. One look at his stiff and rigid profile told her he was furious.

Rhiannon seemed blithely unaware of this. "Kenric," she called, "will you join us?"

His answer was an indecipherable snarl. But at last he put away the brush, patted Lancelot's shining coat, and headed toward them.

When he lowered himself to the ground, it was on the opposite side of the fire. He kept his face averted from both of them, choosing instead to stare into the depths of the crackling flames.

At once Rhiannon's expression went from unconcerned to serious. "It is past time we had this talk."

"If it is another plea from you to try to make me feel guilty and return to Rune, you are wasting your breath."

Megan lowered her head. The icy crispness of his tone made him sound every inch the hardened warrior.

"Listen to me."

Rhiannon sounded every inch the Faerie queen, regal and commanding.

" 'Tis the truth I must tell you now, both of you. Whether you want to hear my words or not, it matters little. The hour grows late, later than either of you realize. And you both must know of the pivotal role you play in the events that will happen. These events will shape our future."

Already enthralled, Megan leaned forward. Glancing at Kenric, she saw that Rhiannon had captured his reluctant interest, though his expression was still hard and unyielding.

"It has been prophesied since ancient times of the coming of one who is of both worlds, Faerie and mortal, and of the power developed from his joining with his soul mate."

Megan exchanged a long look with Kenric. For a moment warmth leaped into his dark eyes before he narrowed them and looked away.

"I have brought your soul mate from another place and time, knowing that only you and she could come together in this dire time of great need.

"Like you, Kenric, Myrddin is half-human, half-Faerie," Rhiannon continued. "Unlike you, he has taught himself to use magic. Though where our magic is good, pulled from the healthy elements that rule our lives, Myrddin has gone to the darkness for his source. His soul is as black as his powers, and he believes the prophecy is about him. He thinks I am his soul-half—and he means to rule the world."

Kenric could hardly take it all in. Though every instinct he possessed screamed out at him in disbelief, he knew deep within himself that this time Rhiannon spoke the truth. Even though Faeries were incapable of falsehood, he had known his half sister to stretch facts a little whenever it suited her.

But this . . . this was serious. Though he wanted no part of Rune, he could not in good conscience step back and let Myrddin and his evil magic destroy the Faeries and their way of life. An entire people, destroyed at the whim of one madman?

Were that to happen, something good, something precious, something beautiful, would forever vanish from this earth.

Stunned, Kenric raised his head to find his sister watching him. Megan too, though the soft tenderness he saw in her beautiful eyes told him she somehow knew what he was feeling inside.

He felt as if he were standing on a cliff, about to take that one step that would catapult him over the edge.

"I have lost too much already. I could not," he said haltingly, "lose you as well."

Hearing his words, Rhiannon's expression crumpled. Gone was the everyday mask she wore: that of regal queen. Tears spilled over from eyes that brimmed with them, and, with a tremulous smile, she moved forward to embrace him.

Kenric suffered her embrace gladly, though he had carefully held himself aloof these many years past. She was, after all, his sister. It was not her fault that she had been born full-blooded Faerie rather than human.

"You are of my blood." He spoke into her hair, as his gaze sought Megan over Rhiannon's head. Megan too wept softly, though she smiled at him through her tears. Her smile seemed as brilliant as the sun, blinding him.

It was time he settled things, once and for all. Kenric realized that unless he did, he would never be able to live the simple life he so craved. He would have to wear the cumbersome mantle of warrior for a bit longer.

"Myrddin has once destroyed my family. I will not permit him to do so again." By these words he claimed what he'd refused his entire life: Kinship with Rhiannon and thus, too, the Faerie folk. Kinship with the part of him that he'd only eschewed. Warrior and mage, human and Faerie. All of it made up the man that he was, the man that he would be.

Finally, wiping at her streaming eyes, Rhiannon stepped back. "You will join in battle then?"

After one final glance at Megan, Kenric gave a slow nod. "I have no choice."

"You will have to learn how to control your magic."

Again he nodded, trying not to wince at the thought of willingly allowing such power as that which he sensed within himself free rein. And there was more he would know before he could commit himself wholly to the task at hand.

"Now tell me what you meant when you said you brought Megan from another place and time." Though he laced his voice with humor, he was not prepared for what Rhiannon said next.

"She comes from a time of no magic, a time we are all moving inexplicably toward. She comes from a place where machines are valued as highly as life, and where Faeries—and Rune—have vanished from the world."

Shocked, Kenric looked at Megan. "Is this true?"

Megan did not speak but, with a quiet nod, confirmed Rhiannon's statement.

He had been a warrior too long to put into words the thought that came next, so terrifying did he find it. Though Rhiannon claimed her magic shielded them from Myrddin's scrying, to exhibit such a weakness could be his downfall.

Still, the thought would not leave him. If Megan belonged in another place, another time, would she return there once their task had been completed?

Such a thing was unacceptable. He would talk to Rhiannon later and gain her agreement.

It wasn't until later, when they had eaten a meager meal of greens and nuts provided by Rhiannon, that it occurred to Kenric to ask about Roger.

He waited until Megan seemed peaceful, straightening her short hair with a brush Rhiannon had given her. As she brushed, her dark hair crackled and shone, alternating gold and sable in the shifting light of the fire. Her delicate face, too, was in shadow one moment, light the next, bringing to mind what a wonder he had found in her. Lighthearted and full of a child's heedless joy one moment, a passionate, sensual woman the next.

His mate. The other half of his soul.

He watched her until he could stand no more, until the stark beauty of her ignited a fire of its own deep within his belly.

" 'Tis time we talked." He spoke quietly, taking care not to disturb Rhiannon, who busied herself with something in a clearing nearby.

Was that fear that flashed into Megan's lovely eyes as she nodded?

Throat aching, he held out his hand. She took it, her smaller hand slipping into his as if it belonged there. *God's teeth.* a tremor went through him at this smallest of touches, and he had to clench his teeth against the urge to haul her up against him and kissed her senseless.

With a heavy heart, he tugged her along after him to a space surrounded by saplings that would shelter them from Rhiannon's wise gaze. He wondered what Megan would say if she knew that he, Kenric of Blackstone, a warrior feared throughout the land, had to struggle to force words past the lump in his throat.

"You are truly from another time?"

"Yes." She caught her bottom lip between her teeth, drawing his gaze. "From the future, about nine hundred years from now."

With difficulty, Kenric forced his mind back to the task at hand. Though he had a thousand questions, questions about what life was like so far in the distant future, now was not the time. Though both he and Megan had been pawns in Rhiannon's schemes, he needed to know what Megan really wanted.

To keep from touching her, he clasped his hands behind his back.

"Do you wish to return to your time once we have completed our task and vanquished Myrddin?" *Or*—and though he left the words unsaid, he thought she heard them—*do you want to remain here with me?*

"I don't know." In a broken whisper she answered, her eyes filling again with tears. "Rhiannon has not told me if I might remain, or if I must return to 2001, where I belong."

He wondered if she knew how it would be with him were she to go. He would be condemned to a hollow life, half an existence.

They stood in silence while he waited to see what else she might say.

"I love you," she whispered.

Still she made no promises. He waited and then, when he was certain she had finished speaking, Kenric inclined his head and strode away, trying to calm the maelstrom that raged within him.

Rhiannon watched her brother stride away and sighed. Raw anguish palpitated off him in waves, which she easily deflected. Though it pained him now, it was a good thing, this powerful emotion from a man who wanted only to be free of such things. Hurt would cleanse him, free him from old restraints, old shackles. Thus he would be prepared him for the awful and beautiful shape of things to come.

She heard a quiet sob and turned. Megan sat, hunched into a miserable little ball, trying to hold back tears.

Crossing to her, Rhiannon laid a comforting hand on her shoulder. "Do not mourn, little sister. Kenric is a wise man. He will think on your words. He will realize you had no choice in any of this."

Megan lifted sorrow-filled eyes to Rhiannon's face. "But I did. I didn't have to lie to him, to promise him land when I have none to give. Do you honestly think he will trust me now? I promised him his heart's greatest desire, then yanked it away."

"*You* are his heart's greatest desire."

"He wants the land more." Megan sniffled. "I am a distraction to him, nothing else."

With the restraint born of being a queen, Rhiannon kept herself from rolling her eyes. *These humans!* How could Megan not understand the silken bond that tied her and Kenric together?

"Has he not told you that you are his woman?" she asked with patience, pleased with her ability to mask her exasperation.

Flashing her a startled look, Megan gave a slow nod. "He has said those words. But I think he meant . . . you know . . ." She blushed and looked down at her hands.

"My brother has never claimed anything as his. Not since the Black Faeries took the lives of his human family. Have you not noticed he does not even name his horse?"

"Lancelot?" Megan smiled wanly, looking toward where the big animal cropped contentedly on grass. "*I* named him."

Grinning, Rhiannon showed her approval. "Lancelot. I like it. Does Kenric use the name?"

Megan's smile faded. "No."

" 'Tis because he fears to grow too close to the beast."

"I thought it might be something like that."

Ah, so the tiny human woman instinctively understood the man she was fated to love. Things were looking better.

Rhiannon leaned close, all traces of humor gone from her face. "Do you love Kenric, Megan Potter of Dallas-Texas?"

In the heartbeat that it took Megan to compose a response, Rhiannon had her answer. She watched as longing and love, despair and defeat, strong emotions all, chased themselves across Megan's mobile face. As she opened her mouth to speak, Rhiannon saw hope fill Megan's lovely amber eyes.

"Yes, I love him." Megan sighed, her voice trembling with the force of her feelings. "I love him more than life itself."

"What of this Roger?"

Megan flinched. "He is an evil man. I still haven't told Kenric everything."

"Kenric will understand."

"I don't know if he will." With a loud sigh, Megan rose and murmured a good night.

Rhiannon watched her walk away, aching for both of them, certain neither of them understood the depth and scope of the battle, of the things yet to come.

As soon as Megan vanished into the woods, a necessary prelude to bedtime, Kenric strode over to Rhiannon. His rough-hewn face was a study in nonchalance, telling her he was actually supremely worried. But about which—the upcoming clash of magic or the palpable distress of Megan, his soul-half—she didn't know.

Watching him, Rhiannon held her tongue and waited for him to speak. He stared at her so long in silence, his dark eyes haunted, that finally she was compelled to help him.

"What is it, brother?"

"Megan." He said her name like a curse, half with frustration, half with longing. "Will she return to the future when this is done?"

Rhiannon cursed under her breath. It was not within her nature to lie; indeed, it was forbidden by a Faerie law as old as time. She had not lied to Megan, merely skirted around the answer. Even this she could not do now, not to Kenric, not in the face of his anguish.

"I do not know," she admitted finally, her voice low.

He narrowed his gaze. "Does she want to go?"

"You had best ask that question of her."

"Do you know how to send her back, should she ask?"

"No," Rhiannon admitted. "But I am sure the spell exists somewhere, buried in the Hall of Records."

Lady help her, she saw the surge of hope her words brought him, hope that he ruthlessly quashed, making her watch powerlessly as it flared, then died in his eyes.

"Is there one who does know how?"

Rhiannon shrugged. "Not yet. But anything is possible."

He swallowed, expelling his breath in a gusty sigh. "Once this is finished, I will ask her if she wishes to leave."

"Do you not know the answer yourself?" Rhiannon asked gently, reaching out and touching him on the arm.

His mouth twisted. "I am not sure. Where Megan is concerned, I am no longer sure of anything."

"I am sorry." She knew her words of apology were inadequate, yet she had to speak them, for they were truth. "What she did was necessary, to her mind."

Both of them glanced at the woods, neither wanting Megan to hear.

"But you brought her here."

Trying desperately for a casualness she did not feel, Rhiannon shrugged. "Because the prophecy decreed it. It was time. What my council and I initiated can be done only once."

Kenric frowned, his expression thoughtful. "Does she know this?"

"No. She does not."

He sighed again and ran a hand through his thick hair, a ruffled lion's mane of sable, so unlike her own blond locks. "Think you it will sadden her, once she finds she is trapped here?"

"No, Kenric." Rhiannon laid a hand on his massive forearm. "I don't believe she wants to leave."

Again the hope flared in him. Rhiannon saw it and rejoiced.

"What of this Roger?"

"You need to speak to her about him. All she would tell me is that he is an evil man. He has no hold on her here."

"Did she tell you this?"

"Not in so many words." Now it was Rhiannon who took a deep breath. Dare she speak truth to him, her half brother who always ran from what she was about to hand him?

Looking at him, seeing the anguish and fear and a kind of calm acceptance that had never been there before, she knew she must. "She loves you, Kenric. With all her heart. The same way you love her."

About to answer, he apparently thought better of it and clamped his mouth closed. His lips a straight line, he looked away, not toward the woods this time, but to where his warhorse grazed, serene and content.

Now, Rhiannon knew, she had to make him understand the seriousness of what was to come. Perhaps then he could accept the emotions that swirled inside of him.

"This battle—" she began.

"It will be fine, Rhiannon." He cut her off, drawing himself up until he looked every inch the magnificent human warrior that she knew he was. "I will take care of this Myrddin for you; then you will let me live my life in peace."

Again she found herself using Faerie swear words under her breath. If ever she could pick a time when she would be allowed to speak a lie, just one tiny white lie, now would be the time. Instead she knew she'd been charged with the task of making this stubborn man understand the truth.

"I'm afraid it will not be that simple."

He froze, cocking his head to watch her, the arrogance

of his stance telling her he would not receive her words well.

"Explain."

"As you know, you must fight Myrddin with magic—"

Again he interrupted, waving away her concerns with a careless move of his hand. "I have done so once. I will do it again. With some training from you, of course."

"Nay, brother." She drew herself up too, wrapping around her the mantle of queenship that she so despised. " 'Tis not that simple. In order to best this wizard, you must not only *use* magic, but become it."

"I do not understand."

" 'Tis like a young warrior preparing for his first battle. You would not hand him a sword and send him out into the thick of things unprepared, would you?"

He laughed, relief showing in his face. "So I must train? I have already agreed to do so."

"Aye, Kenric, that is the way of it." She held up a hand when he would have interrupted yet a third time. "But that is not all. In order to train, you must come to Rune. You must acknowledge who you are to the people—the warrior of prophecy. Only then will they agree to teach you."

"No." His voice flat, Kenric turned away. "You are saying that I must agree to become their savior. I do not like accolades or worship. This battle must be kept secret."

Her heart pounding, it took every ounce of restraint she possessed not to go after him. "You *are* the savior, Kenric of Blackstone. The prophecy has decreed it. You know the words as well as I. *Half-Faerie, half-man.* This person is you, whether you wish to admit it or not."

In the very act of moving away, he spun around to face her. The harsh rage he let show on his face had her taking an involuntary step back.

"Have done with your lies, sister. Tell me the whole

of it now, so that I will have no other surprises awaiting me beyond every turn in the road."

Though the light from the full moon seemed bright, it was dark by the time they finished speaking and the fire had burned low. Surprised, Kenric gathered some more wood and built it back up. He had agreed to nothing, knowing deep within himself that there had to be another way. He could never become one such as his sister, wholly of the world of Faerie. There was too much human in him. Nor would he accept being held up as something he was not. He was no savior—merely a warrior with one final task, one last battle, before he might find peace.

There had to be another way. He promised himself that he would find it.

Gradually he realized something was not right. It was too quiet. Glancing around their small campsite, he saw nothing amiss. The warhorse had finished grazing and now watched the edge of the woods, his ears cocked forward. With a start, Kenric realized the animal watched for Megan to reappear.

"Rhiannon." Trying to calm the fear that rose in him, he motioned to his sister. "How is it that Megan has not yet returned?"

Immediately she strode toward him, her expression concerned. "I did not realize. We talked for so long, she should be back by now."

His blood thrumming, Kenric grabbed his sword. "I will find her."

Lancelot nickered, as if in agreement.

"I will go with you," Rhiannon told him. Immediately she cloaked herself in her protective magic, becoming a vague outline of shimmering light. He knew she could make herself entirely invisible if she so desired. He knew also that she claimed he had the same power, were he willing to use it. Somehow.

No. In the world of men, he was a legendary warrior. He would fight as a man. Now and until the battle to come.

At the edge of the woods he paused, listening. Though the bright moonlight helped, darkness was full upon them, making the forest a dangerous place. Wild animals had begun to prowl; with the instincts born through years of danger he sensed their hunger.

Still, the part of him that was attuned to Megan sensed that she had not gone far. If he was careful and quick he could find her.

A sound broke the silence, then came others: the crash of many footsteps, a loud whisper immediately hushed, then a man's low voice.

Hand on his sword, Kenric froze. This danger was real and immediate. Whoever it was tried to be silent, and failed. Whoever it was meant to sneak up on them under cover of darkness. Too bad the power of the moon foiled their plans. Still, whoever it was meant business.

Chapter Fifteen

He heard her soft cry and fought back the urge to charge
blindly into the dark shadows, his sword raised. Such an
action would be foolhardy, and Kenric had not gotten his
reputation as fearsome warrior by letting emotions over-
rule his head. No, he would wait and listen. Once he
knew what he was up against, then he could save her.
Would save her.

Despite her lies, despite the truth of what she was and
where she came from, nothing could alter the fact that
she belonged to him, and he to her.

She was his. He would save her. He had to.

Tonight he felt ready for anything. Invincible. Though
he hated to give credence to it, there must be some truth
to Rhiannon's claim that the full moon lent magic its
power.

A soft incandescence moved past him. Rhiannon, going to investigate. Maybe these fools, whoever they were,
would see her and think she was a ghost.

For now, he could think only of saving Megan. Strange as it seemed, he fancied he could smell her scent on the night breeze, light and floral.

As his eyes adjusted to the darkness created by the canopy of oaks, he could make out shapes. One of them lit a torch, a small one to be sure, but something no one bent on attacking by stealth would be foolish enough to do. Whoever these men were, they were not professionals.

The torch helped the moon illuminate the small clearing where they huddled, conferring. Slowly Kenric moved closer, searching for Megan. He saw the glow that was Rhiannon shimmering behind a huge, leafy tree.

"I'm sorry." Megan's voice, sounding both apologetic and frustrated, stopped him in his tracks.

Kenric froze as she walked into the clearing, unbound and unharmed. From her stance he could tell something had angered her; she stood apart from the other men, arms crossed in front of her chest.

It took a moment for the significance of this to sink in; then when it did he did not want to believe it. Here was no prisoner, no unwilling captive. Nay, Megan seemed to know these men. Another betrayal?

Gritting his teeth against the surge of emotion this thought made him feel—jealousy, or simple rage?—he moved silently forward. There would be time to analyze his emotions later.

Then a large, bulky man moved into the light, halting Kenric in his tracks. Lord Brighton. And there, next to him, the stoop-shouldered man who straightened himself, standing remarkable tall. Edmyg, the old mage. Though it might be a trick of the silver moonlight, he looked less elderly now.

"How," Lord Brighton's pompous tones rang out, "can anyone manage to get lost so close to their own camp? When you encountered us, long before dusk, you said it was a short walk away."

Ah, so this had not been a preplanned meeting. Kenric did not want to think about how the weight on his chest lightened at this knowledge.

"It is," she insisted. "Or was." Running a hand through her already mussed hair, she kicked one foot at a small rock, sending it scuttling across the ground. "I've always been bad with directions, but I don't know how I managed to take a wrong turn. I wasn't that far from the camp; I swear I wasn't."

One of the men, a foot soldier from the looks of him, muttered something about enchanted woods. Edmyg quelled him with a glance.

Something about the ancient mage seemed different. Kenric watched, trying to ascertain what it could be. He stood taller, for one, and his face did not seem nearly so lined, nor his body so bent with the weight of his years.

Edmyg moved to stand next to Megan, lifting his hand and placing it on her shoulder. Watching this, Kenric tensed, then realized the man meant to comfort her.

"Mayhap we should wait until sunrise." This suggestion came from Lord Brighton, who somehow managed to sound both pompous and weary at the same time.

"I think that would be best." Megan's voice rang with disappointment. "But I don't want Kenric and Rhiannon to worry. No doubt they are searching for me."

"Rhiannon"—when he said her name, Edmyg's voice no longer sounded ancient nor querulous—"and Kenric will find us. They need us, my dear, though not as badly as they need you. We must help them in preparing for the battle to come."

"Oh, yes." Lord Brighton threw up his hand. "The battle. The one where your Kenric must become some sort of king. And what of your betrothed, this Lord Roger? What will you tell him?" Mockery ran in his voice as he seemed to wait for Megan to speak.

Megan blanched, but said nothing.

A slight breeze stirred the leaves on the trees, making

them chime like silver bells or Rhiannon's laughter.

Watching, Kenric narrowed his eyes. He had begun to feel as though everyone in the world conspired to make him take on the unwanted mantle of power. Yet his Megan, who perhaps had the most to gain were he to do so, did not seem overly thrilled with the prospect.

His Megan. There it was again.

About to move forward and announce his presence, Kenric stopped as Megan moved closer to Edmyg. Shoulders touching, they both watched Lord Brighton, who seemed by his very actions to wish he was elsewhere.

"Why are you here?" Megan asked softly. Beside her, Edmyg put his arm around her, a visible show of support.

Kenric wanted nothing more than to knock it away. With an effort, he forced himself to remember that Edmyg was an old man, even if the moonlit night was kind to him.

"What do you mean?" Lord Brighton still mocked her. If he kept it up, Kenric would step forward and challenge the fool with his sword.

"If you don't like Kenric, if you don't believe in him, if you truly don't want to help him prepare for the battle that is to come, why are you here?"

Instead of answering seriously, as the question had been meant, Lord Brighton threw back his head and laughed. His laugh seemed to echo in the sudden stillness of the night.

"Why, I thought you knew, dear." Still chuckling, he appeared not to notice how Megan shrank away from his outstretched hand. "I want only one thing. You. I came for you."

Rhiannon chose that moment to appear, shimmering into existence right in front of Lord Brighton.

With a soft cry, Megan turned to her. "Rhiannon! Thank God. Where's Kenric?"

His sister glanced at him, then away, her gaze focused

on something else, someone else. "He is here, somewhere."

Kenric noticed that his half sister had eyes only for Edmyg. He vaguely remembered someone mentioning they knew each other.

Megan turned in a circle, searching for him in the shadows outside of their little well-lit circle.

Kenric tried to hang on to his anger, tried to remember that she had lied to him about the land, but when her amber eyes somehow spotted him in the enveloping darkness he forgot everything but the need to touch her, to hold her, to assure himself that she was unharmed.

With a muffled sound of joy, she ran to him. And he, God help him, opened his arms and gathered her close. With her trembling body in his arms, her soft breasts against his chest, he knew a stirring of such strong emotion that he trembled with it.

His.

Breathing in the feminine, floral scent of her, he bestowed kisses along the top of her dark hair, along her cheekbone, her throat, until finally she turned her head and touched her lips to his in an openmouthed kiss. And then he was lost.

Megan wondered for the twentieth time how Edmyg, Lord Brighton, and his retainers had escaped the spell that had kept them locked in Lord Brighton's keep. And she wondered how they had come to find nearly the exact spot where she, Kenric, and Rhiannon camped.

But then magic, or so she had learned, could do both wonderful and terrible things.

After she had somehow wandered too far into the forest, stumbling around for what had to be an hour or more, she'd known absolute terror. How could she have been so stupid as to have gotten lost, barely yards from the small fire Kenric had built?

She put it down to her emotional state; she'd been so

worried that Kenric wouldn't want her anymore that she hadn't been paying attention to where she walked.

Finding the small group had at first seemed like a blessing. She was both surprised and delighted to learn that they'd somehow mastered the spell and had been able to leave the keep. Then, once Lord Brighton had made apparent his intention to possess her, she'd wished for Kenric with every fiber of her heart. It was almost a physical ache, this need for him.

Kenric.

When he'd appeared, she'd felt such a rush of joy, or need, that she'd run to him without thinking.

If at first joy had consumed her, passion followed. When they'd kissed, she thought she could drown in him, get lost in the taste and the touch and the glorious feel of him. It wasn't until someone—Lord Brighton most likely—had cleared his throat that she realized they had an audience.

If she'd harbored any uncertainty in her heart, it vanished in that instant. Kenric was her soul mate and would not leave her. She could no more live without him than live without the very air she breathed.

Wrenching her mouth from his, Megan gulped in air and tried to find the strength of will to pull away from him. But Kenric merely tightened his arms around her, holding her so close that she knew he had worried about her and missed her too.

"How did—"

"What happened to—"

They both began to speak at once. She knew she sounded breathless, knew too that she revealed tenderness and joy in her voice.

Lord Brighton stepped forward, his florid face set in a grimace. "I would bargain with you for the woman," he told Kenric.

Kenric's hand went to his sword. "Megan is mine. Have care with what you say."

The older man's expression changed, from antagonism to anguish. "But she is how I escaped my keep. I have discovered love, just as she said. I . . . I love her."

Despite himself, Kenric pitied the man. Megan was easy to love. Still, he could not have Lord Brighton thinking he could have her.

"You will find another," Kenric said arrogantly. "Megan belongs with me."

The breeze that had lightly caressed their skin picked up, startling the leaves and stirring a cloud of dust in the small clearing. The small fire sputtered, nearly dying.

"Hold." Rhiannon's voice rang out, bolstered by moonlight and wind.

As one they turned, facing her. With Kenric holding her so close, Megan knew he shared her unspoken desire never to be separated again.

"He comes."

Was that fear in Rhiannon's silvery voice? The wind seemed suddenly wintry, the bite of it making Megan shiver.

Next to Rhiannon, Edmyg inclined his head in agreement. Megan glanced at him, then back. Was it her imagination, or had his gray hair gotten darker, more black than silver?

Beside her, Kenric stiffened. "Now?"

"Yes. He has overcome my spell of cloaking." It seemed the Faerie queen stood in the center of a whirling funnel, the likes of which Megan had seen only in barren West Texas in the middle of a dust storm.

"I need Lancelot." Kenric moved away from her, leaving Megan feeling cold and alone. Then she realized what he had said: he'd called the warhorse by the name she'd given him, without thought.

"Now is not the time—" Rhiannon began, shouting now to be heard over the force of the wind.

Kenric seemed frantic. Knowing him as she did, Megan knew he would never agree to leave Lancelot.

"I'll go with you," she yelled, moving to his side.

"No time." Rhiannon began to spin, her hair lifting madly about her head. "Myrddin will find you and destroy you. You are not ready."

"My horse—"

"I will bring him with us."

"I will help you." Moving swiftly for one so ancient, Edmyg crossed the clearing to stand at her side. He grabbed Rhiannon's hand, stilling her.

"We must go." The last word was a shriek, as clouds as black as the surrounding sky covered the moon. The silvery light that had made their clearing such a magical place winked out. So did the feeble torch and fire.

Instantly it was dark. Not a comforting kind of darkness, but an enveloping, smothering, heavy blanket that reeked of evil.

Rhiannon and Edmyg joined hands, chanting incomprehensible words into the face of the storm.

It got darker. Colder. Ice froze their very breath.

The sense of doom lay so heavily upon them that Megan staggered, clutching Kenric's arm for support.

Then everything shifted and the darkness vanished. And she knew no more.

The instant his sister had begun chanting, Kenric had wanted to stop her. He knew what she was doing, though he still had not agreed to it. He did not want to go to Rune, not yet. Only concern for Megan's safety had kept him standing within the circle of power Rhiannon had created.

Clasping Megan close to him, he closed his eyes, readying himself for the swoop of stomach and tingling of bones that crossing over always brought.

When he opened them again, they were in Rune. And Megan, his lovely Megan, had fainted in his arms.

"Is she all right?" Lord Brighton asked, concern rendering his normally ruddy complexion a sickly white. He made a move toward her, as if he meant to take Megan from Kenric's arms.

Kenric stopped him with a simple look.

"She will be fine." Rhiannon waved her hand again, a delicate sifting of shimmers caressing Megan's face. At once Megan opened her eyes, confusion darkening the amber color to nearly a chocolate brown.

They reminded Kenric of how she looked while lost in the throes of passion. Unfortunately his body responded instantly. He shifted her in his arms to hide this from the others.

Megan's eyes went wide, telling him she felt his arousal. He found himself smiling tenderly into her upturned face, wishing they were alone so he could kiss her.

"There will be time enough for that later," Rhiannon said, her voice a sharp sword. "For now, we are hidden once again, safe from Myrddin's evil workings. Our power is still strong enough that we can keep him from Rune."

Lord Brighton tugged at his collar, shifting his feet and frowning. "Edmyg has told me of this Myrddin. What does he want from you?"

"He plans to rule the world"—it was the voice of a queen Rhiannon used now—"so that he might destroy everything beautiful in it. We have ancient legends, prophecies that speak of this. Even the humans have knowledge of this."

"Evil," Lord Brighton said glumly. "I don't like the sound of that. And my men? Where are they?"

"They are no longer needed."

He opened his mouth, then closed it, looking for all the world like a fish out of water. "No longer needed," he repeated, then lapsed into silence. His normal color had returned and he appeared to be perspiring profusely, though the air of Rune was pleasantly mild.

Another man, human from the looks of things, stepped

out from behind Lord Brighton. Tall and ruggedly handsome, he nearly resembled a man of Faerie, so beautiful
were his features. Crossing to Rhiannon, he knelt grace-
fully at her feet, head bowed.

What was this? Kenric straightened, not liking the way
Megan's eyes seemed locked upon this interloper.

Even Rhiannon wore a look of confusion—until the
man lifted his face and gazed up at her.

"Edmyg?" She gasped, one hand to her heart. "How is
it possible?"

His answering smile was as bright as that of any man
of Rune. "Another spell, Rhiannon. Don't you remember
years ago when I was taken from you?"

Speechless, she nodded.

"You thought I had aged so greatly?"

Rhiannon shrugged, her mouth trembling. "You are
human. I didn't—"

Edmyg kissed her, silencing her. When he pulled away
he smiled down at her with a look of such tenderness it
generated heat.

Kenric watched with interest. His sister's normally
porcelain complexion was suffused with red.

Megan turned within his arms and grinned up at him.
"Edmyg loves her."

Even as aware of magic as he was, Kenric still had
trouble understanding. "Edmyg?"

Megan nodded, her gaze full of love. For him, Kenric.
In that instant he realized his momentary jealously of
Edmyg was more than foolish.

"Edmyg is not old."

"No."

"Another spell."

Nodding again, Megan pressed against him so that her
soft breasts pushed into his chest and his arousal nestled
against the juncture of her thighs. Tightening his arms
around her, he found himself grinning at her like a young
lad.

"Careful," he said in a growl. "Or I might take you up on it no matter where we are."

Lord Brighton cleared his throat.

Kenric looked up to find Rhiannon and Edmyg locked in a passionate embrace similar to what he had been contemplating with Megan.

"There will be time enough for that later." Casually Kenric threw his sister's own words back at her.

Flushed, Rhiannon broke out of Edmyg's arms. Still, she clutched his hand as though afraid to let him go. Or maybe she was unable to stand without his support. Kenric certainly could relate to that.

"What is this?" he asked, making his voice the stern one of a concerned brother. To his surprise, it was Edmyg who answered, moving toward Kenric unafraid, though his slender body proclaimed him no warrior.

"We are soul mates too," Edmyg said. "For many years, an evil spell has separated us. It not only kept me confined to Lord Brighton's keep, but made me an old man. Thanks to you and your mate, the spell has been broken. It could be that our coming together is also part of the prophecy."

Kenric remembered Megan's words. *Love is the most what powerful magic of all,* she had said. Holding her close, he found he could easily believe it.

"Love is a powerful magic."

The air shifted and shimmered around them. In an instant they were surrounded by three other Faeries who wore the auras of their power like cloaks. Uncommonly beautiful, as was the way of their kind, they said nothing. Instead they simply stared at him and waited.

"He has come," Rhiannon said simply, still clutching Edmyg's hand. "Willingly."

"Is he ready then, to begin the training?"

Since his sister could not answer for him, she met his gaze. From her expression he knew what he needed to say, though he could not say everything she wished.

"I am ready." With Megan at his side he was prepared for anything. He would protect her with his life if need be.

"And do you understand all that acceptance of this training entails?"

He gave a regal nod, pinning each of them individually with a bold stare. "I do, though I must decline part of it. I accept my Faerie blood, acknowledge that it flows through my veins equal to the blood that is human. However—"

They began to mutter, a low buzz of sound. Patiently, he waited until they had finished.

"However, I will not be your savior. Not now, not ever. I will do what is necessary to help you fight this battle, but I will do it as a warrior, not as someone to be worshiped. Do I make myself clear?"

Behind him, he heard Rhiannon gasp. Megan squeezed his hand in encouragement. The elders of the council, however, said nothing. It almost seemed that they had expected this.

Finally the oldest of them, a wizened Faerie named Arwydd, stepped forward. "Come with me then, Kenric of Blackstone. We have no choice but to accept your terms, for you are our last hope. It is time for your training to begin."

Rhiannon would not look at him. He sensed her disappointment. Did she not see that he had no choice?

Kenric stepped forward, pulling Megan with him.

"Leave your woman here," the old one said without looking back at them.

Kenric stopped. Megan tugged her hand free.

"But—"

"The training is for you alone," Rhiannon whispered, her dissatisfaction plain in her voice. "I will watch Megan. Go."

Torn, he hesitated. Megan and Rhiannon exchanged a

long look; then Megan gave him a small shove in the back.

"Go, you big lug." She laughed, though he could detect no mirth in the sound. "I'll be fine. I told you before that I wanted to explore Rune."

So he went, praying under his breath that he did the right thing.

Sending Kenric away was the hardest thing she'd ever done. When his concerned eyes touched upon her face, she wanted nothing more than to throw herself into his arms. Only there did she feel safe; only there did she know that, no matter whether he wanted to admit it or not, she was cherished. She was his soul-half.

Yet, because she had to, she let her gaze travel over his beloved face and laughed casually, while inside she couldn't help but wonder how it could be that such a man could be meant for her and her alone. He was powerful, radiating confidence in his masculinity. With his broad shoulders and massive arms, he looked like the warrior he was. She found him beautiful, from the chiseled perfection of his face to inside his soul.

And she had to send him away.

No matter that it was only temporary. At this moment, at this crossroads in time, she felt his loss as keenly as if it were permanent. For Rhiannon had told her, on that night when they had spoken, of what this training entailed. For days, maybe weeks, Kenric would not be allowed to see her or touch her or even think of her. He needed to become entirely focused on his training, on the power. She could not, would not, hinder him in this quest.

But it struck her now, watching the man she loved walk away, how dangerous this battle could be. Her heart in her throat, she tried to contemplate life without him, and utterly failed. Having found him, she could no more go back to her shadow existence than she could live once her heart had been cut from her chest. It was then that she realized she wanted to stay in this time forever, to live with the man she loved.

As if she sensed the thoughts that tormented Megan, Rhiannon came and enveloped her in a hug. Still, Megan strained to see one last glimpse of him, knowing it would have to sustain her until he returned to her side.

When Rhiannon indicated to Megan that she was to follow, Megan squared her shoulders, took a deep breath, and went. Perhaps there was something she could learn, something she could do that would help in some small way.

"He will be fine," Rhiannon assured her, Edmyg trailing along behind them as though he was afraid to let Rhiannon out of his sight. Megan could definitely relate.

"How long will this training take?"

Rhiannon smiled gently. "Two weeks?"

Two weeks? Megan sighed. Two weeks without Kenric? She didn't know how she would survive.

The other council members followed at a discreet distance. For the first time Megan wondered whether, if they had used some spell to bring her here, they could use some spell to send her back to her own time.

"Rhiannon, I—" Hearing the panic in her own voice, Megan stopped, took another gulp of honeysuckle-scented air, and began again. "I need to talk to you."

"Go ahead."

Glancing at Edmyg, then at the others, Megan shook her head. "In private."

With a regal nod, Rhiannon smiled. "I understand." She cast a look over her shoulder to where Edmyg waited. For a moment the mask of queenship slipped, and Megan saw naked longing reflected on Rhiannon's lovely face. She understood. As a matter of fact, Rhiannon's preoccupation with Edmyg was making Megan down-right uncomfortable. She almost felt guilty breaking it up.

Still, what Megan wanted to discuss was important. "It will just take a few moments of your time."

With apparent reluctance, Rhiannon dragged her gaze away from Edmyg. "For now, duty calls. You need to rest. But later this evening . . ."

Duty, my foot. Megan had seen the red-hot looks the two were exchanging when they thought no one was watching. But Megan couldn't really blame her. With this major battle looming over all of them, Rhiannon might be wise to grab what few opportunities she had. Were their places reversed, Megan would do the same.

They arrived at the multifaceted crystal door to the room Megan had used last time. With another hug, Rhiannon left her, closing the door behind her.

Too keyed up to remain in the room, Megan began to pace. Certainly it would do no harm if she decided to do a little exploring. Rune was so beautiful she should have wanted to see more of it.

But all she wanted to see was the one thing that had been denied her: Kenric. While she understood intellectually the necessity of his isolation, that didn't mean she had to like it or understand it. If it would take her and Kenric together to save Rune, why separate them now?

Chapter Sixteen

Rhiannon found her in the gardens. Megan had wandered among the lush, exotic blooms feeling as though she were on some tropical island, which, unfortunately, made her think of honeymoons—which only made her long for Kenric even more.

In the midst of inspecting the fragrance of one particularly ripe flower, Megan heard the tinkling sound of small wind chimes, looked up, and saw Kenric's half sister.

"Rhiannon." Megan managed a smile. Her sudden, fierce longing for Kenric and her continual attempt to keep her panic at bay left her feeling at the end of her rope.

Rhiannon inclined her head regally, though her answering smile was not unkind. She waved her hand and a bench appeared, made of cool, white marble.

Grateful, Megan took a seat while she struggled to put her thoughts in order. She'd spent hours rehearsing what she wanted to say, needing to make sure she got it right. Now, though, every one of her prepared speeches seemed to have flown out the window. All she knew was that she had to make certain Rhiannon understood what she wanted, and pray the Faerie queen had it within her power to grant it.

But before Megan could open her mouth, Rhiannon spoke. "Do not worry about Kenric. He has within him the makings of a great mage. Once he is trained, with you to enhance his power, I believe he will defeat Myrddin easily."

"It's not so much Kenric that I'm worried about," Megan said. "It's me. I don't want to go back to my own time." The words came out in a breathless rush. "And I am worried that once my task here is completed, I will have to."

Rhiannon laughed, the bell-like sound oddly soothing. "Well, if you do, it won't be through me." The humor in her voice was dry. "Though I brought you here, I can't send you back."

Dumbfounded, Megan stared. "Are you serious?"

"Yes. I don't know how. Kenric asked me the same thing."

"Did he"—cautiously, Megan asked what she most wanted to know—"want you to try?"

Again Rhiannon laughed. "Quite the opposite. But Megan, he is concerned that you yourself want to return."

Megan hung her head. "That's my fault," she said in a small voice. "I kind of let him think that."

"Why?"

"I thought I wanted—" Her voice broke and she couldn't finish.

Rhiannon said nothing, waiting until Megan had composed herself.

"I didn't know." Raising her gaze to meet Rhiannon's, Megan beseeched her to understand. "I didn't know how much Kenric meant to me."

"Have you told him of Roger?"

"Roger." Even speaking the name made Megan cringe inside. "I never want to see him again."

"Aye, but have you told Kenric that?"

Megan chewed on her bottom lip. "Not yet."

"Why not?"

"There wasn't time. I *did* tell him I planned to break off the engagement."

Curiosity shining in her violet eyes, Rhiannon cocked her head. "Do you mind if I ask why?"

"He is not a kind man." *That* was the understatement of the year. Thinking of Roger and his myriad methods of cruelty, Megan could only feel relief that she had somehow escaped him.

"Many men are not kind."

Unkindness did even begin to cover the way Roger had treated her. He had manipulated her, somehow convincing her that she deserved no more than the harsh treatment he doled out. The ridicule and the threats had escalated over time, becoming outright abuse until finally she had retreated inside herself, enduring it because she believed she should.

And he'd wanted her to change her will. Did he plan, then, to eventually kill her instead of simply hurting her?

She'd wondered and suffered and tried to decide what to do. Until one day she'd risen with the sunrise and a swollen, black eye and realized she didn't want to live that way anymore. That was when she had known she'd have to tell Roger she didn't want to see him again, or die trying.

Instead she'd been struck by lightning and somehow transported back in time. Freedom from all the constraints of her relationship with Roger was a heady feeling. The love of a good man like Kenric was even more so.

She looked up to find Rhiannon watching her closely.

"Roger was worse that most. I think he meant to kill me. I don't want to ever see him again."

Smiling broadly, Rhiannon reached over and patted her hand. "I believe everything will be fine."

"I hope so."

Rhiannon's smile faded, replaced by a frown that made fine lines appear in her flawless forehead. "As long as we win the battle. Only then will everything be fine."

Megan thought of Kenric and of the powerful love they shared, even if Kenric himself wasn't ready to admit it. And of Edmyg and Kenric's sister, who seemed well on their way to their own love.

"Love is a powerful magic," Rhiannon said, startling Megan.

"Did you read my mind?"

Rhiannon's laughter trilled on the night air. "No, dear heart. I didn't have to. If you'd have seen the lovesick expression on your face, you would understand. It didn't take magic to know what you were thinking."

Though he had been forbidden to by the rules of his training, Kenric came to her that night. He could no more stay away than he could stop breathing. These Faeries and their foolish rules would not govern him. He would learn what they had to teach, practice until he could wield his knowledge of it like his finely sharpened sword. And it would not take as long as they thought it would. Inbred in his very soul, magic came naturally to him, even though before he'd always fought against it. He would be ready long before a fortnight had passed.

They could train him until he could no longer stand. But they would not, could not, keep him away from his Megan.

In the deepest part of the night, he found her room. Creeping quietly in the darkness, he disrobed swiftly. Though half-asleep, she welcomed him with a glad cry, holding out her arms to him and pulling him to her.

Megan.

He felt a sense of homecoming, along with a fierce, deep possessiveness. She was his. When he took her, plunging deep inside her, she was warm and soft and ready for him.

All through the night he loved her silently. Though she made soft sounds of gladness, they did not speak. One hour before the dawn began to color the silver sky an angry scarlet, he left her sleeping.

Trudging back to the place where they kept him, he knew that, no matter what they said, he would come to her again.

He began his practice feeling renewed, alive. Happy. But the first few spells he tried failed miserably, and he couldn't seem to summon more than a few sparks of power that quickly fizzled.

Somehow they knew. All morning long Arwydd shot him angry looks of disapproval. After two hours of practicing, Kenric stormed out of the sanctuary in frustration. The truth of the matter was that they'd been right: making love to Megan had depleted him of the energy necessary to make magic.

Alone, he sat cross-legged, emptying his mind of everything but the core that was his inner power. Then, as he'd been taught, he focused, waiting for it to build within him, strong and sure.

Instead, he felt . . . nothing.

"You've been with the woman." Arwydd's crusty voice crackled with age. Moving much slower than Kenric, the elderly mage had taken ten minutes longer to reach the small copse of trees where Kenric had taken refuge.

Weary, Kenric looked up at the older man through narrowed eyes and nodded. He was not in the mood for the lecture that seemed certain to follow, but since he deserved it, he would suffer it in silence.

"So now you know"—Arwydd inclined his head, flashing what looked to Kenric's astonished eyes to be a half smile—"why we told you to stay away from her."

"I cannot bear to be without her," Kenric admitted ruefully, wondering when such weakness for a woman had become part of him. Still, it was only a powerful need, lust, not love. He could thank the Fates for that.

"She is your soul-half," Arwydd agreed, again surprising Kenric. "It is understandable."

"Then . . ." Waving his hand, Kenric rubbed his temple.

Arwydd waited, his expression enigmatic.

"What about this?"

"The magic?"

"It will not work." Kenric hadn't known he could feel such despair over something he'd spent years trying to deny. "How can I fight this battle with no magic?"

"The answer is simple." Arwydd spread his hands. "You must stay away from the woman."

Stay away from . . . Every fiber of his being rebelled at the thought.

"No." Kenric's very soul cried out in agony. "I tell you, I cannot."

Arwydd frowned, his normally dour expression becoming even more morose. "If you must go to her, then you must not love her with your body. That is the only way."

Astounded, Kenric could only stare. What Arwydd asked would be torture. To hold Megan, to caress her skin, touch her hair, taste her lips, to become fully aroused and then . . . nothing.

Arwydd pressed his advantage, laying a gnarled hand on Kenric's shoulder. "There are other ways you can pleasure her, which are allowed, but you must deny yourself release. You must win this battle. The entire fate of Rune rests on your victory."

The rest went unsaid. If he did not do as Arwydd—no, the magic—demanded, he risked not only the fate of Rune, but the fate of the entire world as well.

So he, no stranger to discipline, would have to learn to control his raging desire for Megan. And, in doing so, he would experience the greatest sexual frustration he had ever known.

"It will make you stronger, help to build up power." This time the gnomelike man actually laughed, a dry gurgle of sound that had Kenric wanting, irrationally, to punch him.

Kenric found nothing amusing in the situation, nothing at all. "Fine," he said in a snarl, uncoiling his legs and rising. "I will do as you say I must. Now, since it is apparent that I am no good to you for the rest of the day, let me take my leave and go in search of Megan. I must tell her of this latest development, to make certain she understands."

He knew talking to Megan was imperative. *God's blood.* She could tempt a saint if she set her mind to it. He didn't want her turning those feminine wiles on him. What he had to do would be difficult enough without her tempting him further.

Arwydd inclined his head. "Until the morning."

Kenric bowed stiffly. "Aye. Until the morning." Then he spun on his heel and went in search of the woman that drove him to distraction.

He found her in the gardens, seated on a white marble bench that gave off the glow of freshly created magic. One shining tear rolled down her cheek.

"Kenric," she murmured in a broken whisper, burying her head against his chest, "I never want to leave you."

His heart fluttered. He knew she wasn't talking about their brief separation whhile he trained.

"Leave me?" The thought seemed untenable. "Never. I will not allow it."

Even before he finished speaking, she was shaking her head, sending her short hair flying. Her entire body trembled, making him curse under his breath.

He breathed in the floral scent of her, closing his eyes against the forbidden desire that rose in him like some untamed beast. He would leash it; he had no choice. Grimly, he wondered at what cost.

"Kenric."

Her broken voice made him pull back, searching her face.

"Aye?"

"I don't want to go back to my own time." Lifting her chin, she made her announcement firmly, the hint of defiance making him wonder if she truly believed that he would ever let her go.

"Megan—"

"Wait." Regal as any queen, she held up one hand. "I want to stay here with you, forever."

Relief and pride warring within him, Kenric hugged her close. Was this what made her cry? The mistaken belief that he would send her packing into the future as soon as the outcome of the battle was assured?

"Of course, my dear." Tenderly he kissed the top of her head. "All we must do is tell Rhiannon, and she will make certain it is so."

"No." She pulled away from him, leaving him staring at her back. "I have spoken to Rhiannon. She does not know how to send me back."

Kenric shook his head. As long as he lived, would he ever understand the female mind? "Then there is no problem," he told her reasonably.

She spun on her heel, shocking him with the terror bright in her amber eyes. "But she doesn't know how to make me stay, either. I have this feeling, this terrible feeling that once it's over, once we have accomplished what we need to do together, I will have to leave."

Stunned, he froze while a roaring filled his ears. Narrowing his eyes, he set his chin. "I will not allow it. Now come." He captured her small hand, holding it firmly within his. "Let me show you Rune."

Kenric did not return to the training ground that day. On the morrow he would resume his training. Though he did not say so to Megan, the time grew shorter; he could feel it on the wind. Myrddin would not hold off much longer.

He spent that day showing Megan a Rune he barely remembered. Odd how much of it came back to him; the lush tropical foliage, the fresh scent of rain that seemed always to hover on the air, the wild beasts that knew no fear and so wandered close, lowering their heads willingly to be caressed.

Megan's eyes grew wider with each new and hauntingly lovely place they visited.

"How could you—how could anyone—bear to leave this place?"

Kenric thought of his former home. Despite the bleakness of its name, Blackstone Keep lay in the midst of fertile fields of rolling green. A sparkling stream rushed over rocks as black and shiny as some undiscovered gem. The air contained more of a bite than this, to be true, and the days were more often misty than bright, but to him that place was every bit as beautiful—and more of a home—than this one.

But it was his home no longer, thanks to the evil invaders who had destroyed everything he held dear. He would have to make a new home someplace else. With Megan.

The thought brought him such happiness that the day went quickly. Before he knew it, night had fallen.

The evening meal was eaten in a small room off the dining hall, with only Rhiannon and her grim-faced council of three. Kenric felt edgy, on guard. Worry gnawed at his mind. This battle troubled him because it was not a normal battle. Of his skill as a swordsman, he had no doubt. So far he had yet to meet the man who could best him.

But of late, each time he fought with the sword, he had found himself battling his magic. Always it had threatened to overwhelm him, to turn him into the kind of mindless killing machine some called a berserker. Such a thing would be his worst nightmare.

Thus he had known he would lay down his sword and take up a plow. He would be finished with killing and magic and become a simple farmer, a raiser of crops and of children.

Until this final task had presented itself, this task that would make him learn to use the one thing he feared above all others.

Magic.

Magic. Ethereal as the wind. He could not fight that which he could not see or sense. Yet he must. According to his sister and her solemn council, the fate of the entire world hung in the balance.

All he wanted was to be left alone with Megan. And therein lay another problem. He wanted Megan by his side for the rest of their lives. Yet, by her own admission, she did not belong here. Not in this place nor this time. If her fear was true, if after the battle had been won she would be returned to her own place and time, he would be helpless to fight against it. Fully occupied by the great battle, he most likely would not even realize it until it was too late. Until she was gone.

Gone.

Kenric shook his head. He could not imagine it. Without Megan at his side, it would seem like some giant whirlwind had sucked all the color from the world, leaving it in muted shades of gray.

"I will let nothing take you from me," Kenric swore,

hoping he would be able to keep this vow. "Nothing."

A tiny frown creased her smooth forehead. "How can you stop it?" Fear flashed into her velvety eyes.

"If somehow you are sent back to the time and place from which you came, I will find a way to follow you." He looked deep within her eyes to make certain she understood the seriousness of his vow. "I swear this on my honor."

With a slight smile, she relaxed and squeezed his arm.

"Love is a powerful magic," she reminded him, her voice steady, her beautiful golden brown eyes serene. "We will not be parted."

He kissed her then, unable to help it. "God's teeth, how I need you."

She leaned into his side, moving suggestively. "Tonight." Her voice was a throaty whisper. "You can show me tonight."

Instantly his blood ran hot, as though flames raced through his veins. In the midst of all this, he had somehow forgotten that he could not let himself make love to her. He could not slake this fierce desire. He could hold her, pleasure her with his mouth and his hands, but must forsake his own pleasure.

Torture. He sighed, closing his eyes and battling his desire. It might be torture, but it was necessary.

When the shadows grew long and Megan smiled sweetly up at him, hinting that they should go to her room and retire, he reached for more wine instead.

"That is your fifth glass," she protested, her lovely eyebrows arched. "You will be asleep before we even have time to—"

Gulping the wine in one swallow, Kenric forced a smile. *If only she knew.* Though he attempted to dull his senses with the potent alcohol, the need still burned strong in him. He had only to look at her to want her. Touching her would be impossible.

Again he reached for more wine.

She frowned.

He sighed, conscious of the others watching. Arwydd in particular seemed amused by Kenric's plight.

Leaning close to Megan, he whispered, "I will explain in the privacy of our room."

Megan gave a jerky nod, reaching for the wine carafe herself. He drank two full glasses in rapid succession, the hurt on her heart-shaped face blurring after the second.

It struck him that she thought he didn't want her. If only she knew that he wanted her too much. He faced the greatest test of his willpower: to hold her but not love her with his body.

Again he reached for the wine. This time Rhiannon's hand forestalled him.

"Enough. Both of you."

The room went silent. The entire council watched.

Arwydd cleared his throat. "He will go with her to their sleeping chambers. I have agreed to allow this."

The council erupted, all talking at once.

Kenric waited, finally standing and pounding his fist on the table. "Silence," he roared.

Rhiannon smiled her approval. And Megan—he dared not look at her just yet. How he wished he had told her in private, before this, about his self-imposed celibacy. And all for the very thing he'd once sworn he'd have no part of, the very thing that might save them now: magic.

When he had their full attention, Kenric cleared his throat. To his shock, Megan slid her small hand underneath his, giving him her quiet support. He felt pleasure at her touch, pleasure and a warmth that had once seemed unfamiliar, but which he now recognized as a deep caring. She was a true friend, perhaps the truest he'd ever known.

Keeping his face expressionless, he looked around the table at each one in turn. "I am aware of the limitations of my power."

"It is forbidden," Drystan intoned mournfully.

"I wish to remain with my soul mate." Now he let his gaze touch on Megan, tightening his hand on hers as he saw the love in her amber eyes. "Yet because of the battle to come, I will remain celibate."

He felt rather than saw Megan stiffen beside him.

"How is this possible?" Vychan, the unbeliever, crossed his arms and glared at them.

To Kenric's surprise, Arwydd came to his support. "With a warrior such as he, used to discipline, it will be possible. Difficult, yes, especially since they are soul mates. But Kenric is strong. He knows the magic will leave him if he does not remain celibate."

Touched by the elder Faerie's faith in him, Kenric inclined his head. "It is so."

"The fate of our people—and that of humankind too—rests on this battle," Vychan reminded them. "Do you really want to chance it?"

Lord Brighton, who had been allowed to sit in on this council meeting by virtue of his connection with Edmyg, stood. He addressed the entire room, careful to keep his gaze fixed on Kenric. "There is no need for him to chance anything. I would have the woman. I can keep her well satisfied."

Megan gasped. Beside her, Kenric went still, one hand going to the hilt of his sword. Other men had died for lesser insults than this.

Lord Brighton marked the gesture with a wary smile. "Wait before you run me through; hear me out at least."

Kenric tamped down his fury. "There is nothing to hear. She is mine."

No one spoke. All the Faeries, Rhiannon included, watched to see what Lord Brighton would do.

"I have land," Lord Brighton said, his voice casual. "As you have seen. Miles and miles of fertile, untouched soil."

261

Kenric inclined his head in a stiff nod. "So you do."

"Though you are not her father, nor her guardian, I would give you much land in exchange for her. As a bride price."

Land. Kenric smiled grimly. Once his heart's only desire, the offer no longer tempted him. What good would the land be without Megan to live beside him?

Worthless. He would have land of his own someday, but not like this.

He saw Rhiannon's gaze sharpen. She knew how badly he yearned to build his own keep.

But the truth was that he yearned for Megan more.

Laying his sword hand on the top of Megan's head, Kenric stared at the pompous Lord Brighton. "Megan is not for sale, nor is she unpromised. She is to be my bride."

"What of this Lord Roger you mentioned before? Her betrothed?" The other man's smug tone further infuriated Kenric, but he would not waste his valuable energy punishing one as harmless as this conceited lord. Lord Brighton, though tall and broad, had the soft body of a man of leisure. Kenric doubted he even knew how to defend himself, never mind using a sword.

"Lord Roger is no longer an issue."

"Ah, you have found him then?"

"Megan and I have settled this between us." Kenric held up his hand. "Speak of this no more. Megan is the other half of my soul, and as such we cannot be parted."

Slowly the other man's smile faded. "This cannot be. It is because of her that I was able to escape the spell that kept me trapped in my keep. I love her."

"Nay." Rhiannon stood, making a queenly gesture of dismissal. "You only think that you do. Your own soul-half waits for you, if you will but search for her. You were allowed to escape the spell because you *believed* in love. Not because Megan is your soul-half."

"Fools." With a disgusted growl of protest, Lord Brighton stomped out of the room.

Kenric squeezed Megan's shoulder in a gesture of comfort.

"Thank you," Megan told him, her voice soft, her eyes luminous. "He does not understand about things such as love."

He thought about kissing her then, Lord Brighton and the council be damned, but he had another matter to settle: the issue of him and Megan spending their nights together.

He waited until the room had quieted, then fixed each Faerie assembled there with his gaze.

"We cannot be parted. Even," he said deliberately, knowing they all listened and watched, "at night."

Rhiannon nodded her agreement. Arwydd and Vychan immediately resumed their argument. Again Kenric waited while the talk eddied and flowed in murmurs around him. Through it all, Megan kept her hand firmly in his, though he sensed the questions that she longed to ask.

It was Rhiannon who finally cut to the heart of things. "What choice do we have? They are soul-halves, after all. If my brother wishes to do this, how can we deny him?"

Smiling grimly, Kenric settled a look upon his face that dared any of them to try.

It was Drystan the sorrowful who led them off into an intense discussion on the merits of temptation and how it could strengthen the will.

Kenric watched with amusement as, the original issue forgotten yet again, they clustered around Drystan, arguing fiercely.

Tugging gently on his hand, Megan stood, her ripe lips curving in amusement. "Shall we go?" she murmured.

Though he knew she had not meant the husky suggestion to sound . . . well, *suggestive,* his body still responded instantly. He groaned. It would be a very long night indeed.

Kenric growled his answer and, tugging her along beside him, made his way toward her room.

Chapter Seventeen

Megan had never heard of anything so preposterous. Not make love? What possible difference could that make?

Maybe it was something like the restrictions placed on athletes. She'd heard they had to restrain themselves before a big competition.

But how would anyone know? Eyeing Kenric's broad shoulders and muscular arms, she knew *she* wasn't disciplined enough to lie beside him and not want to love him.

When they reached the door to her room, she preceded him inside. As soon as the door closed, she launched herself into his arms and pulled his head down to give him a deep, satisfying kiss.

As she'd known it would, passion instantly flared between them. She felt the fine shudder go through Kenric, felt too the hard evidence of his desire pressing into her belly. Now he would take her; now he would carry her to the bed and lie beside her and bury himself deep inside her.

She shivered, anticipation and desire making her feverish.

His hands roamed over her, stroking her skin, inflaming her already heightened sensitivity. Though it was she who had begun the kiss, he took over, deepening it, possessing her mouth with a fierceness that thrilled her to the bone.

Melting against him, she molded her breasts against his chest and gave into his passionate demands.

"Nay!" He pushed her away gently, his voice cracking with regret. "We must not."

Stunned, Megan could only gape at him. "You really mean this?"

He frowned, looking every bit the fierce warrior she'd first met—except in his eyes, where she could see the pain warring with a fierce desire equal to the one she felt.

Still he said nothing, merely continuing to gaze at her, his jaw set and his body rigid.

Megan remembered what they had said in the council chambers. "They spoke the truth?" she whispered, still only half believing. "The magic really won't work?"

Kenric nodded, keeping his hands clenched in fists at his side. "Today I could do nothing. I had no power, none at all."

She stared. "You—"

"We made love last night."

"But how do you know for certain?"

"God's blood, woman," he roared, "think you that I want this? I have thought of nothing but my need for you all day. Yet, would you have me cede victory to Myrddin so easily?"

Her own body throbbing, Megan forced a smile. With every ounce of dignity she possessed, she took several deep breaths, willing herself to calmness. If she felt shaky and weak, she was determined not to show it.

Keeping her chin up, she marched over to stand in front of the man she loved. Careful not to touch him, she gazed up at him, hoping he could see her love shining in her eyes. The idea that she could tempt a man such as Kenric gave her an odd feeling of power, one that she would tuck away inside her for now and take out and examine later.

"Maybe they were right, then. You should not sleep here."

He gave her a look of such anguish that she took a step back.

"I cannot bear to be away from you," he admitted, his voice a low rumble.

Her heart swelling, Megan shook her head. Never had she loved him more, this giant warrior who cherished her so well, even if he could not yet bring himself to speak the words.

"I don't want . . ." She hung her head, ashamed to tell him.

One large finger gently lifted her chin. "You don't want what?"

"To be responsible for . . ." She waved her hand in the air. "I'm not sure I can lie in your arms and not want you."

To her stunned amazement he threw back his head and laughed. A wicked glint in his eye, he leaned closer, brushing the tip of her nose with his mouth. "Aye, but nothing was said about your finding your own pleasure. 'Tis only I who must not indulge."

"I cannot . . ." Her words faded as he captured her mouth in another deep, drugging kiss, making her burn. Still exploring her mouth with his tongue, he effortlessly lifted her in his massive arms and carried her to the bed.

She moaned, both aroused and shocked, yet unable to keep from moving her body against him. Part of her wanted to be strong, like him—if he must deny himself such pleasure, then in all fairness, so should she. The other part of her—that wild, wanton, secret part that she hadn't even known existed—urged her to take what bliss he offered in the same unselfish spirit in which he gave it.

Then he loosened her gown in an effortless motion and removed her clothing, exposing her overheated skin to his burning gaze and his clever, clever touch.

Ah, Kenric, her mind cried out, while the hot fire he caused in her blood overrode her silent cry.

When his mouth left hers she made a weak sound of protest, until he captured her nipple and suckled gently. Heat suffused her and, mindless, heedless, she arched against him, no longer conscious of her nakedness and the fact that he was still fully clothed.

As she did, a tormented groan escaped him, and this finally gave her pause. Opening her eyes, she rose up on her elbows and tried to push him away.

He raised his head, his gaze hooded and burning. "Do not," he said in a growl, sounding like a man in pain, "deny us this."

"But . . ." And, unable to help herself, she looked pointedly at his braes, and the awesome bulge of his arousal that swelled there. "You cannot—"

"Hush, my Megan." Bending his head, he touched her lips lightly with his own, effectively silencing her. "I want to pleasure you. I will survive; in fact, this will make me stronger."

Warrior. Lover. Soul-half.

His mouth teased her, searing a path from the curve of her cheek to her throat and shoulder. Again he pleasured her breasts; again she found herself arching to meet him. The stroking of his fingers sent jolts of lightning through her, and she parted her thighs eagerly at his touch.

Aching, on fire, she gave herself up to the sheer delight of his amazing hands, then gasped when she felt the moist heat of his mouth as he kissed her where moments before only his fingers had caressed.

"Kenric!" She gasped, entwining her hands in his thick, dark hair, meaning only to push his head away, but instead holding it in place as he stroked inside of her with his tongue. Oh—that such bliss existed, she had never known, never imagined.

It built like a storm, like lightning and rain and thunder all at once, and she cried out loud from the sheer power of it. Release overcame her, flowing through her, a honeyed river of her essence, to Kenric, where he feasted like a man starving, stopping only when she thought she could take no more.

Limp, exhausted, she wanted him inside her then, wanted to feel the swollen hardness of him fill her, though she knew it was forbidden.

With a crooked grin, Kenric backed away from her, holding up his hand to stave her off when she would have gone to him.

"Not . . . now." His breathing sounded loud and labored, his expression contorted like that of a man in torment. "Give me a moment."

Backing away, he left her then. She felt both satisfied and guilty, complete and frustrated. He did not return until several hours later, climbing stiffly into bed beside her and rolling onto his side while she pretended to sleep.

It was in the dark of the night that it happened. While she watched Kenric sleep, the unwanted knowledge came to her in a blinding flash, the way such things as intuition and brilliant insights often do. She and Kenric *would* make love—at least once before the battle to come. They had to in order to generate the necessary power to ensure that he won the battle. Hadn't the prophecy said that the two soul-halves must join?

And then, once they had joined bodies and spirits, once they had produced the necessary magic, she would no longer be needed here. Somehow she knew her earlier fear was on target, that despite what she or Kenric wanted, she would be returned to her own time after the battle was won.

Either way she was lost. If she didn't make love with Kenric, the power would not be summoned, the prophecy would go unfulfilled, and Rune would be destroyed. However, if she did unite with Kenric, Rune might be saved, but she would be destined to a life without her soul-half. She took comfort in only one thought as she recognized her future: at least she would make love with Kenric one last time—for after the battle she would never do so again.

What a night. His willpower tested to the limits of his endurance, Kenric had not slept much. Though, he thought with a savage grin in the rose-tinted dawn, Megan now slept the deep sleep of the thoroughly exhausted.

He had pleasured her in every way known to man. Just thinking of the musky taste of her, the gentle rain of her desire upon his lips, made him hard and ready. Again. As if he hadn't spent the entire night aroused and throbbing.

But he had spent it with the woman he loved.

Every inch of Megan's delectable body now knew the touch of his mouth, the gentle raking of his teeth. He had explored her and aroused her until she had arched her back and begged him to enter her. He had wanted to bury himself in her more than he had ever wanted anything in his life.

From somewhere, somehow, he had found the strength of will to refuse, bringing her to ecstasy instead with his mouth and his hands.

For himself he took nothing, other than the pleasure of knowing he had satisfied his woman.

And now, with the dawn creeping silently up on the horizon, the sexual frustration inside him made him want to take his sword and battle someone. Anyone. Anything to rid himself of the raging fire that burned inside him.

Arwydd would be pleased. The magic would explode from him like lightning this morn. He could only imagine what he would be like after a week or two of this.

Myrddin had better watch his back. He would be no match for Kenric once this time of training was finished.

Arwydd was already waiting for him. His hands folded serenely in front of him, the wizened Faerie smiled gently. "You survived?"

"I did," Kenric said grimly. "And now we'd best begin."

A week flew by. Kenric was so exhausted by the intensive training that, more often than not, he dropped into sleep as soon as he climbed into bed.

There was no repeat of the night when he'd pleasured her in so many ways, taking nothing for himself. She told herself she did not really want one; it wasn't fair to Kenric, after all.

It didn't help that every night, before he fell asleep, he gathered her close in his muscular arms and held her. Never had she felt so cherished. And never had she felt so sexually frustrated. She wanted him so badly it hurt. She lay awake for hours, listening to his deep, even breathing, inhaling the spicy, masculine scent of him, and aching.

Yet once they gave in to the nearly uncontrollable passion that simmered between them, their time together would be over. This moment was both her worst fear and her greatest desire.

This morn, she'd seen Kenric off with a forced smile. He'd been gruff himself, taut and full of a restless energy that she could certainly relate to.

All around them, things returned to normal. Lord Brighton, finally accepting that Megan would never be his, left Rune to return to the mortal world and search for his own soul mate. Megan was glad. After all, she had enough to worry about without adding one more concern.

As though her thoughts of him had called him, Kenric burst through the door. Barely inside, he stopped, his legs spread apart in a warrior's stance, his eyes hard and full of sorrow.

Immediately she rushed to his side. "What has happened?"

He stepped back. "Do not touch me, my love." He issued the warning in a low voice, vibrating with emotion. "It has been decided I am ready."

She stared blankly up at him. "Ready?" Her heart began to pound. "But it has been only one week. They said you needed—"

"I am ready." His tone was so bleak, she trembled.

"When?" she asked simply, because there was nothing left to say.

Kenric lifted one shoulder in an attempt at a casual shrug. The very air seemed to resonate with stirrings of some primal power.

"Soon. Even now they release the spell that kept us hidden from Myrddin's scrying. Because of this, I will stay apart from you this one night. Then together we will seek out Myrddin and finish it. We leave Rune in the morning." With those words and one last look of desperate longing, he turned to go.

"Wait." Her heart heavy, Megan knew it was time for her to play her part. "You must stay with me this night."

One dark brow rose as he waited to hear her explanation.

She licked her lips, trying to summon up the right words.

"The prophecy says we must join for the magic to be made. Tonight you and I must make love to ensure you will be victorious in the battle."

After a moment of stunned silence, he shook his

shaggy head, chuckling. "Ah, my Megan. If only you knew how many times I have told myself such things to be able to join with you. But we have already loved, already made the power. It hums in me, resonates in me, all because we have found each other."

"But—"

"Nay." He fixed her with a look so intense, her heart skipped a beat. "When it is over, and I have bested Myrddin, I will love you all through the night. Until then I must jealously guard my power, and not let the sweet temptation of you sway me. This is why we will spend this night apart, lest the days of abstinence become too much for me."

With these words, he left her, exiting the small room as violently as he had entered.

Megan moved to a chair on legs that would no longer support her. She'd been allowed a respite. More time with Kenric, more time with her love.

What he said made sense. Could she be wrong? If she was, and they did not have to make love again for the power to blossom, then maybe her feeling that she would be sent back to Dallas in 2001 was wrong also. Maybe Kenric was right. Maybe she had nothing to fear but the battle itself.

The battle . . . *Kenric could be killed.* The thought stunned her. She'd never really allowed herself to think about the coming conflict, though it was akin to an apocalypse, to hear Rhiannon and the rest tell of it. A battle like none she'd ever heard of before.

When she thought of war, she imagined tanks and armies, and bombs dropping from stealthy jets. However, fighting in medieval times would mean men on horses, swords and arrows, personal, hand-to-hand combat.

Yet this struggle between Kenric and Myrddin would be none of those things.

Instead it would be a clash of magic. She shivered, haunted by the thought of Kenric in danger. She would make sure she stayed by his side at all times. Though she wasn't sure how, somehow she knew that her love would help him.

Love *was* after all, the most powerful magic.

The moment of truth was upon them; the battle would be soon. Kenric didn't know where it would take place or how it would begin, but the instant they rode through the veil that shielded Rune from the mortal world, he could sense it on the air, hear it in the wind.

The day was dark, the roiling clouds that scudded across the sky an ominous portent. Thunder boomed in the distance, and jagged strikes of lightning followed no pattern. Evil poisoned the air. Kenric's every nerve felt raw, exposed.

He rode Lancelot at a steady pace, waiting for Myrddin to find him. Place would not matter, not in the realm where they would fight, though Kenric would feel stronger if he could ride to the land that had once belonged to his human family, the land near his cave. He didn't know if he would make it—as he rode he sensed Myrddin's essence, seeking him.

Riding behind him in the saddle, Megan held her silence. Occasionally he heard her utter a faint sound of distress, telling him that she too felt the evil that tainted the air.

If Kenric felt fear at all, it was fear for her. Myrddin could not be allowed to win.

To his right rode Edmyg and Rhiannon. His sister had taken human form for this journey. When Edmyg had insisted on coming with him, claiming he had an old score to settle with Myrddin, Rhiannon had refused to leave his side. Kenric did not know if the human mage would be a help or a hindrance, but with Rhiannon's quiet insistence, he had no choice but to allow Edmyg to accompany him.

Now he had one last thing to do before the confrontation. Kenric reined his warhorse in, motioning Edmyg and Rhiannon on. Turning in the saddle to face Megan, Kenric waited until the others had ridden off before speaking.

"My soul mate, I don't have much to offer," he began, "though someday I promise I will give you the world. I intend to buy land with the coin I have, to build a keep, and to raise a family there. Our family." He cleared his throat, his heart pounding in his ears. "If you will have me."

Never had a silence seemed so long. He chanced a look at Megan. In this moment he was not a fearless warrior, but merely a man—her soul mate—who needed her more than he had ever needed anything, past or present.

She gazed at him in wonderment, her magnificent eyes full of joy—and sorrow.

"You are everything I want," she told him softly, her voice shaking, her expression fierce, as tears began to stream down her cheeks. "Everything."

From somewhere in his tunic, he found the ring. Not the token she had given him as payment—nay. This was an ancient ring, a ring of binding. Rhiannon had given it to him the night before.

Shimmering in his palm, it was a simple thing, a circle of moon-silver and thousands of tiny crystal beads, star tears. His heart in his throat, he took her hand and slipped it on her slender finger.

"Metals such as gold are not used in Rune," he apologized, praying she would accept this gift. Though he found it beautiful, surely it was a poor substitute to a woman used to gold and gems.

"Though not as ornate as the ring you once wore, this is the traditional betrothal ring of Rune—a symbol of my need for you. Will you—" His voice broke and all he could do was stare in hopeless wonder as she took his hand in hers, gripping tightly.

"It is beautiful—magical." Megan shook her head,

holding her hand aloft and watching with enchanted fascination the arc of sparkling colors. "Too beautiful, my love. A ring made of twigs would be fine," she murmured, "as long as it binds me to you."

Tears continued to run, unchecked, down her smooth cheeks.

Though Kenric knew they were tears of happiness, they touched him, making his own eyes feel suspiciously full. He cleared his throat.

"You are mine," he told her, sealing the vow with a kiss. "From now until the end of time."

She nodded, echoing his words. "From now until the end of time."

He wondered why she sounded so sad.

Without any urging, Lancelot picked up the pace. His warhorse, Kenric thought with a wry smile, who now had a name. It had taken Megan and her unwavering love to show him that detachment wasn't living. Lancelot was important to him, had always been, nameless or not, and the fondness Kenric felt for the strong-hearted animal deserved to be shown.

As he demonstrated his love for his Faerie kin by fighting this battle.

Fat drops of icy rain began to pelt them. Kenric covered Megan with his cloak as she huddled against him. The wind howled, driving the hail into their skin like daggers. His head down, Lancelot plunged doggedly forward.

So it had begun. From afar, Myrddin sought to torment them. With a casual gesture, Kenric created a shield around them. They were instantly dry. Rhiannon did the same for herself and Edmyg. A simple matter of magic, this. It would take more than bad weather to win this battle.

As if Myrddin could see their easy resistance of his first challenge, the wind calmed and the rain stopped. The trees, no longer bowed by the onslaught, stood straight and tall. Not even the faintest breeze stirred their leaves. Though the sky remained the color of slate, the clouds held their places, no longer racing across the horizon. To all outward appearances, it looked peaceful, yet somehow it seemed more ominous. A feeling of dread, of watching and waiting, hung over the landscape like fog.

Still, Kenric did not relax the shield. He would keep it until they reached the battle place of his choosing, a full day's ride from here.

"Does he come?" Megan asked in a low voice as she rested her head on his back and sighed. She sounded weary, though he knew she would never admit it.

"Soon." He would tell her later of the fierce pride he felt for her. Even knowing what they faced, she showed no fear. Instead she rode at his back, her love and trust evident in her every gesture, from her smile to the way she held her head high.

He had never known a woman like her; few men, either, who could match her for valor and integrity. There was no one he would rather have at his side than Megan, his soul-half. Rhiannon, queen of all Faeries, ran a close second.

Edmyg's horse, a beast nearly as large as Lancelot, kept pace with them. Kenric found it surprising that the mage, who had once seemed so elderly and frail, owned such an animal. Though it was no more surprising than the muscular warrior's body Edmyg now wore. The spell that had made him old and weak had been a strong one, and, though Edmyg had never said it, Kenric knew it was one of Myrddin's. Perhaps that was why the mage insisted on riding with them.

"The time grows near," Rhiannon warned.

Kenric glanced at her, searching for signs of fear in his sister's lovely face. If she felt anything, she hid it well. Her violet-eyed gaze seemed serene, her expression calm and peaceful.

Without even an increase in the wind to warn them,

the day turned to night. Utter blackness settled upon them like a shroud. There was no moon, no stars, nothing to light their way.

"Halt," Kenric ordered, reining Lancelot to an immediate stop. "If we go forward now, we could ride over the edge of a cliff and not know it."

"There are no cliffs in this part of the country," Edmyg scoffed. "If we stay here, we wait like lambs to be led to the slaughter."

For Megan's benefit Kenric forced a laugh, though it was a dry and humorless sound. "There may be no cliffs now, my friend. But who's to say Myrddin would not create them?"

"This is not what I expected," Megan said, her voice low with what sounded like suppressed fury. "This Myrddin fights like a coward, with thunder and lightning and darkness. Is he afraid to face us like a man? Is he so afraid that we will best him that he will try to make us stumble around in the dark?"

After a moment of stunned silence, Kenric chuckled. Ah, his brave soul-half. In her anger she sounded like a female warrior, like one of those Amazons of legend. About to tell her that Myrddin would use whatever means he had at his disposal, underhanded or not, he held his tongue as the darkness instantly lifted.

"Myrddin has heard you." Satisfaction colored Rhiannon's tone. "He does not like being named a coward."

"He will try to avenge this insult." Edmyg sounded worried. "We shall have to guard Megan, and guard her well."

"I had intended on it." Now that he could see, Kenric urged Lancelot on again, this time at a controlled gallop. Though Megan had but spoken truth, he wished she had not singled herself out to the evil mage. Now Myrddin would have two reasons to try to hurt her—the other being the knowledge that Kenric would die for her. This insight gave their enemy a slight advantage that Kenric did not care to contemplate.

Edmyg spurred his own horse until it drew apace.

"You will have to strike fast." Rhiannon glanced at Megan and smiled. "Do not give Myrddin any opportunity to touch her."

With a nod, Kenric tightened his shield. He now felt a double urgency driving him to reach Blackstone Keep. He only hoped they would have time before Myrddin truly attacked.

As it turned out, they nearly made it. Kenric didn't know whether Myrddin was licking his wounds or gathering his power, but by midafternoon on the second day they drew near to the jutting boulders and rocky landmarks that surrounded his cave.

Megan, recognizing them, grew restless. She shifted and squirmed so much that Lancelot faltered in his stride.

"What is wrong?" Kenric spoke low, knowing she would not confide in him if the others could hear.

"This place—" Her voice broke. For the first time she showed fear, though not of the battle to come. "This place is where I woke up, after the lightning struck me and brought me through time. What if—"

He would not let her speak it. Words had their own power, something few people knew. "You will be safe with me," he told her firmly. "I will let nothing happen to you."

Her gaze slowly locked on his, and she nodded. "I trust you," she told him, her voice a husky murmur.

His heart swelled at the honor she so casually gave him. But then he remembered his human family and how they had perished at the swords of his own kind. They too had trusted him to protect them, to help keep Blackstone Keep safe. He had failed them then.

But he would not fail Megan.

Straightening, Kenric pushed away his doubts. Desire for this woman raged through his blood, mingling with the ever-present simmer of the power he now knew he could command.

Impatient for the battle to begin so that he might finish it, he reined Lancelot to a halt near the hidden entrance to the cave.

"This is a place of great power." Dismounting, he held out his hand and helped Megan down, letting her body slide down the length of his so there could be no doubt in her mind how badly he wanted her. Still. Even with the tremendous task ahead of him, he yearned to take her into the cave—*their* cave—and make fierce, passionate love to her.

"I would have first blow," Edmyg declared, his face hard.

Immediately Kenric shook his head. "This is my battle."

"No." Edmyg pulled Rhiannon close. "The legend says *half-human, half-Faerie*. That is what Rhiannon and I are, each of us making the half to complete the whole."

Rhiannon immediately nodded. "There are many ways to interpret the legend. Myrddin believes it is he who defends his right. Edmyg believes it is two individuals, separate yet one. Soul-halves. Like you and Megan."

His eyes narrow, Kenric thought on Edmyg's words. Could this be possible? Mayhap this was not his battle at all, but his sister's. All that training . . . But he would not take the chance that they were wrong.

"We will all fight then. Together."

Megan made a small sound, whether in protest or agreement he could not tell. It happened then, just as Kenric let go of his lady, just as Edmyg released Rhiannon from his embrace. A noise filled the air, sharp and shrill, like a thousand hawks screeching as they sighted the kill. Megan clapped her hands to her ears, her face contorted in pain.

"He comes." Rhiannon had to shout to be heard over the din.

It grew dark, then light, then dark again. The very air they breathed seemed heavy and dank, pressing at them as if to crush them into powder.

Chapter Eighteen

Then Myrddin stood in front of them, his darkly handsome face contorted with hatred. Kenric could feel the evil emanating from him, great waves of it so strong that he staggered back a step.

The noise grew louder, bringing back the wind and the turbulent skies. Edmyg, his own face contorted with rage, rushed at Myrddin, but before he got within a spear's distance he was repelled with such force that it tossed him across the clearing, into the rocks near the cave. Rhiannon rushed to him, drawing Myrddin's glare.

"She and her kingdom belong to me." The guttural words sounded unnaturally loud in the din of the storm. "All of it—Rune, the earth, the prophecy, truly belongs to me."

Startled, Kenric saw how the wizard's dead eyes filled with such pain that it made him appear human. But the emotion was fleeting; it flashed into Myrddin's gaze, then vanished, replaced once again by the flat, dead eyes of a man who had nothing to lose.

As Kenric himself had once been. Before Megan.

Had Myrddin loved his sister that much? If so, it had not been mutual. Her loving attention to the fallen Edmyg attested to that fact.

"This is between us," Kenric yelled, drawing Myrddin's ire. "We are both the same, of two worlds—human and Faerie."

Myrddin jerked his head in a nod, showing he understood and agreed. "Aye, it is between us. Prepare to die as your human family died, Kenric of Blackstone."

By those words Kenric knew for certain that it had been Myrddin who had led the assault against Blackstone Keep. He fought to keep his rage from consuming him—to do so would be foolhardy, with so much else at stake.

Prepare to die. Myrddin had said as much to him before, when they'd met by chance in the marshes. Even then, untrained and weary, Kenric had been able to turn away his magical ire.

"I do not understand," Kenric shouted, as the unholy noise shrieked and eddied around them. "What have I ever done to you that you bear me such ill will?"

With a narrowing of eyes, Myrddin laughed. His laugh was a horrible thing, both bitter and full of an agony that Kenric doubted the other man even knew he exhibited. "You have stolen my birthright, my place in the annals of time. It is I who fulfill the prophecy, I who should take Rhiannon to wife as my soul-half, I who should be worshiped as a savior by the people of Rune."

In a flash Rhiannon stood beside Kenric, a shaken but determined Edmyg standing tall and straight by her side. She opened her mouth to speak and the air became still and silent, so that all might hear her ice-toned words.

"You are both wrong and right, Myrddin. I am not your soul-half—how can I be when Edmyg is mine? And you

283

are mentioned in the prophecy, though not as the savoir, but as the evil that must be defended against. Look deep within your heart, if you still have such a thing beating within your chest, and you will find the truth of these words that I speak."

With one arched brow, Myrddin aimed a look at Rhiannon that promised retribution. He lifted his hand, gesturing so rapidly that his movements were a blur.

Edmyg staggered, doubling over. The wind howled, echoing his cries of anguish.

Rhiannon made no sound, simply stepping forward and taking Edmyg's hand. With a softly chanted spell of her own, she vanquished Myrddin's. Edmyg immediately straightened and drew his sword.

A look of baffled rage came over Myrddin. "Do you think that I will not hurt you, Rhiannon, Queen of Rune?" He made the simple title sound like an insult. "I will rule without you, and not just Rune, but the entire world. After all, who better? I am of both places, Faerie and mortal. So tell me, how is it that you truly believe I will let you go unharmed?"

Still Rhiannon said nothing to him. Still chanting, she held fast to Edmyg's hand and watched and waited.

Love is the most powerful magic. Remembering the truth of these words, Kenric held out his hand. With a shaky smile, Megan took it, her devotion shining bright and true from her amber eyes. With his other hand, Kenric took Rhiannon's, and Megan took Edmyg's, linking all four of them together with the bonds of love.

"I will have retribution!" One with the awful keening of the wind, Myrddin howled. "Victory as well. This I swear."

Kenric tensed. "You forswear then. I will not allow it to be so." He inclined his head, the impact of the invisible blow sending Myrddin staggering back.

Myrddin let out a cry of rage and pain. Straightening,

he lifted his hands, both simultaneously. Twin bolts of jagged white lightning flashed at them.

Without a single movement, Kenric deflected it. As the love, contentment, and joy of their linkage flowed through him, filling him with raw power, he knew awe. Never had his magic been so strong, so powerful as it was now.

Myrddin issued another challenge, growling words so tangled up with furious emotion that they were unintelligible. Flinging spells at them in rapid succession, spells so full of darkness and evil that they fouled the very air, he howled curses as each and every one of them bounced harmlessly away, deflected from the shield of compassion surrounding Kenric, Megan, Rhiannon, and Edmyg.

They seemed as one entity, joined in love. As such, they could not, would not kill unless it became absolutely necessary.

Slowly, with an infinite patience that came from somewhere outside himself, Kenric opened a tiny chink in the armor their joined love created. He sent love, patience, and kindness at Myrddin, small waves of it at first, then gradually increasing in strength until the light it created was blinding.

Resisting it, Myrddin continued to fight, his visage dark and unforgiving. His aura, black and unwholesome, swallowed Kenric's attempt to make him see, feel, and understand, turning the love into something unholy.

Kenric saw and mourned. And still, the mighty strength of love flowed through his every pore.

But Myrddin would have none of it. Darkness clashed with light as the powers of love and good warred with hatred and evil. Above them the sky mirrored the struggle below, dark clouds roiling furiously against the pure cobalt blue of a perfect sky.

The power increased, solidified. Exultation flowed through Kenric/Megan/Rhiannon/Edmyg.

A crack appeared in the earth, a jagged fissure that

snaked between Myrddin and them. With a cry of triumph, Myrddin moved toward it. From it, indeed from the bowels of the earth below, came an unearthly wailing, a stirring of beings so evil that their names must never be spoken out loud.

"He summons help," Rhiannon cried. "We must be strong."

Pure blackness seemed to envelop Myrddin—an inky darkness that flowed from the bowels of the earth. The chants and moans and cries of the voices below grew louder, more certain.

And Myrddin began to change.

Kenric had heard of such evil—dark fairy tales, mere stories meant to frighten children into behaving. But never, even in his training with the Faeries, would he have believed the beast that Myrddin became.

Twisted and misshapen, Myrddin moved in some sort of jagged dance. Steam poured from the cracked earth, reeking with the stench of refuse better left alone. No longer appearing even remotely human, Myrddin embodied the very emotions that he would not release. If bitterness and hatred, evil and rancor could take shape, so Myrddin's visage and body transformed to give them that vessel.

Then Kenric knew he had no choice—knew they all had no choice. Myrddin—or the thing that Myrddin had become—would have to die.

"You're no longer alone," Megan told him, whether out loud or inside his head he could not tell.

"We are here, all of us," Rhiannon/Edmyg confirmed.

Though he didn't want to—indeed, every fiber of his being fought against it—Kenric fused their energies into a sword of light, even as the evil thing that Myrddin had become loomed over them.

Still, he hesitated.

"Now," Rhiannon/Edmyg/Megan urged.

But the minute hesitation was enough for the evil

forces to attack. Kenric/Megan/Rhiannon/Edmyg felt the force of it course through them, soiling them on contact.

"Now." And Kenric, no longer doubting, sent the sword of light into Myrddin, striking him down with one blow.

The power it took was enormous. As Myrddin fell with an inhuman howl of fury, the black bowels of the earth yawned open even wider to receive him.

Kenric/Megan/Rhiannon/Edmyg were knocked back. A loud groaning filled the air as the earth began to close again.

Everything changed in that instant.

The earth moved together with a loud clap and a shudder. The clouds fled before the blue sky; the sun peeked over the horizon and then rose in a glorious blaze of gold and orange. The foul stench vanished, replaced by the heady scent of wildflowers and green grass.

Once more the birds began to sing.

Unutterably weary, Kenric climbed to his feet. Next to him, Rhiannon and Edmyg did the same. He turned to his right, to help Megan up, to pull her close for a well-deserved embrace.

Something should have warned him, even if at first he believed the awful emptiness he felt inside came only from the destruction of another human being. But the horrible truth dawned on him as he searched right, then left, behind him and in front. Disbelieving, he sank to his knees, his head tilted back in a silent howl of anguish.

Megan—his soul mate—was gone. And this time he could not sense her anywhere.

One moment she had been standing at Kenric's side, her hand linked with his, her heart as well. The next, she knew only blackness, then woke to a sound she had nearly forgotten—the low-pitched sound of electricity humming. Opening her eyes, she saw that she lay in a hospital bed, hooked to numerous machines, an IV in her arm. The air reeked of antiseptic, the smell of hospital and illness. A riot of flowers of every color lined the windowsill and shelf. The elaborate arrangements seemed lacking somehow; none of them looked as vibrant as the flowers had in Rune.

Rune. Kenric. Had it been a dream? She glanced at her finger. The silver ring of crystalline beads seemed to shimmer and glow. Her betrothal ring, Kenric's ring. She sighed with relief. *Fine.* Now all she had to do was wait. Rhiannon had brought her to him once. Surely she could do so again.

But when Megan had asked her, Rhiannon had said she couldn't send her home. What if Megan's traveling through time had been a fluke, a onetime spell whose effectiveness had faded?

Panic coursed through her. She had to get out of this bed. Now. Surely there was something she could do to get back to Kenric, some way she could help ignite the magic that would send her there.

At her sudden movement, one of the monitors hooked to her began beeping a frantic warning. A nurse came running into the room, skidding to a stop when she saw Megan sitting up.

"Oh, my." The plump, fortyish woman put a hand to her chest. "Let me call the doctor."

"I don't want a doctor." Megan knew she sounded peevish, but didn't care. "I want my clothes. I need to go home." She needed to go home, all right—home to Rune and to Kenric.

The monitor quieted of its own accord. After checking it, and several others, the nurse nodded. "You wait right there. I need to call the doctor. He left explicit instructions that he was to be notified if there was any change."

She shook a finger at Megan, clucking. "You're a very lucky young lady. It's not every day that someone comes out of a coma, you know."

A coma. Megan's heart began to pound double time.

Only by touching the crystal beaded ring, turning it on her finger, was she able to keep calm.

"How—" Licking lips gone suddenly dry, Megan cleared her throat. "How long was I in a coma?"

The nurse looked pleased by the question, as though by asking it Megan demonstrated that she was in full possession of her faculties.

"Nearly a week."

Megan frowned. A week. She'd been back in the past much longer than that, close to two months, maybe even longer because of the time she'd spent in the land of Faerie. The seasons had even changed. And Kenric had told her time passed differently in Rune.

She swallowed. "What happened?"

The nurse smiled then, a kindly smile that made Megan want, irrationally, to cry. "Don't you remember? You were hit by lightning. You were barely alive when they brought you in. Now lie quietly while I go page the doctor and your fiancé."

Fiancé. Roger. Dear God. She'd forgotten about Roger. She'd been about to hand him back his ring, the huge diamond that she'd used to gain Kenric's help initially. What had Kenric done with it? She'd never seen it again after she'd given it to him as a token of good faith. She knew Roger would insist she return it to him.

And now she wore another's ring. The tiny crystals reflected the artificial light, shimmering with a glow that seemed so magical it made her heart ache. The ring of her soul mate, her soul-half. Kenric, the only man she would ever love, in any place or time.

Urgency seized her. She had to do something, get away from this place. She didn't want to see Roger or a doctor. She only wanted Kenric and Rhiannon and Edmyg. She wanted Lancelot, to pet his shaggy neck. She wanted to go . . . home.

Tears ran down her cheeks. With a muffled cry, she swung her legs over the side of the hospital bed. Dizziness hit her the instant she did, and she had to hold on to the edge of the rail until her head cleared.

Only it didn't. Every time she moved, the room moved with her. With a groan, Megan gave up. She lay back down, fighting the nausea that came with the vertigo. For now she had no choice but to rest, gather her strength, and pray.

Roger arrived within thirty minutes of her awakening. In his arms he carried a hugely elaborate bouquet of blood-red roses. Shoving aside the other arrangements, he placed his in a conspicuous place on the windowsill. Once he had finished setting this up to his satisfaction, he dusted his hands off and turned to face her.

Megan considered pretending sleep. But no, she needed to finish this so she could go to Kenric with a clear conscience.

Once she had found Roger terrifying. Now, after all she'd been through since being hit by the lightning, she felt nothing. Not even fear.

She attempted a weak smile. Staring, Roger did not smile back. Something about his pinched expression and narrowed eyes. . . . Megan stifled a gasp. He looked like Myrddin, though Roger wore a thousand-dollar suit instead of Myrddin's dark robes.

And, as Myrddin had been before the final battle, Roger looked furious. Why, she had no idea.

"Hello," she said softly.

Casually, Roger glanced around to make sure no one watched. Capturing her hand, he squeezed it so hard tears came to her eyes. "I've been worried about you," he told her, though the hard glint of his gaze belied his words. "At one point they thought you might die."

Megan nodded, unsure how to answer. More than anything she wanted to tug her hand free, but she knew that if she did he would find some other inconspicuous way to hurt her. Roger, she had come to learn, delighted in tormenting creatures weaker than he.

"Well, I didn't." Her attempt at pulling off a cheery response fell flat.

Increasing the pressure, Roger leaned closer. "I checked with your attorney. He said you never went in to have him redo your will."

Closing her eyes, Megan tried to breathe slowly. She knew better than to exhibit fear or rebellion. Her only hope of getting through this without him hurting her worse was to somehow remain calm and focused.

"I didn't have time." It was a lie, but she didn't want to tell Roger she had no intention of changing her will. Not now, not ever. Her original will left everything to charity, to shelters for abused and battered women. She meant to keep it that way.

"You will make time." Increasing the pressure on her hand, Roger watched with satisfaction gleaming in his eyes as she bit her lip to keep from crying out.

"Let go of me."

Surprise flickered across his face. Then he laughed, a low, chilling sound that made her want to flinch.

"Certainly." With one final hard squeeze, he released her. Moving back from the bed, he glanced at his watch and smiled.

"After they called to tell me you were awake, I asked your attorney to come by here and meet with you. He should be here within the hour."

Megan pushed herself back, using her elbows to sit up. She ignored her throbbing hand, telling herself that he couldn't seriously harm her in here. There were too many machines monitoring her condition, too many nurses at the station outside her room.

"You've wasted your time. I won't be changing my will."

Roger's gaze narrowed. If he'd had a sword in his

hand, Megan had no doubt that he'd have lopped off her head with it.

Then his handsome face smoothed. "Obviously they have you on some strong medication. I'd better ask the nurses to discontinue it before your attorney arrives."

"Don't bother." Megan thought of facing down Myrddin and felt a surge of boldness. Still, she kept her voice even and reasonable. "I won't be marrying you, Roger. I'm sorry, but I need to break off our engagement."

She thought she saw a surge of panic flicker across his expression. Then it was gone, replaced with the arrogant determination that Roger used when engineering a hostile takeover.

"You will marry me." His tone told her he believed she would have no choice. Again he glanced around, then leaned close. "You belong to me," he said in a hiss, his cold gaze traveling over her, pausing when he reached her hand.

Cursing, he grabbed her hand again, staring at her ring finger with an expression of furious disbelief.

"What the hell is this?" He yanked at Kenric's ring, attempting to take it off. "What have you done with the diamond I gave you?"

Megan curled her hand into a fist and yanked it away from him. She didn't even like Roger to touch Kenric's ring.

The truth, she told herself. She would tell Roger the truth.

"I've met someone else." Swallowing, she heard her pride in the simple phrase. "I'm going to marry him."

His mouth twisted, he raised his hand then, a reaction that came naturally to him. Her reaction was equally instinctive: she flinched, anticipating the blow.

But they were in a hospital, with monitors and nurses and people who would see. Roger was a public person, well known in the upper echelon of Dallas's movers and shakers. And she had never dared to defy him so boldly before.

Forcing a smile, he lowered his hand, the glare he shot her telling her that he would extract his retribution later, when they were alone. Another reason, Megan thought with a shiver, that she'd make certain she was never alone with him again.

"You don't sound like yourself." Though his eyes were hard, he spoke in a soothing tone that she knew he meant to sound conciliatory. Instead he sounded patronizing. "I know you don't really mean that."

"But I do." She closed her eyes, no longer afraid of him, no longer worried about hurting him either. She'd seen everything she needed to in the expression on his face when she'd told him the news. Roger didn't love her. No, he loved her money, the money he could use to boost his company's assets. He loved controlling her, cowing her with fear and threats of retribution. She suspected he also loved inflicting pain, that he was one of those men who secretly enjoyed hurting others, who'd pulled the wings off flies as a child and tormented small, helpless animals.

"Well." Roger stood. "I'd better be going. I think they must have you on some heavy-duty drugs. You don't sound like the Megan I know. Maybe I'll check in with you later, see if you've regained your senses yet."

Patting her shoulder, he turned to leave. His carefully jovial tone rang false to her ears. From past experience she knew he hadn't given up. To the contrary, now he would go and plan a strategy, one that he carefully designed to make certain he was a winner. As usual. So many things had come easily to him. No doubt he expected to obtain her capitulation with relative ease as well.

"Don't bother," she told him, enjoying the surprise she saw in his expression. She didn't sound like the Megan he knew because she wasn't. Before she'd gone to Rune, she'd been a frightened, terrified girl, taking months to summon the courage to leave an abusive relationship. Now she'd become a woman, bold and confident in Kenric's love. Roger would find she wasn't so easy to intimidate now.

Without another word, he spun on his heel and left.

Megan sighed, relief flooding her. She'd made it over one hurdle. Though she knew he would be back, in good conscience she had told him the truth and broken things off.

Weariness overcame her. She fought sleep, knowing she had to concentrate on matters of real importance, like figuring how to get out of here and back to Kenric.

"This has happened once before." Pacing, feeling like a caged lion in the too-small confines of Rhiannon's council chamber, Kenric continued talking. His words were more to reassure himself than the others. He had to find Megan. The alternative was unthinkable.

"The last time I met Myrddin on the road. Before I knew how to control my power. Before—" His voice cracked, broke. Taking a deep breath, Kenric straightened his shoulders and continued. "Before I believed Megan came from the future."

"That was when you found her in Lord Brighton's keep?" Edmyg, calm and serious, sat at Rhiannon's right hand.

Kenric knew a flash of irrational fury. Of course Edmyg could sound composed. He had not lost his soul-half.

Immediately ashamed, Kenric bit back the angry retort he'd been about to make. Instead he nodded. "Yes." He held up a hand, anticipating the next question. After all, they'd been over this ground once before, to no avail.

"You claim you don't know how you found her." Arwydd, the sage teacher spoke. Of all the beings present in this room, man or Faerie, Kenric believed Arwydd would be the greatest help.

"No." Stopping long enough to answer the question, Kenric fought back panic. *Panic.* From him, one of the fiercest warriors in England or Wales. He resumed his pacing, knowing it was probably driving the others crazy, but not caring. Right now, it was the only thing keeping him sane.

"Do you think Lord Brighton has her?" Edmyg continued to use his soothing voice in much the same manner as one trying to tame a savage beast. "After all, he did offer for her."

"And was turned down," Kenric replied with a snarl. "Lord Brighton would not dare. He knows the repercussions should he attempt such a foolish thing."

"Then where is she?" Arwydd scratched his head.

Rhiannon stood, bringing them all to silence with one regal wave of her hand. Kenric stopped moving to give her his full attention; she'd not spoken since they had entered the room.

She looked only at Kenric when she delivered her opinion. "I believe she has been returned to her own time."

His heart sank. He had not wanted to think of it, not wanted to even consider the possibility that . . . Ah, but there it was. He did not sense her here; no trace of her essence lingered to show him where to follow.

She was not here. Not in this place, not in this time, not within his reach.

Stifling a growl of frustration, he barely kept from showing his rage. If she had gone forward in time, then he would follow. Immediately.

He didn't realize he had spoken out loud until Arwydd shrugged, his expression carefully blank.

It could be done. There had to be a way. And he, Kenric of Blackstone, would find it.

Relaxing, Kenric forced himself to look upon his options dispassionately. It was all a matter of learning how. This he could do. After all, he'd learned how to fight and vanquish Myrddin.

The others, taking his silence as permission to go, began filing out the door. As the council chamber emptied, Kenric focused his thoughts inward. He searched methodically through the magical knowledge he had learned for something, anything, that might help him find the answer he sought. But he came up empty. Inside he felt empty too, hollow and yearning for Megan.

When all had left except Arwydd, Rhiannon placed a small, elaborately carved wooden box on the table.

"What is this?"

She motioned for him to touch it. Kenric did, feeling ancient magic in its smooth curves and polished surface.

"This comes from the Hall of Legend."

Not comprehending, Kenric continued to run his fingers over the wood, wondering if the warmth emanating from it was real or imagined.

Arwydd stepped forward, his expression reverent. "It is older than anything in this palace. Since time began it has been bequeathed from Faerie queen to Faerie queen."

Kenric frowned. "But Faeries live . . . forever."

Sadly Rhiannon shook her head. "It may seem like that, to a human with their short life span. But you my brother, know better than that. Our mother's passing is why I have had to assume the heavy mantle of queen all these years."

After a moment of respectful silence, Arwydd cleared his throat. "The box," he reminded them.

Once again Kenric smoothed the sleek wood. "How does it open?"

Rhiannon shook her head. "I do not know. Some time ago, a dream led me to the Hall of Legend. The entrance was not barred to me as it usually is. I found the box inside. It was already open, as if it waited for me. When

I touched it, I knew the time had come to use what I found inside."

Curious, Kenric searched for a latch or some hidden mechanism that would release the lid. By accident or by design, he must have found it, for it popped open.

It was empty, save for a scroll of yellowed parchment bound by a faded ribbon that might long ago have been blue, and a scrap of paper, curled with age.

Kenric read the scrap first. "The scroll herein contains a powerful spell. It may be used only once, in the hour of greatest need—when half-human, half-Faerie become a whole, and the power of love is called upon to vanquish darkness."

"Yes." Rhiannon nodded, her voice a shaky whisper. "And so I used it to bring Megan to us."

The words she did not say echoed in the chamber.

It may be used only once.

Megan. Even her name had his throat aching with longing. "How did you know?"

Rhiannon and Arwydd glanced at each other, both of them appearing uncomfortable.

"A vision," Rhiannon said finally, seemingly engrossed in the study of her fingernails. "The same vision I always have when it is time to link soul mates, only this one spoke of the fulfillment of the legend, of love and of war."

Though more questions hovered on the edge of his tongue, Kenric pushed them away. Impatient, he untied the faded ribbon with clumsy fingers. A sense of foreboding stuck him, the same sense that apparently gripped both Rhiannon and Arwydd.

He hesitated before unrolling the scroll. "This is it, then." No question this, but a statement that needed only his sister's confirmation.

With reluctance, Rhiannon gave it. Odd, but she seemed almost afraid for him to know the spell, as if now that the battle had been won it would not be safe to use it. How could she not know that he would brave the fires of hell itself if it would bring Megan back to him?

Fumbling, he opened the scroll.

It was blank.

Chapter Nineteen

"It's blank." Shock gripped him, shock and the absurd sense that someone played a horrible jest. Fighting back panic, he turned the paper over, searching for the magical words that would bring Megan back to him. Nothing. "Blank."

"I was afraid of that," Rhiannon whispered. Kenric could barely hear her for the roaring in his ears.

"What?" he bellowed. "What does this mean?"

Her shoulders shaking, Rhiannon turned away from him.

It was Arwydd who spoke, Arwydd who told him. "The spell was meant to be used only once. Rhiannon used it to call Megan to you."

"Use it again," Kenric beseeched his sister's back. "Please. Surely you remember the words. Use it again. Bring Megan to me."

"I cannot." She turned tear-swollen eyes to him. "I do not remember it."

The roaring in his ears grew louder. "Some of the words, then. Surely you remember some. Say them. Return her to me."

Rhiannon only hung her head, crying softly.

"I am sorry." Arwydd moved closer, laying a fatherly hand on Kenric's shoulder. "We do not know how."

Kenric could only stare at them in shock, in disbelief. "There is a way," he told them firmly, keeping his voice even when all he wanted was to howl from frustrated anguish. "There has to be a way."

Neither contradicted him. For a moment the only sound was of Rhiannon softly weeping.

"There is a way," Kenric said more loudly, knowing the power of words. "And I will not rest until I find it."

In the weeks following Megan's disappearance, Kenric did not return to the world of humans. He remained in Rune, Arwydd patiently tutoring him in every bit of magical lore they could find. Nothing, not one spell, addressed traveling through time.

Rhiannon took him to the Hall of Legends, which remained open to her. He wandered there, among artifacts so ancient that their meaning had been forgotten, books and scrolls written in a language no longer understood, and engraved runes so worn by time they were no longer legible. Nothing spoke to him; nothing explained the way to bring his soul mate back.

Countless times he read the story of the legend, in all its versions, and every telling ended the same way. The war between evil and good would be fought by half-human, half-Faerie. He and Megan, Rhiannon and Edmyg; each had been so clearly outlined that he wondered how any could have failed to see it. The manuscripts stopped short of naming them.

He found oblique references to Megan's journey through time, though the legend mentioned only that she would travel a great distance, one never before traveled by humankind.

As the weeks turned into months and he learned more, absorbed more knowledge, Kenric's magical powers grew, but his hope began to fade.

"I am worried about you." Rhiannon came to him one eve, as he sat in his usual place in the Hall of Legends, scanning through yet another ancient manuscript, hoping to find some clue, some hint of the magic that would help him.

Kenric blinked in the dimming light. "There is something I am missing here; I can feel it. God's teeth, if only the spell would reveal itself."

Rhiannon shook her head sadly. "You no longer eat, you have lost weight. Your hair"—she reached out and touched one long and tangled strand—"looks like that of a wild man. I would give much to see you smile again."

"Half of me is missing," Kenric agreed grimly, knowing she would understand. "I cannot rest until I find her."

"There is something . . . It haunts me at night." Rhiannon sank to the ground next to him, her lovely expression disturbed. "Sometimes I hear her voice in my dreams."

This was new. Laying the manuscript carefully down, Kenric felt hope for the first time in weeks. Rhiannon's dreams were always prophetic. It was part of the blood of queens. "What does she say?"

"I cannot make out the words."

The hope that had flared within him flickered, but Kenric refused to let it die. "Try." He laid his hand on his sister's shoulder, hoping she did not see how it trembled. "Please."

They sat in silence as the shadows lengthened. At one point an attendant came and lit a wall torch, the flames sending an eerie sort of glow over the place. The air smelled sweet, the scents of a fading summer, when autumn hovered just beyond the next hill.

With the part of himself that was still human, Kenric

301

noticed these things and thought of how Megan would have rejoiced in them. He wondered how much time had gone by in the world of humans—had the months in Rune become a year outside? Did time pass the same wherever Megan was? In his studies he had come to believe that time was like a river, flowing continuously throughout the aeons. All he did now was search for a way to make a boat to travel the river to her.

"She holds out her hand to me," Rhiannon murmured, reminding him that she tried to recount her dream for him. "The way she did when we all joined to fight Myrddin."

Kenric shifted moodily. Well he remembered that feeling of power, the way they had seemed one entity, human and Faerie, united in . . .

Love.

Something nagged at him, something that hovered at the edges of his mind, just out of reach. Something he needed to know.

"She loves you," Rhiannon continued, her voice taking on the monotone cadence of a prophetic trance. "This I sense strongly. And there are words—words she keeps repeating over and ·over—words she wants me to tell you."

What could Megan be trying to say? Kenric concentrated, remembering.

Love is the most powerful magic.

"Did you hear that?" His heart pounding, Kenric stared at his sister. "It sounded like Megan's voice."

"Kenric." Rhiannon shook her head, breaking the trance. "Do you love Megan?"

Affronted that she even needed to ask, Kenric nodded. "I *need* Megan. How can you not know this, when every breath I take is for her? She is all I can think about."

Her smile was wise. "Yes, you have said many times how much you *need* her. But do you *love* her, Kenric?"

Love. Once he had been so sure that he didn't believe

in such a thing. But that had been before, when he'd been dead inside. Now he knew there were things he loved— Rhiannon, his Faerie family, Lancelot, and, most of all, Megan.

"I love her," he said firmly, meeting his sister's fond gaze. "More than life itself."

"Does Megan know this?"

"I have shown her in a thousand ways." Kenric crossed his arms defiantly across his chest. "She has to know."

"Ah, yes. But have you ever whispered the words to her as you held her? Called her 'my love,' told her that without her, life to you is not worth living?"

"She knows," he roared, rapidly losing patience. "I have given her a ring and asked her to be my wife."

Rhiannon waited patiently until he had finished. "Do you not recall the words you used then? Think on them, Kenric; then tell me if Megan knows."

You are mine, he had said. *The ring . . . is a symbol of my need for you.* He had never mentioned love. That explained the sorrow he had seen mingled with the joy in Megan's beautiful eyes.

Love is the most powerful magic.

He leaped to his feet. "That's it. I know what to do."

Satisfaction colored Rhiannon's smile. "What?"

The glow in the cave seemed to brighten. The chill that had haunted his bones lifted, making him feel strong again for the first time in months. A warrior once more, Kenric knew this idea was his last hope of regaining his soul-half.

He reached for the yellowed scroll that he always kept with him, the one that had contained the original spell Rhiannon had used to bring Megan to him.

With trembling fingers, he unrolled it.

The parchment was no longer blank. One word was written there, one word in a flowing script that told him his instincts were right.

Love.

The most powerful magic of all.

Rhiannon bent her head to listen as he told her what he believed he must do.

Together they watched as the words to the spell formed on the scroll.

That night, Megan's dreams were full of Kenric: Kenric holding her in his arms, Kenric covering her mouth with his, Kenric telling her to wait for him, that he would find a way to reach her.

When she opened her eyes that morning, it was to an empty hospital room full of soulless machines and smelling faintly of disinfectant.

"Good morning!" The young nurse, way too cheerful for six A.M., pulled open the curtains. "Looks like we're in for a storm today."

Outside the morning sky looked gray, turbulent clouds blocking out any bit of sunlight. Biting her lower lip, Megan blinked back tears as she remembered that final battle, when they had vanquished Myrddin once and for all. And then she had been ripped away from the only man she'd ever love.

"I think the doctor might let you go home today."

Megan nodded, her throat too tight to speak. Since they had unhooked all the machines the night before, she'd guessed she'd be released soon.

The nurse, perhaps seeing something in Megan's face, left without another word.

Lightning flashed in the distance, followed seconds later by the crash of thunder. A surge of energy went through Megan, a powerful jolt that reminded her of the bolt of lightning that had sent her to Kenric initially.

Was it her imagination, or did her hospital room seem to be filling with swirling mist? Her heart pounding, Megan swung her legs over the side of the bed and clutched her hospital gown closed.

A man materialized out of the shadows, taking shape

slowly. A tall, muscular man, a beautiful warrior.

Kenric!

With a glad cry, Megan moved toward him.

"You," a voice cried from the doorway in a snarl. "So you're the one who poisoned her against me."

Megan froze. *Roger.*

Kenric's beloved gaze met hers, steady and sure. In one stride he reached her, pulling her close with his massive arms, telling her without words that he would protect her if need be.

It was tempting, so tempting to let him shelter her, and the woman she had once been would have accepted gladly, shaking with sheer terror.

But Megan was no longer afraid.

She kissed Kenric lightly, and turned, stepping out of his arms to face Roger.

"Roger, what—"

"You are mine." Though he spoke to Megan, he watched Kenric. "Mine."

"No, Roger." She spoke calmly, her voice steady. "I've already told you that I can't marry you."

Outside, the storm continued to rage. Lightning flashed, and the accompanying thunder was so loud it shook the building.

Kenric stepped forward so that he stood at her side. Still silent, he handed her the ring she'd given him so long ago as a token of her debt to him.

"Here is your ring back, Roger." She held it out, praying he would take it and leave. "Please go."

His austere features grim, Roger's jaw worked. Megan recognized that expression; that and the clenching of his fists told her how much he'd like to hurt her, to hit her.

Once she would have cringed—bracing herself for the blow. But not now, no longer. Never again. She tossed the ring to him.

"Go." Kenric spoke for the first time, sounding controlled, full of unshakable authority. "Go peacefully."

Roger drew himself up, looking even more like a close-shaven Myrddin than ever. "And if I don't?" His voice, though smooth as silk, contained a vague threat, a hint of violence.

Kenric sighed. "Megan and I belong to each other now. I have no wish to fight you for something that can never be."

"Fight me?" Roger laughed. From his suit-coat pocket he pulled out a small black gun. "It won't be much of a fight, since I have this. It's no contest, buddy. No contest at all."

Megan took a step forward, moving slowly, careful not to attract Roger's attention. So there would be another final battle. She had the eerie feeling of reliving the same event over again, in a different time against a different opponent.

There in Rune, she'd been a part of it. This time she would stand alone. This time *she* would have to fight. Kenric and his magic would be no match against a weapon of which he had no knowledge, no match against the deadly killing accuracy of a pistol.

She took a deep breath, drawing strength from the memory of the love that had filled her when they had fought Myrddin. She was ready.

"Don't do it, Roger." Her voice steady, she knew a fleeting sense of pride, even as she banished the quick jab of fear she felt as Roger turned his head to glare at her.

"It will ruin you, destroy everything—your business, your reputation, your life. Do you really want to throw it all away? For nothing?"

"Nothing?" His laugh chilled her blood. "Without your money, it's all gone anyway. You are mine, Megan. Mine, understand?"

Megan bravely took another step forward. If she could put herself in front of Kenric, she might be able to stop Roger, to make him go away.

"I never changed my will."

At her softly voiced comment, Roger's eyes narrowed. "I know. That's why I've taken steps to have you declared incompetent. As your fiancé, I have that right."

Then he would control her money. It was a brilliant plan.

"Enough," Kenric said in a growl. "You no longer have any rights to Megan. Now take your toy and go."

"My toy?" Momentary confusion darkened Roger's expression, but it cleared as Kenric again moved to Megan's side, making it easy for him to keep them both covered by his gun.

"You're as crazy as she is. Good thing you have to die."

"You'll never get away with it."

Roger chuckled. "Ah, but there you're wrong, Megan, my dear. "Especially when I get injured trying to keep my crazy fiancée from killing her new boyfriend with the weird clothes and long hair."

Then Megan knew what he meant to do—shoot Kenric and make it look as though she had done it. Because his name carried a lot of weight in prominent Dallas circles, no doubt the authorities would believe him.

She couldn't let him do it.

Roger brought the gun up, aiming at Kenric.

Kenric muttered a string of unintelligible words.

Megan threw herself forward.

Lightning flashed. Thunder boomed.

Mist swirled up to fill the room.

The gun went off.

And Kenric and Megan vanished.

Chapter Twenty

"Megan. My love."

As if from a long way off, Megan heard Kenric calling her name. She shivered at the emotions she heard in his deep voice, which was oddly hoarse, fearful, and tender all at the same time.

There should have been more pain. Instead she felt as if she were floating. None of it made sense. When she'd thrown herself in front of Kenric, she had felt the bullet graze her shoulder. She'd heard Roger's shout of triumph change to shock, heard Kenric's cry as the spell he'd uttered took effect too late to save her from being hit.

"I love you."

Those words had her opening her eyes. "Kenric?"

His grin was lopsided, full of more sorrow than joy. "Aye, my Megan." With hands that visibly shook, he touched her, his fingers coming away red. "Tell me what manner of magic did he use on you, so that Rhiannon and her council may say a spell to counteract it."

"Spell?" Confused, Megan peered through the haze that seemed to be clouding her eyes, trying to make out Kenric's beloved features. For the first time she became aware that his tunic was bloodstained.

"Did it hit you?" She gasped, horribly aware that her last-ditch effort to protect him might have failed.

"No." Rhiannon appeared, her expression worried. "The blood you see is your own. We have found a scrape on your shoulder, but nothing to show what caused it. I cleaned it and it bleeds very little now."

Megan sat up, her dizziness lessening. "The bullet only grazed me, I think." She looked up at Kenric, startled to see a single tear travel slowly down one rugged cheek.

"Kenric . . ." With a trembling hand, she reached up and wiped it away. "What's wrong? What happened?"

Cradling her in his arms, Kenric swallowed, visibly composing himself before he spoke.

"I spoke a spell to bring us back here, but I feared it was too late. Your Roger fired his strange weapon and hit you instead of me."

Satisfied that Kenric was not hurt, Megan nodded.

"You put your body in front of mine." Kenric sounded suddenly fierce, though his voice still came out rusty. "Why would you do such a thing?"

She shrugged, then winced as pain hit her. "Because I love you. I couldn't let him hurt you."

"I love you, my Megan." Again he said the words that she'd waited so long to hear, though this time Megan saw no sorrow or fear in his handsome face. Instead she saw the dawning of joy, and pride, and the sensual beginnings of the powerful heat the two of them felt when they were together.

She smiled. "I knew that you did, Kenric."

"Are you not surprised to hear me say it?"

Her heart sang. "No." With difficulty she kept from laughing aloud as her brave warrior cocked his shaggy head and frowned in puzzlement.

"You are not?"

"Nope. I've always known you loved me. It just took time for you to admit it to yourself." Well satisfied, she gave a sigh of blissful contentment.

Her happiness must have been infectious, for Kenric threw back his head and laughed.

"If I had not been so thickheaded, I would have been able to find you much sooner."

"What do you mean?"

"Remember what you told me once?" He kissed the tip of her nose lightly, the heat in his eyes promising her that more was to come.

Bemused, she shook her head. "What?"

"That love was the most powerful magic." He kissed her ear, then her neck, making her shiver.

"Yes," she said softly.

He held up a rolled piece of yellowed parchment. "Once I realized that I loved you, the spell appeared on the scroll. I knew then how to travel to you and, conversely, how to bring you back."

"Let me see it." Her voice not quite steady, she held out her hand.

Slowly, after placing another kiss on the hollow of her throat, he unrolled the parchment.

"It's blank."

With a savage grin, Kenric tossed it over his shoulder. "It has served its purpose." He kissed her again, this time full upon the lips, with a lingering heat that left no doubt that he loved her and needed her and wanted her. Forever.

As if she'd ever doubt it.

"I wonder what Roger thought," she mused out loud, "when we vanished like that."

Kenric frowned, a shadow of annoyance crossing his face. "That is my one regret—that I cannot punish your Roger for hurting you."

"He is not *my* Roger," she corrected automatically.

"And I'm sure he will have some explaining to do after firing that gun."

"And your being gone."

"With blood on the floor." Megan grinned. "I bet they will think Roger murdered me."

"He would have," Kenric said darkly, "and me as well, if he could have gotten away with it."

"The inquiry will make the news." Thinking aloud, Megan shook her head. "Roger will hate that kind of publicity. They might even unearth his financial problems. It's not enough, but in his own way Roger will suffer."

"Nay, it is not enough."

Megan reached up, ignoring the twinge in her shoulder, to cup his beloved face in her hands. "I would have no shadows between us, my love. I am glad that you did not kill Roger, especially since you wish to be done with killing."

Kenric looked surprised, then turned his head, kissing the palm of her hand. "You are right," he told her finally, gazing at her intently. "No shadows."

"Only love."

He kissed her then, murmuring against her mouth, "Only love. Now you will stay here forever."

"Forever," she agreed, parting her lips in dazed anticipation of his next kiss.

And the next. And the next.

Forever.

The Magician's Lover — Flora Speer

Determined to locate his friend who disappeared during a spell gone awry, Warrick petitions a dying stargazer to help find him. But the astronomer will only assist Warrick if he promises to escort his daughter Sophia and a priceless crystal ball safely to Byzantium. Sharp-tongued and argumentative, Sophia meets her match in the powerful and intelligent Warrick. Try as she will to deny it, he holds her spellbound, longing to be the magician's lover.

___52263-2 $5.99 US/$6.99 CAN

Dorchester Publishing Co., Inc.
P.O. Box 6640
Wayne, PA 19087-8640

Please add $1.75 for shipping and handling for the first book and $.50 for each book thereafter. NY, NYC, and PA residents, please add appropriate sales tax. No cash, stamps, or C.O.D.s. All orders shipped within 6 weeks via postal service book rate. Canadian orders require $2.00 extra postage and must be paid in U.S. dollars through a U.S. banking facility.

Name_____
Address_____
City_____State_____Zip_____
I have enclosed $_____ in payment for the checked book(s).
Payment <u>must</u> accompany all orders. ❑ Please send a free catalog.
            CHECK OUT OUR WEBSITE! www.dorchesterpub.com

More Than Magic

Kathleen Nance

Darius is as beautiful, as mesmerizing, as dangerous as a man can be. His dark, star-kissed eyes promise exquisite joys, yet it is common knowledge he has no intention of taking a wife. Ever. Sex and sensuality will never ensnare Darius, for he is their master. But magic can. Knowledge of his true name will give a mortal woman power over the arrogant djinni, and an age-old enemy has carefully baited the trap. Alluring yet innocent, Isis Montgomery will snare his attention, and the spell she's been given will bind him to her. But who can control a force that is even more than magic?

__52299-3 $5.99 US/$6.99 CAN

Dorchester Publishing Co., Inc.
P.O. Box 6640
Wayne, PA 19087-8640

Please add $1.75 for shipping and handling for the first book and $.50 for each book thereafter. NY, NYC, and PA residents, please add appropriate sales tax. No cash, stamps, or C.O.D.s. All orders shipped within 6 weeks via postal service book rate. Canadian orders require $2.00 extra postage and must be paid in U.S. dollars through a U.S. banking facility.

Name_____

Address_____

City_____State_____Zip_____

I have enclosed $_____ in payment for the checked book(s).

Payment <u>must</u> accompany all orders. ❑ Please send a free catalog.

CHECK OUT OUR WEBSITE! www.dorchesterpub.com

BUSHWHACKED BRIDE

EUGENIA RILEY

"JUMPING JEHOSHAPHAT! YOU'VE SHANGHAIED THE NEW SCHOOLMARM!"

Ma Reklaw bellows at her sons and wields her broom with a fierceness that has all five outlaw brothers running for cover; it doesn't take a Ph.D. to realize that in the Reklaw household, Ma is the law. Professor Jessica Garret watches dumbstruck as the members of the feared Reklaw Gang turn tail—one up a tree, another under the hay wagon, and one in a barrel. Having been unceremoniously kidnapped by the rowdy brothers, the green-eyed beauty takes great pleasure in their discomfort until Ma Reklaw finds a new way to sweep clean her sons' disreputable behavior—by offering Jessica's hand in marriage to the best behaved. Jessie has heard of shotgun weddings, but a broomstick betrothal is ridiculous! As the dashing but dangerous desperadoes start the wooing there is no telling what will happen with one bride for five brothers.

___52320-5 $5.99 US/$6.99 CAN

Dorchester Publishing Co., Inc.
P.O. Box 6640
Wayne, PA 19087-8640

Please add $1.75 for shipping and handling for the first book and $.50 for each book thereafter. NY, NYC, and PA residents, please add appropriate sales tax. No cash, stamps, or C.O.D.s. All orders shipped within 6 weeks via postal service book rate. Canadian orders require $2.00 extra postage and must be paid in U.S. dollars through a U.S. banking facility.

Name_____
Address_____
City_____State_____Zip_____
I have enclosed $_____ in payment for the checked book(s).
Payment <u>must</u> accompany all orders. ☐ Please send a free catalog.
CHECK OUT OUR WEBSITE! www.dorchesterpub.com

The CHANGELING BRIDE

LISA CACH

In order to procure the cash necessary to rebuild his estate, the Earl of Allsbrook decides to barter his title and his future: He will marry the willful daughter of a wealthy merchant. True, she is pleasing in form and face, and she has an eye for fashion. Still, deep in his heart, Henry wishes for a happy marriage. Wilhelmina March is leery of the importance her brother puts upon marriage, and she certainly never dreams of being wed to an earl in Georgian England—or of the fairy debt that gives her just such an opportunity. But suddenly, with one sweet kiss in a long-ago time and a faraway place, Elle wonders if the much ado is about something after all.

___52342-6 $4.99 US/$5.99 CAN

Dorchester Publishing Co., Inc.
P.O. Box 6640
Wayne, PA 19087-8640

Please add $1.75 for shipping and handling for the first book and $.50 for each book thereafter. NY, NYC, and PA residents, please add appropriate sales tax. No cash, stamps, or C.O.D.s. All orders shipped within 6 weeks via postal service book rate. Canadian orders require $2.00 extra postage and must be paid in U.S. dollars through a U.S. banking facility.

Name_____

Address_____

City_____ State_____ Zip_____

I have enclosed $_____ in payment for the checked book(s).

Payment <u>must</u> accompany all orders. ❏ Please send a free catalog.

CHECK OUT OUR WEBSITE! www.dorchesterpub.com

Bewitching The Baron

Lisa Cach

Valerian has always known before that she will never marry. While the townsfolk of her Yorkshire village are grateful for her abilities, the price of her gift is solitude. But it never bothered her until now. Nathaniel Warrington is the new baron of Ravenall, and he has never wanted anything the way he desires his people's enigmatic healer. Her exotic beauty fans flames in him that feel unnaturally fierce. Their first kiss flares hotter still. Opposed by those who seek to destroy her, compelled by a love that will never die, Nathaniel fights to earn the lone beauty's trust. And Valerian will learn the only thing more dangerous—or heavenly—than bewitching a baron, is being bewitched by one.

___52368-X $5.50 US/$6.50 CAN

Dorchester Publishing Co., Inc.
P.O. Box 6640
Wayne, PA 19087-8640

Please add $1.75 for shipping and handling for the first book and $.50 for each book thereafter. NY, NYC, and PA residents, please add appropriate sales tax. No cash, stamps, or C.O.D.s. All orders shipped within 6 weeks via postal service book rate. Canadian orders require $2.00 extra postage and must be paid in U.S. dollars through a U.S. banking facility.

Name_____
Address_____
City_____ State_____ Zip_____
I have enclosed $_____ in payment for the checked book(s).
Payment <u>must</u> accompany all orders. ❏ Please send a free catalog.

A GAMBLER'S MAGIC

EMMA CRAIG

Gambler Elijah Perry is on a winning streak, until he is shot in the leg and fears his good fortune is at an end. Then he awakes to find the straight-laced Joy Hardesty scowling at him and he sees he's been dealt another tricky hand. But as the lovely nurse tends his wounds, he discovers a free, joyful spirit beneath her poker face and a straight flush that bespeaks an enchanting innocence. There is magic in the air, and Elijah realizes that it is not a sleight of hand that has brought him to New Mexico, but Lady Luck herself. As he holds the beauty in his arms he knows that in winning the love of a lifetime he'll more than break even.

___52358-2 $5.50 US/$6.50 CAN

Dorchester Publishing Co., Inc.
P.O. Box 6640
Wayne, PA 19087-8640

Please add $1.75 for shipping and handling for the first book and $.50 for each book thereafter. NY, NYC, and PA residents, please add appropriate sales tax. No cash, stamps, or C.O.D.s. All orders shipped within 6 weeks via postal service book rate. Canadian orders require $2.00 extra postage and must be paid in U.S. dollars through a U.S. banking facility.

Name_____
Address_____
City_____ State_____ Zip_____
I have enclosed $_____ in payment for the checked book(s).
Payment <u>must</u> accompany all orders. ❑ Please send a free catalog.
     CHECK OUT OUR WEBSITE! www.dorchesterpub.com

A LOVE
BEYOND
TIME
FLORA SPEER

Accidentally thrust back to the eighth century, Mike Bailey falls from the sky and lands near Charlemagne's camp. Knocked senseless by the crash, he can't remember his name, but no shock can make his body forget how to respond when he awakes to the sight of an enchanting angel on earth. Headstrong and innocent, Danise chooses to risk spending her life cloistered in a nunnery rather than marry for any reason besides love. Unexpectedly mesmerized by the stranger she discovers unconscious in the forest, Danise is quickly roused by an all-consuming passion—and a desire that will conquer time itself.

___52326-4 $5.50 US/$6.50 CAN

Dorchester Publishing Co., Inc.
P.O. Box 6640
Wayne, PA 19087-8640

Please add $1.75 for shipping and handling for the first book and $.50 for each book thereafter. NY, NYC, and PA residents, please add appropriate sales tax. No cash, stamps, or C.O.D.s. All orders shipped within 6 weeks via postal service book rate. Canadian orders require $2.00 extra postage and must be paid in U.S. dollars through a U.S. banking facility.

Name_____
Address_____
City_____State_____Zip_____
I have enclosed $_____ in payment for the checked book(s).
Payment <u>must</u> accompany all orders. ❑ Please send a free catalog.
        CHECK OUT OUR WEBSITE! www.dorchesterpub.com

Love Just in Time

FLORA SPEER

After discovering her husband's infidelity, Clarissa Cummings thinks she will never trust another man. Then a freak accident sends her into another century—and the most handsome stranger imaginable saves her from drowning in the canal. But he is all wet if he thinks he has a lock on Clarissa's heart. After scandal forces Jack Martin to flee to the wilds of America, the dashing young Englishman has to give up the pleasures of a rake and earn his keep with a plow and a hoe. Yet to his surprise, he learns to enjoy the simple life of a farmer, and he yearns to take Clarissa as his bride. But after Jack has sown the seeds of desire, secrets from his past threaten to destroy his harvest of love.

___52289-6 $5.50 US/$6.50 CAN

Dorchester Publishing Co., Inc.
P.O. Box 6640
Wayne, PA 19087-8640

Please add $1.75 for shipping and handling for the first book and $.50 for each book thereafter. NY, NYC, and PA residents, please add appropriate sales tax. No cash, stamps, or C.O.D.s. All orders shipped within 6 weeks via postal service book rate. Canadian orders require $2.00 extra postage and must be paid in U.S. dollars through a U.S. banking facility.

Name_____
Address_____
City_____ State_____ Zip_____
I have enclosed $_____ in payment for the checked book(s).
Payment <u>must</u> accompany all orders. ❏ Please send a free catalog.

ATTENTION ROMANCE CUSTOMERS!

SPECIAL TOLL-FREE NUMBER
1-800-481-9191

Call Monday through Friday
10 a.m. to 9 p.m.
Eastern Time
Get a free catalogue,
join the Romance Book Club,
and order books using your
Visa, MasterCard,
or Discover®

Leisure
Books

GO ONLINE WITH US AT DORCHESTERPUB.COM